WE ARE STARDUST

BY

KG BROME

WE ARE STARDUST

Book 1 of The Soman Chronicle

Cover design by studio haus

ISBN 979-8-9947367-1-5 (paperback)
ISBN 979-8-9947367-0-8 (eBook)

DEDICATION

To LY, my best teacher ever

...we are destined to know the dark beyond the stars before we comprehend the nature of our own journey.
  Loren Eiseley

Part One: Into the Darkness

Chapter 1

At first he simply breathed, astringent air on tender lungs. Fingering the letters on the nameplate, S-O-M-A-N, he whispered, "What did I…" A hanging flight suit undulated at his touch. Zero G. The insignia on the breast drew him, a tapering staff topped with an ornate knob. Shadowy recollections rose, the emblem on the side of a ship. *Sorcerer.*

Naked, peering at the ovoid chamber set into the floor of the room, another word came to him—*descroid.* He touched the moist handprint fading on its open lid. Must be his. Why was he emerging from a descroid. He stared off, memories distant, fireflies in the black night. The descroid's done this, scrambled everything. Emptiness beyond the present moment.

Soman's bones ached of time and distance. Joints dry and gritty. Spotting the water station, he sucked, his need urgent. Then he dressed, the fabric stiff like leather left years in the sun.

A sound. Every hair prickled at the faint throb, distant, discordant. On the console, a pulsing red light. A flicker of recall—*Alarm.* He reached for the hatch, then stopped, disoriented by the shimmering grey surface. It came to him; a nexport, the latest thing. He pushed off and floated through the nex. The grey stretched ever so slightly, then crackled as he passed through, a few tendrils clinging as the field snapped tight behind him.

A racket of klaxons. Down the tube, a flash of purple fabric and black hair, a woman pulling on a pressure suit. Then smoke engulfed her, a seething wall bearing down. No clear air near the deck—not without gravity. The acrid smoke struck; his lungs burned. He grappled with the lid of a floor locker big as a coffin, his fingers tangling in the fittings of an oxygen pack, everything happening too fast.

A sharp tug pulled his head back. Cold plastic circled his face. A strap snapped the base of his skull. He gulped cool relief and turned to see the woman disappear into the gloom. The alarms clanged on. Where the hell were they. His mind shot full of holes; memory tattered. Only the machine part of the brain working, and how far would that get him. At least the tube looked familiar, arcing gently away, and he clutched at an image of the ship—the habitation disc, spokes to the central axis, the collector open-mouthed in front, the nozzle of the drive behind. He was somewhere in the disc of *Sorcerer*. And *Sorcerer* was burning.

"Fire assignment!" he yelled. A voice jumped from the imcom in his skull. "Level Three. Recharge junction, L deck." He used long pulls on the webbing to race down the tube, straining to recall the layout.

Over the blare of fire alarms, a new sound, motors revving, spingrav kicking in, rotating the mass of the disc. A clash of gears. The ship shuddered, slamming him against a bulkhead. Something had seized up. Damn ship's tearing itself apart.

An ocher glow ahead. Soman slowed and grabbed an extinguisher from its recess. Gripping it, he peeked around the corner. Searing heat drove him back. Damn. A fire that hot could burn right through the hull, and that would be it. Their brand-new ship, burning up like an old tenement. Soman's frenzied breathing outran the oxygen pack; he hunched over, gasping.

A new alarm split the air: three blasts like a foghorn. A calm female voice repeated in his imcom, "Air purge. Air purge." The last resort against a hull-threatening fire. Soman spun, searching the length of the tube. One minute to find a pressure suit—and no locker in sight. He sped along the webbing, leaving the useless extinguisher floating, its nozzle curled in a question mark.

Ten seconds gone. Around him the hull groaned. Twenty seconds. He collided with something in the smoke. A locker. Thirty seconds. Tugging out a pressure suit and helmet, yanking to untangle a spare boot lodged in a pant leg. A roar echoed down the tube—their air venting to space. The suit thrashed in the wind like a man possessed. A second sound joined the roar, his own scream, and he couldn't stop it, even knowing in a thinking corner of his brain that he was wasting the last of his air.

Something cold brushed his face, and he touched his cheek. His hand came away with a skim of frost. At the sudden sensation of cold, a scene from Earth flickered on, of snow and wind, a slab of stone protruding from fresh soil, melancholy like the smoke swirling down the corridor. Who...

Then he was flailing like a bug in a killing jar, shoving arms and legs into the balky suit. Because when that frost sublimed, eyes would bulge, blood vessels burst, lungs heave to a halt. His yell diminished to a croak, no longer enough air for human voice. He slammed the last cams closed. The regulator hissed and he gulped air, old, sour.

The cacophony of alarms, whistling air and screeching steel faded in the vacuum. Silence. Soman grew still. A single memory rose like a bubble, bursting to the surface. A snow-swept street, a woman stepping away, gazing back. Anne! He bent over the locker. What was he doing out here.

The open com channel bombarded Soman with frantic crosstalk, every voice strung tight. A hot spot on K deck, spingrav down, a problem in forward descroids, and four missing crew. Foreboding filled Soman. This might not be winnable. Maybe they should evacuate in the LEV's and call for a rescue, or drop down to Lunar Colony One. But another thought crept in. You don't use descroids in orbit. Descroids were for vast distances.

Urgent call. Firefighters to J tube, aft deck. Vent valves had failed; air still fed the fire. He pushed through a nex to J, energy flagging. God he was hungry. They were supposed to eat on emergence, then rest.

A shudder shook the ship. A voice on open channel: "Burn through—aft descroids!" He grabbed an extinguisher and raced aft, all the lights out, his helmet lamp barely penetrating the smoke. He swept the beam from side to side as he advanced, wriggling past sharp edges that would rip his suit open, red-hot splinters of metal glowing from the gloom like ghosts.

Valves thunked. They'd opened the vent. Air whistled past. Soman held on to avoid being swept against the wreckage.

Red flash from the dark ahead. A glowing shard burst from a pod, red-hot metal arrowing straight at Soman. He spun away and collided hard with a crewman who had come up behind him in the dark. The gobbet flashed inches from Soman's faceplate and disappeared into the fabric just below the crewman's helmet. The man's arms rose to his throat, then stopped, as if afraid to touch. Soman peered into the faceplate. The man didn't appear hurt, merely intent, as if concentrating on a tricky bit of calculus. Red spray fizzed from the man's suit. The crewman crumpled, his suit deflated. Soman stared. Seconds ago, a man had dwelt among the meat and bone. Now he was gone. Why do they say gone. Gone where. His mind raced across the calendar of years to the moment when the universe would glide on with no Soman—he gripped his helmet with both hands. Gone. The breath squeezed from him. Around him the fire cooled in the vacuum, fading to nothing.

He picked his way toward the faint glow of a lighted corridor that would lead him out of this destruction.

Soman froze when his light fell across a pair of crushed descroids. How many had been destroyed. How would they return home. Staring at the descroids, he sensed a memory rising: a huge vault filled with row upon row of descroids, curving far into the distance. A little girl lying on a white sheet, straining to smile, tubes running into both arms. Soman faltered, clinging to a dislocated handrail, remembering a name: Anoka. He gasped in dread, like the mother who wakes from the grace of drugged sleep to remember she buried her child yesterday. No wonder the sight of descroids terrified him. He had left his child in one—but where. He looked around, taking in the ruined pods, the scorched bulkheads, the dead crewman wedged against debris. Surely not here. "Auton," he said. "What's my duty station?"

"Nav One," came the reply, emanating from the bone behind his ear.

He pulled himself along the webbing lining the tube. Deck plan, Nav One, he thought, and the plans materialized. Along the way the ship re-pressurized living areas, air whistling, hull creaking. Unrelenting cacophony on open channel, work details mobilizing to plug the worst leaks in the hull.

The nexport to Nav One crackled as Soman pushed through. Peeling off his pressure suit, he scanned the cabin. Terminal screens glowing green on black. He pulled himself along the guide rail toward the center console. A man floated in the left-hand seat, his bald head familiar, like a shadowy figure from a past life. Sliding into the vacant seat and fastening the zero-G restraint, Soman peered at the man, trying to dredge up something more than this vague sense of recollection. The man's eyes flickered across Soman's features. For a moment they studied each other like dogs sniffing assholes.

A spark flashed behind them. A man screamed. A tang of ozone wafted out of the Nav electronics rack, its access panel hanging open, lights flickering inside. Someone shouted, "Fry the rest of the coolers why don't you." Two men squirmed out, one moaning and holding a hand over his eye, the other saying, "Fuck" over and over. The name Moss on his coveralls. Soman took in Moss's wiry frame, the tendons standing out from his neck. Moss would look at home on a submarine; his wiry crew-cut and gray-green eyes recalled gunmetal and stormy ocean sky.

"Great. We got no cooling now," Moss said in disgust. He pried the injured man's hand from his eye. "Let me look at it…fuck. Gotta get him to medical." The nex crackled and they were gone.

Soman stared after them. Then he jumped as the nex came alive and someone burst through, a man with a great shaggy head and a pocked face. Cabot.

"What's our position?" Cabot wanted to know.

Soman turned to his controls. A holo sprang up in the space above the console. Dominating the star field was the sun. Soman exhaled, relieved at its proximity. An instant later his relief chilled as he registered the sun's hue, a few wavelengths too red. On the display, a name glowed in blue script: Epsilon Eridani. Goddamn, it can't be.

"Position?" Cabot repeated.

"Is this a…" Soman glanced to Cabot, then back to the coordinates of the star. "…a simulation?" No, goddamn, crew don't die in a simulation.

Coordinates blinked on, blue figures floating in the air before them. He told Cabot, "Five point six million miles from…" *Sorcerer* approached a planet glowing orange, not blue-white. The second planet of Epsilon Eridani. *Sorcerer's* crew reduced to dust and hurled at a distant star. Ten point five light years from Earth.

The man gripped Soman's arm and said, "Easy man."

Suddenly Soman knew him. How many times had Hakim said 'easy man' when they'd manned the old lunar freighters, before the rail launcher replaced them. One minute the guy's a total stranger, the next he's Hakim.

Cabot pointed at the image on Hakim's console screen. "What are we looking at there?"

"Our hull," Hakim said. "I'm running the damage inspection."

"That can't be our hull."

Soman leaned over for a better look. A surface scoured and pitted like an asteroid. A faint remnant of the scepter insignia.

"Holy shit," Hakim said.

In Lunar orbit *Sorcerer* had felt solid beneath the feet, the massive curve of a familiar planet nearby, surrounded by swarms of smaller craft. Now *Sorcerer* limped alone, trailing a cloud of frozen smoke, its skin worn to the quick, its metal bones vulnerable to the immensity of deep space.

A movement on the screen startled Soman. "Hakim, look. Something's out there." Hakim zoomed in. A blob of white crept toward the base of an antenna mast. His skin crawled. Something was on their ship.

"That's Ley," Cabot said. "She's breaking down the antenna. Leak at the mount."

Ley stopped at the mast, seized a tool from her belt, and attacked the mount. Beyond, the Milky Way blazed against the obsidian universe.

"She's alone?" Soman said, watching Ley perched precariously on the edge of the ship. "With no tether and no backup?"

Ley's motion stopped, and Soman's imcom came alive with a derision-laced Aussie accent. "You're worried about protocol when the ship's leaking? I'll be done before you finish the damn checklist."

Soman cringed; he'd forgotten about open channel.

A voice crackled on open. "Captain, problem at forward descroids. Three pods down." A pause. "Crew inside."

All channels went silent.

"And a code D, group three."

Cabot rushed through the nex.

A woman entered, a long rope of black hair trailing behind. "Did they say a code D?" she asked.

"Yeah. What's that?" Around them the low hum of electronics, the soft rustle of air circulating, a distant hammering felt through the feet, someone making a repair or going berserk.

"Descroid malfunction. The person didn't show the required, um, human awareness. Auton locked the compartment down."

Talk of descroids stilled Soman, that memory dogging him. Rows and rows of descroids, pods beyond counting. He tried to hold the image, but it was gone, in its place a terrible longing. Where did memories go, staggering back in ones and twos like casualties of war.

"What do you think about this date line?" the woman said, pointing. "It can't right."

Soman stared. November 28, 5241. Like looking at a misspelled word and knowing it was wrong, but everything you try looks wrong, too. How can you not know what century it's supposed to be.

"Well?" she said, cocking an eyebrow.

"Why can't we remember anything?"

She chewed her lip. "Maybe a leftover from the re-hydration. Let's try this."

She focused inward, working the auton. The console screen refreshed.

"My personnel record," she said.

Rula, Siba (no middle initial).
Sorcerer assignment: crew psych 1, medical backup 2.
Grade: 3SP9.
Classified Information Level: 10.
DOB January 1, 2020.

Siba... A fragment of recollection flew by, Siba introducing herself that first time, the day of his interview, long black hair and bronze complexion. He remembered how his throat had caught at the aroma of a woman after the years working the freighters, a forgotten fragrance of hair and warm skin. Now the only odor any of them emanated was a tang of disinfectant from the descroid.

"I was...thirty-six when we left," Siba said. "That would make it 2056. A hundred twenty-five for the transit, right?"

Hakim nodded tentatively, as if chasing something fleeting. "Yeah," he said finally. "I used to say long enough for everyone that hates me to die."

Siba said, "That would make it 2181. The record's off by over three thousand years. A glitch in the display?"

"Must be," Hakim said.

For the first time, Soman noticed Siba's purple blouse. "Was that you in the corridor? Strapping on my respirator?"

"Good thing I saw you."

An urgent call burst across open channel: Moss requesting the doctor.

"Forget it," someone broke in. "Explosion got him in aft descroids."

So that had been the doctor. Soman couldn't forget the expression on the man's face as his final seconds drained from him.

"Oh, God," Siba said. "I have to go. I'm the back-up."

At that instant a woman rammed through the nex jaw first, taking in her surroundings in an instant, then pushing off to float toward the console while calling on open channel. "Moss, this is Ley. Status of those chilling units?" Soman tried not to stare at the small hole in the right side of her skull where an ear should be; and something odd about her eyes.

Moss replied, "Haven't found a spare board yet that wasn't damaged."

Ley pointed at Soman's console. "How close in are we?"

Soman ran the distance to the star. "Not good," he said as the distances flashed in the holo. "A hundred thirty million kilometers."

"Too damn close. We're going to fry without those coolers."

"We could abort the insertion," he offered. "Move off to make repairs."

She turned to him. "Mr. Soman. At full thrust, how long until we'd start gaining distance from this damned sun?"

Soman looked away, drew into the auton and ran the curve. "Hmm. We'll need orbital insertion to slow us that much. That's in four days."

"Right. We're carrying all that speed from the crossing. At the rate our temperature is rising, we'll hit fifty-five degrees in thirty-nine hours. That's when your lungs start to burn up. We don't have the luxury of maneuvering. We have to get those coolers on line." She folded her arms, a pose that accentuated the hump in her back. "Or the mission will be over before it starts."

Mission. Another fragment came to Soman. The construction of *Sorcerer* in lunar orbit.

At Soman's puzzled look, she said, "We're all nutzed up for some reason. Here," she pointed to the screen, "I had to look it up."

A news story flicked on. *Astronomers confirmed today that periodic flashes emitted from the vicinity of the star Epsilon Eridani are not random, but a complex series of mathematical progressions indicating an intelligent origin.*

Ley said, "I don't know how the descroids fucked up our memories, but in our off shifts we all need to read the archives. Now that we're here, we've got to prepare." She turned to Soman. "And you're going to tell us why it took so long."

"What?" he said.

"Explain to me why it took us over three thousand years."

"Oh, that's a glitch in the…"

"Don't be ridiculous. The hull is so damaged I could almost poke my hand through. And the log's been over-written six times."

"That's crazy. There's five hundred years of memory there…"

"Exactly, Mr. Soman. The chronometer reads 5241, and the log is in its sixth over-write. You do the math. We've been gone a hell of a long time, and I want to know why."

"No…"

"Mr. Soman, one century or thirty. What do we care. Just recover the damn log."

Soman knew it mattered to him. But why... He glanced sideways at her. The reflection of the holo glittered in her cropped gray hair and flickered in her eyes—eyes with unnatural clarity for a woman her age. Then he spotted the faint ridge along the eyelids. Eye clones.

Ley caught him staring. "What are you looking at?"

"Your, your…" and the word came to him. "…wedjats."

Ley gazed into the distance, mouthing the word—*wedjat*. She touched an eyelid, exhaling audibly as she found the thin scar. "Damn."

Soman's glance slid, with a tingle of revulsion, to the melted skin of her cheek. A scene came to him of a smoking crater where once a city center throbbed, refugees stumbling along its crumbling edge.

"What have you got? Well?"

He sped through screens. "There's supposed to be a way to recover this. But…wait."

Ley scowled at the delay.

"Whatever happened, auton would have exchanged messages with Colony One base. Let me check the com log. Here—" he stopped. A paltry half page, routine telemetry exchanges. The last receipt from Earth in 2097, a simple acknowledgement of data. "Then *Sorcerer* sent a burst to Earth in 5119." Soman did the arithmetic. "A hundred twenty-three years ago. But…no response."

"Mr. Soman, they've written us off as dead and derelict."

"They wouldn't."

"Then why haven't they sent another ship after all this time?"

"Oh, maybe they have." He looked up hopefully.

Ley chuffed. "Don't be a moron. They had plenty of time, right?" She called up an electromag scan of the local area. "You see another ship?"

Soman shook his head. No electromag of a ship, no emissions of any kind. Thirty centuries to mount a second mission, and no one here.

But wait. "That was three thousand years ago. They would have been here and returned to Earth."

"You don't think they'd have picked us up along the way?"

Chapter 2

It took Soman until his second Nav shift before he figured a way to assemble a flight log from raw instrument data. Sleep and truly awful food hadn't eased the fatigue.

Hakim scanned for rocky objects that might cross *Sorcerer's* path on the glide into EE2. "Strange, nothing there," he said, shaking his head. "I got a suspicion the proximity tracking's not working. We ought to pick up debris."

"Not good," Soman said. That would leave the ship vulnerable to any fragment of asteroid that might smash through the central disc of *Sorcerer* and vaporize three thousand years of voyaging.

"Might have to eject some test objects," Hakim said.

Soman made sure he wasn't on open channel. "We could shoot Ley out an airlock."

When Hakim's head shuddered again, Soman didn't think anything of it. He was focused on the flight log. After three failed attempts to recover the lost information, the algorithm was finally spitting out data. The history of the voyage unfolded before him in fuel records, thrust vectors, and centuries. The dateline was not a glitch.

"Hakim, cut it out," Soman griped when a string of spit slapped him across the face. But hearing a guttural sound, Soman turned to see Hakim's head swinging so hard it seemed it might tear off, saliva slinging, eyeballs rolled back.

Soman lunged at Hakim to stop his head from banging against the console. Hakim's thrashing carried them tumbling across the cabin. Soman flicked into open, shouting, "Medical help Nav One!"

Hakim flailed with unnatural power; Soman couldn't stop him even though he had an advantage of six inches and eighty pounds on him. Tangled with him, Soman feared he'd break both their arms. He buried his head in Hakim's chest and held on, yelling "easy man." Hakim gurgled and gasped. He wasn't getting any air; he was going to suffocate. The cabin air grew acrid with his stomach juices.

Then a long wheeze; Hakim's muscles slackened, leaving him gasping for air.

Soman held him by the shoulders. "You all right man?"

Hakim then croaked, "Hell of a headache."

"Soman, is it an emergency up there?" It was Siba on open.

"Hakim had a seizure."

Hakim held weakly to the webbing that had stopped their tumbling, his breath ragged, his limbs trembling. "I'm okay," he said.

"He's not okay," Soman snapped. For a few frightening seconds Hakim had seemed inhuman, a senseless force tearing through his body.

"I'm in the clinic with a patient.

Soman worked Hakim back toward the console. "This ever happen before?"

Hakim hesitated, then said, "Had one last night. Well, two."

Soman slid Hakim into his seat. Then, "Ley, I've got the flight log. I know what delayed us."

"On my way."

Hearing the exchange between Soman and Ley, a few haggard crew trickled into Nav One. They floated at the edges of the cabin, somber and exhausted.

Siba burst in, a medical kit over her shoulder. Floating to Hakim, she checked his vitals, spoke quietly with him, drew blood.

Ley slid through the port. Soman brought the graphics into the holo, lines in red, green, and blue. A murmur ran through Nav One, everyone craning for a look.

"Hang on a minute," Siba interrupted. "While we're doing this, I need blood samples." She pulled out a case of syringes.

"From everyone?" Ley asked. "I thought Hakim was the sickie."

"We may have descroid residual." Siba readied a syringe.

"What do you mean residual?"

"Neurological imbalances left over from the emergence. I'm seeing symptoms that worry me."

The Nav One cabin stilled. The holo of the Epsilon Eridani system glowed in their midst, the only sound the popping of the hull as it expanded in the heat of the yellow-orange star.

"What symptoms? The rest of us are okay," Ley said.

"I hope so. I was just in medical. Rami's having trouble moving today. Some kind of neuromuscular problem. And Hakim had that seizure. The rest of us could have suffered damage as well." She unfolded her kit, syringes and glass vials. "The descroid has a tricky job during re-hydration," she said as she worked. "It has to balance hundreds of neurotransmitters and enzymes. It's complex, and with the age of the equipment and its stored chemicals, things could go wrong. And then you add to that the accelerated cycle."

"What accelerated cycle?" Ley said.

Siba looked up. "Lorca says the rehydration cycle was accelerated in an emergency. The fire triggered it."

Soman said, "Why was there no problem with the ship all that time, and then as soon as we emerged, fires broke out...oh." It dawned on him. "The O_2."

"Exactly," Siba said. "The ship was evacuated to slow corrosion and conserve energy. Just before emergence, the auton powered everything up, and apparently three systems failed." She ticked them off on her fingers. "Recharge junction, spingrav motor, and the breaker on aft J deck."

Ley cackled, "Apparently we exceeded the recommended service frequency." No one laughed.

Siba said, "That's why I want to run complete blood workups. Salts, proteins, neurotransmitters, autoantibodies, endocrine balance, everything." Siba looked around at the tired and anxious faces. "Who's first?"

Ley shrugged, held out an arm. "Right here."

Siba ran her needle into Ley, while in the back of the room an argument broke out over whether there were enough descroids for the return trip.

Ley spun to face the crew arrayed behind her. "Okay everyone, hang on," she said, wiping the blood coagulating on her arm. "So, there aren't enough descroids just now. At least not until Mr. Lorca cobs a few together from the spare coffeemaker and the melted switchgear. He's the best there is when it comes to descroids." She scanned the room, meeting each pair of eyes with her steady gaze. "I promise you, everyone who needs one will have a descroid."

Soman flinched as Siba found his vein. Ley obviously hasn't visited aft deck. Or...what did she mean by *everyone who needs one*. Soman ran the arithmetic again. It always ended the same. Twenty-three original crew. Three never emerged. One code D. One perished in the fire. Leaving eighteen crew and only the thirteen pods.

Siba slid the needle out of him, moved to the next person, working fast.

Ley thrust her jaw at Soman's graphs quivering in the air. "So, Mr. Soman, what do these mean?"

He turned to the holo. "The blue line is hydrogen concentration in the solar nebula, measured by the collector. See it drop to zero? We hadn't even left the solar system. Then within days the energy reserve follows— the red line. It's—"

"Wait a minute. That's gotta be a mistake. That was supposed to be the densest part of the nebula. It's why we chose that trajectory out of the solar system. Are you sure it wasn't a malfunction of the collector?"

"There's no indication of that."

"Fuck, that was our reactor fuel, how could they get that wrong? We're like hunter gatherers out here, living off the land, sucking our fuel from space."

"Sometimes hunter gatherers starved." Everyone turned to Lorca in the back of the room.

"Fucking astrophysicists," Ley growled.

Soman pointed. "Right here the drive shut down to ensure power for life support." He pondered that. An odd name for systems preserving the crew in an undisturbed state of death. "The hole in the nebula came at the worst place. The drive had barely got going. See, this green line is velocity. But with reserve near zero, there was no way to turn around." Soman grimaced at the cruelty of the timing. *Sorcerer's* speed had barely nudged above the baseline. They'd drifted uselessly away from Sol, almost becalmed. No chance to revive the crew. And no reason to— there'd be nothing to do but play cards, fight, masturbate, coast through a useless lifetime until the supplies ran out. Might as well wait it out in descroids.

"What must they have thought on Earth?" Siba said.

"Have a nice trip, bye bye," chuckled Lorca.

Like watching a rip tide tug their child out to sea. *Sorcerer* coasted through the void, too slow to cross the gap in a lifetime, ten lifetimes, twenty. Souls on Earth winking on, burning through, flickering out, while twenty-three desiccated shapes drifted beyond the heliopause.

Soman ran his finger along the blue line to a spot where it spiked up. "There. We finally hit a fresh lobe of the nebula. Fifty-one nineteen. The ship powered up, which tells us the collector was working fine." In five years, *Sorcerer* hit design speed. On to Epsilon Eridani, holding its cargo of dried protein, cold and still.

No one moved in Nav One: three thousand years and still alive. Impossible.

Siba slapped the last blood sample into her bulging satchel and rushed for the nex. Someone called out to her, "When will we know something?" But she was gone. The crew filtered out. Hakim left for the clinic, needing something for his worsening headache. Ley opened a com channel and barked at Moss for an update. When Moss didn't reply immediately, she turned to Soman, eyes flashing. "Under a day left, Mr. Soman. By this time next work shift it'll all be decided. If we don't stop this temperature rise, we can't stay here."

"Where would we go?"

"We'll have to abandon ship in the LEV's."

"We can't live in the LEV's." And they sure couldn't get back to Earth in them.

Ley contemplated the holo of EE2, growing each hour as *Sorcerer* neared orbit. "Of course we can't. We'll have to evacuate to the planet." Ley launched herself at the nex, cursing Moss and the damned heat.

Holy shit, that meant never getting back to Earth. Soman wondered what Cabot thought about Ley's plan. And where was Cabot anyway; hadn't seen him yet today. Soman stretched his sore shoulder, wincing at the ache, already exhausted, only hours after waking from the longest sleep in human history. He wiped the sweat from his face with the crook of his elbow, and in the gathering heat double-checked the course correction that would place them in orbit around EE2.

Soman got to thinking about the descroids. What could he recall—almost nothing. He flicked into the auton and opened an archive. *History of the Descroid*, he thought, and the words scrolled into the search engine. Articles flashed before him, and he scanned hungrily, the facts triggering memories. The press conference. DeSarvo striding the stage holding the glass of water, his fluttering lab coat and tousled black hair, his commanding gaze and hooked nose. They'd called him "The Hawk".

Soman played it in the holo. "We have discovered how to preserve humans for space flight, and to rejuvenate them at their destination," he said, speaking English with a hint of his Buenos Aires Spanish. "We can now make the journey to this star that has captivated us these years."

Raising an arm to hush the noise, DeSarvo said softly, "And the key—" he lifted the glass, his eyes twinkling— "is water." DeSarvo drank slowly, with relish. "If we remove the water—under the correct conditions, of course—we can transport humans for decades and re-hydrate them at his destination. I can tell you this with no doubt or reservation. How could I ask someone to travel into the depths of space, trusting to this process, if I haven't the courage to try it?" DeSarvo turned to the back of the stage. "If the theater technicians would be so kind as to turn on the visual equipment."

An imaginative observer might recognize DeSarvo's features in the shrunken form projected on the screen at the back of the stage, a creature like a dead wasp left to bleach in the desert sun, Glass of water in hand, DeSarvo contemplated his desiccated form, the smile gone. No electrical impulse, no heartbeat. Dead but not gone. Where could a soul reside during all those years.

Soman shivered, then opened the next archive. The first commercial use for the descroid: *Future Lives, Inc.* The name triggered an upheaval of memories, scenes of the crowded tunnel filled with descroids. Anoka lying in the abandoned Fermilab complex, taken over by *Future Lives* when the new generation of supercolliders made obsolete the atom smasher under the western sprawl of Chicago.

He remembered her last words to him, lying in her pod in the moments before the tranquilizer swept her away, I.V. tubes snaking into both arms. "Daddy, will I dream while I'm dead?"

"No, sweetheart." He'd given up trying to stop her from saying that; Anoka thought death was simply a place you waited while they found a cure for your disease, too young to comprehend the end of existence.

"Will I have to wait long?"

He had looked out into the broad curving tunnel, where gleaming descroids arced into the distance, rows of pods lined up like huge insect eggs, each the size of a small room. Just beneath the bubble, each held someone's desiccated child, parent, or lover, the rustle of metabolism silenced. "For you it'll seem like only a minute," he said.

Holding his thumb in her hand, Anoka asked, "How long will it seem for you, Daddy?"

In the swelter of Nav One, Soman held his head in his hands. Thirty centuries.

It had been a desperate plan, joining families scraping together down payments on a pod in the underground vault at *Future Lives*, hoping to stave off the death of someone they loved, then laboring to earn the cash to reclaim them when a cure became available. He'd taken that five-year stint hauling ore from the asteroids for the hazard pay that would reclaim Anoka when the treatment for her medulloblastoma was perfected. Five years away from a cure, they'd said. So why couldn't he recall anything after that. Recovering her from the descroid, her treatment, everything that must have followed. And what about Anne. All he could bring back was Anne standing on that icy curb. The moment hung there, her expression telling him something he couldn't quite grasp. And then…what could possibly have flung him out here.

The nex crackled and his relief arrived, a woman named Selen with cloudy blue eyes and a tired look, who strapped into the zero-G restraint and promptly closed her eyes. Soman hesitated to leave the ship in her hands. But he was needed on the chiller crew. He wiped the sweat from his neck. The temperature aboard *Sorcerer* reached 43.

Hurrying down J tube, a sound interrupted his concentration, and he peeked through the open nex of descroid chamber seven. His chest filled at the sight of Siba, stripped to her underwear in the heat, the length and curve of her glistening with perspiration. A second pair of legs protruded from a service opening at the base of the electronics cabinet, scrawny limbs matted with dark hair. Siba squinted into the shadows, one hand on the man's bony knee, the other pointing at something inside the cabinet.

The hairy legs twisted, and something snapped deep inside the enclosure. A hand appeared, holding a small part—a micropump Soman judged. Siba tossed it into the parts cage. "Is that the last one?" she asked. The man slid from the enclosure, using Siba for leverage as she braced against the console, their arms and legs tangling. Soman recognized the long face, the hooked nose, the olive skin. Lorca.

"I don't know why we bother," Lorca said. "Everyone expects miracles."

Siba patted his cheek. "You're doing great."

Lorca's eyes lingered on the swell of her breasts beneath her tee.

Soman felt like an intruder, the room grown small and quiet. He must have made a sound, because they glanced over.

"We're scavenging parts," Siba said. "Lorca doesn't think we can repair this one."

"You're giving up already?" They'd be down to twelve working pods.

"You are most welcome to try," Lorca said. "You are now the big descroid expert?"

"Half the pumps are ruined," Siba said, "And the warming circuit was burned out." She sighed. "Poor Jane."

Lorca wrapped an arm around Siba. "Thank you…for the help…my dear." He planted a languorous kiss on her lips, then began kissing his way down her throat.

She pushed him away playfully. "I don't often get this kind of thanks," she said. "But back to work."

"What about the other descroids," Soman interrupted.

Lorca glared at Soman for a moment. With a soft growl, he planted one last kiss on Siba's bare shoulder, then untangled himself. He unclipped the cage of parts and moved along the webbing.

Soman grabbed Lorca's shoulder as he passed. "What about the other descroids?" he repeated.

Lorca glanced at Soman's restraining hand. Soman let go. Lorca held up the cage of parts. "Should have enough parts to rebuild number eight," he said. "That was yours, right?" Lorca studied the parts. "I think most of these are good. We'll see."

Soman clenched a fist. Lorca showed mock surprise as he watched Soman struggle for control. Soman shoved him away down the corridor. Lorca stopped his momentum just shy of the port to pod eight and squinted back at Soman. "You're not counting on going back, are you? Have you noticed we have eighteen crew and nine working pods? Well, at least we think nine might work. How should we decide who gets one? Rank? Maybe we run a little lottery. Or women and children first. That would be quaint."

Soman gaped. Down to nine.

Lorca smiled. "Of course, don't worry, it's been decided already, everyone will have a descroid." He pushed off into the port. A crackle as the nex opened. Number eight—Soman's pod.

Soman growled, "What the hell's got into Lorca?"

"You know Lorca. He's awkward. Give him a chance. It was his way of being humorous."

"That wasn't humor. It was fun at my expense."

"That's what humor is." She touched Soman's cheek and chuckled. "We just appreciate it more when someone else is the butt."

"He was right? Only nine pods work?"

"As long as we can be certain what caused the residual cases like Rami."

Soman had run into Rami at Nav Two. The poor guy could barely move, gripping his seat as if facing a re-entry gone wrong. "Have you figured it out?"

Siba positioned the access panel and flipped down latches. "It's his sodium channels."

"What are those?"

"Proteins on the surface of nerve cells that control sodium transfer. The channels move electrical impulses along the nerve. When they don't work, the nervous system is compromised."

"Can you fix it?"

Siba ran an unsteady hand through her hair. "I don't know."

"How about Hakim?"

"I didn't find anything. He's coming in for a brain scan."

"And the rest of us?"

"Well…"

The open port carried sounds of banging, Lorca working on descroid eight. Soman flinched at each bang, Lorca hammering on the delicacy of the descroid. His descroid.

"…half a dozen others have, um, some neurological deviation. But I'm not sure it's anything unusual."

"What about my blood test?"

She moved close and pressed a palm to his chest. "I have to check a couple more things. I'll find you."

Soman's gaze drifted to the tattoo of a dove in the hollow of her throat. She followed his glance and touched her collarbone.

"Beautiful. What does it mean?"

Her eyes welled up. "I can't remember. There are things that just won't come back."

Her words triggered something, a snippet of an old book, by a long-dead twentieth century author, who claimed that the brains of humans in ancient times were bicameral, two halves operating independently, one half telling the other what to do. People interpreted this voice as the gods talking, the origin of Greek and Roman mythology. With time the connection between the halves improved; human consciousness flickered on. The gods receded, replaced by One God, invisible, aloof, silent. For Soman, life before the mission seemed unreachable, trapped in a detached half of the brain, his only reality the voice of the auton living in his skull, talking through his imcom like the gods.

A drill started up in the next chamber. Siba glanced that way. "I'd better help." She squeezed Soman's shoulder and slipped out.

As he watched her disappear into the tube, he rubbed the sore arm. Damn this shoulder. He wanted to believe it was just a sprain. But maybe it was something else, this pain spreading down his arm each hour, this jangling of nerves, this corrosion of the neural pathways.

Chapter 3

Soman whistled softly. Two days from orbital insertion, he realized a landing would be more challenging than anyone imagined. Ley wasn't going to like this. "Um," he said, "These reflection data indicate EE2 has no atmosphere…"

"Nonsense, Mr. Soman. Someone down there signaled us. There must be atmosphere."

"I don't see how…"

"By now they've surely noticed us," she said, studying the holo. "I expect we'll see ships heading our way any time. Can we enlarge it? I want to see more detail of the surface."

The way she was jumping to conclusions one on top of another disturbed him. But he wasn't going to argue with Ley. "We're beyond usable resolution. With the primary scope wrecked, we're stuck with this low power backup. It'll have to wait until we get closer." And he had a chance to talk to Cabot about Ley.

Never satisfied, Ley had to fiddle with the settings, blowing up the image to prove to herself it didn't help.

Soman cast a glance at Ley. She was hard to figure, scary to look at. She sat at attention, but one shoulder sagged, and a bulge marred her back, as if she'd had a difficult birth and never straightened out. But give her a whiff of battle and she's in her element. The recollection of that smoking crater returned. In a flash he remembered the news report he'd watched back on Earth. After panning across the destruction of an entire city, the scene had switched to a wet nighttime tarmac somewhere in West Australia, emergency lights flashing, sirens warbling, sleek warplanes lined up in the glare of arc lamps. A pilot strode from a burning plane, yanking off a helmet. A correspondent with a microphone said, "We're going to speak with Commander Melinda Ley, who led the squadron just returning from the Indonesian capital. Commander Ley!" She shouted over the whine of jet turbines, the microphone thrust out, "Can you tell us what happened over Jakarta today?"

Ley never slowed as she said, "We showed them we're ready to fight terror with terror. And if you'll excuse me, I must plan the next sortie."

The newswoman fell behind. "Commander," she shouted, as she ran to catch up. "Is it true your parents were killed in the attacks on Perth last week?" The reporter's high heel broke and she stumbled. Ley disappeared into the smoke and noise.

The memory faded. Soman squirmed at the thought of sharing a ship with this dangerous old warrior. Why had Cabot chosen a first officer who preferred to fly and shoot at the same time. The Butcher of Jakarta, they'd called her. Over three million casualties, just to make a point, war over ideology and revenge. Soman remembered how Ley got that hump in her shoulder, when she'd stood her burning aircraft on end returning from the final Jakarta raid, when she'd lost that ear—and her birth eyes. Damn Ley. Shot out of the sky three times, yet there she sits, lungs pulling breath, heart pumping, tongue slashing. And unlucky Anoka, plucked from a five-year old life before she learned to fear its misleading appearance, before she knew she held a one-way ticket.

Ley gave up on the image of EE2, exhaling in exasperation. She tried to raise Cabot on open channel. Grunting, she unfastened her restraint and headed for the hatch. "Our captain is having one of his bad days," she said as she disappeared into the tube.

Soman stared after her at the nex. Not Cabot too.

Hakim stirred and pointed to his screen. "Look," he said, his voice shaky. "Here's what I was working on before all hell broke loose. Remember we thought the proximity tracking system was busted?"

"Yeah."

"Well, it works fine."

"You found something out there?" He leaned over for a better look. Sure enough, a cluster of objects, eighty kilometers out, moving slowly away from Sorcerer. "A near miss?"

"Mac," Hakim said. "The burial."

Five objects, each a couple meters long. Holy smokes. Three hours ago, the crew had met at C hold for the burial, ejecting the sealed containers through the lock. That had been the agreement; no remains brought back. The voyagers deserved to spend eternity at their hard-earned destination. At least that was the official story. Rumor held that mission planners wanted to minimize the risk of returning an alien infection. Couldn't always be sure what had killed a person.

"I looked to see if the proximity tracking system could find 'em," Hakim said. "Yep, right there. System works fine. Now you explain to me why in ten million miles of glide there's not one rock."

He pulled up the nav plot, rubbing his sore shoulder. The lack of an atmosphere was maybe for the best. He had no enthusiasm for a landing, and without an atmosphere, forget it. Update the course correction.

Bring the ship to orbit. Try to find out who's living on EE2 and how they built all those mirrors. Then get the hell home in one piece. He knew he had to get back. He hoped he'd remember why.

He got to work on the insertion burn. But the extra shift working on a repair team, on four hours' sleep, had sapped his energy. And it was easy to doze in zero G—no drop of the head to snap you back from sleep. He startled awake at the crackle of the nexport. It was Moss, worn raw.

Soman hadn't noticed Lorca asleep on a couch until he roused at the noise. "Why don't you fix that noisy damn nex?" Lorca said to Moss, as he smoothed his rumpled flight suit. "A person can't get a decent nap around here." He wore a faded cap that read *Descroid: driest martini in the known universe.*

Moss looked Lorca up and down.

Lorca pointed to Moss's tool belt and laughed. "You still using wrenches? It's the fifty-third century."

Soman held his breath as he took in Moss's blistering gaze and tightening muscles, hoping Lorca was smart enough to button it up. Despite what Siba had said, Soman couldn't see this as harmless fun. People take psychiatric drugs for this.

Moss said, "You want spingrav working, grab a wrench." He pushed past Lorca is if he weren't there.

"I like it this way," Lorca said, sprawling across the couch, feigning nonchalance. "It's easier on the legs."

A flicker of annoyance crossed Moss's face. "We don't get spingrav working, we're all going to atrophy. And we better get these seals replaced and fix those servos, or we're asking for another venting failure."

Soman's dry joints hurt bad enough without spingrav. He couldn't imagine trying to put a full G on his knees. But Moss was right. Already he could feel the muscle tone draining.

Moss reached the far couch, clipped his belt to the restraint, and turned his back to the room.

The nex opened again, allowing in for a second the warble of a sonic saw from down the tube as someone tore into the seized bypass valve. Siba glided in, pushing tendrils of damp hair from her face, her blouse sweat-stained. She glanced at Soman, her expression serious. "Good, I wanted to talk to you."

Lorca studied her. "Looks like someone's been exercising you, sweetheart. When's my turn?"

"Jesus Christ, Lorca," Soman said. "Keep it to yourself."

Lorca laughed. "What's this, a new rule?"

Siba's glare made it clear she didn't need Soman's help.

Lorca said, "And I suppose you're here to enforce the rules." When Soman said nothing, something mean flickered in Lorca's eyes. "No? That's not it? Come on, Soman, why *are* you here?"

Soman faltered, recalling when he'd faced that question once before: his final interview for the *Sorcerer* mission, held in the massive orbiting assembly station. Ley across the gleaming steel table, arms crossed, asking why he wanted to leave Earth for two hundred fifty years. He knew he had lied. But now he couldn't dredge the truth.

Lorca's eyebrows rose in mock astonishment. "I'll bet you came to answer the great mystery of Epsilon Eridani. Let's all sing kum-bah-yah."

"So why are *you* here?" Siba asked Lorca.

"Ah," Lorca said, turning his attention to her. "I heard there are women at Epsilon Eridani. Beautiful women."

Siba met his stare. "I'm serious. Do you have any recollection why you joined?"

Lorca gazed up, pondering the maze of conduit and ductwork snaking across the ceiling. "Oh, I wouldn't miss Cabot's second voyage."

Siba dismissed Lorca with a wave. "What I wouldn't miss right now is my turn on this couch," she said. "Go clean some filters so we can get the rest of the CO_2 units on line."

"Can't. I've got descroids to analyze." He grinned at Soman. "Wouldn't want any more code Ds in group three, would we?"

Soman knew he would never dare crawl into that descroid again.

Lorca unclipped and floated through the nex.

"The man's sick," Soman said.

"What?"

"Lorca." Soman said, gesturing toward the nex, irritated that she looked more amused than angry. "He went after Moss, then me, then you. I thought Moss was going to smash him in the face."

"Oh, it wasn't that bad. I thought you overreacted."

"Come on! He badgers you for sex in public and you don't think it's that bad?"

She waved a hand. "That didn't bother me. He comes from a culture where that's normal."

"He pushed Moss right to the brink of a fistfight. It was psychotic."

"Leave Lorca to me. We don't need any fights." She pointed at his screen. "What are you working on?"

"Well," he muttered. "Ley wants me to develop a landing scenario. But I'm getting nowhere. And she's so unqualified for space she doesn't get it."

"Get what?"

"We expected a planet with an atmosphere. If she wants to land, we'll have to use the two-stage descent and leave most of our lift capability on the surface. She's so mule headed. I never understood why being the Butcher of Jakarta was a qualification for First Officer."

"What did you say?" Siba faltered as if he'd slapped her. Soman recognized the sensation—a memory swimming to the surface.

Soman instantly regretted what he'd said. "It's just...I hope Cabot keeps her on a short..." An instinct told him to move on. "Speaking of Cabot," he said, "What's the news on him?"

Siba took a moment to gather herself. "Well...his vitals are good, but...he may have a bit of the sodium channel problem." She grew pensive. "And Selen had a blackout last shift. They found her floating in LEV bay. Her acetylcholine was sky-high."

"Who's going to run Nav One in the off shift?"

"Rami. He can't move around much, but he can fill in here."

Soman rubbed his elbow, grimacing.

"What's wrong?" she asked.

"This arm is killing me." He rubbed his thumbs across his fingertips. "And my fingers are a little numb.

She probed his arm, working along the muscle up to his shoulder. "These are rock-hard," she said. She tried to knead his shoulder, but without gravity the effort only floated her toward the ceiling. "Here," she said. "I need to get some leverage. Hold me down" She placed his hands on her hips, then began working his arm. "Brother, I'd forgotten how big you are. These are some real muscles." She dug into his shoulders with the heels of her hands. Soman felt her warmth. Knots loosened across his back, and he rolled his head. "Mmm, that feels good. Like you're injecting a drug right there."

As she worked, she asked, "Were you ever told you had a B-12 imbalance?"

"I...I don't know."

"It's called pernicious anemia. Apparently, you had a Lokey procedure."

"Oh...that sounds familiar."

"You'd remember it." She stopped for a moment. "Well, normally you would." She resumed the massage, her fingers digging into his neck. "It starts with tingling in the fingers, then numbness moving up the arms and legs. When it reaches the core muscles, you can't swallow or breathe. It was always fatal until they synthesized B-12 in the twentieth century. They used to treat it with a monthly injection. Now there's the Lokey implant."

"What's that?"

"A patch of your own cells is genetically modified to produce B-12 receptors, then stitched into your stomach lining. They absorb it from your food, so you don't need the injection. But your blood test showed abnormally low B-12. Your treatment's no longer working."

"So, I need to come to the clinic for a shot?"

"We didn't stock B-12. It's strange, but I couldn't find it in your medical file. If we'd known, we could have brought B-12 as a precaution."

Soman cringed. Somehow, he was certain he had deliberately withheld the information, wanting nothing that could disqualify him. Just like they didn't know he had a daughter. Hadn't disclosed that either.

Soman swallowed hard. Always fatal, she'd said. "They didn't know a descroid cycle would do this?"

Her expression grew dark. Something churned in her.

Her touch felt so good. Forget the B-12. He glanced to the corner, where Moss proved that gravity is not required for the mechanics of snoring. He pulled Siba close and kissed her. He pulled her tighter, aware only of the fluid pressure of her lips. She wrapped her arms around his neck and kissed him back.

It was a small change at first, a tightening of her back. Then she broke off, distance in her eyes. "No," she said, a moan more than a word. She trembled, a hand to her mouth, looking past him.

"What's wrong?"

"I remembered..."

Studying her face, he was surprised to see lines radiating from the corners of her mouth, the furrows of a much older woman. She was wearing herself down, working day and night under the pressure of keeping everyone alive and functioning. "What?"

Her eyes rimmed with tears. "I...I can't." She pushed away and dove through the nex.

Chapter 4

Soman made his way back to quarters. Suddenly a new sound. He stopped, looked around. Then he felt it. Air movement. Blowers. He flicked into open channel. "Is that the chillers?" Someone answered, "That's right. Now we see if one chiller can do the job."

Soman was asleep before he could finish undressing. The dream started everything churning.

He was on a different ship, in a tiny cabin, wearing a comlink helmet. Something in the helmet's heads-up display held him transfixed, the glow of revelation suffusing him. But before he could grasp the revelation, a shudder ran though the ship's skeleton. The craft yawed, and he tore off the heads-up helmet. Metal shrieked around him. He dove for the hatch as the shock wave hit.

He woke thrashing in the dark. Soman knew the incident was real, though he couldn't recall the name of the ship, couldn't piece together when it had happened; a free-floating memory with nothing to anchor it, ambushing him from the depths of sleep. But he recognized the compartment in the dream, and he chewed it over. A spin tunnel, the kind they used in ore freighters to get a few minutes of G's every day to stave off atrophy. He had used a comlink helmet just like that to scan the daily data burst from Earth when he'd been out...

The sleeping sack rocked. A sudden noise, settling into a low whine. The sack swung like a windsock in the breeze. Soman sank deeper into the fabric. Spingrav. Moss had finally got it working. He checked the time. Three hours of disturbed sleep. Might as well keep Ley off his back by starting the LEV prep. Soman slid to the floor. His cabin had an up and down again.

His flight suit had collapsed in a heap when spingrav created weight out of thin air. He pulled it on, moving unsteadily. The dream had shaken him, torn attachments loose.

Almost time for insertion around EE2, a correction so minor he could barely feel the nudge as he limped down the tube. He made his way to LEV bay. Powered up the first LEV and started its diagnostics. He ran it up the rail into launch position. He could return later and review the boot data. He'd check every detail of this now-ancient craft before trusting his life to it.

Entering Nav One, Soman stopped at the unexpected crowd. Rami and Ley sat at the console, gesturing toward the flickering holo. Cabot stood behind them, holding Rami's seatback. Lorca leaned carelessly against the electronics rack, a toothpick hanging from his lips. Siba stood beside Ley, watching something on the holo as Ley pointed.

After days of weightlessness, it was strange to see everyone standing like toys stuck to the floor. Soman grew aware of his height; everyone looking up at him. He'd forgotten about being the tallest person on ship, weightlessness taking away the distinction.

"Mr. Soman," Ley said. "Your landing simulation doesn't work." Her voice lacked its usual spine.

He pondered the image of the planet in the holo, immense now that they had swung into low orbit. No longer the fuzzy data blob of Earth's interferometers, EE2 lay under them huge and hard, its polished edges stark. No cities and no spaceports, only bare, gleaming skin, a polyhedron of mirrored surfaces. A beacon, not a world.

"That's what I tried to explain yesterday. Our LEVs are designed to land on an Earth-mass world and return to orbit without refueling, assuming airbraking on entry. But there isn't much safety margin. So first we send down an unmanned fuel drop. Then the LEV lands nearby and refuels from the drone. The problem is you can't airbrake when there's no atmosphere."

Ley rubbed her face, exhaled heavily. "We got any more coffee here?" she said, looking around. Soman was struck by Ley's drawn face. No wonder she needed coffee, spending her off-shifts trying to figure out a landing instead of sleeping. Those eyeballs might be brand new, but the face was worn.

Siba said, "I'll get some." She squeezed Ley's shoulder, then patted her arm. Ley and Siba exchanged a tender smile. Like mother and daughter, Soman thought. No way, those two couldn't be more opposites. Siba headed for the nex.

Ley rubbed her temples. "Is the airbraking really such a big deal? Just adjust the fuel loads, like we do landing transports at high elevations."

"People who fly airplanes take the air for granted." He tried to keep the derision he felt out of his voice. "Watch." Soman ran the simulation on the holo, the flash of the rocket burn lighting their faces. The drone made its descent, falling away from *Sorcerer* toward the planet. "The drone hits the surface of the planet at three times design force." The simulated drone crashed and exploded. "There's just no engine efficient enough to make a single stage drop to an airless planet the size of EE2 and return."

Lorca stirred. "You mean we weren't smart enough to plan for this?"

Ley said, "So we need a lower stage for the drone, right Mr. Soman?"

"Yes, we can do a two-stage drop," Soman said. "Strap a LEV underneath the drone, load it up with fuel, burn it and jettison. Essentially it sacrifices a LEV to land a full drone in one piece." It had been an unlikely contingency, but they had designed the parts for a two-stage vehicle, just in case.

"Good," said Ley. "And of course we refit the LEV with one of those mark nine engines. That'll get the impact down to a hundred twenty percent of design. There's enough safety margin to survive that."

Soman recalled his calculation from yesterday: 123.7%. Close enough. He pondered those mark nines stacked in C hold, black nozzles twice as high as a man, their tapered ends enveloped in a snarl of piping. None of the LEVs carried a mark nine, yet here were four of them secured and ready. The specs told him they could deliver twenty percent more thrust. Why weren't they already mounted on the LEVs.

"I still don't like it," he said.

"What's your problem. It works."

"It's a matter of safety."

"Safety? You put yourself in a descroid on a prototype ship and travel ten light-years from home, and you're worried about safety? I got news for you, Mr. Soman. This mission isn't about safety. It's about first contact."

"That doesn't mean we have to be stupid about it. And starting off with one-third of our LEV capability gone is just stupid."

Ley glared at him.

Lorca said, "Use a drone as the lower stage."

"Then we'd be out of drones, with no way to get fuel on planet in an emergency."

"Why didn't we bring more equipment. We come all this way, and we can't finish the job. Now that's stupid."

Soman said, "It's all mass we have to accelerate and decelerate both ways. You never get as much payload as you want."

"We shouldn't have to do this all ourselves," griped Ley. "There's supposed to be a civilization here. Where the hell are they?"

Soman said, "Until we spot some evidence of life down on the surface, I'd hate to gamble all our resources on a landing. We might need every LEV, if only for spare parts. And we'd lose our rescue capability. We don't have two more LEVs for a second fuel drop *and* a rescue."

"But you'll already have fuel on the surface," Ley shot back. "We just send the third LEV to pick everyone up, using the fuel from the first drone."

An expression from training came to Soman. "Every manned mission must preserve double redundancy."

Lorca laughed. "You *are* here to enforce the rules."

"Fuck the rules," Ley said. "We're here to explore a planet. This is no place for cowards, Mr. Soman." With an air of dismissal, Ley turned to Cabot. "Captain?"

After an overlong silence, Cabot said, "We *are* here to find whoever signaled us." His voice, always built of gravel, was now halting. "Rami, where else could we look?"

Rami moved agonizingly to bring up a new display. Skinny little Rami had resembled a teenager before he'd crawled into his descroid back in the comfortable light of Sol. Now he moved with the slow deliberation of an old man. Unbalance a few neurotransmitters, alter the sodium channels, and a different person appears behind the familiar folds of flesh clinging to the bones. Soman looked from Rami to Cabot with a sudden premonition—these two traveled the same path of decline.

The holo of the planet with its black smudges collapsed, replaced by a model of the Epsilon Eridani system. At the center lay the mother star. Close to it orbited the two solid planets, EE1 and EE2. Then the disc of an asteroid belt. Farther out circled two gas giants, obscured by swirling, ruddy-brown clouds.

The nex crackled and Moss stepped in, eyes bloodshot, wearing the faded coveralls with the same grease stains as yesterday. A quick nap in Nav One was probably the only sleep he'd managed in the past few days.

Moss took in the group. "Heard we're planning. I'd sure like a vote."

Lorca shoved his palm in Moss's face. "Invitation only."

The nex slid open, Siba returning with a vacuum bottle on a tray and four steaming mugs. "Coffee's a lot easier with spingrav, isn't it," she said brightly. She pulled up short, Moss and Lorca blocking her path. She barely had time to register their stare-down before Moss swept up his hand and knocked the tray into Lorca's face. Lorca screamed as the hot liquid splattered him.

"Hey, that was my coffee!" Ley yelled.

"Fucker burned me!" Lorca bawled, sidling away from Moss.

Ley waved an arm toward Lorca. "Why the hell you wanna needle Moss anyway? Haven't you got something better to do?"

For an instant Lorca's glare fell on Soman, an extra narrowing of the eyes. Then he fled, banging his shoulder on the hatch frame as he stumbled toward the nex. Lorca's expression stayed with Soman, the look of a man without a friend in the world.

The aroma of coffee permeated the room; its stain ran down the wall like tears.

"Idiot," pronounced Moss. He threw himself onto the couch with a grunt and rubbed the back of his neck. "He asked for it."

"Okay, Rami, the children are quiet now," Ley said. She looked back to the holo. "Fuck the coffee. Rami, what do we have?"

Slowly, excruciating, he got out, "EE2 has been…built from scratch, or…re…surfaced. No debris in the inner system. Look. Not an impact crater in sight."

For a moment they watched the curve of EE2 slide across their screens.

"What does it mean?" Ley asked.

"I think…they cleared all the junk. Gathered the scrap, parked it in a closer orbit so it couldn't crash into their beacon and wreck the surface. That's EE1: the trash heap from the construction."

Moss said, "You're talking about clearing away a disk 200 million miles in radius. That's a hell of a civilization."

Soman said, "So that's why Hakim hasn't found any debris." He pondered what it would take to haul away the entire asteroid belt between Mars and Jupiter. Then he remembered—asteroid belt—that's where he'd been in that ship, hauling ore, when he'd learned about…Soman gripped the edge of the console, certain he would fall any second to a memory rising faster than he could hold on.

"And" Rami said, pointing to the tiny black moon of EE2. "I don't believe…that's a moon."

Soman couldn't be sure about the next sequence of events; memory so imperfect, held in living cells, needing oxygen every minute of an uncertain life. As all attention hung on the holo, the room lights flicked off, plunging them into darkness. The holo collapsed to a tiny point, then winked out. Pounding through the dark, the sound of valves slamming. A rushing noise like a blizzard howling across the prairie.

Soman staggered in the pitch black. Memories welled up in a breaking wave—the dream of forever. His knees failed.

"Moss!" Ley yelled over the shriek of wind. "Didn't you fix that overload limit?"

"That wasn't an overload." The pitch of his voice rose. "Where's the backup?"

"It'll kick in."

"It's taking too long."

"Why are those blowers running?" A hint of worry in Ley's voice.

Moss shot back, "That's not blowers. That's our air."

"Pressure suits!" yelled Ley.

Someone ran into Soman, upending his shaky balance. His head struck something as he fell, spraying sparks across his vision. He crawled forward, finally glimpsing the revelation he'd found that day in the freighter.

Siba called, "Auton, auton, auton…" Then she went silent.

Soman's extremities tingled from hypoxia, nerves shutting down. The last of his air gone, chest ballooning, guts convulsing, the strengthening vacuum sucking his organs out—spacer's heartburn. His cheek against the icy deck, frost forming on his eyelashes. Soman lay still and empty, stunned by the realization that he was about to expire on this cold slab of steel seconds after remembering why he'd joined the mission: immortality.

Chapter 5

Something fell to the deck beside Soman's face. A whiff of cold air roused him. An oxygen mask. He clutched it to his mouth. Click; a light blazed above him. Siba stood there, sealing herself into a pressure suit with practiced motions, twisting into the helmet. She must have tossed the mask to him. Then she disappeared.

Soman gulped from the mask, recollection pinning him to the deck.

When that asteroid had hit his freighter, Soman had been in the aft spin tunnel, winding some extra Gs after the scan warned of depleting bone mass. While he spun, he sifted through the day's news burst. The heads-up display had flashed a warning, but Soman missed it for a few seconds, so intent was he on one item. *"Scientists Unravel the Telomere,"* the headline read, but it was the quote near the end that so riveted Soman's attention that he was slow to recognize the insistent skew in the ship's attitude. *"This breakthrough"*, *said Dr. Leonard Szalby of the Salk Institute for Biological Studies, "will allow us, within twenty years, to halt the aging process."*

Soman had been thinking a lot about death, and it almost cost him his life.

He tore off the helmet and listened. You don't twist one point seven million tons of rock without one hell of a collision. Metal shrieked, the disturbance growing closer. Soman dove out the hatch of the spin tunnel into the LEV hold as the first shock wave hit. By the time he'd turned to look, the concussion had crushed the tunnel; only a thin sliver of blue light shone through the flattened structure—from the display helmet he'd just been wearing. It flickered and went out.

The freighter's hull groaned and shook. He snatched the suit he always secured within a few feet of his workstation. Crewmates on the lunar runs had teased him for dragging a pressure suit around, but there had been many a crew surprised by the speed a small hull can decompress. Surprised and dead. Especially single handing like this, no help within ten million miles. He suited up in under fifteen seconds, then squirmed into the the drive module. Silence. No buzz of lasers melting the rock to plasma. No roar of ions blasting through the nozzle. He slid into the console, his hands shaking, sent a burst to Colony One.

Asteroid strike destroyed the control module. Shock wave split the mass feeder for the drive. Drive disabled. Collision perturbed trajectory. Present course will miss Earth by one point six nine million miles. Require relief.

While he waited for the return burst, Soman returned to the news feed. He read it twice, with awe, then gall. Twenty years. He'd be fifty-four. And what if it took thirty years; he'd be an old man. What good would it do to extend life when it was almost over.

Soman waited in the silence of deep space. While he waited, he pulled in more research. Teams all over Earth were racing to find a cure for aging. The most promising route: prevent the shortening of the telomeres that tip each chromosome. Because when the telomere is gone, the organism can no longer renew itself. They were closing in on the answer, but how long would it take. Unfair, this short lifespan.

A burst arrived from the lunar transmitter.

Abandon load. At closest Earth approach, transfer to Colony One in the LEV. We calculate you have sufficient air and supplies.

Soman stared. Sufficient air. Maybe by taking every other breath. Just thinking about it increased his respiration rate. Fucking company. Won't spend the money to pluck their pilot before he spins beyond the ecliptic.

He ran a few trajectories, then gazed out the port, the starfield so bright it hurt his eyes. Eighteen months until he could launch the LEV, then six months in the LEV to Colony One. He'd need to store extra O_2 on the LEV, O_2 produced from the rock. Just stay alive.

The frost on the deck sublimed away, exposing grime and bare steel. Pressure built behind his eyes. He rolled over, crawled toward the suit locker. Nearby, Moss and Ley, already suited up, helped Cabot with his helmet, their visor lamps casting shaky pools of light.

Soman yanked down a suit and struggled with fabric and balky latches, sinuses bulging, skin and cartilage straining to hold back the pressure of his swelling face. Faster. Finally, the helmet, the familiar aroma of plastic and machine oil. Air billowing the suit, pressure tamping his face back into shape. He clawed at the faceplate in agony.

A barrage of noise on open channel. Clanging alarms. Hakim calling from somewhere. Grunts and moans. In the background, a faint voice croaking, "Help."

Then Siba, on the edge of panic. "Quick—I can't do this myself. Hurry, Hurry." She knelt over Rami, struggling to jam him into a suit as his limbs flopped from her grasp.

Soman staggered over and dropped to a knee. Then, as he shoved one of Rami's skinny arms into the sleeve, he slowed. It reminded him of

Anoka's tiny arm as she lay in her pod, moments before surrendering to the sedative. He'd watched an artery pulse in her throat, her hair shimmering, the fine texture of her skin like melted pearl. The doctor pausing, then nodding at Soman as he opened the drip to her IV. Hearing the squeak of the valve, Anoka had flung herself at her father, throwing the white sheet partially off her bare body, burying her face in his arm. "I'm going to be afraid now," she had said.

"You're going to be brave," he told her. Her breath slowing; her pupils dilating. The pod's lid hinged open above her like a gaping mouth. She gazed up, concentrating as if trying to catch the last diminuendo of a faraway choir. She lifted two fingers in a feeble wave. "See you in a minute, daddy."

Recalling that moment, Soman sagged, losing his grip on Rami. It had seemed foolproof, the revised contract with *Future Lives*—its language carefully researched and crafted, assuring the continuation of the trustee from Julian through succeeding generations. Time wouldn't matter to Anoka; it would still seem like a minute to her. But now he was long overdue. Written off as dead and derelict. Their ship failing, the old hull coughing out its puny puff of Earth air to fog the mirror of EE2. Since emergence, he had thought he'd joined the mission for her—to allow time for her cure. Now he knew the truth.

Siba elbowed Soman away and sealed the last of Rami's latches.

Ley's voice crackled on open channel. "Mr. Hakim, what's your status?"

"Four of us in LEV hold two."

"Pressure?"

"Yes."

"Are we hit?"

"Don't think so. No alarms."

"Your whole detail accounted for?"

"Missing Lorca."

"Yeah, he was up here making trouble," Ley said. "Moss, come on. We've got to get the backup on. Soman, you find Lorca."

Soman heard that faint moan again in his auton, the mournful noise of a man yielding to his last extremity. The same voice that had called earlier for help. "Lorca!" He jumped up and stumbled through the nex. They needed Lorca, or the descroids might never...

Soman raced down the dark tube, stumbling into bulkheads, his legs clumsy after days in zero G, his knees in agony at this abuse in the first hour of spingrav. As he ran, he flicked into the auton and opened the locator. There was Lorca's marker—outside living quarters. He plunged through the nex, blinded by the lights—there was power on this side. Then why was Lorca prone on the deck of the tube, an arm tangled in the webbing. Soman hesitated. Lorca was having fun at his expense again. Asshole. But something about Lorca's posture drew Soman near, the angle of his neck or the heaviness with which he sprawled. Soman checked his suit gauge. What the—there was no air pressure here either. He'd been fooled by the lights into thinking this tube was unaffected. He fell to his knees beside Lorca, and what he saw clotted the air in his lungs. Lorca's face split open; blood pooling in his eye sockets.

He scooped up Lorca and ran for the clinic nex. Better be pressure there or Lorca's dead. He dove through to L deck, and he knew instantly there was pressure, from the momentary convulsion that ran through Lorca, and the moan. Soman flinched at the pain Lorca must feel. After that brief spasm, Lorca hung in Soman's arms like dead weight.

Bursting into the clinic, Soman eased Lorca to the floor, then tore off his helmet and gloves. Hands shaking, he glanced around at the unfamiliar medical gear. "Sibaaaa!" he hollered into open. "Clinic!" Unable to form a coherent sentence.

No pulse. Chest still. Get him air. Looking down at Lorca's burst and bleeding lips, Soman faltered, then spread his mouth over Lorca's and breathed into him; Lorca's chest swelled like a worn balloon. On the exhale, a stench gurgled out of him. Soman's stomach turned over. "You're gonna owe me," he said. When the nausea passed, he blew again, and again. He focused on the routine. How many breaths. Three. No, five. Pump the chest. Fist in fist. Five pumps. More breaths. Need a rhythm.

The nex crackled, and Siba was there, straddling Lorca, taking over the pumping. Soman continued breathing into him, trying not to think about the thickening slime of blood and saliva he and Lorca now shared.

Numb to the routine, Soman's recollection from Nav One flooded back. No wonder he hadn't told Ley why he'd joined. He had used the mission to get a free descroid. With the delays in a treatment for Anoka, he had considered using a portion of his hazard pay to place himself in a descroid for a decade or two. But in the four years after he'd committed Anoka to her pod, news of the breakthroughs in telomere research had started to leak out. Those who could afford it were quietly buying up the available descroid slots, a hedge in case the development of life-extension treatments took too long. By the time Soman returned from the asteroids, the waiting list for a descroid was twenty years, and the price far beyond his means. *Sorcerer* held the only descroids he had any chance of occupying—and as the most qualified LEV pilot on Earth, he knew he had a shot.

But now…three thousand years. The advances on Earth would be unimaginable. Maybe that's why there were no messages from home—the new realm on Earth made it difficult to understand beings who still counted life in days and weeks and years.

Siba shouted, "Got a pulse! Get him on the table." Soman hefted Lorca up. Siba grabbed a length of tubing, then tore off a piece of tape with her teeth. It took her three tries to position the tracheal tube. She taped it down, strapped on a mask, and flicked up the monitors. Lorca's chest rose and fell eight times a minute to the rasp of the machine.

"We did it," Soman shouted. He stepped back, watching Siba adjust the machine, in admiration of her skills. "I thought you were gone," he said "And then you were the first into a suit. How did you do it?"

"Meditation," she said. "While you and Moss were opening the suit locker, I got my heart rate down and saved my air. I had enough for one burst." Then she began to sob. Soman peered over her shoulder, and his elation plummeted. Beneath the oxygen mask, Lorca's face lay bloated and purple. One eye glinted white and crystalline like a shattered gem, the other obscured behind hardening blood.

Siba stroked Lorca's chest, gaping at his ruined face, her breath coming in shudders. "Oh God," she murmured, tears running down her cheeks.

Soman scanned the incomprehensible screens. "Got a brain picture?"
Siba shook her head.

He gripped the edge of the gurney and leaned over Lorca, more afraid than at any time since emergence. How was he going to get back.

Another crackle of the nex and Ley plunged in, tearing off her helmet as she came. She leapt across the room and kicked the gurney, screaming, "You son of a bitch!" Lorca's limp body lurched, his head lolled, and the respirator tube whipped. She booted the table again, knocking it against the wall with a crash.

"Stop it!" Siba flung herself across Lorca to keep him from rolling off. A rivulet of blood ran down his temple.

Ley fought her way at Lorca, her fingers digging into Siba's shoulder. "You better hope you never wake up, Mr. Lorca, or I'll kick your scrawny ass all the way to fucking Sol."

Soman knocked Ley backwards into a chair. "Leave him alone!" he shouted. She tried to fight back up, but he pinned her down.

Siba touched Ley's hand. "Please," she said.

Ley grunted and stopped fighting him. For a moment her breathing matched the plunk and hiss of the respirator.

Moss came through the nex, pale and haggard.

Soman looked from Ley to Moss. "What happened?"

"He pulled the backup power, then flipped off the main breaker to Nav deck."

"Lorca?" Goddamn Lorca, retaliating for the coffee. Make them scramble in the dark. "But…that should just cut the power, not blow the air. The vents close automatically in a power failure." Soman saw Ley thinking it through. "That's right, Moss. What the hell happened?"

"I'll tell you what happened. Everyone's over-worked. Hartler cycled the con valves after a double shift on the spingrav motor windings. She must have left the valve control in the wrong mode. They're supposed to fail closed, but she left them in fail open. Fuck." He kicked at Soman's crumpled pressure suit sprawled on the floor.

Soman looked down at Lorca. He wouldn't have known; he must have thought it a harmless prank to take out the con lights.

"Get Hartler down here!" Ley barked.

"She's dead," Moss said.

"What?"

"She went to her quarters before the next shift. Everyone else in quarters got caught, too. Hartler. Huang. Marton. Tedar. All gone." Moss almost lost his balance, leaned against the wall.

"How did this take out the air in quarters?"

Moss sighed. "Yesterday…we shut down living quarters' air system to repair that bypass valve. It was temporarily connected to the con header. When the air blew, it took theirs with it. They never had a chance."

Soman watched Lorca's chest expand and collapse. He probably didn't believe it when his ears popped. And then, instead of grabbing a suit and coming back to help, he'd left everyone trapped while he fled through the nex to quarters, thinking it would be safe. It should have been. Soman steadied himself against the bulkhead. It gets you just like that, no warning, no time to prepare. What would you prepare, anyway.

Ley screamed, "Mr. Moss, how many times can you screw up in one day?"

Moss launched himself at Ley. Soman leaped up to hold him back. Trying to fight his way past Soman, Moss screamed, "I've told you how many times we didn't have enough people to get all the repairs made. But no, you want to land on the fucking planet."

"You're trying to blame *me*?" Ley showed a pilot's reflexes as she reached around Soman and punched Moss in the face. Moss staggered, shook off his surprise, raised his fists and swung at Ley.

As much as he would have liked to see Moss deck Ley, Soman pushed Moss away, shouting "Don't!" A melee would make things worse. Moss's punch caught Soman below the eye. The pain from his damaged face almost took Soman down, but he managed to keep his feet, pinning Moss against the bulkhead until his will to fight drained. Then Moss tore himself from Soman's grasp and disappeared into the tube. Ley turned on Lorca. "Must've been a sweet moment when you realized there was no air on the other side. I wish I could have been there to see your face."

Lorca's body heaved rhythmically.

Soman's eye throbbed where Moss had clipped him. Dizzy, he pictured the group of them in their spinning can, trying to kill each other, ten light-years from home. A sudden motion—Ley punching off the power to the respirator. He leaped for the panel. "Wait! He's the only one who knows—" Ley blocked him, and he lost his balance, falling heavily against the adjacent bed; the bed and Soman toppled with a crash.

Fending off Siba and ignoring her screams to stop, Ley tore the mask from Lorca's face, the tube slithering out of his gullet, blood and saliva spraying across the room. She slung the bloody mess at Soman where he sprawled in the tangle of the gurney. "I just hope he knows he's dead." She crouched before Lorca like a lioness defending her kill, while Siba wailed.

Lorca's lungs gave up the last of their borrowed air in a long shuddering exhalation.

"Sorry, Mr. Lorca, we seem to have had a power failure," Ley said. Then she stormed through the nex, leaving Soman and Siba staring at Lorca's remains, imagining the row of descroids one deck down, lined up like open graves.

Chapter 6

At the end of a sleepless rest period, Soman remembered where he'd hidden the holocard. He tore off the access panel behind the O_2 sensor in his cabin and reached deep into the crevice. For a moment he froze, recalling the motion holo that would float above the card, a sham of life. Little Anoka, smiling, joyful, absorbed in the moment, holding down the mauve beret, golden hair blowing about her face. His fingers bumped the card, and he withdrew it with trembling hands. "No!" he whispered when it wouldn't power up.

In search of a power lead, he tracked down Moss, found him just as Moss left his cabin.

"Have you got one of those universal leads?" Soman asked.

Moss glanced down the tube as if he wanted to get away.

Soman said, "I've got a dead transmitter in one of the LEV—"

"Just a minute," Moss said, and he went back into his cabin.

Soman waited, frowning over an impression that Moss had been concealing something.

Within seconds, Moss returned with the lead. "Here," he said, then shooed Soman away.

Back in the privacy of his cabin, Soman plugged it in. Nothing. "Goddamn," he said, shoulders sagging. He knew he shouldn't show the card to anyone, but he ached to see her. In desperation he took it to Rami. Rami would be discreet.

Rami turned it over in his hand, wincing with the effort of even that simple motion. "This memory…only good…a few decades," he said as he handed it back. If Rami was curious at Soman's anguish over a dead holocard, he didn't show it. Of course, Rami had his own problem. He could barely move.

Shoving the card deep into his pocket, Soman went straight to forward J deck, to the spot where a view of descroids always teased memories of Anoka closer to the surface…

He jumped at a hand on his shoulder.

"A favorite place of yours, it seems," Ley said.

She had hit the mark, and it rattled him.

"Why didn't you volunteer?" she asked.

Soman looked away. The truth was out of the question.

For a moment they pondered descroids.

"Mr. Soman," she said firmly. "We need you."

"Hakim's as good a LEV driver as anyone."

"He's almost as good as you. But you've seen his convulsions. Cabot insists this be a volunteer flight, so I can't force you. But we need a steady hand. We need you."

Soman cringed. "He hasn't had a seizure in a couple days." He knew how lame it sounded. "Siba's giving him something." That small accomplishment had buoyed Soman, a first step in reversing the degradation. Now Ley was saying she didn't trust it.

She gazed at the view down the tube. "Does this help you to remember something?"

Soman felt the lure, someone to confide in. He almost said *I need to get home,* but bit down hard instead. No unguarded moments with Ley. "Not much," he said. Uncomfortable under her gaze, as if she knew he was lying, he asked, "Do you remember anything from before?"

Ley shook her head. "And you know what? I like it this way. No regrets, no guilt, no false obligation to the past."

Pondering her scarred face, Soman could only imagine what regrets Ley must have left behind. And what enemies.

She gripped his arm. "Come on, Soman. An easy cruise to the moon and back. You can catch up on your sleep or read girlie magazines, I don't care. But I don't want to go without you. You are a part of this mission. Stick together, and we'll get you home."

He looked up. "How?"

"In case you haven't noticed, we're now only four descroids short. Nine pods, thirteen of us."

"Nine if Siba can get them working."

Ley shrugged. "It's the best offer you're likely to get."

He locked eyes with her. "Are you promising me a descroid if I volunteer?"

Ley's gaze turned steely. "Would you take it?"

"Well..." he looked down.

"That's correct, Mr. Soman. I shouldn't offer, and you shouldn't accept." Her eyes bore into him. "But you were tempted."

"I wasn't sure..." His ears reddened.

"Forget it. It turns out we don't need a descroid for everyone."

"What?"

"If Siba brings eleven on line, we'd be only two short. With eleven pods working we can all get home."

"How?"

"Rami worked out an alternating system. Eleven of us in pods, two crew running the ship. After twenty-one years, they revive two from their pods and take their places. Every twenty-one years there's a new switch, so that each crew member takes a rotating twenty-one-year shift running the ship. As long as you could manage a two-decade coffee break without your partner murdering you, you'd get home alive. A little longer in the tooth, is all."

It could work. But…his mind raced. Twenty-one years; how could a person survive that. Could there possibly be enough rations. And how would you fill the minutes. Anyway, he'd arrive almost sixty years old. Could have stayed on Earth for that.

"So, are you with us?" She tightened her grip.

He found himself nodding. He'd done dozens of routine recon flights like this, surveying asteroids. Rocket out, rocket back, follow the checklist.

"Thank you, Mr. Soman. Now I'll brief the captain on our plans."

She strode down the curve of the tube. Idiot. How had she maneuvered him into this. Damn her.

Soman headed for his cabin. But as he passed the lounge, he heard lively voices and a clink of glass. He poked his head in. Like two puppets on the couch, they swung to look, Siba and Moss, raised glasses sloshing two fingers of amber liquid. Soman's glance flickered from the bottle on the low table to Moss. So that's what he'd been hiding.

"What's the stuff?" Soman asked.

Moss waggled his glass. "Lagavulin, sixteen years old. When they bottled it, that is. Now it's the oldest scotch in the known universe." He gazed at the whiskey, more grimace than grin, a man who looked like he needed a stiff drink. "Sorry, can't get a glass for you just now."

Obviously not, one hand wrapped around his drink, the other around Siba's thigh.

Moss turned to Siba. "Bad luck to waste a toast," he said. Siba peered over the rim of her glass and sniffed dubiously. Moss tossed his back, then exploded in coughing, bent over Siba's lap. An odor spread through the room of battery acid and dirty socks.

"Nasty!" Siba said. "Don't bother looking for a glass."

"One more fucking thing broken down," Moss said as he threw his glass onto the table. It rolled to the edge, teetering.

Siba touched Moss's shoulder. "Come on. Don't take everything so hard." She studied his haggard face, his stiff posture. "You're really wound tight. I'd like to see *you* at the clinic."

Moss stiffened.

"I never got your blood work-up, you've been working so hard. Come down for a check-up and I'll throw in a massage. Today's special." She plucked his glass from the table just before it would have fallen, and carried it to the sink. "Deal?"

Moss grunted. "I think Cabot's seizing up like our old hydraulics. He gets much worse, he won't be fit for command." His eyes narrowed. "And you know who'd take over."

Siba's eyes flashed. Seeing her anger, Soman said, "Easy Moss."

"That bitch will kill us all."

Siba hurled the glass into the sink. It exploded in a shower of shards as she stalked out.

Moss glared at Soman. "Guess I ain't getting laid today."

"I tried to warn you."

"Yeah, sticking up for Ley again. I ought to punch you in the other eye."

"I was just trying to—oh, go to hell." Soman hurried after Siba, the insistent tapping of her boots echoing along the tube.

She spun as he drew close. "You just want to get laid too?"

He almost said yeah, heard it's today's special, right after the massage, but stuffed it away at the last instant. He always said the wrong thing when a woman was involved. Better to just shut up. But she looked so good, back straight, eyes blazing, that flush glowing through her bronze skin. "I just wanted a checkup."

Her anger seemed to cool. "All right, come on."

Finally said something right.

At the clinic nex he said, "You really got mad over Ley.

"You're all so *mean* to her."

Mean to Ley. Now there was a concept. Ley lived for mean; she couldn't possibly care, or notice. Then again...maybe her tough exterior was a defense against a lifetime of meanness toward a woman who didn't fit. But Moss was right. If she took over from Cabot...scary. She spent half her time at the Nav one holo display, running simulations. She seemed resigned to exploring the moon first, but inside she's gunning for the planet. "I'm worried about her obsession with landing," he said.

Siba motioned Soman onto the diagnostic platform. She peeled his flight suit back to expose his chest, and rammed the plug into his sternum socket with a snap. "I don't have time to worry about the people still functioning. I'm treating tremors, melancholy, and work injuries. Not to mention stitching up after fistfights."

"Fistfights?"

"Bruni and Dowd got into it." She flipped on the machine. The skin covering his ribs quivered; the tube filled with blood. He shuddered. To get home, he'd have to trust a machine to suck every drop of liquid through that socket.

"No luck with the captain yet?" he asked.

Siba shook her head.

Soman had researched Cabot, refreshing his memory of the man. He'd led the first expedition to Mars and back, then endured five years of criticism when earthbound scientists refused to believe his results. The science had been clear: no life, ever, on the fourth planet. But Cabot's peers wouldn't tolerate that conclusion—the hope for life elsewhere in the solar system had supported a growing corps of scientists and their grants. They needed nearby planets to search. Not that any of them wanted to travel for a quarter millennium to pursue their specialty; they had families and comfortable lives to finish. Cabot left NASA to command *Sorcerer*, knowing it would mean two and a half centuries of exile. Cabot had been the best. But look at him now. Look at them all.

"Hey," he said. "Remember Lorca's crack about Cabot's second voyage?"

Siba nodded as she set up the diagnostics.

"I looked it up. I think he meant the English explorer. Discovered Newfoundland, thought he'd found the route to China. Came back to England a hero, then sailed a second time to find the Northwest passage." He looked up at Siba. "Never heard from him again."

Siba stilled. From a distance came a faint clanking.

Maybe Cabot had made his way through the Northwest passage and found exotic lands too enthralling to give up for clammy old England. Maybe he'd found a woman and a warm island. Soman grimaced—he didn't have that luxury. He had to get home.

The machine ran its probes. Siba inspected the tube carrying his fluids, a pulsating crimson stream. Satisfied, she turned to him. "So what's your obsession, Soman?"

Before he could control it tears welled up; Siba blurred.

"Look at this," she said. "There's juice in the big turnip." She wiped his eye. "What are these all about?"

He hesitated. He didn't dare reveal Anoka. Siba might tell Ley. Ley would use it as a weapon. And he'd concealed it. Mission planners had worked hard to assemble a crew without deep psychological ties to the present age. They'd wanted people who were ready to leave everything behind and commit themselves to a long voyage along time's arrow.

Siba watched him; he watched back. He had to tell her something...

"Okay," he said. "Not an obsession, maybe, but a side benefit of the mission. By the time we return, they'll know how to stop aging." It was the first time he had put it into words for anyone, this vision that had grown in him after tucking Anoka into the pod in her stalemate with death.

Siba's eyebrows rose.

"Think how bad it would be to live in the last generation before they learn the secret. Gone forever, just when there's an alternative."

His heart rattled. The machine beeped. On the display a trace wobbled and fell. Soman drew a sharp breath.

Siba said, "Gone forever? You don't believe in the soul?"

He shrugged. "No one knows what a soul is. Why else are there a thousand different religions. Soul is just a word we use to fool ourselves. Some day science is going to figure out where the universe comes from; why there's a universe at all. I'd like to see how it all turns out."

"So you're looking for God."

"Not a god in man's image. The real god, the prime mover. Something had to create the big bang."

"I wouldn't get your hopes up. All our advances in medicine have never increased the age of the oldest people. Medical care just helps more of us live that long."

"No—"

"Let me finish. In the first half of the twenty-first century, there were more centenarians than ever, but the oldest people still lived to only a hundred twenty or so."

Soman shook his head. "That's because lifespan increased only as we cured disease. That's different than targeting the aging process. Believe me, I looked into this for two years when I was stuck on a wrecked freighter. You've heard of telomeres?"

"Of course. Strings of DNA on the ends of chromosomes that shorten with each cell division."

Soman nodded. "There was a lot of promising research on how to stop the shortening process. I can show you. They were so close when we left." He raised up on an elbow. "They had mice that lived twenty-five years, ten times their normal lifespan. They had rabbits thirty years old and still fucking like rabbits."

Siba scowled. "Too bad for the girl rabbits—can't even enjoy their old age."

"They're not going to have an old age—that's the point."

Siba looked at him skeptically. "How did they do it?"

"They figured out what was going on with the petrels."

"Petrels?"

"Birds whose telomeres never shorten. They don't age."

"Come on. There aren't any immortal birds."

"Well, it's a tough life. They migrate over the ocean. Eventually something gets them. But they can live thirty years or more, when most birds live a tenth as long."

"Something eventually gets us, too."

"Our three-thousand-year delay is a gift, don't you see? This ship can be our time machine. It can take us to a future where we don't have to…" Her words sank in. Eventually something gets us too. Damn. An immortal human could spend an entire lifetime avoiding risk—never swim, never board a plane, never cross a street—and die falling down stairs or choking on a piece of meat. Just like that. Like Hartler in her bed.

Siba looked into the distance. "I believe that aging is the natural state of things, whether we're people, or mountains, or galaxies." She patted his chest. "We're stardust, Soman. Stardust. Don't pretend you can cheat entropy. Inside we all know time is short. When we're mindful of that, it makes our choices worth something."

How could she resign herself so easily to death.

"What a selfish world if everyone tried to live as long as possible."

Is that how she saw him.

Siba's look grew dark, the leaden expression he'd seen that morning in Nav One. "Besides, you can't pursue your personal goals for long before others have to pay."

His chest rocked again.

Siba turned at the machine's beep. "Oh my." She scanned the screen. "Quite a palpitation there. Everyone has an atrial fibrillation once in a while, but two in a row we need to keep an eye on."

Soman gasped, short of breath. An elusive recollection had crystallized, of a conversation with Julian.

He had abandoned his crippled ore ship after calculating a trajectory that would, just barely, place him in lunar orbit. It turned out to be the longest time any man had survived in a LEV. Nearing the end of six months, almost out of oxygen, he was decelerating to match the speed of the pale white moon swinging toward him, close enough to use real time voice instead of burst. He'd arranged a down-link to Julian, and at first it seemed nothing much had changed on Earth in four years. Then Julian mentioned his new job on the ground team of a space mission.

"Julian, did you say two hundred fifty years?"

"That's right."

"What star is it?"

"Epsilon Eridani."

"And they're going all the way out there just because of some unusual light modulation? What do you think? Is it for real?"

"Oh, yeah. It's coming from one of the planets. Clearly an intelligent signal. They have the propulsion figured out, some kind of fusion scramming."

"What's your job?"

"We're figuring out how to automate the descroid. When they re-hydrate the crew out there, the descroid has to rebuild the entire endocrine system, all the neurotransmitters, everything. So they need an endocrinologist. That's me."

"And here I am hauling goddamn ore around."

Julian laughed. "Making ten times what they're paying me…"

Neither spoke for a moment; both understood the money's purpose: to pay for recovering Anoka from the descroid. And for the medical care she'd need once the cure was at hand. Soman could picture Julian in that sparse Chicago apartment where they had last met, the living room empty but for the stone Buddha and prayer mat. But Soman hadn't needled Julian about this new phase in his promiscuous spiritual life; Julian had been the best godfather Soman could imagine for Anoka.

"Julian?"

"Yeah."

"Any progress on the medulloblastoma?"

"Actually there *is* some good news."

"Not that good, I take it."

"They've isolated a gene. They think they know the proteins involved."

"But no treatment yet."

"Not in humans, but there are clinical studies in mice."

"Mice."

"It's a first step."

"It's been four years."

"At this stage we can expect human trials in maybe four more years. So we're halfway there."

"You're giving me best case. And then a couple years evaluating outcomes, a few more until the first round of patients tell us if there are nasty surprises."

"We discussed all this before. Better to be patient. We've got to make sure the treatment really works before we bring Anoka back."

"I know. Patience. It could be ten more years. One setback and it could be twenty."

Julian said nothing at first. Soman knew Julian would never lie to him, but he would put the best light on it.

"No, not that long," Julian said.

He'd be an old man before he saw his daughter again. He and Julian had thought she'd spend at most five years in the descroid. They'd been too optimistic. What would she think of him, a tottering gray-haired man standing over her when she woke after re-hydration. Soman bit down, imagining being old, watching the body degrade one organ at a time. He'd seen enough death to last a lifetime. Life a constant scramble to hang on a little longer.

Soman had looked around at the wreck of the LEV cabin, a craft not intended as half-year living quarters. "So, Julian, are you going to Epsilon Eridani?"

"Are you kidding? Who would do it?" Julian laughed. "The poor bastards have to depend on a descroid and a computer to reconstruct them twelve light years from Earth. Not to mention they're going to be gone at least two hundred fifty years, plus exploration time."

Soman sat up. Two hundred fifty years. The oxygen monitor beeped. After four months in the LEV, laying low, minimizing consumption, this was the highest he'd seen the O_2 drain. "Easy man," he muttered to himself. Even sleeping half the time, the O_2 was going to be close.

"What?" asked Julian.

Soman lay back, heart racing. "Oh, just something a buddy of mine used to say." He gazed out the port at the disk of Earth glowing blue-white. Two hundred fifty years. More than enough time for Anoka's cure to be ready. And by that time...

That night Soman dreamed of forever. He stood at the end of time, his arms spread wide, the universe splitting open, suffusing him with the glow of infinite stars, bathed in the wisdom of a billion years.

He re-wrote the contract with *Future Lives*, assuring the continuation of the trustee after Julian's death and beyond. The hazard pay from his run to the asteroids went into a modest bank account that would multiply two hundred thousand-fold during the quarter millennium of the voyage, two and a half centuries of compound interest. The treatments to halt aging would be expensive—people would pay anything. He'd be ready.

Julian had not been happy, but Soman had swept aside his objections. He couldn't stand this waiting for doctors any longer, the agonizing delays. He'd give them all the time they needed. For Anoka.

Now Soman looked up at Siba. "Look," he said. "It's something to think about."

"Seems to me you've been thinking about it quite a lot."

Soman shrugged, but her words pricked him.

Another thought occurred to him. That bank account had been compounding ten times as long as he'd planned—the figure was inconceivable. He and Anoka would be fabulously rich. If they still had banks, or even money. How different the world would be. Three millennia before his birth, civilization tottered at the brink of the Iron Age, and the mythic figures of the biblical patriarchs. When they returned, would anyone remember the twenty-first century, or would it be shrouded in ancient mystery.

The sound of the nex brought Soman back.

Hakim stood there with a grim look. "It's Ley," he said.

Siba dug her fingers into Soman's arm.

"Something happened. She's tearing up her cabin."

Chapter 7

Soman looked up sharply at Hakim. "I thought the episodes had stopped!"

Across the cramped cabin, Dowd looked up from his diagnostics check on the sensor helmet.

Hakim swung around to place his back toward Dowd, and lowered his voice. "Easy, man. Just want you ready to drive if I need to find a quiet place to relax for a few minutes. No big problem."

"No big problem?" Soman hissed. "Have you noticed there's no quiet place around here?" Even before they lit the engine, the LEV was crowded and noisy, the rasp of air purification, the beep and warble of instruments, the smell of nervous sweat that would soon enough grow sour. Soman and Hakim sat in the nav and driver seats. Ahead of them slumped Cabot, facing the viewscreen, and Dowd, swiveled sideways, his muscular shoulders bulging through the black T-shirt with the skull and crossbones on the sleeve. Set into a well between Cabot and Dowd was the only way out, the airlock door. Behind Soman, beyond the two unused seats folded down, hung four silver pressure suits in the rack, their shiny helmets tipped down as if in prayer.

Hakim flashed a crooked grin and punched Soman in the arm. "I'm in better shape than most a' you goons." He peered at Soman's eye, the shiner fading from black to yellow. "We really shouldn't let you drive anyway, with that bum eye. Wouldn't want you running us into something."

"Let me drive, you back up."

"Oh, no. I've come a long way to drive this boat to their doorstep. Shouldn't have said anything. Besides, I volunteered first." He winked at Soman. "Heard you took an arm-twisting."

"What's up guys," Dowd called over. A line of black stitches marred his face.

Soman wondered how Dowd had survived the blow. Never realized Bruni had the fist to lay open a man's face like that.

"Mac's telling me about his love life." Hakim winked at Soman. "Very boring."

"That's what I hear."

Hakim grinned, then flipped off the cabin light, plunging them into the dim instrument glow of the operational LEV.

Hakim lifted the LEV off the platform, positioning thrusters filling the cabin with their tinkle, like a symphony tuning.

They slipped from the bay, and Soman's palms grew sweaty. He recalled the woman who'd found herself unable to board the airplane, paralyzed by anxiety, by the sudden and certain knowledge the plane would crash. She'd been escorted away when her legs had been unwilling to carry her up the jetway. And then, somewhere over the vast ocean, the plane had disappeared. Soman remembered it too well—he had put his parents on that plane.

Hakim lit the main drive. Soman tasted the familiar dry bitterness of old dust shaken free from every crevice by the vibration of the drive—spacer's mouth. Then the thrust of the single engine pushed him deeply into his seat. He thought about Siba trying to pick up where Lorca had left off with the descroids, Moss resentful of his short crew, Ley seething, left behind by Cabot. Cabot, in one of his lucid moments, had bumped Ley from the sortie. No wonder she'd trashed her cabin. Soman was relieved he didn't have to spend several days in a LEV with Ley. He allowed himself a smile; let Moss deal with her.

Hakim rocketed them away from EE2, aiming for an empty bit of space where the Pearl would circle in a day and a half.

He watched Hakim, alert for the onset of an episode, puzzling the possible source of Hakim's heavy-lidded gaze. Then, on the second day out, Soman spotted furtive movements while the others slept, Hakim sneaking something from pocket to mouth. When confronted, in hissed whispers, Hakim admitted he'd been taking tranks. "Let Siba think it was her roots and herbs helping him," he said. "If they'd put Lorca on this stuff, more people would be alive right now."

And after thirty-eight hours, the moon of Epsilon Eridani two swung toward them, black and enigmatic.

Long-range scans had showed it to be a dark, lustrous sphere without recognizable features, a smooth black pearl. As the LEV moved in, Dowd studied the surface in greater detail, finding silicon, oxygen, iron, beryllium, traces of organics. The internal structure of the material was amorphous, a supercooled liquid. "Glass," Dowd said. The black helmet bulged in front like insect eyes. "But tougher than glass. Tidal forces would crack glass the first day in orbit."

When the LEV approached within five hundred kilometers of the featureless Pearl, instruments detected a faint dot on the equator, a subtle difference in reflectivity. The LEV closed in, moving into the cone of the moon's shadow. Everyone leaned forward. The holo cast its flickering light across Cabot's face. His eyes glittered bluer, more focused. The looming Pearl seemed to have stirred something.

"Whoa," Dowd said. "Blank spot. No return from the laser."

Hakim moved the LEV toward the spot.

"An opening," whispered Dowd.

"How big?" asked Hakim.

"A hundred sixty two point three meters diameter."

Hakim whistled. "We'd fit."

The holograph drilled contour lines deep into the Pearl as the LEV hovered directly over the hole.

Dowd pinged it. "We've got ourselves a hollow moon. 2K thick shell, 60K deep."

"Amazing." Soman said. "How do you build something like this?"

Hakim grinned. "Tax dollars."

The LEV hovered above the center of the hole.

"We should probably recon the surface," Soman said.

Hakim readied the controls. "Captain?" The viewscreen showed only black; they watched their instruments.

"Go in."

Three heads swung to face Cabot, Hakim frozen over the controls. "You mean go in *the hole?*"

Cabot gestured toward the display. His words were labored but clear. "That's why we're here."

Hakim slid his hand over the yoke. "So we are."

Soman looked around. "Hey, wait a minute here, why not make a traverse, then decide what to do."

"Captain?" Hakim repeated.

Cabot pointed at the black spot on the viewscreen.

Hakim leaned forward and concentrated on the holo. "Here we go."

Soman looked between Hakim and Dowd in the dim light of the cabin, their indistinct shapes focused on instruments. Damn. Cabot's trying to outdo Ley. He wanted to say more, but the LEV was already dropping below the lip. He felt a pang of claustrophobia. Spacecraft were for between planets.

Hakim descended slowly, keeping his distance from the walls.

"Whoa!" said Hakim. "I'm lost. No walls"

Dowd worked the sensor controls. "We're inside the shell." Soman pictured the LEV's sensors flashing beneath their feet, sending a million bursts of laser light to shower the inside of Pearl with a mist of photons. Gradually the holo built a new picture. The outline of a hemispheric chamber grew. On the floor, sixty klicks down, four hollow arms ran like spokes toward the periphery.

Soman didn't like it; he flicked into the auton and checked behind them, wanting the reassurance of stars, to know the exit was still open. Instead, there was a shimmering orange glow where the exit hole should be. "Get out of the way!" he shouted.

Hakim slewed the LEV sideways with a hiss of thrusters, all eyes fixed to the viewscreen, eight hands gripping armrests. The holo outlined their faces with a faint green sheen.

Hakim spoke from the dark. "Nothing moving."

Soman frowned. "There was something behind us in the opening. Let's get some distance between us and the hole. Then we can move back under it and have a look."

Hakim continued the LEV down, staying off-center.

The electromag scanner on Soman's console flickered alive. Before he could investigate, Hakim said, "All right, let's have a look." The LEV moved sideways.

Soman strained to see anything forming on the viewscreen. Just black, and spots where his eyes played tricks. Then a thin sliver of orange. "There!" As the LEV centered beneath the hole, the orange sliver grew, its edges rounded, stabilized into a perfect circle.

Hakim stopped the LEV, the deceleration pushing the four of them sideways against restraints in perfect unison like some dance routine. While the others straightened against the straps in a motion of second habit, Cabot kept tipping, flailing for a moment, and Soman heard something crack in Cabot's neck before he finally regained his balance.

Dowd spread his arms, his helmet shaking. "Scan says nothing there."

"There's *something* there." Soman studied the orange circle. It seemed to be moving toward them. He forced himself not to duck.

"I'm pinging it, but I'm not getting a return. Wait a minute… Man, are we edgy or what?" Dowd pulled off the helmet, laughing. "Fuck!" he said as the edge of the helmet snagged his wound. A splotch of blood bubbled up. As he stanched the flow with his sleeve, he growled, "Something's there all right. A solid object, two hundred seventy thousand klicks away. Which object would that be? And by the way, it's orange."

Soman laughed. Of course. EE2. Pearl must orbit in tidal lock, rotating once per revolution, the only way the hole could stay lined up with the planet. Not unusual for an old planet-moon pair.

Hakim descended slowly, taking the remaining fifty-seven K in an hour. The walls of the hemisphere drew gradually away. Hakim pulled up five hundred meters from the bottom.

Something about the shape of the chamber nagged at Soman. The scanner continued to show a steady electromag background. He flipped on the searchlights. The switch felt strange. He ran his thumb across the ends of his fingers. Numb. He clenched his fists, digging his fingernails into the flesh of his palms. No feeling.

"*What* are you doing?" Hakim watched Soman's hands.

Soman stopped. "Nervous, I guess."

"I can give you something for that." Hakim laughed.

Trying to avoid thinking about his fingers, Soman studied the chamber below them. Why was that shape so familiar. Then he remembered: the new Volny lasers, developed to drive space probes to the outer planets. Well, new in 2048. And the hole pointed right at EE2, which was…a collection of mirrors. "Guys. I think we should get outside."

Dowd cocked his head. "I've got RF." He pulled the helmet back on, cursing again as it caught on his stitches. Blood smeared his jaw. "Induction," he said. "Electric motors. Big ones. Really big."

Soman watched the sensor, its needle pegged.

Hakim grabbed the control yoke and eased back. The LEV started up, Hakim intent on the viewscreen.

No one breathed. The aroma of sweat and anxiety spread through the cabin.

The front viewscreen brightened by ten magnitudes, then flicked off like an imploding drivecell. The brightness in the cabin grew, searing through the ports. Pain sliced Soman's eyes. He covered his face with his hands, and saw the shadow of bones through blue meat as the flash penetrated soft tissue. A roaring sound filled the cabin, and he braced himself for a shock wave as the LEV rose, accelerating, grinding his tailbone into the seat.

Hakim screamed.

The LEV shook as if it would disintegrate. Dust filled the air. Soman struggled to breathe, slammed by g's that tore his hands from his face like two bricks. The LEV hurtled up, the four of them pinned to their seats, faces stretched like Halloween masks. Soman couldn't move, thinking about the approaching ceiling two K thick, made of the toughest material humans had ever encountered.

The blue light dimmed; the x-ray image faded, leaving yellow splotches in Soman's vision. He glanced at the viewscreen. Diagonal lines flickering across it. Probably ruined by overload. Soman peeked at the airlock port. On the bottom of the chamber below, four rows of circles radiated like spokes, glowing deep blue, the more distant circles flattened to ellipses by perspective. The circles shrank under the LEV's furious rise; the floor of the chamber receded at frightening speed. Hakim screamed on, gripping the control stick, head thrown back, eyes swollen shut.

Finally Soman grasped what was happening. Hakim clenched the stick in full up, locked in the throes of a seizure. There had been no explosion, no shock wave. The roaring sound was the LEV's engine straining at full throttle, driving them straight toward the ceiling.

"Hakim! Let go!" Soman unbuckled and lunged for Hakim. The floor rushed up and crashed into him. The roar of the straining engine filled his ears, blood ran into his eye, the cold deck froze his cheek. Lifting his head against the force holding it to the deck, he yelled, "Hakim!" Hakim kept screaming.

They had to hit the ceiling any second. Soman scrabbled harder, finally reaching Hakim's hands, locked tightly around the stick. He pulled on Hakim's arms, trying to use the g-force to his advantage, the furious vibration of the engine tearing at his grip. Hakim didn't budge.

Someone grunted. Dowd was pulling Hakim from the other side. Soman found Hakim's restraint clip and released it. Hakim's grip broke and he tipped away, slamming into Dowd in a knot of arms and legs.

The whine of the engine stopped. Quiet weightlessness enveloped the LEV.

Soman felt a moment of relief. Only their hoarse and heavy breathing filled the cabin. Then the rippling hologram caught Soman's eye. The spokes below were now distant blue lines. The LEV still sped toward the top of the chamber.

Soman slid into the driver's chair. "Strap in!" he yelled as he made a frantic scan of the controls. He needed to flip the LEV over and decelerate. He flicked into the auton, found the nav screen, and spun the LEV hard, moving the positioning cursor as fast as he could, knowing each fraction of a second counted. The inside of the Pearl's shell barreled toward them. Behind him he heard someone grunt, but he dare not turn to look, every bit of concentration on the maneuver. "Strap in!" he screamed. The LEV spun. Finally he moved the cursor to 180 degrees. There! Soman yanked back on the yoke.

The engine roared. Behind Soman a crash, then a cry of pain. G forces pulled the skin over Soman's eyes and sucked the blood from his head. His vision darkened; the cut above his eye throbbed. Flicking in, he selected radar image. Data to nav program. Distance to the ceiling…6.3 kilometers. He flicked in the current speed and deceleration rate. Stopping distance: 12.1 kilometers. Damn! Nineteen seconds to impact. Soman's mind raced.

Someone moaned. Soman spared a quick glance behind. Hakim lay atop Dowd near the airlock. At this deceleration rate, Hakim crushed Dowd with the weight of seven men. Cabot stared out the port. Did Cabot even know what was about to materialize, rushing out of the blackness faster than they could flinch. Soman imagined the ceiling out there, its hole aimed directly at EE2. That blast of blue light would have bounced off one of EE2's reflective surfaces and was on its way somewhere. Where. Why.

Wait. The hole. Follow the laser out. Re-focusing on the console, he flicked through the radar returns. There. Eleven degrees off their trajectory. How to maneuver the LEV into that narrow opening at this speed. Then a rush of hope. Autopilot. He slid the autopilot cursor onto the hole and activated, his mind moving the controls, his body paralyzed by Gs.

The LEV slewed sideways as the autopilot fired steering thrusters. He hung on to the control yoke. A crash against the bulkhead, a double exhalation, a snapping of bone. Over the engine noise, Soman heard the rasp of a man's desperate breathing. Five, six, seven times, each croak shorter and less determined, until the next breath never came. A stench of excrement filled the small cabin.

The engine whined, the hull groaned.

A sudden flash of light. Soman flinched. The viewport flickered back to life. Ominous blackness. In the autopilot display, the glowing crosshair crawled across the moon's ceiling, slowly making its way toward the hole.

A klaxon sounded: clang, clang. Collision alarm.

Soman's face blanched, his knuckles white on the yoke.

The viewscreen flashed crimson, the ceiling racing toward them, illuminated in fiery red by the main thruster. Soman's gut tightened from his anus to his throat. He closed his eyes in the instant before all those neurons splattered against alien construction. What will happen to this thought, stored briefly, a fruitless exercise, a final involuntary response, like the twitching of a severed limb. Consciousness subsided to a soft buzz, the overload and comfort of unavoidable death.

The buzz shattered in a cacophony of grinding metal. Cabot's limbs leaped like a marionette and his great hairy head snapped back. Dowd and Hakim flew past Soman's head to crash against the ceiling with a sound like a coconut dropped from great height. A noise of tearing metal. The alarm clanged and the engine roared.

The LEV hit the wall of the hole at an angle, ricocheted, and spun. For an instant he glimpsed the long tube of the tunnel. Then they hit again, spinning.

Like a shell from a naval gun, the LEV shot from the hole into open space, whirling directly at EE2.

Chapter 8

Pounding spin, vertigo, Soman screaming, clinging to the yoke, searching the auton for the damn autopilot routine for stabilizing a spin. Never recover from this manually. The edge of vision turning black, growing each second. He knew in seconds he'd black out.

There! Select. Hope it was the right one. His vision closed down.

The whine of thrusters. Cabot thrashed faster. The sound from aft grew. If that was the engine nacelle separating it would tear a hole in the cabin. He was feet from a pressure suit with no chance to get it without ending up in a pile with Hakim and Dowd.

The LEV spun down. Gradually his vision returned.

Hakim and Dowd floated in the airlock well among a tangle of flight suits. Soman unbuckled. "Guys," he said. Blood smeared the inside of the well. Black globules floated up. Then he saw Hakim's head, the impossible angle of the neck, eyes swollen shut, mouth open. Soman weakened at the sight, moaning, slid a hand behind Hakim's head, gingerly. Shouldn't move a neck injury. It wouldn't matter.

He'd had to do it or they would have crashed into the ceiling, there wasn't any choice, come on guys. "I had to!" He yelled. Dowd's head emerged from the pile, split wider than his helmet, glistening in white slime. His shirt torn through the skull and crossbones, his arm flabby and loose. Soman clutched Dowd's shirt and moaned. Could he have given them a few more seconds…his mind whirled, trying to spin a new reality, one in which Hakim would climb out of that well with a shake of the head and a clever word— "bit of a stiff neck there"—one in which Cabot had never—

The radio crackled. "LEV One." Ley. "LEV One, what's your status."

He looked forward. Cabot wasn't moving. Soman leaned close. He was unconscious but breathing. Soman flicked into the com channel. "LEV One here."

"You're telemetry's gone nuts. What's going on?"

"Um, flight emergency. Hang on a second." He closed the channel with Ley and shook Cabot. "Captain!" Cabot's forehead was bruised from banging the console. "Captain!" No response. Soman looked around the cabin, taking in the debris. His eye caught the viewscreen, where the Pearl had receded to a lustrous dot in the immensity of space. The LEV was moving off fast.

He flicked back to Ley's channel. "Sorry. Had to do a little…first aid thing there."

"I'll speak to Cabot now."

He glanced at Cabot's unmoving form. If Ley thinks Cabot is incapacitated, she'll take command. "He's…asleep."

"Asleep? In a flight emergency?"

Hi bit his lip. "Well, that's over now. I'd best give you my report."

"Yes, Mr. Soman, you'd best do that."

As he finished, his voice trailing off, Ley whistled softly. "So you've got two casualties and a ruined LEV your first time at the controls."

Soman swallowed hard.

"You didn't mention the captain. He's alive at least? Or have you killed everyone out there?"

Soman tore his eyes from the casualties and considered Cabot, his mind running in circles. "Alive," he said finally. "Yeah, alive and kicking. Banged his head in the spin, had a hell of a headache. I gave him morphine from the kit here. He's sleeping now."

"I hope you're better with drugs than you are flying the LEV."

Finally anger replaced the emptiness in Soman. "If I hadn't been here they'd be splattered on the inside of the Pearl."

"So you see I was right to recruit you," Ley said. "And you're returning to ship now?"

"Yes, sir."

"That's all I need. Out."

That was easy. Then he frowned. Too easy.

Soman hovered over Cabot. His mouth hung open like a man waiting to have a tooth pulled. Soman moved to the locker and found the medical kit. Holding the morphine injector, he studied Cabot. Ley would check every detail; better have a used injector. How much though. He stood over Cabot, hesitating. Finally he dropped into the airlock well and discharged the injector into Dowd's exposed arm, flinching at the sharp hiss. Then he tucked the empty ampoule into one of Cabot's pockets.

Soman sat in the driver's seat. It had been difficult work cramming them into pressure suits, especially with his arms now numb to the elbows. He hadn't been able to bring himself to jettison them; he wasn't sure why.

Outside the black of space spread endlessly around the LEV.

Soman tried closing his eyes, but instantly he saw Hakim holding the yoke in that death grip. When the laser pulsed, Hakim holding the controls when the light blast seared his eyeballs and drove him into a seizure. Soman began to tremble. Easy man.

That memory of Anne swam up to confront him. Oh, God. Not now.

Anne had looked back at him with an expression that rooted him to the sidewalk. Just for an instant, an instant too long. In the snow and fog of that gloomy London winter evening, she stepped off the curb, looking to the left though she knew better, to a blare of horns and a smashing of metal and bone. And by the time he'd slipped and crawled to her at the base of the lamppost where she'd come to rest, lit by a single dislocated headlamp, all he could do was hold her cooling body, the night still and quiet in those moments before sirens would wail.

Soman raised his head, taking in the squalor of the LEV cabin, retracing the worn path of despair. Anne's insurance money had paid for Anoka's journey into the descroid. He couldn't escape the timing of Anne's death, three days after visiting the offices of *Future Lives*. Seventy-two hours after Soman and Anne had faced the crushing cost of a descroid for their dying child. He remembered their last hour together, Anne's lingering touch as she'd dressed Anoka that morning. How she'd started to cry before pulling herself together.

To save their child, women would pay even with their lives. He pressed his forehead to the console. He had to get back. Whatever it took.

With trembling hands, Soman dug into the medical kit. Tightening his seat belt, he placed the injector against his thigh and pressed. Pffft. Tendrils of relaxation snaked through him. He lay back and let it carry him away.

An alarm squawked. Hakim had shaken loose from the suit anchor—he was opening the hatch. Soman lay rooted to the seat, unable to leap up and close the swinging hatch, staring in terror, looking directly into the black of space—impossible—he'd be dead. Lorca floated in the void, breathing from the escaping bubble of air, laughing, "It seems there's been a malfunction."

Soman flailed in his seat, his eyes snapping open.

One nightmare waned, another returned.

Soman shook off the dust of the dream. An alarm had sounded. Or had it. Soman scanned the cabin. A malfunctioning light flickered in the corner. Cabot lay motionless in the co-pilot's seat. The LEV creaked and rattled.

The alarm beeped again, the sound from the dream. Soman swung around. The hatch was still closed. *Idiot, of course it is.* A light flashed on the console. Proximity alarm.

In a corner of the viewscreen hung a bright object, partly obscured by a diagonal line of black, permanent damage to the screen from the blast of light. Soman flicked in. *Screen control. Zoom in.* And there hung *Sorcerer*, the torus and maw of the collector unmistakable. Soman's heart leaped as if it were the blue and white swirl of Earth.

He switched to open channel, waiting for the familiar sense of contact, the zephyr of thought always present on open. Nothing. He frowned. "Auton!"

"Ready."

"Why can't I patch in to open?"

"You are."

No one on open channel. A deep foreboding stole through him. Half the mother ship blazed titanium white, illuminated by the nearby star. The other half smoldered amber, reflecting the planet's alien hue. As the LEV moved round the ship for docking, *Sorcerer* revealed more of that tawny face to him, like jaundice creeping over the ship. This was not the ship he'd navigated through the asteroid belts, not the crew he'd joined.

Bay control hadn't acknowledged the autopilot. The LEV hovered five hundred meters in front of closed doors. His palms grew sweaty. He flicked into the emergency channel.

"*Sorcerer!*"

"*Sorcerer!*"

"*Sorcerer* here." It was Moss.

Relief flooded through Soman, until Moss spoke next. "Why are you on the emergency channel?"

"Th…the guys are dead and…the captain needs medical attention. That might qualify as an emergency." A long silence. "Moss?"

"Yeah, yeah, just thinking. Got a little problem with the bay door. Can you hold there? And let's stay off emergency. Don't need the whole ship listening to you lose your grip. Nav channel will be fine." Then he was gone.

Damn Moss. Who's losing their grip. All he wanted was to get back in. Now.

Nothing more from Moss. The bay door stayed closed. And he couldn't slip across to bay two—the other LEV sat in the rails there. He touched the scab above his eye, tracing its jagged outlines with his finger, fragile clots holding back the blood. It would need stitches. Under the eye, the flesh was still tender from Moss's jab. Must look like hell.

He flicked over to nav channel. "Moss, what's the update on the door?"

Silence.

A second channel opened with the telltale falling tone of a private communication, the auton locking the frequency and spinning it through the encryption algorithm. "Soman here."

It was Siba, her voice missing its fluidity, chopped and synthetic from encryption. "I heard you on emergency." She was breathing hard, and her voice quavered.

"What's wrong over there?"

"You need to get the captain back here now."

"What happened?"

"I was coming back from—" she stopped abruptly and paused so long, Soman wondered if they'd been cut off. Then she started again, her voice rising as if she fought back tears. "I heard noises from C hold, and I went to look. Next thing I know Bruni storms out and hits me."

"He hit you?"

"Knocked me into the bulkhead, trying to rip off my shirt. Then, Moss… uh, showed up. He got Bruni to back off and pushed me into the nex. He said there had been a chemical leak, that I should get to quarters."

"They don't keep chemicals in C hold."

"And you don't smash a woman in the face for that."

"Are you okay?"

"To judge from Rami's look, I must be quite a sight. I thought I'd be safer up here than alone in the clinic. Don't know if Moss can control the rest of the crew."

"Shit." His stomach churned.

"And Ley's left the ship. She took the second LEV."

Soman eyed the bay door while he tried to imagine what was going on. "She wouldn't land without building the rig first."

"They're building it. Moss showed me. They patched things up."

He thought back to Ley's last-minute meeting with Cabot. And that odd, truncated conversation just after clearing the Pearl. She'd been satisfied the instant she knew Cabot was returning to the ship.

At least he wasn't making this descent with her. He grimaced. Not yet.

"Siba?"

A quaver in her voice. "Rami just locked down the Nav One nex and shifted control to our console. He's been watching the locator, and we have a crowd on the way. He said he doesn't want them in until he's done with something."

Soman flicked to nav channel. "Moss." Keeping his voice even. No response. "Moss."

"Right here, Soman." A bit out of breath.

"What's up with the door?"

"Still trying to figure it out. Keep on holding. Shouldn't be long if you stop interrupting us."

Then Moss was gone.

Soman flicked back to Siba. "What's your locator say, is Moss with the gang at the nav door?"

"Yes."

Lying son of a bitch. He's trying to buy time. For what. "Siba, I don't think you can count on Moss. He won't let me in. Check the bay one door. Can you open it?"

He heard her murmuring to Rami. Then nothing.

"Well, can you open it?"

"We're trying!"

Soman punched in the auto-dock sequence again. Again no response from bay one.

"Rami says it's been locked down at bay one control. He can't do anything."

Soman remembered what Moss had said in med bay—we've got to get *Sorcerer* home. What better time, with Cabot and Ley gone and plenty of descroids for those aboard—if they leave now. He thought furiously. Wait—if Ley took the other LEV, bay two is vacant. "Siba, can you open the bay two door?"

"Oh, it's open. Ley banged it on her way out, they couldn't close it. They were all cursing down there."

No wonder Moss had wanted him to hold here at bay one, out of sight of the open bay two door. "Thank you, sweetheart," he said to Ley under his breath. She'd spent a lifetime driving hot jets, straddling that big engine, but was never good with thrust in three dimensions.

He needed to get to LEV bay two. But a trip around the rim would place the LEV in view of every port and screen on Sorcerer. Then Moss could get ready for him. He watched the crew torus rotate around the bay hub, the four spokes swinging past him every few seconds. It was a huge risk. One of those spokes contained the elevator. Miss the timing, mortally damage the Sorcerer and cut off LEV bay from the rest of the ship. Soman closed his eyes. When he opened them, they were stony. He was still the best LEV driver on the planet. Two planets.

He backed the LEV away, timing the passage of spokes, squinting as the harsh shadows played tricks with his depth perception. A spoke passed; he touched the thruster lightly. Under his numb fingers the control felt clunky. He was approaching too slowly. He jammed the thruster. The LEV jumped forward. The spoke swung ponderously away. The next spoke grew alarmingly fast in the port. In seconds he could make out every detail of the scarred and pitted skin, flayed by time and distance. He squeezed the thruster, but it was already at maximum. The spoke swung at him. He could read the warning sign on an access cover—DANGER HIGH VOLTAGE—twisted in the seat, as if body English could save him when that spoke rammed the LEV. An airlock grew in the screen, and he braced for the crash, a hand on the safety belt release so he could dive for a suit as soon as the collision sent the LEV spinning away. Should have got into a suit before trying this. There had been no time, just as there had been no time to wait for Dowd to strap in. He held his breath.

The spoke reappeared to starboard. The impact never came. The LEV was through.

Reversing thrust, Soman turned the LEV like a skidding car, then slid it into alignment with number two bay. Relief flooded through him at the sight of the gaping bay door. And there was the dent, a small protruding lip of the door curled out from Ley's impact, his one piece of luck on this miserable voyage.

Siba crackled back on. "They're trying to get in here—"

Soman concentrated. Auton to autopilot. Green cursor to docking pad. Activate. The LEV started in, the bay dark, the navigation lights of the LEV providing dim illumination. Like an abandoned ship, dead and derelict.

The LEV thunked down on the pad. Docked.

He unstrapped. "Captain?"

Cabot lay still as the vacuum outside, staring straight ahead.

Siba's voice crackled on the private channel, low and urgent. In the background was another sound, the low hum of a sonic saw. "They're cutting through the bulkhead. I can't raise Mel." Her voice betrayed panic.

Soman moved faster. Ley wasn't the only one they'd leave behind. He fought with a suit. "Goddamn you all!" he bellowed, fumbling with seals, struggling to feel the latches.

Something occurred to Soman: He and Moss wanted the same thing. He flicked into Nav channel. "Moss." Silence. "Moss! Look, I'm ready to get home too. I'm—" He almost said he was in bay two, then thought better of it. "Cabot's in no condition to take command." What should he say about Ley. He couldn't bring himself to suggest…"There's no need to do this. I…can be inside in a minute, and we'll get this boat headed back as soon as…soon as we can."

And soon as we figure out if there are enough descroids. Soman felt cold in the pit of his stomach. That's the real problem.

Nothing from Moss. Why would he buy any of that. After all, Soman's the guy enforcing the rules, the guy standing up for Cabot, taking punches for Ley. If only Moss knew. Soman stopped. Did anyone really know Soman, the man who kept everything inside, who held back why he was here. The one who wouldn't talk about personal matters. So what did everyone do—they filled in the blanks from their own personal assortment of belief and bias. And when the chips were down, who would stand up for him. No one.

Siba crackled back on. "Rami's acting strange. He just turned to me, grabbed my arm and said, 'Get everyone back."

Donning a pressure suit, squeezing through the airlock, Soman rolled onto the LEV pad, catching a glance out the open bay door. Blazing stars filled the rectangle. His chest filled at the beauty and danger of it.

He yanked his way across the bay, using the handholds. No time for a safety tether. Breathing hard, he reached the airlock and punched the button. Nothing. He began pounding the button, yelling obscenities at Moss. His breath came fast, his chest heaved. Goddamn Cabot, wouldn't install nexports for the external airlocks, wanting only proven technology on the outside skin of *Sorcerer.*

Then Siba was talking to him, calming him down. He'd been on the private channel and she'd heard the whole thing. He gathered himself, trying to quell nausea. In a spark of hope, he saw the emergency panel. *For Manual Entry*, the sign read. Okay, do it the hard way. Yeah, Lorca, we still use wrenches in the fifty-third century.

He snatched the door wrench from the emergency panel, an unwieldy tool that would weigh twenty pounds on Earth. At the first turn of the bolt, the torque spun him around. The wrench slipped off. He lunged for the bolt just before he drifted beyond reach. Damn! Out here with no tether and no backup. Be careful. Could have been drifting out the bay door.

Something caught Soman's eye at the back of the bay. He squinted into the dim light at a low structure of beams and cross braces. He recognized the gear: the skeleton of the two-stage superstructure. Siba was right; they'd started to assemble it. But Moss had worked at it only until Ley left. Then he'd raced to take over the ship. And if Ley hadn't hit the bay door, they'd both have been trapped out here. He remembered the way Moss had held Siba's leg; probably figured he was getting laid today.

Trembling, Soman slid into the foot locks and worked the bolt, cranking the hatch open, the lifepack unable to keep up with his metabolism. On a normal EVA he'd stop for a few minutes to let the suit catch up. Not now. Nothing was normal. Nothing's been normal since that day in the doctor's office, Anoka in the reception area watching the closed door, Anne staring at the antique golf balls on the doctor's desk while he told them, in his tone of practiced apology, that there was no treatment for her particular tumor, that he was referring the family to a counselor who would advise whether the child be told, that he was very, very sorry. Soman remembered the man's hands as he spread them helplessly beside the golf artifacts, gutta percha and wound goat hair and all the others nestled in the mahogany base with neat inscriptions in faux Celtic script. Useless hands.

The hatch open, he squeezed into the lock, then peered through the port into the corridor beyond. No one in view. Twenty more turns to close the outer door, then the manual air bleed. It hissed loudly in the closed space and Soman cringed, peeking through the port again. Anyone near the hatch had to hear that racket. The pressure gauge hit thirteen psi. Can't wait for full pressure. He heaved on the wrench until he had a crack wide enough to slip through.

Sliding into the tube, finally a feeling of lightness lifted him. Back on board.

Soman's relief shattered with a clang. The floor rushed up and struck him hard, the impact driving the breath from him and smashing his face against the inside of the helmet. Pain from his eye; spheres of blood floated into view. He twisted around. But Bruni wasn't waiting, he swung again. Soman wondered briefly how Bruni had taken his wrench away. Then he tightened his hand. Still there. Of course, Bruni had the inside wrench. Soman yanked on a stretch of railing. The deadly mass of the wrench blurred past his helmet. The speed of that swing drove it home to Soman: these people are deadly serious.

Here at the hub there was no spingrav. Bruni's momentum flipped him, arms and legs kicking as he struggled to right himself like a beetle upside down in the dirt. Crew training hadn't included fighting in zero g, but Soman saw what had happened to Bruni. He grabbed the rail to keep from spinning, then struck with his own wrench. Bruni's head bounced against the deck. Red sprayed into the air. Soman recoiled at the sight. Then Bruni jerked, an attempt to strike back or a spasm from his cracked skull. Not waiting to find out which, Soman struck again, fear narrowing his vision, pounding until his spent arms wouldn't move, his lungs seizing up from lack of air. Gradually his vision cleared. Bruni drifted toward the wall of the tube, his damaged head dangling from his limp body.

Soman felt an overpowering rush of raw power, and he glimpsed for an instant what had brought Ley back to the cockpit of her killing machine for three decades; why she mourned the end of war. He crouched in the center of the ship, while the red pounding blood cleared from his vision. The heat drained from him, leaving him frozen to the depth of his bones. They left him no choice. He flicked into the private channel. "Siba, can you do your breathing thing again?"

Siba gasped. "Why?"

"Did we ever take those suits back to the Nav deck locker after the thing with Lorca?"

"Are you kidding? They're still in the corner of the clinic."

So there were no suits outside Nav One. Good. "How long can you go without air?"

"With preparation, six, seven minutes. Right now, I don't know. My pulse must be one twenty. Maybe I could manage three or four."

"Get ready. You may need more. And let's set up a passcode for the Nav One nex."

He pulled along the webbing, spotted a suit locker, and threw it open. Only one suit. He needed two; one for Siba, one for Rami. But no time for a search, no time for a detour to medical. Any moment now someone would call for Bruni or check the locator. A sonic saw wouldn't take long on that bulkhead. Soman snatched up the suit.

Climbing aboard an elevator pod, Soman clenched the bloody wrench, the empty suit hanging like a wraith in his service.

The motor whirred. The pod accelerated to match the spin of the torus, then injected into the vertical tube. Soman rose toward the outer rim. He flicked in to Nav channel to call Moss one last time. Then he considered. Fucking Moss, sounding so reasonable, hold just a minute, chemical leak. Soman brought up the locator. And there Moss was, a black shape at the Nav hatch. Soman held the wrench tighter, blood dripping from it under the artificial gravity of the lift. No more chances for Moss. Soman's heart palpitated at the decision. A feeling of lightness passed through him, a sudden need for breath. Pain stabbed the length his arm. He leaned against the wall; eyes closed. The flutter passed. The pod lurched to a stop.

Holding the wrench ready, he lunged through the nex and spun around—if they were using the locator, they knew where he was. But no one waited. They thought he was still sitting in the LEV like an idiot.

He ran down the corridor, clumsy in his suit, and reached the M deck nex. Next to the nex was the emergency panel, and dead center, the backup power breaker.

Soman brought up the private channel. "Siba, you still there?"

"Yes," she whispered.

"What's happening?"

"They have a hole. Won't be long before they're in. I don't think they're planning to blow the air."

Soman yanked out the breaker and flung it down the tube. Backup power gone. There would now be a small indicator flashing on every console.

He dove through the nex to M deck, his bloody arm smearing a red streak like a scimitar on the bulkhead where he bumped it. On the other side stood a man, shock on his face at the sight of Soman bursting into the tube. Soman recognized him—Miller, the astrophysicist. Miller backed away, eyes wide at Soman covered in blood. "Miller," Soman screamed. "Get into a suit!" He wondered if Miller could hear him through the helmet. Miller tripped and fell, then scrambled to regain his feet and ran. Soman faltered. There were others here besides Moss. He'd known it, but seeing Miller…goddamn. But he didn't have another plan. Only seconds now before the gang came for him.

Soman ran down the tube, veered left, and reached the wall terminal. Clumsy in his gloves, he scrolled to the relief valve status screen. Select Default Open. Fire system, purge mode. He closed the screen and raced down the tube to the main breaker. Soman stood before it, sweat running down his face, the cut above his eye throbbing. He heard muffled voices behind him—here they come. He stared at the bright yellow handle, at the grime in the crack between the edge of the breaker and its enclosure. Lorca had stood on this spot, looked at this handle. Soman's mind spun, searching for an alternative.

"Hey!" A voice from behind. Soman quelled an urge to turn. If he had to look someone in the eye, he wouldn't be able to do it. He threw the breaker. "Now, Siba," he whispered.

Sudden dark. Servo motors wound, valves pounded, ductwork whistled. The first pop of the ears for those not in a suit.

Maybe they'd stop to dig into the empty suit locker. He pictured Moss on his knees, leaning over the locker, fumbling with the latches in the dark—as his air disappeared. Or if he was smart, if he'd paid attention, he'd keep barreling down the tube. Soman turned and spread his feet for balance in the total dark, ready to defend the breaker. How many would there be. Too confusing to do the math. How many dead and jettisoned, how many on the LEV, two in the control room, then there was Ley.

Soman guarded the breaker in a wail of fleeing air, picturing Siba descending into meditation. How long to wait. Don't start up the tube too soon, someone might reach the breaker and turn it back on. Don't wait too long, or Siba will be dead.

The single suit hung over Soman's shoulder. How best to use it. Suit up Siba, they could both carry Rami. No, Rami wouldn't last as long as Siba. Suit up Rami first. But Rami could never help carry Siba through all the empty corridors to medical. And while he suited Rami, Siba could die. Damn, should have taken that detour for a second suit—

A jolt on the shoulder. Reflexively he swung the wrench. Contact, crushing flesh, cracking bone. The sickening feel of it made him draw back—but then he took a blow to the helmet, and he swung the wrench again, all reservation gone. He heard a scream and swung harder, lunging up the tube. The spare suit slid off his shoulder, but he couldn't stop to grab it. He stepped forward, feeling with his foot for the suit, striking something with the wrench again, the force of it knocking him off balance—and he realized the scream was his own voice, its primal sound filling the helmet. He swung, again and again.

Soman's arms grew heavy. Breath ran short. Something struck his leg and he fell, swinging as he went down, another crunch under the mass of the wrench. He lost track of the breaker, on his knees in the pitch black, arms burning.

He stopped. Listen. Only the ragged pull of his own breath. He flipped on the helmet light, Beside him lay an inert figure, a second nearby. Dark pools of blood spread from their contorted forms. Down the tube, others lay in less violent poses, the peaceful collapse of oxygen deprivation. Near one lay a sonic saw. Moss's hand still gripped it, not eight feet from where Soman had guarded the breaker in the dark, unaware of the weapon creeping up on him. Soman spotted his spare suit, its helmet sliced through, the telltale curled edge left by the sonic cutter. Only luck that Moss had got hold of the wrong helmet in the dark. Maybe Moss thought he'd won, just before his air ran out.

"Siba," he called hoarsely. No answer. Soman's grip on the wrench loosened and it dropped to the deck with a clang. Around him the ship yawned cold and empty.

He accelerated up the tube. Glancing down, he recognized Miller.

At the Nav One nex he tore open the panel on his sleeve and yanked out the patch cord. With shaking hands he connected to the jack. "Auton," he barked.

"Ready."

"Open the door."

"Passcode please."

Soman hoped Siba had set it up correctly. "Lucky." Then he dove through.

He spotted Rami first, leaning far forward in his seat, chest spread across the control panel, arms reaching for the floor as if just short of salvation.

Where was Siba.

There, in the corner, splayed on the couch. He rushed over, lifted her, and raced back to the nex, her limbs bouncing, her head sagging so far back it seemed it would fall off. He gasped at the bruise on her face where Bruni had punched her, the skin split and oozing, her cheek swollen and red, vacuum opening the wound, tearing it inside out as he watched. Her blouse, ripped in half, hung from her in tatters.

He hurtled down the tube.

Twelve seconds to the M deck nex, past the fallen. Too late he thought about flipping the breaker back on and activating the emergency recompression. He wasn't going back; any more delay now could cost Siba her life. Down the tube. Twenty more seconds, tick, tick, tick. Siba slipped from his grasp as his strength dwindled, his arms like stumps.

Ten seconds to the clinic nex, tick, tick. He gulped for breath. Blackness crept in from his peripheral vision. The clinic nex came into view. He dove through. Dropped Siba on the bed, threw his helmet bouncing into the corner. With a rip of zippers and latches, he tore open his suit. It fell away in a heap.

Blood trickled from Siba's nose. Her cheek had been laid open from eye to jaw. Her face was ruined. No rise and fall to her chest. How long had it been. Seemed like fifteen minutes. Couldn't have been. Too long.

Tipping her head back, Soman pinched her nose. Her skin felt dead under his fingers, but he knew it was his own flesh dying, every finger now numb. Covering her mouth with his, his chest caught at the touch of her lips, at the recollection of that kiss. God, seemed a year ago. He pumped her full. Three, four, five breaths. He breathed into her ten more times, fifteen, until breathlessness forced him to stop, and he lay his head on her chest, gasping. It had been too long.

Alone in an empty ship, half the corridors blown to vacuum.

Then he heard it: thump, thump, thump. Siba's chest rose in a spasm. A deeply drawn breath, a moan. Her hands gripped his head. He met her open eyes. She looked around like a person waking from a coma in a strange room, whispering words he couldn't understand, names he'd never heard.

Chapter 9

Siba's eyes rolled, then gained focus. "Rami," she slurred. Sliding off the gurney she stumbled, a hand cradling her wounded cheek.

"It's too late," Soman said, trying to hold her back.

Siba pushed past, staggered to the corner and stooped to lift one of the suits. She pulled on the first leg, her eyes barely focusing, a dark nipple visible through the jagged rip in her blouse.

"Siba, wait."

But she kept on yelping as the helmet caught her swollen cheek. Then all sound from her stopped as she locked down, her voice sealed in with her thoughts, her expression unreadable through the visor.

Soman wrestled back into his suit, then hurried to catch up.

On the far side of Nav airlock, the tube was cold and dark. Helmet lamps illuminated the bodies on the deck. Siba stopped at Moss and knelt, touching him with a tenderness due the dead. Her hand shook. "How could he," she whispered, her voice quavering.

Siba rose and walked on, weaving among the fallen, disappearing into the dark of Nav One.

Soman reset the breaker; lights flickered on. Retrieved the backup breaker, restored the normal valve positions. Normal.

A vibration, barely felt through the soles of his boots: valves slamming shut, air flowing to re-pressurize. Squinting in the sudden brightness, he looked around. Only four crew down in the tube. Seemed there should be more. He picked up the discarded wrench. Someone might still lurk out there.

In Nav One, Rami clung to his station, head sideways on the console, frozen juices cementing him down. Siba sobbed, tugging ineffectually to free him from his coagulum.

Soman went to the galley lounge for a knife. Siba cried as he slid the knife between Rami's head and the panel to pry him loose.

They gathered the corpses at the shuttle elevator. The stiff bodies bumped grudgingly through airlocks, their blank eyes staring. Ley and her colleagues should have been forced to see their battles this close. From the bomber cockpit it was just buildings, bunkers, bridges. Targets. On the ground, among the carnage, there was this.

In the LEV, Cabot lay like a prehistoric idol unearthed, cooling, hardening. Siba stroked and prodded. No heartbeat, no breath, only a hard look in the eyes that wouldn't fade. His second voyage nearly at an end.

Tethered to the edge of LEV bay, open to the stars as if at the gates of heaven, they watched EE2 rotate beneath them. One at a time they released the dead, to begin their perpetual orbit. Eight tumbling forms trailed *Sorcerer* in an arc, the machinery of the universe operating silently around them.

On the way back to Nav 1, Soman peered into every dark space, unsure they had accounted for everyone. Three times he counted—a different answer each time. How difficult can it be, adding to twenty-three. Stripping off his suit, Soman said, "We have to search the ship." When Siba said nothing, he added, "We have to be sure no one's hiding somewhere."

Siba said, "We're only missing Ley, and Selen."

Soman looked at her in surprise. She had appeared dazed; wandering, touching doorways, barely acknowledging his presence. But she had the count figured to the person.

She added, "I medicated Selen for seizures and put her to bed two days ago. Now she doesn't show on the locator. Maybe she's with Ley."

There was no answer to repeated hails for Ley.

They searched the ship. Neither believed Ley would have taken Selen, drugged and subject to seizures. But after two hours' of fruitless poking into every space aboard the ship, fatigue overcame them. The locator told the truth—there was no one else on the ship. A human being had vanished.

They locked themselves into quarters, a motion detector rigged. Maybe Siba had counted right, maybe she hadn't. They shared the bunk, Siba curled against him, her breathing steady, her warmth loosening tense muscles. The wrench lay close.

Twenty hours they slept, spent and twitching.

Siba stirred and turned to him. He stroked her hair; she nuzzled his throat. A softening of the muscles, unwinding. A throb of pleasure from the groin as Siba slid closer. But remembrance intruded. He stiffened with dread. The blessing of sleep had lasted only seconds.

Siba jerked as if stunned to reality. They stared at each other for an instant like strangers, then climbed from the bunk and headed for Nav deck without a word.

More messages to Ley. Still nothing. Soman stared at the terminal, certain what Ley's silence meant. *Sorcerer* orbited pole to pole, pass after pass. In polar orbit it would take a day, one rotation of the planet, to pass over the entire surface as the planet spun beneath them. A good orbit for getting a look at every spot on a planet, but lousy for staying in contact with a landing party, especially on a planet with a rotation period of seventy-seven Earth hours. She must be on the surface, waiting for the planet to twirl her under the orbiting ship. Or—she'd crashed. That would solve a lot.

Siba sat on the couch, sipping what passed for coffee, her cheek blue and purple around the bandages. She stared off, began to sob. "I wish I hadn't remembered."

"What."

"Most of us had no family. It was part of the selection process. No ties to Earth that could endanger the mission."

He looked away. *Most of us*, she had said. Could she know about Anoka?

"Except me," she said, looking down.

"*You* left someone behind?"

"Mom and dad."

"You had your folks? Then why?"

"I had no choice."

"What?"

She studied him. "You've heard of the company called *Future Lives*?"

Soman nodded slowly, spooked.

"They were the sales arm of a development company. I worked for that company."

"You helped develop the descroid?"

"No, I did the psych models. Validation of the calibration." At Soman's blank look, she said, "You have to get the neurotransmitter balance right or the personality's wrong. There were problems. But they didn't want anything to interfere with the licensing plan for retail sales. There was a lot of money riding on it. They already had six thousand units in use when we began to see the pattern of damage. I couldn't stand by while people trusted their family members to a defective product."

The color drained from Soman's face.

"So I went public."

He'd never heard about a scandal. Though if it had happened after Anoka was interred, while he was out among the asteroids. "Well, uh, good for you."

She dropped her face into her hands. "Tell that to my husband."

"Your—"

"They came after me. They got *him*." Through tears she said, "You can't pursue your personal goals for long before someone has to pay."

"Oh, Siba."

"Mel took me in."

"Mel?"

"Commander Ley. She suggested joining *Sorcerer*. Honey, she told me, you know they're not going to stop. And there's Lane to think about." Siba pressed her lips together for a moment. "My mother."

"Mel knew your mother?"

"They're sisters."

Of course. That touch. Almost mother and daughter.

"Now mom's gone. I never got to see her again…" Tears flew as she bunched her fists against her thighs.

Siba steadied herself. "Cabot had approached Mel earlier about coming with him, but she'd turned him down. They'd been wing commanders together, way back, before Cabot joined NASA. When my mess happened, she changed her mind. She cooked up the deal with the company—she'd take me off-planet, the company would back off."

Soman was amazed that Ley would do this, that she had the generosity in her. "Did they fix it?"

"What?"

"The descroid problem."

"What do you think?"

"But…there were regulatory agencies. There were laws."

"Sure," Siba said, "I ran. I let them get away with it. For my parents' sake, I let the criminals go."

"They must have done something. I mean, a lot of people were using these things. DeSarvo would have made sure it got fixed. DeSarvo believed we could run all the bad guys in the world through a descroid to rebalance them."

Siba turned. "People who claim things are that simple usually have an agenda. His agenda was money for research."

"No, he really believed the technology could be used for social problems."

Siba fixed him with a withering look.

"You know, balance everyone's chemistry. Help children learn better, stop the psychopaths."

Siba scoffed. "That's just how he got support for the mission."

"No, DeSarvo was passionate about it."

"I can't believe you're defending these people."

He raised his hands. "I'm not defending anybody." Soman thought back to the times he'd heard the great man pleading his case. No, DeSarvo was committed. Siba was just beyond reasoning.

"You and your pal DeSarvo can go to hell!" She spun away.

Sorcerer crossed over the pole of EE2 and glided toward the equator.

Siba slapped the screen and wailed, "Why doesn't she answer?"

A jolt tipped them sideways, flinging Siba against the console. Her mug slid off and smashed, sending shards sliding along the floor, clattering against the bulkhead.

"Auton, what was that?" he said.

"Drive start."

His eyes met Siba's. "Why?"

"Orbital termination."

Soman hissed, "Someone else must be on the ship." The skin of his neck began to crawl. "Auton. Who's doing it?"

"Automatic flight plan."

Siba gripped Soman's arm. "That's what he was doing. Auton, who programmed it?"

"Ramon, R."

"My God. Mel. Abort it."

"Password, please."

Soman looked at Siba. "He pass coded the—" And now Rami was dead. Ley had better be racing for the bay.

Siba called out, "Auton, did Rami leave a log entry?"

"Yes."

"Display it."

The emergency channel crackled, startling them both. "Ley to *Sorcerer.*"

"Thank God," Siba said.

"Commander Ley," Soman said.

"Mr. Soman. You had me worried. I didn't realize how long it would be between com windows. You finally rode over the horizon. How's construction proceeding?"

Soman felt cold to his deepest parts.

"Moss and his crew must be done, yes?"

"Where are you?" Though he knew.

Her voice sounded like a big grin. "Perfect landing, 30% fuel reserve. Even without the mark nine."

"You're supposed to drop the fuel *before* you land."

The pressure from the drive grew.

"There you go again, quoting me the rules. LEV, drone, you're so worried about the exact order. And you won't believe what's down here. The thumper shows a maze of caverns and corridors underneath. All kinds of mechanical sounds. But I haven't figured out how to get through the surface yet. There's so much to explore down here."

Soman shook his head. "Commander, I need to give you an update on…our status here." Just hours ago, from the LEV driver's seat, facing the closed bay door, he had confronted the prospect of *Sorcerer* receding as he orbited, helpless. Now it was happening—to Ley.

"Your status?" Her tone of voice changed.

"Remember I told you all the things that could go wrong? And one of those was the unexpected, the wild card? But you didn't want to hear any of that."

"Is Selen with you?" Siba asked.

"Selen?" Ley's voice rose on the word, incredulous. "Noo…what's going *on* up there?"

"Moss told you he was going to build the two-stage fuel drone, didn't he," Soman said.

"He finally…saw things my way." But her pauses between words said she was recollecting that conversation in a new light. "Mr. Soman, where are you?"

"Nav One."

Silence. Then Ley said, "I'll speak to the Captain now." It was an order.

"Cabot never returned to consciousness."

"You told me he was fine!"

"I told you he was alive." His cheeks flushed hot. *Alive and kicking.*

"I'll speak to Moss then."

"Sir, you've been had. He tried to take over as soon as he got you off ship."

"Mr. Soman, don't give me this bullshit. They were moving the gear into…" She stopped. For a moment, only her breathing came through from the planet.

Soman wondered how she could have been fooled. Battle-hardened Ley. Got to hand it to Moss, exploiting her weakness, her need for action, turned into compulsion by her trip through the descroid. Even without the nudge of chemistry gone awry, Ley was prone to impulse, only alive because of luck, chutzpa, and the best surgery taxpayers could buy.

"All right Mr. Soman, tell me what's been going on since you returned."

Soman's throat tightened. Think. Skirt the details of decompression. He forced himself not to look at Siba, afraid she'd see it in his eyes. He explained his forced re-entry to the ship. "Bruni attacked me inside the airlock. Lucky for me I had my suit on, and he didn't. My helmet saved me."

Siba's mouth dropped open as she finally pieced it together. "*You* blew the air! I thought it was Moss."

"So you sacrificed everyone to get control of the ship," Ley said. "Impressive, Mr. Soman."

Siba turned away, and Soman moved around to stay in front of her, pleading, "They were taking over! They wanted the descroids."

But Siba's attention was somewhere else, as she moaned, "Rami…"

"I had a suit for him! Moss cut it open with his torch!"

She wailed, a sound of anguish filling the air of Nav one. "All those people dead…they just wanted to get home."

"I tried to reason with Moss! He left me no choice!"

"When?"

It felt as if she'd slapped him. "He—he moved me to nav channel." God, Moss had it all figured out.

She squinted at him.

"The thanks I got was Bruni trying to beat me to death with an airlock wrench." He could see she didn't believe him. "I thought they were going to kill you for the descroids!"

Siba's spoke through clenched teeth. "We had enough descroids. I had the parts to put ten back into service. He wasn't going to hurt me. He just wanted to go home, and I wouldn't agree until you and Mel were back."

Soman stopped. Could that be right. With Cabot and the rest of the LEV crew dead, that left how many. Soman, Siba, Rami, Ley. That's four. Moss and three others in the con tube. Eight. Bruni down in the bay tube. Nine. Oh shit. Selen, wherever she is, ten. "Then why were they cutting their way into Nav One?"

Silence.

"Mr. Soman." There was steel back in Ley's voice. "Let's talk about getting the rest of our equipment down here."

Soman looked at the Nav screen, felt the steady acceleration of *Sorcerer*. "Sir, I have bad news."

"I assumed you already *gave* me the bad news."

Siba's mouth trembled.

"Rami programmed the ship out of orbit. He pass coded the instructions, and we—"

"Siba, what's going on."

Siba slid behind the terminal, fumbling over the keyboard. "We…just located Rami's log. Maybe…we're hoping…he left the password there. Give us a minute.

Soman leaned over Siba's shoulder.

> *don't think we can hold out. ship must get home. drive start in 36 hours. Should be enough time for everyone. siba was good to me. thank you. go with god*

"No password."

Ley's voice crackled. "When does this program kick in?"

Soman touched the scab above his eye, saying nothing.

Siba finally answered. "We're accelerating now."

At first, nothing from the planet. Then the radio hissed again, urgency in her voice. "All right, Mr. Soman."

Soman kept his back to Siba. Don't ask, Commander.

"You have to disable the drive."

Siba's eyes lit up. "How?"

He held up his hands. "No idea."

Siba pushed her hair back. "Then let's get started figuring it out."

"Auton. How long until escape velocity?"

"Four hours ten minutes."

Soman could see from Siba's calm manner that she still didn't understand. "Siba. We have only four hours."

"Why? If it takes us longer, we just come back."

Ley came through. "It doesn't work that way, honey."

Siba looked to Soman.

"Once we hit escape velocity, there isn't enough chemical fuel to get us back to orbit. The positioning thrusters weren't made for that. If we disable the main drive, it's going to be useless. And as soon as we reconnect it, Rami's program tells it to head for Earth." He watched the implications dawn on her.

"It has to be done in the next four hours. Sooner really, because the longer it goes, the more eccentric the orbit will be, making it harder to launch and retrieve a LEV. In fact…" he looked away in thought. "At some point there may not be enough fuel on the LEV to make a landing. We have less than four hours…" Soman's mind spun trying to grasp the complexity of the equation, and its consequences.

"Then…" She shook off her paralysis. "Let's get *moving!*" She turned to the console.

"Wait! Let's think it through before we do anything. Do you understand the flux down on drive deck? One mistake, we fry ourselves. Or disable the ship forever in orbit around Epsilon. And if we don't kill ourselves trying to get to the planet and back, then we have to repair the drive, with the power still on, eighty thousand volts."

Siba wasn't listening, working the console in a fury. She'd already called up diagrams of drive deck. "So you're saying you won't help."

Soman's voice rose. "No, I'm just saying, let's think about this, what would the captain do?"

Ley said, "Mr. Soman, I'm your captain now, and don't you forget it."

Soman blanched. Disobey Ley's direct order, return to Earth an outlaw. Anger rose in him. "You put us in this position with your…your—" He turned to Siba. "We have to think about the mission. We have to bring it back."

Siba turned to him, hands gripping the console. Her voice came out low and soft. "Soman, we *are* the mission. You, me, and Mel." Her fingers flew across the keyboard. The engineering specifications flashed on her screen, the access codes to five deck.

Soman pinned her hands. "Wait—listen to me. I risked everything for you."

She pushed him away. "You risked everything for *you.*" She leaped from behind the console and dove through the nex.

Soman raced after, caught a glimpse as she disappeared around the curve of the tube. Flicking in to open, he yelled, "Siba!"

Silence.

"Sibaaaa!"

He ran. A flash of purple, then gone. "Auton, patch me in to Ley."

"That is now a private channel."

Siba was heading for drive deck, and Ley was going to talk her through the disconnect. The airlock spun open; he tumbled in, picturing where Siba would have to go next. "Auton, freeze airlock two."

There was a slight pause. "Negative. Safety violation."

Damn. He barreled down the tube after Siba, leaning into the wall to counter the push of *Sorcerer's* acceleration. "Sibaaa!" He checked the chronometer. 23:11—three hours and fifty-seven minutes to escape velocity.

Chapter 10

Soman reached airlock two, Siba nowhere in sight. Locator. There. Going down. Using the shaft, not the elevator, five airlocks to negotiate on the way to the drive access ring. "Um, Auton, lock down the elevator."

The auton hesitated. Then, "Negative. Safet—"

"Excellent." He sped for the elevator. Saving Ley is impossible—or is it. He tried to remember what he knew about drive controls, searching for a way to disconnect safely, to buy them time. Time to talk to Siba, to think it through. They should be working on this together. "Sibaaa," he called across open channel.

Locator. Damn, she's already through three airlocks.

The elevator reached five deck. He pounded through the nex, feeling light—less than half gravity at ring access level. He knew what that meant from long experience: faster moving with handholds than walking, not enough friction against the floor, too much time waiting for each step to fall. Locator. She was already at the fifth airlock. He flicked up the floor plan, studied it a second, then pulled for the ring access junction, his arms burning.

Soman flew across the tube intersection and plowed into the far wall. Siba appeared around the curve, bounding, arms and legs flailing, not enough experience in half-G to control her stride. She spotted him. "You…" Her voice a growl. And there was something in her hand. She twisted it, bringing a point to bear. With her free hand she searched for the wall while her legs pumped in the air, her eyes locked onto Soman.

Soman froze.

Siba stretched to stab him.

He jerked back. She missed her footing, the half-G step taking longer than she expected. He saw what she held: an injector. She wasn't going to kill him—she was going to sedate him.

The ship lurched; the pressure of the drive increased.

Soman seized the handrail as the new motion pushed Siba into the wall of the tube. She spun and fell, holding the injector the way a woman would protect her child in a fall. She bounced, the impact flipping her. Soman dove and caught her wrist.

She tried to bend her wrist, twisting the point of the injector toward his arm.

"Stop it!" he screamed. God, she's strong. The needle trembled just above his skin. If they hit a wall wrong, the force of it would sink the lance into him. She wailed and lashed at him with her free limbs. They rolled along the tube, driven by the strengthening acceleration. She clipped his nose; he felt the wet warmth of blood in the back of his mouth. Still he held her fist, trying to pry her fingers off the injector. They spun off the wall and landed on the deck, Siba's back taking the blow. Focusing only on the injector, he pinned her to the deck, oblivious to the blows she landed on his head, his ribs, his groin. His pressure on her hand increased. Her wails grew louder. What could Ley be thinking, helpless in the LEV, listening to the struggle.

He managed to pry one finger off and bent it back. Something gave way and Siba wailed in pain. Then he had the injector out of her grasp.

Both hands free, Siba doubled her attack, going for his face, tearing open the wound above his eye. He held the injector behind him. "Stop! We need to talk."

Spit flew from her mouth, blood streamed from her cheek.

She was not going to talk.

Siba recoiled from his thrust, her hands out in defense. She twisted. He missed her arm. She howled as his momentum plunged the injector deep into her breast with a sound like a hissing snake.

Suddenly still, she looked up at Soman. Her eyes lost focus. Her mouth opened and a sound gurgled from deep inside her.

Soman watched, horrified. It was working too fast. Maybe she'd set the dose for his body mass. Maybe she *had* planned to kill him. "Please tell me it wasn't a lethal dose." Her eyes rolled to the ceiling. She softened and settled to the deck.

Sorcerer swung over the south pole of EE2, arcing steeply up, gaining speed, reaching for escape velocity. The ship rolled slightly; Siba's head lolled to the side. Saliva ran from her mouth to puddle on the deck. The empty injector rolled away, coming to rest against a floor locker.

The radio crackled in his implant, making him jump. It was Ley, barely audible above the static that grew worse each second. "…Mr. Soman…what have you…Siba…" and she was gone, the ship beyond her horizon. He flicked into the chronometer: 23:37. Three and a half hours until escape velocity, two hundred minutes until Ley could give up hope of a second ship appearing in the black sky above her.

Soman moved in a daze down the tube toward the ship's drive, through the tunnel to the transfer pod. It spat him across the gap between the spinning crew module and the fixed drive housing, giving him up to weightlessness. In the dark cavern he hovered before the barrier shield, every hair on end, feeling the powerful magnetic field tugging his bones. This had been Siba's destination. Maybe there was a way. Ley must have suggested something. But by the time *Sorcerer* swung above her again, it would be too late.

Soman studied the warning signs on the EMF shielding. Enough flux in there to cook your brain like a hard-boiled egg. He held a dialog with the auton, probing possibilities. None of them hopeful. But there was one without obvious disaster. The ship was built with redundant power nodes. It might be possible to re-route drive power through the ruined Level Three re-charge junction. Destroyed and isolated, it might work to cut the power feed. The weak point was the switching gear. If it fried in the surge, the fireball would burn through the hull in a heartbeat. Even if it didn't, he might be unable to switch it back.

The auton ran him through the probabilities. Nineteen point seven percent odds for a successful switch-over. If it switched successfully, eighty-nine percent it would switch back and restore the drive in working order. Odds for the two in sequence: seventeen point five. One in six chance of living to save Ley. Blood pounded through Soman's head. His heart thumped and rattled; he dropped to a knee. About the same odds he could have piloted the LEV into the hole in Pearl. But there, he'd have been dead if he didn't act. Here, he could die if he did. What the statisticians called Type I error and Type II error. No longer just math.

Soman backed to ring access, moving like a sleepwalker. Silence on open channel, the auton awaiting his instruction. He returned to Siba and crouched close, listening, watching. Finally he saw the movement: a barely detectable swell of her ribcage. Gently he lifted her, corralling her flopping limbs. As the elevator started up, he pulled her to him and clenched his eyes shut.

Soman had watched Siba connect him to the monitors enough times to figure it out. He didn't understand most of the displays. "Auton, what's BMT?"

"Basal metabolic temperature," the auton told him. The trace slipped steadily lower. Siba's core heat leaking away. Soman piled on blankets. He rewound the options for stopping the drive, searching for the easy solution he must be missing, his head spinning. Sever drive module: no— only an option in Earth orbit, only when rescue is a certainty. Enter the drive shield and physically disconnect: no—too much flux. Send a fuel drone down unmanned: no—by the time Ley completed the fuel transfer, they'd be twenty hours past escape velocity. Every option no, no, no. Only the recharge junction held any hope. Siba would try it. But here she lay, her breath slowing, her temperature trailing down. She owed a life to Ley—Soman didn't.

Siba would take the one in six chance for Ley. Just as he would for Anoka. But doubt speared him—would he.

Soman drew a chair close to Siba's bed. He pushed a lock of hair from her face. Placing a hand on her hip, another on her shoulder, he laid his head beside her arm. God, he was tired.

Soman woke to a feeling of dread, looking around the empty clinic. For a moment he couldn't think, staring in confusion at the empty injector on the bed, certain he'd left it at five deck. The contradiction confused him; sleep refused to let him go. A groggy aftermath of sleep that—he jumped up, clapping a hand to the tender muscle, then falling to the deck as his legs refused to work, stiff and useless from the drug. Siba had awakened and put him under.

Soman crawled to the nex as he flicked in. Locator. There she was, in Nav One. What's she done. His heart tripped-hammered. Chronometer. 21:47. How could that be. Almost a day. Siba's had time to—he burst into Nav One and pulled up.

Siba never looked up from the console. Muted music played, an ethereal, haunting hymn. Those crinkles in the corners of her eyes that used to accompany her dazzling smile now scratched deep furrows across her temples.

He looked to the Nav screen, couldn't register what he was seeing, too much black, unable to focus on the object occupying the upper right corner.

The hymn ended. Siba turned to him, her look unforgiving. "I was four hours too late."

Soman stared at the screen. Epsilon Eridani was shrinking away.

"I would have disabled it anyway, but Ley wouldn't let me." Her swelling cheek had squeezed her eye shut.

Siba said, "What did you do with Selen?"

Soman's mouth hung open. "Selen? I haven't seen Selen."

She eyed him skeptically. "I searched again. She's not here. What did you do?"

"I didn't…" Soman stopped, faltering under Siba's accusation, thinking back to the chaos, uncertain anymore what he'd done, what he hadn't done, what he should have done.

"You'll be wanting a descroid."

She was right; he could no longer feel his feet; the arm throbbed unmercifully; the heart stumbled continuously. Degenerating like the rest. No choice but trust the machine. He nodded.

She looked away, busying herself with some task. "It doesn't require assistance."

"Can't you monitor? Please."

Her disregard mocked him.

"Or I could set you up in yours first."

"I'm staying up a while."

"We've got to get into descroids before—"

"I have to be here for Mel. And I need time alone."

Soman sighed. What ancient core of Ley deserved such devotion. He tried to imagine Melinda Ley as a young woman, without the wracked and bent body, before she learned to treat people with disdain, before she became a killer. He couldn't imagine her little niece running to her squealing when Ley arrived for a visit, Siba jumping into Ley's lap to hear stories of distant places.

He walked to descroid deck.

Siba followed him, pausing when he stumbled over his unfeeling feet, offering no help.

Picking his way through blackened, melted bulkheads, past the rubble of pods, all those one-way tickets, the aroma of cold embers catching in his throat.

From the console he shut down spingrav and listened to the motors fade, felt the last vibration of the bearings. In a minute his body would run down like that, as the descroid sucked him dry.

Soman stripped naked and faced the pod. He would use Lorca's descroid.

Siba watched expressionless, disinterested in his body, his terror, his remorse.

He climbed in. Siba lowered the lid. Servos slid the anal tube into him. A mechanical arm dangling tubules swung over his chest. It locked into the socket in his ribcage. Finally the tracheal probe pushed deeply into his throat. With relief he inhaled the narcotic and slid down a darkening tunnel. Siba faded, her eyes offering nothing.

His soul began its long retreat from the weary work of life.

Part Two: Prodigal Child

Chapter 11

Soman had always imagined the world would end in fire: a blaze of hatred and munitions, missiles and napalm, nuclear inferno. And now the temperate regions of Earth seemed wrapped in smoke, as if the Northern Hemisphere burned steadily. He studied the planet for hours, hovering before the screen in Nav One.

For a day and a half he wouldn't allow himself to think about Siba and descroid fourteen, forcing his attention back to the systems needing his attention; to the strange appearance of Earth.

Maybe it wasn't smoke. Clouds, perhaps. But clouds wouldn't remain stationary so long. Whatever is was, it reflected sunlight like a cue ball. The fuzzy blue globe, always so easy on the eye of a returning spacer, now blazed searing white. Enhanced, magnified, IR, UV, it was all the same. Only a band across the tropics showed blue and green. And something else wasn't right on the home globe—no radio chatter, no sign of orbital traffic.

The wad of food in his gut wouldn't digest. He'd forced himself to eat immediately after re-emergence, but the solid items on the menu—beef steak (with or without onions), breaded fish patty, sweet potatoes— raised up an image of the descroid. The food stored the same way, the process less delicate. He'd taken the liquid nutrient. It had tasted wrong; it was old. Or maybe it was—no, just work the repair checklist.

Finally he could avoid Siba's log entries no longer. White streaked her hair; furrows sliced her once-smooth cheeks. He double-checked the time stamp—a week after he'd entered his descroid—yet she appeared to have aged twenty years. "Siba," he whispered. She didn't seem to realize.

Her eyes bore into him; of course she knew he'd be the first to view the log.

Soman found it hard to breathe.

"So you made it back," she said. Anger simmered beneath the surface. "We've made it through week one, Commander Ley and I."

Siba said she was processing Ley's data from her work on the surface of EE2. In case their descroids failed on the return trip, she would leave a record.

She identified the files containing the data. She talked of solar flux, orbital shape, the thousand other measurements captured by *Sorcerer's* instruments. Then her reserve faltered, and she leaned back in her seat, gripping its arms like a reluctant witness. Her eyes slid upward, her head back slightly, two fingers on her lower lip. The familiarity of this gesture pricked him; what she did when she paused to think. Her eyes filled with tears. Then the screen went blank.

Soman sat unmoving in the dark, to the quiet thrum of the ship around him.

After a long time, he said, "Auton."

"Ready."

"Position check."

The holo came alive with a plot of the solar system. "Distance four point five zero seven million kilometers. Orbital selection optimal within twenty-seven hours."

Soman considered. An equatorial orbit would provide the most time over populated regions; a polar orbit more complete access to the entire globe. Geostationary would stay farther from hostile launchings, though *Sorcerer* would use a lot of fuel moving to a lower orbit for a landing. That was the problem: where to land. Impossible to know the political map after three thousand years. The country with the best technology. The best hospital on Earth. His arms numb almost to the shoulders, his walk a ragged shuffle. His heart rattling at least once an hour. He was falling apart.

The questions kept coming: what was the population; would they remember *Sorcerer*; what language would they speak.

What was their lifespan. Three thousand years should have been more than enough time to learn the secret of the human organism. If they haven't burned up the place.

"Polar," he told the auton. Better take an orbit with full surface coverage. Just the way they had at EE2. The auton displayed course correction vectors and deceleration equations, drawing delicate green lines against the black background, curving to a rendezvous with the white sphere.

The list of failures grew faster than he could make repairs, alarms casting him back to that first dark day at Epsilon Eridani, the ship falling apart around him.

Soman and *Sorcerer* stumbled along the last stretch of their marathon.

He dragged himself to Nav one for Siba's second log.

"Look." She clutched a rope of hair, indignant. "Hair can't turn white so fast. And my skin. It's supposed to take years for this to happen." Telltale folds marred the curve of her jaw; the firm flesh sliding down her high cheekbones.

Soman sat forward in the seat. "Get in the damn descroid," he said.

"Yesterday I ran full med. I'm not a young woman in old skin; I'm really growing old. I have an arrhythmia. I have low blood pressure and high sugar. My pancreas isn't working well."

She looked at the bony hands in her lap, blue veins showing through transparent skin. "One more difficulty with the descroids. Make a note of it."

Soman watched in horror, then in awe. She couldn't have told Ley. Otherwise Ley would have ordered her into a descroid.

Siba looked up. "Enough of that. That blast of light from Pearl was a signal, I think. I wondered where the light went after it beamed from the hole. So I simulated it, thinking it must be a message to someone or something down on EE2. It stumped me for a while. There was nothing down there.

"Finally I remembered how we first spotted EE2. Those mirrors reflecting the light from Epsilon Eridani. So I calculated where the reflected light went. And then I recalculated it. You'll never guess." A smile flickered. For a moment she was a schoolgirl, enjoying her secret.

"Earth," she said. "There must be a message in the light beam." A spark in her eye. He noticed the way the tip of her nose flattened as she spoke. "Maybe you can find out," she told him.

The holo faded. Soman swiveled to watch the approaching Earth. The flash would have arrived a hundred fifteen years ahead of him. He studied the shrouded planet. "Auton."

"Ready."

"Display the image of Earth from yesterday, side by side." The image fuzzed, a duplicate materialized. Exactly the same. The clouds hadn't moved since yesterday, since last week. "Full spectral scan on those clouds. And get a reading on the dark spots. Here, and here, where I'm pointing. Check it against all profiles in the database."

Soman floated to the canteen and drew a tube of water. It tasted of stale sweat. Well, that's what it was. He drank. Stay hydrated.

The auton reported. "The dark areas are rock. Ninety-nine percent confidence."

Rock. Sure. Mountains sticking through the clouds. "Okay, how about the clouds?"

"The best match is ice. Ninety-eight percent confidence."

Soman pursed his lips. Then it wasn't smoke. "So we're talking high clouds? Cirrus?" Then he frowned. Mountains poking through cirrus— no way.

Auton responded. "Not ice crystal. Based on reflectance, purity, and IR peak it is solid ice."

Soman's eyes remained locked onto the scene. And suddenly he saw it, like a rattlesnake hiding in the leaves, a deadly reality the eye misses until it moves. The striated white surface had none of the swirl of cloud tops. Those fine lines etched into the surface were crevasses. The dark edge revealed the snout of massive continental ice sheets, the terminal moraine along its southern edge. A moraine piling up the rubble of European civilization almost to the shores of the Mediterranean.

He blinked, then looked around as if to reassure himself of the reality of the ship. The clock: 09:17, November 8, 5381. Yet Earth appeared as it must have during the Pleistocene, an expanse of ice stretching from Spain to the pole. An image flickered in memory: the medieval church in the small city of Falun in central Sweden, home to his Soman ancestors, its pipe organ resonating with Toccata and Fugue in D minor, the music shaking the flesh to his bones. Falun, now under a mile of ice, the land pressed down under the weight of it. All the cities and towns and villages and farms, gone. His mind threw it all back, like trying to imagine the end of the universe, or his last living breath.

The time machine had transported him backward.

Where else to look. Moonbase. At first he couldn't locate Colony Four. He scanned again. It was impossible to miss with its two docking gantries, always a ship in one. Finally he found it. Not from the gantries, but from the rubble of the central dome scattered across its crater. Hands shaking, he panned the telescope. Colony Two was intact, the twisted hull of a fallen ship near the lock. Three was a repeat of Four, its dome wrecked, two ships splayed on their sides, hulls crushed and bent.

Soman studied Colony One long and hard. The perimeter was littered with ships, six, seven or more. The dome appeared to be intact, and a ship stood at the airlock. Soman scanned, searching for signs of life, like a child returning home to find his house a smoldering pile of ash, his family missing. Nothing moved. It looked derelict.

His heart hammered. Anoka.

The edge of the ice sheet cut across the Iberian Peninsula, through northern Italy and Turkey, until it disappeared into the darkness of the terminator. It had to be a European phenomenon. A quirk. A hard winter. In six hours North America would swing into view. He stared at the Earth as it turned slowly beneath him, sextillion tons of rock twirling on its axis. Europe disappeared bit by bit under the terminator, as each new slice of the North Atlantic glistened white. By the time the Americas appeared, he knew what he would see. Rock and ice. White from Greenland to Hatteras. Chicago, center of the stable craton of the continent, buried.

A phrase came to him from the deepest folds of the brain. Some say the world will end in fire, some in ice. Robert Frost. Well-named for the prophecy and its fulfillment. The people of Earth live their poetry. Civilization, crushed and swept away.

Chapter 12

Soman woke to cold. Outside the skin of the ship, space nudged absolute zero. Ahead, glaciers gripped the Earth. A memory surfaced, snow falling, the nose prickling at the driven crystals. A rectangle of marble, black and glossy, rises through the snow, its edges sharp in rebuke. The wind moans across a thousand miles of prairie. His knees press the ground. Before him lies the fresh mound bearing its stone. Beside him stone-faced Anoka, catching snowflakes in her mouth. To save their children, women would pay even with their lives.

And now Anoka lay under immovable tons of ice, buried as surely as her mother.

In bay one, the last LEV was poised for descent. Somehow he had managed to move it there, Fueled it, completed the checklist. What a person can do when they must.

Dropping to the surface of the bay, he tugged the lockdowns, making certain the LEV couldn't shift during *Sorcerer's* insertion burn. Any damage to the LEV, any breakdown, would strand him on the ship. *Sorcerer* glided in, course correction done, fifteen hours to orbit. Soon Earth would dominate the viewscreen. Almost home. Hugging himself against the chill, he headed for Nav One and faced Siba's last entry.

Her voice quavered as if it had few sounds left to it. "I've lived a whole life in two months, like a butterfly." She stared from the screen at Soman, a wrinkled creature with white hair and tired eyes, a tremor to her hands. The purple blouse hung on her gaunt bones.

"Mel's gone."

Soman looked away.

"But there was something odd." Siba held her hands together as if to still them, palms touching. "She had a week's air left. She slept a lot, trying to conserve. Then she called. Talked while suiting up. Time was worthless, she said, the way she was spending it. She was going to control *it.*"

That would be Ley.

"She walked away from the LEV with six hours of air. Two hours, just breathing. I listened to every breath. Then she started talking. The surface was beautiful, she said, everything gold and gleaming. She talked about her life. The things that woman has seen."

Soman watched her cry, tears floating away like bubbles. There would have been no way to penetrate that bond but by risking everything for Ley.

"Anyway." Siba composed herself. "Mel had spotted these knobs, studying images taken during the descent. The nearest was too far for a roundtrip on the air she could carry. Five hours walking. She decided to make it her last exploration. When her first canister ran empty, it surprised her. Talking too much, she said. After that she just walked and breathed. She reached the knob just as her second tank started to hiss." Siba's eyes filled, her voice squeaked. "She never said goodbye." For a moment she sobbed. Then she looked up and wiped her eyes. "But…I keep hearing her radio click. On, off. Like it's flapping in the wind, except there isn't any wind down there."

Soman looked around the cabin like a photographer. *Click*. The console where Rami wrote *Sorcerer's* escape routine. *Click*. The corner under the air vent where Siba slowed her body so she could live to see this moment. *Click*. The bulkhead cut open by Moss. *Click*. The couch where he kissed Siba, where Siba had kissed him back.

Siba spread her arms. "Look at me."

He couldn't. He'd seen the bones poking through the shoulders of her blouse, the skin hanging from her jaw, her trembling lip.

"We know we're going to grow old, but it's supposed to have the grace to creep up on us slowly, time to get used to it." She straightened. "Well, no one can live forever." She stared from the holo, her eyes fastened on him, as if she could grasp his lapels and shake him. "Not even you."

Then her look softened. "Soman. You kept a lot of secrets. I think, I hope, your biggest secret is that you're not who I think you are." The screen went blank.

Soman left Nav One and wandered the empty ship, knowing where the wandering must finish.

Lights flickered uncertainly as he entered descroid cabin fourteen, illuminating the shiny egg embedded in the floor. Tethered in the corner, a crumpled pair of jeans and a purple blouse. A yellow rectangle flashed on the console. He couldn't see her through the opaque lid. He dare not open the descroid, and he must not run spingrav. When he finally risked her rehydration, he would have only hours.

He stared again at the yellow indicator.

NONVIABLE, it flashed.

And Soman vowed: Never again climb into a descroid.

Data streamed across the display panel. There could be no denying the data, or the yellow light: Siba had waited too long. Now the only hope for Siba, for Anoka, for him, was whatever medical knowledge survived in that narrow tropical region, the silent civilization that revealed itself with a few clusters of nighttime lights.

Sorcerer's engine ignited for insertion. When the maneuver finished, a new kind of light surrounded him. No longer the dim green cast of *Sorcerer's* diodes, but a natural light, blue-white and brilliant: the huge, blazing Earth, the view from a ship in low orbit.

Chapter 13

Gliding above the empty Pacific, *Sorcerer* shuddered in orbital correction, adjusting to gain the exact spot where the LEV must eject.

Siba must be ready for transfer to the med suit with only ten minutes to spare before the LEV must launch to hit its re-entry window. Assuming he could fly the LEV to a safe landing, he would have two hours to find medical help for Siba before the power pack in the med suit expired. He would trust the autopilot for landing—his arm would barely move.

No satellites whizzed past in low orbit. That meant none had been launched in at least a hundred fifty years. The auton spotted a handful in geosynchronous, but they appeared dead. Nothing turned up in the RF scan. Yet people lived on the planet; the tropics had held off the ice. Across the band of green circling the equator, settlements blinked at night.

The descroid whirred. Its heavy shield moved, a half-cylinder rotating into the floor, exposing the glass of the pod, speckled inside with condensation. A tang of ozone filled the air. Floating in the descroid was a withered and desiccated old woman, like an ancient mummy, skin like tissue paper clinging to bones.

Siba shuddered. A wave rippled though her, raising her emaciated hips, expanding her ribcage, tilting her neck back. Her jaw opened around the tracheal tube as if it drowned her. Deep in her empty eye sockets, diaphanous drapes of tissue glistened and moved. Siba began to swell.

Sorcerer glided across the North Pole. Just beyond the horizon, the land once called Canada approached. He had to eject during this orbit. He didn't dare wait the twenty-four hours for this slice of Earth to circle below again—he might not last that long. He had trained the telescope on the ancient spaceport at Old Ciudad, in Venezuela, starting point of the *Sorcerer* mission, lifting port for the heavy loads. Nothing remained of the massive gantries, the assembly buildings or runways, those millions of tons of steel and concrete. In its place sprawled a jumble of weathered stone blocks holding off the jungle. In 2056 that spaceport had seemed a technological monument that would stand forever. Forever wasn't as long as he'd thought.

At least there was a town nearby. Not a big one, but there weren't many choices on this world. The old spaceport it would be. If the LEV worked. If there was a level spot to land. If no one shot them down.

The descroid completed its cycle and retracted its probes, With a snap, the overhead arm retracted from Siba's chest socket. Soman recoiled as droplets of blood sprayed a trail down her abdomen. He took in her nakedness, her breasts shrunken across protruding ribs, her face deeply wrinkled, jagged blue veins marring her legs, the skin of her hands thin and transparent. He closed his eyes. This was the future he had hoped to prevent.

He fumbled, lifting her gently, a gelatinous body without substance, like soft remains found at low tide. He lay her on the opened suit. Connected the chest plug, slid it home with a click, careful not to brush nipples with shaking hands. Slid the helmet over her head, grateful when it shrouded her grimace. A gurgling sound—the helmet's probe located her mouth and slid in the tracheal tube. Zip up, fasten the clasps. Punch the machine on. With a whir the respirator chugged on, forcing her chest to rise and fall in a cunning pretense of life. Soman floated her into the corridor. Nine minutes remaining. Move.

The re-entry burn forced Soman back in his seat. The first wisps of air buffeted the LEV. He dropped at the mercy of a three thousand-year-old machine blasting toward a planet with enough gravity and atmosphere to sear them both to a faint trail of ionic trash. Hot plasma streamed by the viewports. Turbulence rattled Soman and Siba against their seats. Then the LEV settled into a glide, and the view from the ports cleared.

The southern edge of the ice passed beneath, giving way to dry steppe, a brown strip sucked of its moisture by the dirty snout of ice. To the east he spotted the dark tops of the southern Appalachians fingering through white. South of the ice, foothills spread brown and bare and bleak. No habitations. Too cold, too dry, no tree, no scrub, only the occasional lichen tinting rock green and ocher. Farther south, over what had been Florida, scattered buildings, a lonely wisp of smoke, a few trees.

The LEV banked. Islands below. The gross, swollen tip of Florida, its shallows left high and dry by fallen sea levels. With a shock he spotted the edge of a large landmass off the Florida coast. He looked again. The Bahama Banks lay above the sea, so much of the ocean's water tied up in ice. Looking down the long receding curve of the eastern Caribbean, he saw a new continent risen.

Ahead, the coast of Venezuela, the ragged summit of Pico Cristobal Colon fronting the Sierra de Perija range. Lying serenely behind the mountains, the Lago de Maracaibo. No longer a lagoon, it was now a lake cut off from the waters of the Caribbean. As the LEV fell, the texture of the land fingered into the sky. Earth began to look like a world of dirt and rock and topography, no longer a smooth glistening globe.

Bang! A slam of metal and a rush of air; the cabin seemed to break apart.

"Drogue one airbrake," the auton announced.

Soman braced as two more bolts blew. Chutes slid from their holders, cables singing, the pitch decreasing like bombs falling. The LEV slowed. Another explosion; drogue jettison. For five seconds, the LEV glided in peaceful, quiet flight. Positioning thrusters stood the craft on end.

A deathly roar: engine ignition.

He searched for a landing site, scanning furiously, moving the aiming cursor across the target zone, struggling to focus on the constantly changing scene. There. A flat area. It looked like an old concrete slab. "Auton, what do you make of this spot, cursor center, now."

"Composite, mineral, angle 2.5 degrees."

"Put us down in the middle." LEV slewed sideways as every thruster added its hiss to the thunder of the main engine. Anyone within five hundred miles would hear this fireball dropping from the sky.

Bang! Landing struts descended. The whine of the engine rose, the ground approached fast. Slam! Crushed into the seat. Siba bounced.

The engine shut down. In the sudden quiet, Soman sat still, not daring to move. The LEV lurched to one side. Soman held on, expecting the sickening fall. He reached for Siba, then froze. Gravity tugged her limbs down. In the weightlessness of orbit she had appeared suspended, waiting for life's resumption. Here on her home world, she looked dead.

With a final creak, the ship held, tilted but steady.

He could barely lift the weight of Siba and the med-suit. But he managed to stagger through the airlock into golden light, so different from the harsh glare of space. Yellow, warm, luxurious sunlight, filtered through miles of atmosphere, the sunlight of beaches and summer afternoons. He startled, thinking something had brushed his face, but it was only thick, humid, sensuous air. Almost too viscous to breathe, it filled his lungs with a satisfying heaviness, carrying a flood of aromas. Moist earth. Growing grasses. Salt air.

Before him lay a jumble of eroded concrete sections invaded by creeping vines. Beyond the ruined launch pad a field of grass waved, then green forest stretching to the lake. Beyond the lake, the sun hung above distant mountains. Clustered along the shore, buildings huddled like anthills. A breeze from the sea carried evening chill. Though much of the planet froze, here Soman could imagine he was home. Back on the site from which he'd ferried loads to *Sorcerer*. His legs grew weak; a lump clogged his throat.

A whir and a buzz. A string of vehicles stood at a distance from the LEV. Three, four of them, squarish, drab brown with tiny windows. Soman stared in shock—vehicles with wheels, all of them, not a Levitron in sight. Figures emerged. Soman tried to catch a glimpse of them, but they stayed behind the vehicles. Words too faint to understand.

Soman clattered down the stairway, then swayed on crumbling concrete, his arms giving way, Siba sliding from his grip, everything on the home world so heavy. His legs failed and he sat, Siba's helmet resting against his face, its smooth surface pressing into his lips. Then it seemed the sun set as the sky turned from blue to gray to black.

Chapter 14

Delirious dreams. Water, mysterious sounds, touch. Calm like a blue sea surrounded him. He slept and woke in cycles. Sounds. A voice. He opened his eyes. A room. He tried to speak but heard only a long, low moan.

He woke again. Raised his head. Tubes and wires tugged at him. Dim pinpoints of instruments surrounded him like constellations. The smell of bedclothes and disinfectant. And then the wrenching memory. He looked around. Where was Siba. Dread clenched his stomach. Then a wave rose inside, lifting him, quenching the bile. What narcotic could confer this absolute calm while leaving the senses sharp.

"Hello?" he called.

Footsteps. A voice.

A woman burst through the doorway with a steady stream of language that resembled song more than speech. She swished about, arranging tubes and fluffing pillows.

Soman touched her arm. "Where is the woman? She glanced to the door, clearly understanding none of it.

Soman swallowed. His throat was razor dry. He mimed drinking, and the woman brought him water. Never had water tasted so good, cool and delicious. He studied the woman. If she was a nurse, she didn't appear to be in uniform, wearing a long green dress with intricate embroidery down one side.

Feeling an urge to urinate, Soman made the woman understand his need. She guided him to a small toilet. Dizzy, he leaned on her. She braced herself, large and solid against his weight. When he hesitated, she pulled his penis from the gown and aimed for him, murmuring encouragement. It seemed the most natural thing to let fly under her steady hand, accepting his vulnerability, creating a bond borne of helplessness. She laid him back in bed, and he was instantly asleep.

Soman woke hungry. He pointed to his mouth and the nurse brought food. A chunk of dark bread, a slab of cheese, fruit he didn't recognize, green-orange and juicy. He salivated at the sight of real food, at aromas he couldn't identify, at the unexpected pleasure of it. Crumbs flew; his stomach gurgled, juice ran down his chin, tears down his face. Alive.

A woman entered the room, an old woman with white hair and a face like weathered wood. She wore black leggings embroidered in silver beneath a long purple tunic. She asked Soman a question. At his blank look she scowled, then pulled something from a fold of her clothing. A black rectangle and a stick. She asked another question, this one longer. "Como esta," he tried. They used to speak Spanish here, though what they spoke now didn't sound much like Spanish.

The old woman spoke to him a third time; the sound a different one again, as if she tried different languages.

Now she handed Soman the pad and stick. He studied it, then wrote: I SPEAK ENGLISH. WHERE IS THE WOMAN WHO CAME WITH ME?

She studied the pad, then held the pad in front of him, her finger on the word ENGLISH.

Soman nodded vigorously. "Yes, English."

The woman's eyes opened wide, and she backed out the door. His energy spent, he slept.

When he awoke, golden light washed down the corridor. Outside the doorway, a knee and shoe; a man sitting in a chair. Soman stirred. The man rose. From the hallway came the sounds of moving feet, people growing alert. The man moved into the doorway, watching Soman, a large black man with a thick neck, wearing a beige suit of clothes cut oddly, the shoulders wide, the fabric gathered on one side. Their eyes met, the man's look without welcome. Behind him, Soman made out the silhouettes of other men in the glow of the morning sun.

Soman's stomach tightened. While he'd slept, they had brought guards. Then, as if a hand reached inside him, his heart slowed; the sweat on his palms dried. Soman lay still, trying to imagine what had just happened. He no longer had the urge to…to do what. Flee. Or fight.

He swung his legs off the bed, then stood, cool floor against bare feet. He raised his arms and stretched tentatively. No numbness, no tingling in the arm. He twisted the arm back and forth. They had stopped the degradation; a feeling of well-being swept through him.

The nurse entered, stopping short as she looked up at his standing height. She hurried to him and tried to press him back into the bed.

"No, I want to walk," he said. He steadied himself with an arm around her shoulder, but she shrank from him. "Aw, come on," he said, and hopped, stumbling, forcing her to hold him up. An arm over her shoulders, Soman moved with halting steps to the doorway.

The thick man in the chair stood, backed one step, and held there. No sign of a weapon, only the plain stare. A half dozen others leaned against corridor walls, all clad in the beige suit, watching him. Soman looked from man to man. Here were the uniforms.

Down the corridor, large windows streamed sunlight. Soman steered his nurse like a large, comfortable boat, squinting against the brightness, unprepared for the radiance of his home world. Reaching the window, he basked in the morning light, soaking in the impossible blue of the sky. The nurse smiled at his pleasure. He pointed to his chest and said, "Soman."

Her eyes crinkled. She repeated the gesture. "Alla."

The sun warmed his face, and the spring deep inside lifted him.

Outside, bicycles and motorbikes passed regularly. Beyond stretched a beach, and a bay where a few sails luffed. Not the Venezuela he remembered, snarled with traffic and blaring horns, the stench of oil refineries, soldiers with automatic weapons.

A vehicle pulled up. Soman recognized the shape; one of the type that had met the LEV. Built of wood, with dark angular inlays set in a lighter wood frame. A dozen people stepped out; all wore the beige suits of the guards. The newcomers greeted three on the sidewalk with touching and much talk, except for a lone man, tall and stiff, who stood apart, scanning the windows. Then they made their way toward the building.

Alla fussed and guided him back along the corridor. From a closet she withdrew clothing: a beige suit. Soman tried to hearten himself with this—prisoners don't wear the same uniform as their guards. Alla pushed him into the bathroom, where she opened a panel to reveal a shower.

He soaked in the steamy cubicle, his hand touching a tender spot on his belly, a hard lump the width of three fingers where an appendix should be. But his appendix had been removed for the mission. He wiped away the soap to get a better look. No incision or suture. But it was hard underneath the skin, like scar tissue. Soman dressed slowly, occasionally rubbing the spot. Whatever they had done, they knew how to heal at a prodigious rate. Or he'd been unconscious a long time.

Alla guided him down a different corridor, stopping before a door, a sound of voices on the other side. The door opened, and Alla pushed him into a room full of people, a room grown suddenly quiet, everyone frozen in mid-gesture, all heads turned toward him. A dozen dark faces inspected him—the only white person in the room—as if he were a zoo animal rather than a returning explorer.

Soman had expected to be met far out in the solar system by people like himself—spacers—and transported to Earth in unimaginable new ships. A wild reunion, backslapping, drinking, a swapping of stories. He'd worried about inquiries and investigations, questions into conduct—explanations would be required. Instead, this was the kind of anxious reception they'd expected at Epsilon Eridani: First Contact. It occurred to Soman that he must now draw on his ancient training, training he'd never used, disoriented that he should employ it first on his home world.

He had traveled to Epsilon Eridani and back, and to his successors he was an alien.

Arrayed around the walls of the room were five of the large men from the corridor. Soman saw no weapons, but the threat of these men was enough to make him move carefully, no sudden moves.

Three people stepped forward: an older man with a rumpled face and white hair falling to his shoulders; the tall man he'd noticed on the street; and a tiny young woman with delicate skin the color of toast and cascades of black hair. The tall man was clearly in charge. One eyebrow rose high into his forehead as he studied Soman. The older man looked more relaxed, an expression hinting of amused interest. The woman was clearly nervous, leaning slightly away from the tall man.

The older man moved without hurry, placing his right hand on Soman's left arm, gripping the bicep. Soman recognized the man's gesture from the greetings he'd witnessed on the street, a cross between a handshake and a hug. Soman raised his right hand and gripped the man's arm. The man nodded, released Soman's arm, and placed five fingertips on his own chest. "Kolar," he said.

Soman named himself, then repeated the ritual with the tall man and the tiny woman. "Ratoul," the man said, thin and reedy. The woman flinched when Soman loomed over her. Then she recovered and said, "Marya." Soman marveled that such a small person could possess that alto voice.

Ratoul motioned them to sit, the three principals in a semicircle facing him, the crowd behind, leaning forward.

Marya began to speak, and Soman's heart fell. She spoke yet another unknown language. That would make four unintelligible languages since waking. Seeing Soman's incomprehension, Marya stopped in mid-sentence. Ratoul scowled. Sounds of dismay through the room.

But something she'd said had sounded half-familiar. He thought back to the individual sounds. One she had repeated several times. Something like eeyew. Then in a flash: 'you'! He held up a hand and said, "Wait!"

Ratoul froze, his eyebrow raised so high Soman thought his forehead would disappear. Marya's eyes widened. She spoke urgently to Ratoul. Soman grinned at her; she had understood. The room broke out in a dozen conversations. Kolar spoke; everyone grew silent. Then he turned to Soman and waited.

Ratoul crossed his arms.

Soman thought back to the training. Always identify yourself. He looked steadily at Marya and said, "I…am…So-man."

"Si," Marya said, then quickly shook her head, as if erasing a mistake. "Ee-ess," she said. "Ee-yew er Soe-mann."

Soman grinned. "Yes. You…are…Marya. My friend."

Marya smiled broadly.

It *was* English she spoke, but a drifted version. He mimed writing. Marya fumbled with a button on her tunic and produced one of the black pads.

He wrote: I NEED TO WORK ALONE WITH YOU SO WE CAN COMMUNICATE. TELL THEM.

She read the note, her lips moving soundlessly, then looked up, her eyes filled with gratitude. She explained the note, and a debate followed, Ratoul skeptical and stubborn, Kolar mediating. Soman felt a welling of anger at Ratoul's manner. Then a surge of something forced him to take a deep breath, and by the time he exhaled the anger had evaporated. It was like the old count to ten rule, but it happened without thinking, and faster. Soman looked around, wondering if someone here could control his mind.

Suddenly Ratoul stood. He and the others left the room, leaving only Kolar and Marya.

"So," he said to Marya. "You speak English." One word at a time, slowly.

"Ee-ess," she replied, more relaxed with Ratoul's departure.

He settled into his chair, pleased to hear even one mangled English word, charmed by Marya's elfin look.

"Yes," he said. "Not Ee-ess. Yes."

She looked at him quizzically.

Soman wrote the word. "Yes," he said again, holding up the pad, pointing to the word. Her eyes grew large. Her lips began to form the E sound, wide and grimacing. She stopped and looked again at Soman.

"Yes," he said. "Yes, yes, yes, yes."

She peered into his mouth. "Y-yes," she said.

Soman was impressed. Almost perfect.

Marya wrote. You. Yellow. Young. Soman pronounced them while she watched and listened. She repeated, starting at some distance but finding the mark quickly, calibrating her speech to the authentic language.

With the method established, she worked the vowels. Marya wrote furiously, covering long and short, before r, after th. She listened and practiced.

Kolar sat calmly for a while, unable to participate in the game but apparently satisfied of its worth. After a time, he touched Marya's shoulder and spoke.

Marya set down the pad. "They want to know why you come."

Soman nodded. Lesson over. "Okay, but I want to know about the woman who came with me."

Marya's forehead knitted.

"Is she all right?" he continued.

Kolar interrupted; his voice soft but firm. A few sentences back and forth between Kolar and Marya. Soman strained to understand some fragment, to catch what they might be saying about Siba. Not one word intelligible, but it seemed Kolar gave instructions.

"Please. Why you come. What you want. We have made no problem for you." Marya and Kolar faced him somberly.

Soman looked out the window at trees and sunlight, giving his tired brain something it recognized. There was some misconception, one he couldn't fathom. Oh well; start at the beginning. "I'm from the crew of the starship *Sorcerer*. Launched from this Earth 2056."

"From Earth?" She pointed down.

"Yes."

She related this to Kolar. Turning back to Soman she said, "You are Ikrit?"

Soman shook his head. "I don't know who they are, but no."

"So you are Monar. There are Monar on Earth?"

"I don't know what you mean by Monar. We left from here, this city.

"From here?"

Yes, then we assembled the ship in orbit."

She blinked. "Where is ore-bit?"

He remembered the fruitless scan for satellites around Earth, and the crumbled spaceport, unused for many generations. They have no space flight, no concept of how it's done. Soman's unease gnawed. A backward Earth wouldn't—he looked at Kolar, registering for the first time the implication of that white hair and wrinkled skin.

"Why do you bring your ship down here."

"To find..." How to explain. "My home."

Marya looked more confused.

"My big ship is in orbit, the small ship brings me from orbit to the

Earth."

"The big vessel is above the Earth?"

"Yes."

Marya loosed a long, low noise. "You *are* Monar."

Soman leaned forward. "Who the hell are the Monar?"

"Where are the others from the ship?"

Soman's couldn't speak for a moment. "Gone," he said finally.

"Where?"

To Marya, 'gone' meant something simpler. "Dead," he said.

Marya gasped. "I am sorry. How? The Ikrit? We thought they were ruined."

Soman stiffened. He almost shouted, I killed them, I beat them to death with a wrench, I suffocated them. I left them on a lonely planet. Then that steadying hand reached inside him. He drew a deep breath. "Please, not now."

Marya asked, "Which country learns to build this vessel? Why do you bring it here to make things dangerous for us?"

It was Soman's turn to look confused. She's using present tense; she must have misunderstood the date. "Marya. My ship is very, very old. We left Earth in the year 2056." At her blank look he wrote it on the pad. It seemed inconceivable even as he wrote it. "We visited another star. Now we're back." He looked at his shoes. "I'm back."

Marya studied the pad, then said, "Not understand." She wrote four figures of her own. "This year," she said, handing the pad to Soman. "There is a mistake."

Soman read. Five, three, six, six. The ship was a couple years off. How could that be. Of course. Time dilation. "No mistake. We visited another star."

"Another star," she said, her eyes distant. "You are a great-child of them."

"No. I was born on Earth. In 2023. Two zero two three."

"You think I believe in child stories. I am not a child."

"It is not a children's story. It's my story."

Marya eyed him.

Kolar shifted, as if he might intervene.

Soman leaned forward again; everyone tensed. He eased himself back. Pretty skittish about their Monar. "I left Earth over three thousand years ago. On my ship our bodies were changed, dried, preserved…" seeing her incomprehension, he cast about and finally remembered Julian's expression. "…made to dust," Soman said. Easy for Julian to say, he didn't have to climb into a descroid.

Marya's eyes grew huge. She folded her arms across her chest, fingertips to shoulders. "The Hawk welcomes you," she said, and bowed her head.

Soman's jaw dropped. "The Hawk? You know the Hawk?"

Marya gasped, a breath pulled so deep it seemed she would suck the air from the room. Then she spoke, voice quavering, addressing a place in the air before her, speaking a rhythmic phrase over and over, like a poem, or a...prayer. Her voice trailed off, tears streaming. Then she threw herself at Kolar, clutching him. Kolar fumbled to keep her from falling, then scooped her up and stumbled out the door.

Chapter 15

Waking to morning light and a return of energy, he prowled.

The guards allowed him to roam, following at a distance. When he approached the stairwell, a guard moved in; Soman backed away. In former days he could have taken the man. Now even the thought of it sapped his strength.

He tried again to piece together some rational explanation of Marya's fear, and flight. How foolish he'd been, thinking her mention of a hawk meant his Hawk, DeSarvo.

Finding a table strewn with black pads, he picked one up. Not unlike holopads. But at his touch a flat image appeared on the surface. Several pages carried photos of people. A fashion spread, it seemed, except that the subjects appeared to be regular people. All of them dark-skinned. Plain faces, no tension of haut couture, the people compelling in their composure.

He touched a second pad. A map opened. Soman pored over every detail. There: the bay known as Maracaibo, now a shrunken lake cut off from the receding sea, the entire coastline of the Caribbean altered.

Then a page with a drawing riveted his attention. A see-through panel into a human body, a three-inch disk embedded in the abdomen. Soman probed his tender spot; his fingers found the hard mass. An implant. With a chill he considered that he might be a prisoner, the implant allowing the appearance of freedom until he strayed too far, until he behaved inappropriately, until they decided what to do with him. But the magazine appeared to be medical. Maybe the disk was part of his treatment, a pacemaker for his irregular heart—it *had* been rock steady.

A rustle nearby. Soman looked up to see Kolar watching him. Kolar motioned him to follow. They climbed stairs to the next level, the phalanx of guards following. Soman brought the magazine.

A smaller room this time. And Marya. She sat in one of three chairs pulled into a circle, wearing not the beige suit but a simple sleeveless dress in white that wrapped high onto her neck and draped the floor about her feet.

She flinched as he drew near, like a mouse beneath the owl.

"Are you all right?"

She nodded.

"You mentioned the Hawk."

At the word, Kolar grew alert. Marya grew even more still. Then she said, "I may not…talk about that."

He glanced at Kolar, about to argue, but Kolar's look told him to play by his rules.

Soman settled slowly into a chair. "Then let's talk about *this*. What is it?" Soman handed the magazine to Marya, the page with the implants displayed.

Marya looked to Kolar. He nodded. "It is the Mah-row," she said.

"What does it do?"

"It gives you balance."

"Oh. Is something wrong in here?" He pointed to his ear.

She shook her head. "It…tell the doctor if you are ill."

Built-in diagnostic, maybe. "What do you mean by balance?"

"I am not sure the word. It keep you in the center. So you do not feel too…sad. Or angry. So you can be…normal. I am sorry—it is hard think the words."

Soman exhaled audibly. So this Maro must be that source of stability, the spring that fought anxiety, that kept him from slapping prickly Ratoul. "It balances the chemicals in my body? In my brain?"

"Yes."

"Ahhh." So this is how they were able to counteract the damage from the descroid. He gazed at a tree outside the window, its leaves trembling in a faint breeze. DeSarvo at the podium. '*And we will use the same technology to transform our world, so that when the travelers return in two hundred fifty years, they are greeted by a new society with achievements unimaginable today.*' Soman touched the disc in his belly. This was exactly what DeSarvo was talking about. But still, maybe it was only for patients, or prisoners. "Do you have a Maro?" he asked Marya.

"Yes. Mine is here." Marya touched the drawing of a breast implant.

Soman shifted his gaze to Kolar, who seemed to be taking in Soman's every move. "Kolar has one too?"

"Yes."

"Everyone has one."

"Yes."

Her glib statement made Soman wonder. It would be like saying everyone in 2061 had an AIDS-4 vaccination. A wish but not a reality. "Everyone in the whole world?"

She frowned. "I do not know about the whole world. Maybe not some people living in the jungle—"

Kolar interrupted, and there was an exchange.

Marya nodded. "We talk much of the Maro," she said to Soman. "Please, we would hear your story."

His brain spun, the tongue clogged, as he faced the story he must tell.

Kolar and Marya waited.

He spoke in generalities, in impartial terms of time and malfunction, of accidents, of neurotransmitters, Soman a minor player in the narrative; a navigator, a lucky survivor. Pausing as she translated. Sometimes his self-control faltered despite the Maro, and he would halt, then cast about for a safe topic, some detail of navigation or propulsion.

He described the blast of light from EE2. Surely the Earth must have recorded such a momentous event. He did some quick arithmetic. "It should have arrived in the year 5268."

Marya and Kolar exchanged a puzzled glance. "Kolar will ask."

Soman noticed that Kolar would occasionally address him directly in the local language, a short question or statement, watching Soman as he spoke. Sometimes Marya would do the same, then after a moment say, "Sorry, I get confused."

They paused for a meal, a slab of cold fish, a chunk of bread. And juice, cool and sweet—he almost choked, it was so delicious. For a few minutes the food occupied him, the spicy fish, the aroma of warm bread, the satisfaction of hard food working his jaw. He looked up, his brow knitted in concentration and pleasure, to see Marya and Kolar watching him. He realized they had just addressed him again in their language.

He swallowed, then asked, "Why do you test me?"

Marya froze, then translated for Kolar. "Kolar apologizes." Her voice small.

"You know I don't understand your language. Why do you do this?"

"Kolar is careful. He say men fear what they do not understand."

"You think I'm your enemy?"

She shook her head in anguish. "I know you are not. But…there are some who worry you are Monar. Please, finish now?"

He resumed. They tested him no more.

At the end, he leaned back and fixed Marya with his gaze. "Now tell me about the woman I brought with me."

Marya twisted her hands. "I am so sorry."

Soman held breath.

"We do not know your customs. We wait for you to decide what… ritual—I think that is the word—what ritual for her. Do you understand?"

An ancient recollection seized him, of his grandparents' funerals, an aroma of formaldehyde and sickening sweet flowers. He couldn't stop the flow of tears. Then he felt the Maro grasp him. His despair softened.

The next few days fell into a pattern. Soman slept mostly, his body healing. For a few hours each day Marya and Kolar came, sometime also Ratoul, and they continued to question him, gaining new details, pondering, talking among themselves. One day he asked, "Where am I?"

"The city is Alta," Marya said.

"And the country?"

Marya hesitated. "I think you mean the paz. The bigger land around the city. Also Alta."

"So this is the capital?" Marya said nothing. "The main city?"

"Yes."

"How big is this country?"

"Until the people end and there is only the forest."

He tried to imagine what events could have so rearranged the political boundaries of a continent, a landmass so unpopulated that wilderness formed the political boundary, as it must have in the centuries before *Sorcerer* departed, before cites swelled and crops replaced the ancient wilderness. And in the North, ice—and Anoka. A sense of longing swept over him for his own time, for a familiar place.

"Do you believe me?" Soman asked.

Marya translated. "Kolar say he has two brains. In one brain, he knows you tell the truth. In his second brain he hears stories he cannot understand. You give his two brains much to discuss."

Finally, following a daylong session with Ratoul, Kolar and Marya showed up unexpectedly in the evening as Soman prepared for bed. Kolar took him by the arm and led him down stairs, across a bright lobby with a floor tiled in a mosaic of fish and crabs, coral and squid, sea creatures in fantastic shapes Soman didn't recognize. Soman had to lean on Kolar as they made their way out the door. The sky was darkening. Kolar joined him in gazing up, the first stars blinking on.

Soman watched the sky, sensing the strange city around him. Across the water were constellations of lights, some fixed to the far shore, some moving across the bay. Beyond, a hint of dark, massive shapes rising.

Marya said, "We wait for the olden." She gestured toward a light moving toward them. A vehicle pulled up to the curb. Its whirring died; the vehicle stopped. That dread rose again, confronting the simple technology of the vehicle; not technology at all really. He would need serious technology to reach Anoka's descroid. Even then, what are the odds that a descroid designed for 500 years could still function after a span five times longer, even with the nuclear powerplant of Fermilab to sustain it. And then there was all the ice.

Marya climbed into the olden as Soman protested that he was too tired for anything but bed. She tugged. "You will sleep in the shay." One step up, collapsing onto a hard seat. The whirring sound resumed. Soman looked back to see the motor compartment behind the third row of seats. Suddenly he realized they had left the guards behind. "You're not afraid of me any more?"

Marya smiled. "We have heard your story. We see how you behave. And we see that the Maro works the same in you as in us."

They rode in silence, buildings drifting past like dreams.

The bus soon stopped. Marya guided him toward a house glowing in the night air. It stood far back from the street, a blend of farmhouse and apartment complex, three stories of porches and dormers and competing rooflines, soft pools of light illuminating a wide porch filled with people lounging in low wooden chairs. The smell of moist earth rose to him as they moved across spongy grass. Children ran past, yelling then disappearing into the dark, and Soman thought of Anoka, chasing fireflies.

They climbed steps to the porch, and everyone rose for shoulder clasping. Soman tried to concentrate, but fatigue made it hard to focus. Marya pulled him into a large room with cushions and chairs and more people to meet. It seemed an entire village squeezed around him, pushing and craning, every face a different shade of black or brown or gold, as if all the colors of the Earth had risen to greet him.

Finally Marya said, "You sleep?"

"Thank you."

She led him upstairs to a room, sparse, small, the only furniture a tawny futon, a dresser, a wooden chair. Simple furniture and square, but with intricate carvings, the wood dark, rubbed to a sheen. An open window invited a rustle of night air and the murmur of people conversing below. Marya opened a closet to show him hangars with clothes. Not the beige, but black slacks and a thin shirt in green with leafy patterns woven through it. "You wear these tomorrow."

"Come." She led him down the hallway to a lavatory. Once again Soman felt as if he'd been transported back in time, no holo decorations in the walls, lights with hand switches, no evidence of autons, or even ear-coms. Only the disk in the belly to remind him he was in different world.

Marya squeezed out and disappeared, the murmur of voices downstairs growing louder with her arrival. What conversation there would be on the porch tonight.

Five minutes later he was in bed and descending into sleep.

The bed shook. Something gripped his arm. The heat of a person close, an aroma of dust and leather. Soman's eyes snapped open. A man's face hung inches away, a finger to his lips, his features fuzzy in the wan light of the last quarter moon, everything in the sepia tones of night.

The man whispered, "Puhleze."

Soman's heart pounded. Someone else in this house spoke English, someone who wanted to speak in secret. Fully awake, every sense alert, Soman willed himself not to move, not to startle this man.

"Speeeek slow."

"What... do... you... want?"

The man smiled broadly. "Speeeek eeyew."

Soman looked at the door. Closed tightly. He glanced at the open window, curtains fluttering, dirt on the sill. A chill crept up his spine. This man was not from the shay.

"Ieeyam Horg," the man said. "We know you come from outside." He pointed up. "We are in...de...pen...dent." Horg grinned. "Like you."

"Like me?"

"You come from before the Maro." Horg stood and pulled down his waistband to reveal an ugly, red, six-inch wound in his lower right abdomen. "We come from after the Maro."

"You've removed your Maro?" said Soman, weak at the thought of the procedure that had dug that scar, terrified that these people could slip into his room. *People living in the jungle.*

"Maro evil," Horg hissed. He glanced toward the door. He sniffed the air above the bed and scanned the blanket as if he could smell Soman's Maro, as if he could discern it through the bedclothes.

"What do you want?" Soman pulled the blanket higher.

Horg dropped to his haunches—Soman flinched. "Take you."

"Where?"

"Far away. Secret."

"When?"

"Now."

Soman's mouth dried. The Altans might never find him. Soman bunched a fist under the blanket and edged back to swing. But weakness overcame him, his arms fading as if he'd just finished twelve rounds in the gym. And he knew the Maro wouldn't allow him to attack; the implant of the Altans rendered him defenseless. He should holler and bring the house awake. But something made him hold back. Horg had called the Maro evil. Soman sensed the alien bulge of it under his skin. There might be more to this Maro than Marya had revealed. Anyway Horg wasn't threatening him; he simply crouched, listening, waiting. Soman studied Horg, his long face and droopy eyes—not the face of a dangerous man, not the look of a man living in savagery. Except for the scar.

"I can't come now."

Horg's expression grew grim.

Soman gestured to the beige suit he'd worn that day, draped on the chair. "Horg, you know about the people who wear those clothes?"

Horg nodded.

"Do they know about you?"

"They can not find us," Horg said proudly. "You come."

"I can't."

Horg's eyes narrowed.

"Not yet," he offered. When Horg made no move, Soman said, "There are things I must do first."

Horg glanced to the window, then cocked his head as if listening to the house around them. He leaned close to Soman. "You will not tell about tonight."

"No."

"Not the pretty woman? Or the old man?"

Horg's people know exactly what was happening here. "No."

Horg studied Soman a moment longer. "I come again. You join us." Horg moved to the window. Before Soman could roll over to look, Horg slid into the night without even a barking dog to mark his passing.

Chapter 16

Soman startled awake. The room unfamiliar. Sunlight slanted between curtains, dust sparkling. Muffled sounds of a house waking, aromas of yeast and spice. For a fleeting instant he was a small boy waking at Grandma Moreau's to the delicious smells of her kitchen, the clicking of the dog's toenails on the tile floor.

Tap-tap-tap.

Stumbling from bed, he cracked the door open.

Marya stood there, beaming, hands folded in front of her. Soman felt his heart quicken. Her hair was braided into a thick rope that hung to one side. Colored ribbons wove through her dress, dancing in and out, joining at the neckline to become straps over bare shoulders. He took in her tawny legs and silky hair, her dark smiling eyes, and his heart pounded in his ears, not the irregular knocking of before, but a smooth surge. "You…this…is beautiful."

"Thank. It is my design."

"You made this?" As he spoke, he detected the Maro slowing the swell of desire, slicing off the peak, and he stood admiring her swinging braid and laughing eyes, but without the urge that, a moment before, had begged him to touch, to pull her in and close the door. He swayed in the swirl of chemistry, cheated of lust like a sneeze that never arrives. Amazing that a thin disk in the belly could intervene in a heartbeat. The response of the Maro depended on the strength of his emotion. Mild upsets it left alone. Powerful swings, lust or anger, it blunted. And…he placed a hand alongside the Maro. It was the most intrusive form of regulation ever. What other capabilities of the Maro might have driven people to tear them out and escape to the jungle.

"Everyone make clothes," Marya was saying.

Remembering Horg's visit, a thread of a dream tugged him. Hordes of people stripping the LEV, hauling away its parts like an ant army. Horg's people. What if they…the LEV was his slim lifeline to *Sorcerer*. He might need all its resources to reach Anoka. In this technology-starved world, it stood in the open like an auto broken down on an L.A. freeway.

"Marya, today I want to see my vehicle. It's…" hesitating as alarm crossed her face. "…the only way back to my ship."

She backed a half step as if told dread news. "You are leaving?"

"No. I just…the LEV is my responsibility. The only way to reach the big ship in orbit."

She wrung her hands, her face a mixture of bewilderment and anguish.

"I want to make sure the LEV's cool."

"Cool?"

"It means everything's fine. It's slang."

"Suh-lang. I do not know this."

Soman threw up his hands. "I just want to go to the ship."

Her expression turned grave. "It is dangerous."

"Nonsense. We're not going to launch. I just want to look."

"I will speak to Kolar." Turning abruptly, she descended the stairs in a flash of swinging fabric and dark limbs, her swish and patter trailing away. A clatter of dishes rose where she disappeared.

He breakfasted with a dozen members of the shay at a table of mahogany inlaid with geometric patterns. Morning sun streamed across a floor of ceramic, each tile unique in shape and color, shards fitted like a kaleidoscope. A tortoiseshell rug, nubby and asymmetric, basked in a spot of sun like a sprawling cat.

A woman with grey-speckled hair spoke a word he assumed to be a morning greeting. He tried the word. "Bwonda." This earned him approving murmurs. Marya appeared in a stained apron, placing a bowl before him and a plate of breads within reach. Soman dug in, suddenly hungry. Hot porridge drizzled with sweet sauce, slices of an orange fruit, soft rolls of spiced bread. And coffee, dark, rich. He held the mug in both hands, breathing its aroma. Real coffee.

Outside, people worked the gardens, and Soman felt a desire to join them, to dig in the earth, to sweat in the morning sun. From the size of the gardens, he judged they could provide most of the fresh produce needed by the shay. What a change, growing locally, instead of transporting produce from a distant land. No wonder everything tasted so good; it hadn't been harvested hard and green and shipped halfway around the world. But—he *needed* to travel halfway around the world.

An olden pulled up, Kolar sitting behind the driver. "We see your machine now," Marya said.

Once in the olden, Marya and Kolar huddled in conversation. Soman watched out the windows, his first look at Alta in daylight. The olden passed a couple Soman had seen earlier at the street corner. They looked away at his glance, but as soon as the bus passed, they stared. Thinking back, it seemed they had been loitering ever since he first spotted them from the window of the shay. And here they were, two idle people wearing long white tunics, eyes on the bus as it receded. Watching.

Marya answered Soman's questions. She told him that oldens were expensive to build and operate, so there weren't many. They ran on electricity, generated in the ocean by a process neither Marya nor Kolar could explain. Soman scanned the interior. Not high tech. The seats were lightweight wooden benches with woven cane seatbacks, reminding him of an ancient bus in which he had hitched a ride through the jungles of Guatemala. All it lacked were the fluttering chickens, the squealing pigs, and threat of banditos. At that thought he scanned the open ground along the olden's path, wondering how far Horg's people could reach.

Low stone buildings swept past the windows. The city thinned and fields appeared. Earth should have advanced beyond his wildest dreams. Instead, this odd combination of stone and electricity, wood and the Maro. Turning to Marya he asked, "What brought the ice?"

"You must sit the…" Marya stopped, showing puzzlement. "We call it mem. You must sit the mem. You will understand everything."

"Is it like a holo?"

"I do not know holo. It will take you there."

"A museum?"

"No, no." Placing two fingers against his forehead, she said, "You go in here."

The olden bounced along with a whirr and thrum. He looked out the window at an orchard, where people with pitchforks spread mulch around the trees. "Do you have vehicles that fly?"

"No, no." she said. "Too dangerous."

He grimaced; without winged aircraft it was hard to imagine an expedition north. The LEV was out of the question—it could never land on ice without melting a hole big enough to swallow it whole. From orbit, Anoka had seemed so close, the ice above Chicago gleaming below twice a day. It struck they keep saying dangerous. The LEV is dangerous, flying is dangerous. Before he could ask about this, the olden crested a hill and the LEV rose into view among the jumbled ruins of the spaceport. For a moment, watching the awestruck looks of his companions, Soman saw the LEV as the citizens of Alta must, as an incomprehensible marvel. A marvel that would rust and fall, reclaimed by the jungle; another lost technology. Perhaps his future was to live and die in this community, returning to the soil along with his ancient ship. His head sank into his hands, the dream of immortality swirling up to taunt him.

The bus pulled to a stop with a jerk. Soman started for the door.

Marya called out, "We see your ship is safe. We must return."

Kolar spoke to the driver, who backed the bus to turn around.

Soman pushed the door open and jumped down. "No—I want to go inside."

Marya followed, making noises of distress, clambering down the slope after him, Kolar's reserve cracking as they entered the circle of scorched concrete, surrounded by a ring of burnt vines gradually turning green at a distance from the blast zone. They passed the LEV's landing struts and Soman headed for the ramp, starting to breathe hard, the body not used to exertion.

His thumb press on the entry pad opened the hatch. He flicked on lights, then powered up the console and checked the log: seventeen days since landing. He sat heavily. It felt as if it were only last month they'd departed for Epsilon Eridani. He made a quick calculation. Fifty-five hydrated days in the last thirty-three hundred years, while a hundred forty generations of Homo sapiens lived and died on Earth.

Marya and Kolar stood near the hatch, taking in the complexity of the cockpit, stroking the metal surfaces. Yesterday Soman had been on their ground. Not today. Time to re-open the subject of The Hawk. He waved Marya over. "I want to show you something." Searching ship's files, he found the record—the second half of DeSarvo's famous speech. The holo sprang to life; DeSarvo materialized as if he strode among them. Marya jumped back. Kolar watched open-mouthed.

DeSarvo extended his hands. Marya moved forward, so rapt she forgot to translate for Kolar.

"In developing the technology for a mission to Epsilon Eridani, what have we learned that we can use today?" DeSarvo paused and scanned the auditorium.

Marya followed DeSarvo's gaze behind her as if an audience might have crept into the LEV. But there was only Kolar, holding the edge of the hatch, one foot outside on the ramp.

"Do you know that in developed countries, fifteen percent of students suffer from behavior disorders? And in the under-developed world, the numbers are higher. These children battle constantly with the norms of society. From this group come eighty-five percent of our criminals. And what do we do about it?" He threw up his hands in exasperation. "We throw them in prison.

"What happens when our children grow up and cannot hold a job, or make the vegetable plot productive, or care for *their* children? An entire segment of society is trapped in poverty and hopelessness. For decades, we have known that the limiting factor is the chemistry of the individual, aberrations in the hundreds of neurotransmitters that allow our brains to function. When the chemistry is out of balance, we face learning disabilities, depression, violence, self-destruction. We have developed drug treatments for some of these disorders. But the treatments are haphazard, and available only to the wealthy."

DeSarvo stopped pacing. "Now we have learned to build our entire system of neurotransmitters from scratch. We know how to start the system and how to balance it. All this in order to re-hydrate an astronaut. And we can use that same knowledge for you and me, and for our children. We can balance the neurotransmitter network to help our children reach their full potential. We can lift their depression and fill the void that leads to sociopathic behavior. We can help everyone live more satisfying lives.

"I see a day when we run the diagnostics and fine-tune the psychological state using a device embedded in your skin—" DeSarvo pointed to the back of his hand "—just as today we regulate your insulin, your sleep cycle, or your immune system. Some will call it mind control. But I can tell you it's not. It's mind empowerment. We will give people *more* freedom of choice, because they control their destructive urges."

Soman touched his Maro. DeSarvo made it sound so positive, yet wearing the actual implant...

One last time, DeSarvo fixed each person with his stare. "Yes, we should go to the stars. And—" he slammed his fist into his palm, eyes glinting.

Marya stepped back involuntarily.

"—we will transform our world, so that when our travelers return in two hundred fifty years, a new society greets them with achievements unimaginable today."

Soman paused the holo. *Greets them*, DeSarvo had said. *The Hawk welcomes you.* A strange similarity.

Marya and Kolar stared at DeSarvo's fading image.

"Do you recognize that man?" Soman asked Marya.

Marya shook her head, slowly, a flicker of apprehension in her eyes.

"That," Soman said, "was the Hawk I knew."

Marya stared, mouth open. Then she nodded and made the same gesture she had yesterday, arms crossed, fingertips to shoulders. "It is written," she said.

At her tone and demeanor, Soman felt in the presence of the sacred.

"What is written?"

"It is written that the Prodigal Children were made to dust and flung to the dark beyond the stars. That they will be re-created by our Lord and returned to us in human form, that they will bring the message of God's plan. It is written in the Book of the Last Prophecy."

Her words echoed through Soman. Ritual words. Finally Marya's seizure made sense—she thought the *Sorcerer's* return a fulfillment of prophecy. Made to dust and flung to the dark beyond the stars. "This gesture you make." Soman nodded at her still-crossed arms. "What does it mean?"

Marya hugged herself. "It is…the greeting we say among ourselves. For the return of the Prodigal Children. We should greet them so."

Only something they say. Following their ritual, a habit of three thousand years, until someone arrives from the stars, someone who matches the story, someone who responds to the words. Like an explosion going off, he glimpsed the possibilities. If they thought the returning astronaut to be part of their prophecy, imagine the resources they would make available for a pilgrimage into the North, to resurrect one of the Children. But how…The Hawk…the Maro…made to dust and flung…Soman hesitated. Go slowly. Think this through. Very, very carefully. Soman sensed great risk; this tale would crackle like lightning across Marya's world. Faced with momentous change to their world, people of faith throughout history have resorted to persecution, to violence, to pogroms.

And nothing must interfere with finding Anoka. Maybe revealing DeSarvo was a mistake. He took Marya by the shoulders. "Please do not tell anyone about this." Her eyes showed confusion and anguish. He strengthened his grip to make sure she understood. "Share this with no one, all right?"

Her eyes dropped.

Soman sighed. "You already have."

A quiet nod of the head.

Kolar spoke, standing at the open hatchway.

"We must go," she said, scurrying to follow Kolar down the ramp.

Soman powered down the cockpit while Kolar and Marya rushed up the hill to the olden, eager to get away from the LEV. Soman smiled inwardly at the power of the LEV over the Altans. Strange they feared his machine, but less risk from the curious and the mischievous.

The slanting rays of the early morning sun had given way to a high bright light that transformed the fields to a green so vivid it hurt the eyes.

Soman settled back into the seat. A religion that speaks of The Hawk, that somehow foretold the return of *Sorcerer's* crew. And a young woman shocked to find herself in the presence of the prophesied. "How were you chosen as translator?" Soman asked.

"I am just back from my study in the writings, and do not yet have a…I will make the devotion."

"It must be quite an honor to be chosen before more…experienced translators."

"The older English scholars are occupied in the Church. None wanted to involve when we thought you were Monar."

"All the English speakers are part of the church?"

"Most. We study the writings."

"Your scriptures are in English."

Marya nodded.

Soman looked ahead at the distant shapes of mountains. English, the dead language of ancient scrolls.

The sound of the whirring olden echoed off stone buildings passing on both sides. Quite a week for Marya. Just graduated from seminary. Sent to help with an interview that none of the scholars wanted.

Marya said, "Now we visit the doctor."

Soman faltered, seeing her expression grow somber. "Why?"

"He knows about the woman."

As the olden came to a halt, Soman understood. Siba.

Lar sat in a tiny cubicle, a gangly man with a protruding forehead. The desk groaned under the weight of shelves packed tightly with specimen jars, beakers bulging with human meat and bone, enough flesh to assemble a new crew for *Sorcerer.*

Soman mouthed the doctor's name, so close to Lars, his father's name. Soman pronounced it the traditional way—Lawrsh—and the sound of it brought to mind his ancestral land, crushed now beneath ice.

Lar spoke fast, leaning forward for emphasis, and Soman found himself holding the desk defensively as it creaked toward him, shelves swaying. Marya forced Lar to stop occasionally so she could keep up with the translation.

Lar was among the first Altans to reach Soman and Siba at the foot of the ship. Lar saw that Siba's suit was providing life support and left her in it until she arrived at the hospital. Marya said, "It was just the machine keeping her body. You understand?"

Lar kept talking.

"He say no brain ac…tiv…ity."

Lar grew agitated. His long arms reached high into the air, rattling jars, knocking dust loose. Marya tried to interrupt but Lar grew forceful, jabbing a finger in Soman's direction.

With a sigh, Marya said, "He complains I do not translate everything. He say I must tell all details. I tell him maybe you do not want to hear so much."

"You are correct."

Lar added one more comment. "He say she was so old, of course she could not survive the voyage."

Soman stared at a bit of grey and red tissue floating in an encrusted jar. "She was thirty-six."

Lar rose from his seat and whispered a question.

"He wants to be certain. You said thirty-six years, an age such as you." Soman nodded.

"He wants to know how long it took for her to look like this."

"A few weeks."

Lar exhaled forcefully, hands splayed on the desk. He spoke briefly and dashed into the corridor.

Marya's eyes grew huge. She looked through the doorway, where Lar lunged around a corner on spindly legs., then back to Soman. "Now we see her."

Soman remained rooted to his chair. "See her? I thought…" Then, tentatively, they followed. Expecting to descend into the dark of the mortuary, to the smells of mold and formaldehyde, Soman found himself following Lar up a flight of stairs to a brightly-lit corridor scuttling with nurses. Lar held a door open, motioning vigorously.

A stink like sour milk stopped Soman. His eyes adjusting to the dim green light, he made out a structure filling the center of the room, a glass bubble in which lay a frail, naked, white-haired figure. A clear mask covered her face. Tubes snaked into her nose and mouth. The machine forced air into her; her chest rose tiredly, ribs through skin. Gray, limp nipples quivered flaccidly to the vibration of the machine. More tubes pierced her arms and legs, bruises blossoming around the punctures as if her blood had lost its way.

Surviving this were the soft crinkles around her eyes, vestiges of her perennial smile.

Lar began a new dissertation. Soman interrupted. "Can you help her?" The rise and fall of Siba's chest sparked hope.

No one spoke.

"Marya, they've kept her on the machine this long. Surely there's something they can do."

Marya spoke with Lar, Soman straining to catch a sense of it. Lar was matter of fact. Marya turned to Soman, shaking her head. "The machine gives her the air and pushes the blood. Her body cannot do these things. Her brain…contains nothing."

"Then why does he keep her like this?"

"He say he discussed with many doctors…they saw your great ship. They thought you would tell what to do."

Soman slumped into a chair in the dim light of medical displays. His great ship of metal and fire, from an age of wealth and technology unimaginable to the Altans. None of it any use to Siba.

Marya knelt beside him. "He want your…permission, I think it is the word." She bit her lip. "I am sorry. It is hard to say the right thing."

Soman sat still as stone. Bring her all this way home, just to unplug her, give her up. The machine breathed and pumped; Siba's body writhed to its rhythm. Every rise of her lungs made his chest hurt.

After a while the sounds of the hospital intruded: muted voices, a distant laugh, a cart clattering down a corridor, a cry of agony.

Lar had gone. Marya led Soman downstairs. Approaching Lar's office, they peered in. Lar scribbled notes on one of the black pads. He waved them in.

"He speak of her age. He say it is caused by the…I do not know your word. It is a part of your cells. The small part that tell the cells what to do."

"Chromosome."

"Yes, chromosome. He say this happened when doctors learned to fix cancer."

"Cancer." Soman gripped Marya's arm. "Your doctors can cure cancer?"

Marya glanced over in surprise. "Of course."

A great heat swept through Soman. He still needed the cure once he recovered Anoka. And here it was. Their transport technology was pitiable, but in medicine…"

Lar continued.

"There is a small piece of the chromosome. He calls it telomere."

"Yes, I know of telomeres."

"To stop a cancer, doctors remove the telomere. The cancer dies. At first some patients lost their cancer, but they grew old quickly. The treatment take the telomere from all cells, not only the cancer. Lar think this happened with your Siba. Lar want to know what happened to remove her telomere."

Soman shook his head. "Something went wrong with the descroid." At Marya's blank look he added, "The machine that dried us..."

Marya stared at Soman gravely. Soman could see her grappling with the information that a machine had dried them.

But with her translation, Lar grew more animated.

"Lar want to see your machines."

"Why?"

"Lar says that after doctors learned to kill the cancer, they thought they could stop aging by replace the lost telomeres."

Soman leaned forward. "And?"

"Doctors try to solve this. It is very hard. Lar think maybe your Siba is a new clue."

Lar continued his discourse. Marya said, "I try to explain. They study the loss of telomere as a person age. They find an equation of the loss. A range, they are not all lost at the same speed...you understand?"

Soman considered. "I think you mean a distribution."

"They compare to other dis...tri...boo...shh...shon in nature. They find one the same. He call it neutrino."

Soman frowned. "Neutrino? The particle?"

"Oh, yes, scientists used to think many things were particles. Now we know they are not." She paused. "You understand?"

"Whatever." Particles or waves, every generation has a new answer to that question.

"The telomere loss has a distribution like the neutrino. Lar say this is a clue to the process in the body that cuts the telomere."

Then maybe they were close. And Siba could contribute to a future in which a person wouldn't lay awake with night terrors, or rise each dawn to face his mortality.

"Lar ask for your permission."

"What for?"

"He want to study her, what happened to make her age so fast. He believes..." She hesitated. "He believes that her change to...to dust and back brings the Earth great knowledge."

A message deep in her cells, the way to immortality.

Lar hadn't stopped his unending discourse, and Marya jumped in to catch up. "He would take the body to the laboratory to...I do not know the word...study the organs, and—" Marya stopped, noticing the jars of human tissue surrounding them, swallowing hard.

Some time later he noticed Marya at his elbow, guiding him along the white sidewalk in shimmering heat.

Marya said, "I told Lar you need time, until you can know her purpose."

Chapter 17

At the shay, Marya warmed a thick chowder smelling of the sea and assembled a salad of crunchy greens. The plates and bowls carried the imperfections of handmade, the spoons and forks carved from tough and resinous wood. Marya used a device in the kitchen to contact someone, a keypad with a speaker.

Then she told Soman, "We see your Maro doctor after we eat."

"I have my own doctor?"

"She prepared your Maro. She knows about your…chemicals. She knows how you are operating."

"You make me sound like a robot."

Marya looked puzzled. Her lips rounded. "Roo…what was the word?"

"Robot. An artificial person. A machine that looks like a human."

"You had such things in your time?"

"We had robots, but most of them didn't look like people. The idea was that a perfect robot would do all the dirty work and never get sick, never have a bad day. Everything under control. Maybe a person with the perfect Maro would be the same."

She frowned. "I think a person can never be the same as a machine. Even if you control all the chemicals, there is something else special inside you."

"You mean the thing that lives on after your body is gone?" he asked.

She spooned soup into bowls. "Yes of course."

Soman took his bowl in silence. What we want to believe, need to believe. And if it's not true, what then. Where was Siba's something special right now.

They carried lunch to the porch and settled into rockers. "Why must I see this doctor?" After Lar, the thought of another doctor wasn't thrilling.

"She must check the operation of your Maro. After it is placed in you, it must be adjusted. There is always some little thing. She give you the most careful settings."

Soman noticed she was more direct, less awe as she grew comfortable around him, familiarity easing the distance. He chuckled to himself. Maintaining a godly status might require more detachment. How had Jesus managed it, living so long among the disciples. Well, being an actual

God would be a great help, though from the collection of characters who had attempted the task throughout history, maybe not a requirement.

Children sat close by, watching Soman's every move. Marya spoke to them, touching each one, provoking giggles and hugs. For a few minutes Soman ate quietly, observing Marya's joy with children, and their easy manner with each other, like little adults.

At a pause, he asked, "Why are they here during the day? Don't they go to school?"

"The children go to school a part of each day. For the other part, they take learning here at the shay."

"Pretty unstructured. How do you handle the wild kids?"

She laughed. "What is that?"

"The kids who fight or do mean things, or run away."

"No one would run away."

Soman set down his spoon. "Every group has a few bad ones."

"In the shay, the children learn all their life how to behave."

"It can't be that easy. What about the child who has a hormone problem? Or their brain didn't develop correctly? The people DeSarvo talked about?"

Marya thought. "Yes, we have children with medical problems. But they learn how to behave properly. If they don't, it is a problem with their Maro."

"So the Maro really controls us."

Marya stopped eating, frowning. "No, it does not control us."

"That's what you said."

She looked at him with hurt in her eyes. "Then…I do not explain right." She paused. "The doctor will explain better."

Something perverse made him want to ask about people living like animals in the jungle, but he held back, asking instead, "What if I decide I don't want my Maro?"

"Do not talk so!"

The children grew silent.

Soman swirled his spoon in the soup. Loneliness flooded through him. His gaze fell on a little girl. Setting the soup aside, he lifted her into his lap, surprised expression and all. She snuggled against him, her tiny weight perched happily in his lap, her squirmy bottom settling in.

At the airy feel of the child, a memory swirled up, of Anoka nuzzling in his lap, her nightgown rustling softly. It was the day her doctor mentioned casually that he wanted Anoka driven down to Mayo for a few tests. That evening, as Anoka prepared for bed, the deepening twilight had enveloped Soman and Anne in silent, clawing apprehension.

"Daddy," Anoka had said as she buried her cheek into his chest. "Where did babies come from?"

Anne, standing at the window, turned and tossed Soman a glance of sweet envy.

Soman pulled Anoka closer, a crystalline awareness of the moment. "You know. You came from mommy's belly."

Anoka scoffed. "No, daddy, I know all that, I mean where did the first baby come from? The first human couldn't be a baby."

Soman and Anne exchanged a look of astonishment.

Now Soman hugged the little Altan girl. If he could ever reach Anoka, she could be this girl's friend, never noticing the dislocation of the centuries. She'd pick up the language in a few days' play and slip easily into this world.

"Marya," Soman said.

"Yes?"

"The cities up north, under the ice. Has anyone tried to reach them?"

Marya frowned. "I do not think so. Why?"

"Maybe to…salvage valuable things." He scowled. Why not simply tell the truth. How did it all get started, this habit of concealment, some habit holding him back.

The girl in his lap tensed. Soman stopped. Marya's spoon halted an inch above the soup's surface; Soman followed her gaze. A man with billowing silver hair strolled up the walk, wearing a solemn face and robes of heavy fabric. A cowl trailed down his back, ending in two heavy rows of fringe. With each step, bare feet swung from beneath the robe. He did not smile, but his ease suggested that, for him, each moment of life brought peace and contemplation.

Around Soman, everyone grew quiet like mice stilled by the shadow of an owl.

Chapter 18

Slap, slap, the man's feet sounded as they carried him across the veranda, robes rustling. Marya scrambled to stand, sending a bowl clattering to the floor. The man stopped, crossed his arms, fingertips to shoulders. His words, deep and deliberate, raised hairs on Soman's neck. "The Hoo-wak welcome eeyew."

Marya returned the gesture. Soman stood.

The man spoke, his unwavering gaze on Soman. Soman assumed it was a greeting; he replied with the word he had learned at breakfast. "Bwonda."

Marya hissed at Soman, "He is speaking your language!"

"Um…" He placed a palm to his chest and said, "Soman."

"Mordano," the man said, rolling the 'r'.

Soman studied Mordano's flowing robes, his disciplined demeanor, his meticulous appearance. "Marya, remember our problem with English?"

Marya nodded.

"Please explain to our guest. We do not want him embarrassed."

Mordano's eyebrows rose a fraction. His self-assured smile flickered. Before Marya could say anything, he spoke to her in their language.

Marya said to Soman, "He invites you to meet with him this afternoon."

"And who will I be meeting?"

Marya looked puzzled.

"His position.

"Mordano is the…I do not know the word, leader of the Church."

Studying Mordano's robes, Soman said, "Priest, that's the word. I thought we were to see the doctor about my Maro."

"He insists."

"And the subject of the meeting?"

"He will extend the hospitality of the Church to such a famous person." She gathered the dishes in a rush.

"Why do you fear him?"

"We do not fear him!" she whispered.

Mordano's next words stopped her.

"What is it?" Soman asked.

Her eyes flashed. "He will take only you."

A chill ran through Soman. He watched them, Marya holding the dishes awkwardly, Mordano struggling to follow the English. Soman touched Marya's arm. "Invite him to try the soup. And bring one of those writing pads." At Marya's questioning look, he said, "We must help his English."

Mordano ate while Soman wrote and spoke. Then Mordano practiced. He worked hard, though without surrendering his air of dignity. No linguist, he thrashed through the hurried lesson, his pronunciation at last reaching some level of intelligibility. The soup done, Mordano lapsed to his native tongue and lavished Marya with compliments on the soup, diplomacy Soman needed no translation to comprehend.

Then Soman sensed an end to pleasantry. He took up a bowl, saying to Marya, "Let me help you with these." Then, to Mordano, "I will return."

As they turned the corner into the kitchen, Soman whispered, "Is it safe?"

She looked at him in dismay. "How can you ask such a thing?"

"In my time a person could be in danger from someone's religion."

"But you could not..." She stopped, mouth open, and Soman watched her grasp the politics of the situation. Mordano come to personally check this report of a novice half out of her mind bringing wild stories of Prodigal Children. Marya moved abruptly to the sink, dishes clattering, water splashing.

Soman backed out, rejoining Mordano on the porch. With a bow of the head Soman said, "I am at your service."

They strolled up the walk; the sounds of children at play resumed behind them. Silence at first, only Mordano's feet rustling against the hem of his robe and slapping the bleached sidewalk, brown on white. He walked slowly, white hair flowing down his shoulders in waves, attentive to something distant, far beyond the buildings.

A bicycle whooshed past, the rider's shirt fluttering behind. The bike emitted a soft buzz. Squinting, Soman spotted the motor housing above the rear wheels. Everything was electric. He'd seen nothing so far that ran on liquid fuel. Without it, the LEV would soon be grounded.

Mordano began to chat, his right hand grasping two fingers of his left behind his back, his feet never varying their pace. The dignity of his pose could not compensate his awful English. Soman had encountered people of many accents; he had an ear for picking through the noise to detect the essential sound, for using context and gesture to fill the uncertainty.

But he struggled with Mordano, asking him to repeat, suggesting a different word to check his guesses, or giving up and changing the subject.

"Iss vorrrrm," Mordano said.

Soman thought for a moment. "Yes, warm. Warm today."

With a barely perceptible nod of the head, Mordano responded. "Warrm tooodye."

Mordano must feel a powerful need to speak alone, or he would not have left behind a competent translator.

A cathedral swung into view, rising like a ghost of the 21st century, a vaulted structure of curve and spire, incongruous among the low buildings of Alta. The façade swept upward to a bell tower, topped by a spire that parted the blue sky. A central panel of stained glass rose forty feet above the massive carved door. More stained glass retreated in a row down the side of the church, glittering in blue, red, green, and gold. Though Soman had left the church of his upbringing far behind, a wave of nostalgia rose, this familiar structure from his childhood, on an alien Earth.

Mordano stopped for a moment and gazed up with Soman. Then he strode through the door.

Their footsteps echoed in the vast sanctuary. Wooden pillars like tree trunks held up the vaulted ceiling, pews nestling among them. Color streamed through towering windows. Each panel depicted a scene: a man extending his hand; a man and woman embracing; a group of robed people craning necks upward into a starry night. Nothing familiar, neither the figures nor the symbols. No cross, no crucifix, only spheres of glass suspended from the ceiling above the alter, some white, some black, hanging at different levels in a random arrangement.

Behind the altar loomed the largest window of all. Depicted in it was a man with flowing white hair, arms spread, robes rippling about him, face turned upward, showered by beams of light from a firmament of stars. Soman studied the figure. Apparently not Jesus, the hair white and the skin dark, the expression suggesting wisdom, not holiness.

Just below the window, in a niche set into the wall, lay an object. Something about it caught Soman's attention, but he managed only a moment's glimpse of it before Mordano descended a stairway. He followed the priest down the spiral staircase, its timbers creaking amid an aroma of old wood and sacred must. Soman almost stumbled, thinking about that object. A small wooden box with an arched lid, maybe a meter long, dark and worn, ancient. The image sizzled through him with familiarity. Maybe because it resembled a miniature version of the treasure chests of his childhood pirate books.

They passed the sacristy, shadowy in the dim light from the hallway. Soman peered in at tables laden with gold candelabra and shiny basins, racks hung with robes and colored lengths of rope. And in one corner a row of telescopes, a standard Schmidt design of at least twelve inches, their mirrors staring from the dark at Soman.

Mordano led Soman to an office. A lamp cast a yellow glow on a wooden table, two chairs, a sideboard. Scents of soap and candle wax and the residue of a recent meal. Mordano gestured to a chair. Its seat of woven cane squeaked as Soman settled his weight.

"The Hoo-wak velcoome eeyew," Mordano said, his arms crossed.

Soman studied Mordano's face, trying to discern if Mordano intended a meaning, or if it was simply something he said. Mordano watched for Soman's reaction, then moved to the sideboard, where a silver pot perched on a grate, and earthenware mugs hung from hooks. "Keffay?"

"Yes, thank you."

Flame sputtered under the grate. Mordano fussed over the pot.

Soman studied the room. A tapestry hung on the wall behind Mordano, depicting the same scene as the stained glass behind the altar, the white-haired priest reaching toward stars. The other walls were bare, the only exception a framed inscription. Its letters flowed across richly-textured paper, obviously hand-made. Soman swung back for a moment to study the tapestry, trying to grasp its meaning, then giving up, indecipherable without understanding the precepts. Glancing from the figure in the drapery to Mordano, Soman was struck by their similarity.

An aroma of coffee filled the room. Mordano handed Soman a cup of dark brew.

Soman sipped. "Thank you. The coffee is good."

Mordano fixed Soman with a long gaze. "Eyew have seen many things."

Soman waited.

"Eyew had a cho-arch?"

"Lutheran."

"Loothrun," Mordano said slowly "Eeyew lived well. The world well-thee. People turn from God. They do not need."

Soman studied his mug, round and heavy. Painted on its surface were dark green leaves and thorny branches surrounding an orange fruit. He traced the fruit with a finger.

"Then..." Mordano concentrated. "The dis...the diss..."

"Disaster?"

Mordano nodded. "Eeyess. Disaster. The dark age. We turn back to God."

Soman thought back to the sanctuary, trying to imagine the denomination of this church. At one time, it was all Catholic around here. But there were no paintings of the Virgin, no angelic hosts. "It's not the Catholic Church?" At Mordano's blank look Soman added, "The Church of Rome?"

"Ah," he said. "Rrrooom." He shook his head. "It was in peace."

Soman frowned.

Mordano tried again. "It do not communicate. It is in poorrrts."

"Parts?"

Mordano nodded. "Eeyess. In porrts. Each porrt travel a different way. Now it is…no more."

Soman considered that statement. The Church of Rome gone after a reign of more than two thousand years.

"But I tell of the Church of Dark and Light."

Soman nodded. Those spheres suspended high over the altar.

Mordano turned in his chair, gestured to the tapestry behind him. "The prophet Vawere. God send his prophet again for the hard time."

Soman forced himself to relax as Mordano talked, trying to ease the strain of drawing meaning from fractured speech, allowing Mordano's words to flow over him, soaking it in without grasping at every mangled syllable.

The prophet Vawere emerged ten years before the disaster. He preached, and he fed the poor. He brought the gift of the Maro, telling his small flock, "The calming hand of God will reach inside every man and woman."

"Where was this?" Soman asked.

"Where the edge of ice stand. In…Button Rowg."

Known for his long white hair and bare feet, Vawere walked the city, serving the poor and building his congregation. He gathered around him a group of followers known as The Hundred. They all took the Maro, and provided it to others from their clinic. He drew suspicion. Someone burned the building. Vawere rebuilt. Police arrested him. The Hundred arranged his release. Across the world, stories grew of his prophecies and his charisma. And Vawere predicted, 'The waters will lap upon your feet and you will mourn your lost.' Two weeks later all the land south of Button Rowg lay under water. Vawere drew The Hundred closer, and they prepared. As ice buried the Northern lands and threw the continent into chaos, Vawere and The Hundred disappeared.

A year later they re-appeared in Alta, amid stories of miracles in the wilderness during a year of searching the path of God. They brought knowledge and hope to a village huddled on the brink of starvation. They sent missionaries to recover vestiges of Mankind's technology, and assembled a city of skilled artisans, of technicians, of doctors.

They introduced the Maro and spread it throughout the city, then the paz.

And they revealed the Book of the Last Prophecy.

Soman sat back; the story swirled through him, something flickering. Vawere. Button Rowg. The man in the tapestry, with his slightly mischievous smile, as if he knew something no one could imagine.

Mordano's eyes shone as he continued. "We follow our p…poor-poose three thousand year. We wait the Prodigal Children. We goord the Maro. The Church of Dark and Light protect the way to the life of God."

"Dark and Light? What does it mean?"

"Vawere teach what a man have inside." Mordano held out both palms like pans of a balance, folds of robe dangling beneath. "Dark, Light. To find the way of God, we search the Light. We must…maah-stor the Dark. Our poorr-poose. To walk in the way of God. The Maro is our guide. The Church make the Maro. The people depending on us."

Mordano rose with a rustle of robes. He moved to the doorway, scanned the hall, then pushed the door closed. Pouring more coffee for Soman, he sat, folding his hands on the table. "And now eeyew come." Mordano held his gaze on Soman. "One alive. One dead."

Meeting Mordano's steely stare, Soman understood why children quailed in his presence.

Mordano inclined his head forward an inch, fixing his eyes on Soman as if looking over reading glasses. "Surely eeyew understand."

Mordano sipped again, waiting for Soman to answer.

By force of willpower Soman held still, then said, "Understand what?"

Mordano set aside the cup. "Three thousand eeyears our people wait the Prodigal Children. Much time. And now eeyew come." Mordano leaned forward. "Not the Prodigal Children at all." Mordano nodded. "Eeyess. But people can be con…con…foosed. It can make problem. They can lose the poor-poose." Mordano's look sharpened. "Eeyew bring the wisdom from God?"

Soman sat still as stone.

"You speak with God?" He gestured above him. "Out there?"

Out there. Soman closed his eyes. Scenes of death and wreckage.

Certainly there had been no God, out there. No light, only the dark. Soman buried his hands between his legs, as if Mordano would see the blood on them.

Mordano raised his voice a fraction to bring Soman back. "Eeyew bring a message from God?"

Soman stared at Mordano. There was some connection between the story of the Prodigal Children and *Sorcerer*. And Mordano was making it clear—don't claim any part of it. Soman's thoughts flashed to Marya. She believed in him, but Mordano's implacable gaze willed him to deny. The force of Mordano's will stirred in Soman an almost irresistible urge to comply. And certainly Soman brought no message from God. At least that much was true. Haltingly, Soman shook his head.

Mordano leaned back. "Eeyess. We understand each other."

Sweat trickled down Soman's face. Then time froze as something in the tapestry spun like an odd bit of space debris. Recollection swirled, chaotic, as in those first re-hydrated hours on *Sorcerer* when memories exploded like fireworks. Julian, Anoka's godfather. Why did he come to mind now.

Seeing Soman's attention on the tapestry, Mordano said, "Vawere invite eeyew to join the Church of Dark and Light."

Soman understood Mordano's invitation: if the stranger joins, if he worships alongside the faithful, if he prays for the return of the Prodigal Children, than he cannot be one of them. What harm would that do. When in Rome…

Then a spark of recognition. The white hair and mahogany skin had thrown him off, but the artist had been skilled. There was no mistaking the eyes, that crooked smile. *It was Julian.* And Julian's hometown, how could anyone forget that drawl: Baton Rouge. And in a flash Soman recalled Julian waiting for him in the *Future Lives* lobby when he had emerged, shaken, from the long elevator ride up from the bowels of the vault, minutes after interring Anoka in the descroid.

Julian had steered him into the warm twilight. In the distance a solitary cumulonimbus towered over the prairie, riding on sheets of rain, its dark walls lit every few seconds from within. Soman didn't speak in the Levitron, gliding above the manual traffic, watching the storm approach, in its path a restless humidity. Julian respected Soman's silence. They reached his rooms just as full dark descended over the western sprawl of Chicago.

In the kitchen Julian had poured scotch, then said, "Anne would have been happy."

The amber liquid quivered in Soman's hand. "No," Soman said. "Anne would have asked what have we just done to our little girl."

Through the window Soman watched the last flicker of sunset, crimson clouds darkening to charcoal. Below, people scurried from the rain, carrying around their meat and bone and brain as if they owned all those molecules, as if they'd always own them. Atoms of borrowed stardust, resisting the tug of gravity, holding back the arrow of time. But it would all end so fast, like fish granted one short leap. Leap, splash, gone.

Julian waited awkwardly.

Soman turned from the window, pointed to the corner of the room. "What's with the Buddha?" he asked.

"My meditation room," Julian said.

"What happened to the evangelical thing?"

Julian made a small wave. "They wore me out."

"I thought it was the Wicca wore you out."

"Them too."

He remembered wondering at that moment, what faith Julian would drift to next. Now, sitting before Mordano, he knew. Oh, Julian. Julian who dabbled in religions the way other men collected women. Julian who must have seen it coming, somehow. This was all his making: a long tradition of white-haired, barefoot priests; a structure that would survive war, politics, and natural disaster; a church at the most likely spot on Earth for the *Sorcerer* crew to land—their former spaceport. And what was Vawere but an anagram of Julian's family name, Weaver. Julian, what in heaven's name...

Mordano cleared his throat, uncertainty flickering in his eyes.. Perhaps the priest had glimpsed Soman's flash of revelation.

There had been one final visit to Julian's, four years later, in the short pause between training and *Sorcerer's* launch. Three days to say goodbye to Earth, to touch a human of his age for the last time. Julian had been somber, making his last plea for Soman not to go. If he had been sad over Soman's four-year job hauling ore, he was distraught over his departure to Epsilon Eridani.

"I wish I'd never told you about *Sorcerer*," Julian said bitterly, though he'd wished Soman well, and they hugged.

Damn, what would Julian think now, if he could know Anoka still lay in her descroid, under a mile of solid ice, three thousand years after his futile objection.

Soman stared at the tapestry, his skin prickling. *The message of God's plan.*

Soman considered Marya—she was about to enter the church as some kind of novitiate, devoting herself to Julian's myth, one created from the debris of a failed mission to the stars, from Julian's perverse spirituality. Maybe he owed Marya the truth. Yet…what right did he have to rip away the foundation of her faith.

Mordano leaned forward, studying Soman, as if trying to discern the meaning of this new expression. Then he said, "We stoot the…trining too-maw-roo."

Soman blinked. "Training? Tomorrow?"

"Yyess."

"All right." Agree to anything right now and get out of here. Then Soman remembered. "Um, tomorrow I see the doctor, and then the mem." No need to rush. He was going to be in Alta a long time, trying to organize an expedition.

Mordano did not look pleased.

"Tomorrow night?"

Mordano nodded his assent.

Soman took a deep breath. Tomorrow would be a long day.

Soman followed the priest up the stairway, then slowed, regarding that small chest tucked into its niche. A clear glass pane sealed the niche. He ran his finger along the glass, studying the antique. Then it flashed before him like the blue light from the moon of Epsilon Eridani, and he recalled this exact chest hunkering in the corner near Julian's Buddha.

Soman turned to Mordano. "What is this doing here?"

Mordano's eyes narrowed at Soman's choice of words. "The *fundam*," Mordano said.

"What is that?"

"The *fundam*," Mordano repeated, as if mere repetition could clarify the obscure. "The *fundam* contains g…gifts for the Prodigal Children."

"Gifts?" Soman's heart skipped a beat. "What gifts?"

"We cannot know," Mordano replied.

Soman leaned against the glass. The dark and light spheres suspended from the ceiling cast shadows across the rich wood of the chest. Gifts.

Mordano pulled Soman from the platform. "Please, iss sacred place."

Soman stumbled in Mordano's firm grip, looking back at the stained glass window, at Vawere fading in the twilight.

Chapter 19

Marya's hair flew behind her as she ran to Soman in front of the shay. "What did he say?" she asked, breathless.

Soman started up the porch steps. "I...It's a beautiful church."

Her expression clouded. "Yes. But what—"

He turned. "Marya, what is the *fundam*?" Gifts, Mordano had said.

Marya hesitated, struggling to change gears. Then she said, "It is the found of the Church."

At Soman's confused expression she tried again. "*Fundam*...the base of the Church. No..." Then her eyes brightened. "Foundation. That is the word."

"Foundation?" he asked.

"Yes. The Prodigal Children should receive the fundam. It will reveal the foundation of the Church, and offer gifts for them. It is written..." her voice trailed off.

No doubt she struggled with the incongruity between the writings she had been taught from childhood and the ordinary, uncertain man who had dropped from the stars, who met with the priest only to return alone, asking questions.

That little chest must be Julian's time capsule, his collection of mission history and crew artifacts. He had assembled a few treasured possessions from each of the crew and gathered documents relating the facts behind the mission. Thinking about it filled Soman with a longing to break through that glass and throw open the chest. But that would mean exposing the profane origins of the Church. Julian had set up the Church of Dark and Light for a cosmic disappointment.

Perhaps Julian hadn't counted on his Church ossifying into what churches become—monolithic bureaucracies protecting their existence. The last thing they want is for their messiah to appear—it is the unfulfilled promise of a messiah that energizes the machinery. Julian might have been blind to this—he'd been captivated by spirituality but disinterested in religion.

They entered the shay. "I'm going to lie down for a while," he said, and he started up the stairway, leaving Marya as still as Julian's Buddha.

As he reached the landing, she said, in a small voice, "Ratoul sent someone."

He stopped. Someone scurried from the nearby living room and out the door. From the kitchen, sounds of pots and pans quieted. The shay knew something.

"What?"

"Ratoul says you must take your ship from Alta."

It was so ridiculous, he laughed.

Marya's grave expression remained unchanged. "I tried to tell him. It should not be. You…"

Soman tried to imagine Marya arguing with Ratoul. He came down a step. "Ratoul can do this?"

"The Congress of Alta met today."

Soman leaned heavily against the railing. The ruling body meeting to discuss him. "But what have I done?"

"It is your ship," she said.

He took another step down. "The ship?"

"Ratoul say the ship is a danger to Alta."

"Marya, the ship isn't going to hurt anyone."

"The Monar will see it. It can be bad for the city."

The Monar again.

"What do you mean, bad? How is it dangerous?"

"Fast machines that explode. This is the reason we do not build a flying olden. In my father's childhood, the people of Ik built an engine that flies. The Monar sent something from the sky and now we hear stories the cities are gone."

"But why?"

"It has always been that way. Ever since the disaster."

Soman settled onto the step. Could this be true. He yanked the banister in frustration; there was no time for this—he needed to be organizing an expedition. But…it was going to take flight to get to her. If Marya was to be believed, the Monar would destroy the LEV. Then it occurred to him…whoever these Monar were, they apparently had the means to fly.

"We must speak with Ratoul," he said.

But when Marya tried to contact Ratoul, she learned he was busy for the evening, hosting a dinner of the Altan Congress. "We must wait until tomorrow," she told Soman.

"We can't wait," he said. "Do you know where Ratoul is holding the dinner?"

Marya nodded.

"We must see him tonight." Her face showed her apprehension, but

Soman saw that, for now, the Prodigal Child carried more weight than the leader of Alta.

They left the shay as dusk deepened the shadows of the city.

Nothing prevented them from walking into the dinner—no need for security in placid Alta. Marya led him to a terraced courtyard surrounded on three sides by a great rambling building, the fourth side open to the bluff, the nighttime harbor spread below, black water lapping pools of light. Tables and diners descended the terrace, a great buzz of unintelligible conversation drifting on the warm breeze like summer cicadas.

"What is Ratoul's position?" Soman asked as they peered into the courtyard.

"He is the may-ore," Marya said.

"So he leads the city."

"Yes, and the parts outside the city."

"All of Alta, then…" he tried to remember the word she had used—"the paz?"

"Yes."

So more like a governor, or a president. Or a dictator. How to know which. Soman hesitated, taking in the stunning variety of clothing—stiff black suits and flowing gowns, beige tunics and multicolored wraps. He and Marya stood at the threshold, unsure how to gain Ratoul's attention. They didn't need to—someone detected them and a head turned, then a few more, every face a shade of brown to black; within moments conversation died. Silence spread across the terrace.

Ratoul placed his napkin beside his plate, pushed his chair back, stood. Lifting a goblet he offered a toast, his words initiating a chain reaction of raised glasses and formal greetings that revolved round the head table, then moved to the next. Having started the ritual, Ratoul strolled to Soman and Marya.

Ratoul offered no further pleasantries. He spoke, and Marya translated. "He hear you completed your interview with Mordano."

It was an opportunity to claim support from Mordano. "Yes, he invited me to join the Church."

"And your impression of our famous priest?" Ratoul asked, with the dour expression he wore like a smelly coat.

Soman thought for a moment. "Dignified," he said.

When Ratoul spoke next, Marya's cheeks reddened through her mahogany complexion. "He…call Mordano 'The White Man'."

Realizing he'd witnessed an insult to the priest, Soman felt suddenly aware of his skin.

Ratoul smiled at Soman's discomfiture.

"You are a member of the Church?" Soman asked.

"Certainly not. A member of the Church may not participate in our government."

Soman couldn't suppress a look of astonishment. What a reversal from the theocracies of the twenty-first century. He'd never known a time when membership in some fundamentalist congregation wasn't a necessary badge of honor for a political career. He still had that article in ship's archives: Age of Aquarius opens with a Century of Holy War. Now, apparently, political custom had evolved in the opposite direction. "This applies only to the Church of Dark and Light, or to other churches as well?"

"There is only the one Church. And one Government. We watch each other." Ratoul scanned the lesser tables arrayed beneath the dais, as the toast wove its way to them.

Soman tried to imagine what could have happened to all the faiths of humanity. It must be Ratoul's ignorance. Or could it be that the Maro, by propping up the biochemistry of hope, had excised the despair that drives people to seek solace in faith, any faith.

Ratoul spoke without turning to Soman, watching the dinner party. "You understand my responsibility," Marya translated.

"Your responsibility?"

"Our laws have kept us safe. My job is to uphold the law. We allowed the violation of your ship at first because we thought you were Ikrit, and the best course would be to make you well and send you home with your machine."

"And a new Maro."

"Of course. Do you object?"

Soman cringed at Ratoul's glare. Idiot; don't antagonize him. "I believe it saved my life."

A nod from Ratoul. "Then we feared you were Monar, and we debated what was best. But now you say you are neither Ikrit nor Monar." Ratoul scrutinized Soman, as if waiting for him to come clean. In the distance, the murmur of the ceremony moved to the far end of the courtyard.

Ratoul said, "Now we have a flying unit near our city, and since you do not have the good sense to take it away, we must force the matter. You are ready tomorrow?"

"Tomorrow? No...I—" Searching for anything to put this off. "—it would take me at least a week, maybe two..." Ratoul didn't have to know the ship could launch on an hour's notice.

Ratoul stepped close to Soman. His voice hardened, and even Marya's translation couldn't soften the message. "It has been almost three weeks. The risk is too great for delay. You may have tomorrow to prepare. On the next day, you must take the ship beyond the borders of Alta. If you do not, we will destroy it."

Soman's mind raced. It was only the LEV they wanted gone. What if..."Wait Ratoul!" he blurted, trying to think this through. "What if I take the ship beyond Alta and return on foot?"

Ratoul appeared to consider. "As a theory, that is acceptable. But I think you do not realize." Ratoul looked to Marya as if Soman's ignorance were her lapse. Then he delivered a brief dissertation on travel beyond Alta, a bleak picture of coastal vessels carrying goods only as far as nearby ports. Jungles to the north and south preventing overland travel. Sailing ships traveling farther but infrequently, trade winds unreliable, icy continents creating zones of stable high pressure. And no word from Ik for decades.

Ratoul glanced down the terrace as a mild commotion arose, the toast starting back from the most distant table.

Marya touched Soman's sleeve. "He say he have only a moment more."

Soman watched, adrift, as the ceremony wound back up the terrace. What would catch Ratoul's interest. "My...my home. It was in the North. If..." Something told Soman not to place Anoka as a bargaining chip in Ratoul's hand. "If I can reach the place above my city, we could recover valuable things from the life I left. There is wealth under the ice, metals, factories. With the maps in my ship, I can locate steel mills, smelters, enough metal to last lifetimes, if we can just..." Except that now he had only two days.

"You think," Ratoul said, "that because you travel among the stars, you can do anything. Wake from your dream. We lost the ways to travel to the north a hundred generations ago, and it will be so a hundred generations more."

Soman grasped Ratoul's elbow to keep from stumbling. A hundred generations.

Ratoul pulled his arm free and sauntered toward his guests, the toast now returning to the head table. Raising his glass to his guests, he accepted the offered tribute. With an intricate clinking of goblets the ceremony was over. Without a look back, Ratoul began rounds of the tables, clasping shoulders and listening with a politician's eager ear to the entreaties of the prominent diners.

The shay was still as Soman sagged into a porch chair. Fireflies flickered over the lawn; peepers filled the night with sound. He watched Marya's outline at the railing, her skin blending perfectly with the night. Beyond, a waning gibbous moon rose blood red through the jungle haze.

Soman tried to look beyond the shock of it. There must be a way around Ratoul's conditions.

"Marya. If I understood Ratoul, you couldn't take a position in the government?"

She shook her head, taking the chair beside him. "Our responsibility is to the Maro, theirs is to the...admin..."

"Administration. Mordano said the Church makes the Maro, but I don't think I understood."

"The Church guards the knowledge of the Maro. It is the way to God. Our purpose is to bring the Maro to all people, to become closer to a life lived like God. The Maro help each person search for the Light, and master the Dark."

"Why does it exclude you from the government?"

She gazed across the lawn to lights moving in the harbor. "Vawere created the Institute to improve the Maro, to find better methods. In that time, many people of the Church served the government. There was a...crisis. Some people were afraid if the Church control the government and the Maro. They made the rule that everyone would take the Maro, but no one from the Church would be in government."

Soman pondered the balance of power struck by that ancient compromise. The government managed the state, unable to exert control over its citizens through the most powerful tool of domination ever invented. The Church determined the programming for the Maro, forbidden to take secular power.

"Why do the Monar deny flight to others?"

"No one remembers. It was so long ago."

No one remembers. It would be like attempting to explain what had happened in his world a millennium before Christ.

At a sudden thought, he stood and took her arm. "Since Alta has been at peace, maybe we could convince the Monar we are no threat. My ship's files have the knowledge for building airplanes. If the Monar wouldn't interfere, Alta could be the first to regain flight."

He heard her quickly drawn breath. "We have no contact with the

Monar in my lifetime."

"Someone must know how to contact the Monar. Where do they live?"

Marya stared at him.

"You know, their paz. Where is it?"

"I thought you know. They live on the moon."

Soman pictured the ruined airlocks, the wrecked ships, the desolation of the lunar bases. Surely Marya was mistaken. Tomorrow he would ask Kolar.

He felt the tug of that other question—what to tell Marya. He must learn more about her intentions. "Marya, when you've taken your vow, will you go to a convent?"

"Con-vet?"

"A place where women live who train for the church."

"No, I will live at the shay."

"So in your church you can serve and also marry?"

Silence. Then, "No, I have taken the duro."

"The duro?"

"When we decide to follow the devotion, we ask the doctor to…adjust the Maro so that we do not care for the man. We take the duro."

Soman considered this duro. A step that, once taken, removes the temptation to change one's mind. No need for the forced discipline of the convent. So people turn up or down their Maro's limits to facilitate their life choices. Hone the Maro for success in a chosen field. Butchers dampening revulsion to gore. Teachers ratcheting up empathy. Politicians… Soman tried to imagine which tendencies politicians might choose.

The mist strengthened to drizzle. Soman shivered in the damp.

Marya's duty to the church will lead her to squelch her libido, to spend her life in the study of ancient scripture. Scripture that wasn't scripture at all, but some mad writing of Anoka's godfather. Julian had played many a joke during his time with the mission, but this one…

Marya wept quietly. He realized that, when she told him of the duro, her voice was sad. He remembered her joy with the children. Perhaps she was harboring regret, sensing something amiss with the Prodigal Child.

Chapter 20

Soman tried to rouse himself with coffee. On two hours' sleep, he would visit the Maro doctor and the mem. Might as well stick with the schedule and learn as much today as possible. He would talk with both Kolar and Mordano. Find a way around Ratoul's dictate. Then tomorrow...a desperate possibility swirled in the back of his mind. There was a way to program an unmanned launch. Maybe even an unmanned docking, though refueling was out of the question. Then, if he ever made it back out of the gravity well, there would be hardware available. Although...the Monar might object to a ship in orbit. And when could he ever hitch a ride to orbit in this lifetime. The decision would be irrevocable, no backup, no alternatives. Make a life here, at the mercy of Altan technology and the Monar. At the mercy of age and death.

He realized Marya had spoken to him. He lifted his head from the table. "What?"

"Yesterday you talked of traveling across the ice."

"Yes."

"We will inquire," she said.

"We?"

Her eyes flickered to a group on the lawn.

"They...would help you."

"Who are they?"

Soman met the eyes of a woman in the circle. Caught by his gaze, she swayed forward, raised fingertips to shoulders, and mouthed the words: *The Hawk welcomes you.* One by one, the others followed the woman's example. But this assembly of gentle souls couldn't have the means to take him to the frozen north. Unless he was ready to trust in miracles. Then he recognized where he'd seen that pure white tunic: the couple who had watched the olden depart yesterday. So word had spread; these were people eager for their Prodigal Child. He'd thought they were Horg's people. This was worse. Mordano was his only hope for an ally, but that depended on joining the church, not inspiring a movement. How to deal with a growing throng. Sorry, just a big mistake. No Prodigal Child here, but surely he'll be along any millennium now. Soman watched Marya. She would never agree to a lie. And the truth would rock the entire institution. When Mordano discovers this...

Marya stood. "Now we must see your Maro doctor. We should not miss again."

The Institute filled an immense building, with twin domes over the spacious reception area, one of black stone, one of white. The space above the swirling tile floor was hung with hundreds of light and dark spheres. Just so we know who is running this show.

Sora clasped Soman with surprising strength for such a small person. Her tiny eyes followed his every move, eyes set far back in a face so uniformly black and impassive he could read nothing in it. Around his belly she strapped a belt that held a small disc directly over his Maro. Then she placed three of the black pads before him on the low table. They came to life, and charts began to grow. For a minute she studied the displays, nodding occasionally. Then she spoke, gesturing to the three displays.

Marya said, "She say hundreds of chemicals regulate a human body. She wants to know if you are familiar with these chemicals, or if she should explain the bi…the bio…"

"Biology," Soman finished for her. He waved Sora on. "I am familiar."

She explained the normal range for each neurotransmitter and the intricate feedback loops. Changes in the secretions with age. Impacts of stress and environmental conditions. It is a wonder the human body works at all.

Soman nodded. Especially after tearing it all down and shooting it at a distant star.

Sora continued. Many people are born with chemistry outside the normal range. These differences, along with experience and learning, determine personality: how we respond to stress; how tolerant we are of ambiguity, or deprivation; how needful we are of affection, of structure, of action; how predisposed we are to anger, to violence, to poetry or libido.

"Doctors of the Institute examine every child," Marya explained. "Then the Maro is placed in them, special for each one. You understand?"

Soman nodded.

"We do not want everyone the same. It mean moving each chemical until it is inside the standard range. It mean helping each person to search the way to God, the way they act toward others. If you are not pleased with your path, you request a change."

Soman imagined a person experiencing the mortification of lust, or an urge to slap the child, then trudging to the Institute in search of confession and correction. Penance replaced in the fifty-fourth century by a bit of tuning.

"Now we speak of your Maro." Marya pointed at the pads before them on the desk. "All is…" she smiled sheepishly "…cool. But when you arrived, she has never seen so extreme as you. She say many of your chemicals were beyond her books. She wonders you could live for long. "Probably your machine has ruined your body for controlling the chemicals."

"So the Maro saved my life."

"She says the Maro has saved many lives. There has been no murder in Alta in her lifetime."

Soman walked to the window, squinting against the bright afternoon sun. That would make him the only person alive in Alta who had ever killed. Beyond the city, mountains quavered in the heat like a mirage. No murder or robbery. Really. He turned. "Do you have guns?"

"Yes," Marya said. "Her father uses one for hunting."

Sora watched Marya with a benevolent smile.

Soman could picture Sora behind the scope, stilling every muscle for the squeeze. "In my time many people killed with guns," he said. "We never solved it. Some wanted to take away the guns, but that was hard. Once people have them, they like them." He smiled. "Just like the Maro."

Marya explained to Sora, who scratched her narrow chin and considered.

"She says she can see that without the Maro, the only solution would be taking away the guns. But it is like giving the patient a pill for the pain and never fixing the disease. She reminds me of the words of a great man. 'Peace can not be kept by force. It can only be achieved by understanding'. These words are written in every shay."

Soman snorted. "Nice words. But this man never saw our time."

"I think…he was from your time. Insten." At Soman's blank look she said, "You don't know him?"

"No."

"But he was famous. I write it for you."

Soman read from her pad. "Einstein?" Not exactly from his time, but damn close from the Altan perspective. "Anyone can write the words, it's another thing to live by them."

A flicker of surprise from Marya, as if she were unfamiliar with cynicism. "Of course we live by it."

Soman looked skeptical.

"I will tell you of the fallen mayor. It was more than one hundred years ago. Alta was led by a man named Solin. He was famous even before he fell, for many new things brought to the paz. It was Solin who learned to make the fuel for our boats.

"Alta was visited by a ship from Ik, looking for trade. One night some men from the ship did a…bad thing to a woman of Alta, and she died. She was the wife of Solin. Of course the city was sad. No one knew what to do. Solin walked up and down at the harbor, shouting at the people on the ship. Then he stole a boat and drove it into the visitors' ship. It sank and many people died."

Soman said, "It's hard not to fight when you are attacked." So violence can be done, even wearing a Maro, if one chooses the weapon wisely. This put Mordano in a whole new light. And Ratoul.

"You must hear the rest. The people in Alta were sad for Solin, of course. They understood his anger. But what he did was not acceptable. He was removed from the mayor. All his possessions were taken from him. Each day he must face the people of Alta he once led. Since that time, no one uses the name of Solin for their child. We say the path of Solin begins with a loud voice. Today the Maro is much improved, it would stop Solin."

Soman looked out the window. Removing a violent leader from office. Maybe this *was* a true pacifist society. He watched two of the motorized bicycles fly past on the street. Groups of people left the hospital, strolling down the sidewalk. But a sense grew—they weren't telling everything. He watched the street. "And everyone has a Maro."

"Yes, after the age of two."

That would take care of the terrible twos. "Everyone in the world?" Soman met Marya's eyes, wondering if she remembered that incautious moment when she'd mentioned people living like animals in the jungle.

When she translated Sora's quick answer, her voice was softer. "Sora says it has spread everywhere in Alta and the countries near."

"There are no people living in small villages who do not have the Maro? Maybe they can't afford it?"

"The Maro is provided by the Church, the materials are paid by the government."

"What if someone does not want the Maro?"

"You could not enjoy your life!"

"But *if* I chose, could I have it removed?"

Marya gasped. "No doctor would remove a Maro."

"Sometimes people do strange things." He saw Horg's terrible scar and heard his words: '*Yes they know. They can not find us.*' Maybe the Altans were in denial. Or maybe they were lying. "Ask Sora if she has ever heard of someone removing their Maro."

Silence. Watching a dust devil spin down the street, Soman counted ten heartbeats.

Marya's speech slowed, like a computer burdened with too many tasks. "She says she has not seen it in her lifetime."

Soman watched the empty sidewalk, the afternoon shift change done. Perhaps not a lie, if Sora has never ventured into the jungle. So the Maro does not prevent its owner from being clever.

He turned back to Sora. "And does my Maro require maintenance?"

"She say it is a good idea to check it. An adjustment is sometimes needed."

"What if I make this journey to the North, and I'm gone some months. Would I be in trouble? Could it break down?"

Sora shook her head. "The Maro does not break down. People go for years without a problem."

Soman thought for a minute. Sora seemed a person with broad knowledge and many more years of experience than Marya. "Ask Sora if she thinks anyone can help me travel beyond Alta, across the ice."

Marya and Sora talked for a minute. Then Marya turned to Soman. "She say there is no one in Alta so unwise."

Soman gazed out the window into the early afternoon light. There was one last possibility: Seek the Monar.

Chapter 21

In the center of the room the mem lay like a giant clam, its lid hinged open, a control panel crouching to one side. Soman hesitated at the door. It wasn't just a story the mem would tell, it was the fate of his world. The disaster. A chill ran through him, recalling Mordano's hissing pronunciation of that word.

A man pulled Soman to a room where suits hung. Measuring Soman with his eye, the man snatched one, then gestured for Soman to remove his clothes. The suit was rubbery, an inch thick, and much too big. Folds hung from his waist and ankles as he waddled back to the mem, the white oval of his face peering out.

The attendant clucked, then advanced on Soman, towing a cable like an elephant's trunk. The man slid the plug into a receptacle in the chest of the suit. The fabric crawled; the suit shrank around him, the extra folds gone. A sensation of warmth spread, then disappeared. All feeling faded, and a sensation of nakedness overcame him. He peeked down to be sure the suit had not fallen away.

The operator appeared with four disks the size of thumb pads; these he stuck to Soman's skull. He placed an object in Soman's right hand, keeping up a steady, indecipherable conversation.

Marya said, "Use the first finger to skip forward. Use the second finger to go back to an earlier part. The fourth finger we call the… the crazy button. The mem will be real for you. You will feel you are there, but of course you are not. If you be sick, press the crazy button. It keep you from crazy."

He climbed over the edge and slid into the pool of liquid. The operator swung the lid shut, to pitch black.

Just as panic nearly claimed him, there was daylight. Trees fluttering in the breeze, broad heart-shaped leaves flapping like wings. Soman recognized the scene—the street he had just left behind. Two women in tunics, purple and black, walked past him as if he weren't there, leaning into the wind, shimmering fabric pressed against the curve of breast and hip. The mem granted Soman no time to gawk—it plucked him from the sidewalk and he soared into the sky. His stomach convulsed, and he clenched his eyes shut as he arced high. Thankfully Marya had suggested skipping the noon meal. But he couldn't escape vertigo—vision in the mem apparently didn't require open eyes. Soman's heart pounded. Fourth finger. The scene darkened. Now he looked down on the clamshell. Marya and the operator stood at the console, the operator laughing. Seeing his amusement, Soman released the crazy button, tightened his jaw, and resolved to go crazy before pressing it again.

Air whooshed in his ears, cooling as he rose. The shimmering leaves shrank. Trees crowded into clumps, the clumps merged into jungle. A coastline spread beneath him. The mem soared him far from from the turquoise Caribbean, over rivers brown and muscular, around jagged peaks. Rising, rising, until the continent spread before him. And Soman knew he was in an earlier time, because the coastline had returned to its old contour, the shape of maps in the twenty-first century.

Behind him, North America stretched green and verdant. Soman ached to go there, but the mem took him south. To his right the Pacific appeared, shimmering.

The broken shape of Tierra del Fuego. He gasped at its rocks and jumbled seas, the jagged dangers faced by Cook and Magellan, clippers and pirates, uncounted vessels vanished forever beneath the currents of Cape Horn. If they could have witnessed this scene, they would never have dared the voyage.

A descent began; stomach rising, he gritted his teeth, unwilling to press the button.

Antarctica. Massive flocks of penguins blackened its ice shelves, a croaking din rising to him. He sped over vast, cold glaciers. He sailed over mountain ranges, their immense rock faces challenging snow to cling.

Slowing, he descended to a remote and icy coast. Ships dotted the bay. A slithering sensation at the base of his skull, a momentary blurring, and Soman knew they were ships from that great and growing nation thrust into the Himalayas. An India approaching four billion souls on the eve of the 22nd century, clean water their most critically-depleted resource. There to mine the ice of Antarctica.

The slippery discomfort again. The Indian fleet blurred. And he knew to raise his eyes to the horizon, black with ships, hundreds of them, approached the Indian flotilla, from nations in opposition, publicly concerned for the krill that supports life in the southern ocean. But the objecting countries also possessed ample water supplies, and India represented a vast market for a commodity with a value escalated beyond that of oil and grain. One-third of the world's warships congregated in the southern ocean, fighting the gales that circle the bottom of the world.

But the people of India were thirsty; they would war over water. And they had already invested heavily. Back home in the protected Gulf of Khambhat, the Indians had built a containment to surround the glacier they planned to tow north. After pumping out the seawater, they would allow the ice to melt, producing a vast freshwater lake.

Charges placed deep into boreholes. Indians returning in haste to their ships. The flotilla pushing back from the ice shelf, beyond Heard Island and the Kerguelens. The Indians knew the surrounding navies were closing in; there would be no second chance. Their calculations told them that viscoelastic ice could absorb huge forces before fracturing; staggering amounts of explosives of the most modern type lay beneath the pack. But the Indians underestimated the propagation of shock waves along the thin boundary between ice and bedrock. They did not understand the slipperiness of water under the tremendous pressure of mile-thick ice sheets.

The glacier writhed; its surface pulsed and crackled. A jet of ice riddled Soman and he screamed reflexively. The concussion tossed him five thousand feet in the air, driving the breath from him.

The shock wave reached outward to the West ice shelf where it floated on frigid brine. Its energy finally released, it blasted iceberg-size chunks more than ten kilometers into the air. The rest it shredded into razor shards that sliced the Indian ships with ferocious shrapnel. Casualties fell from exposed decks like the first pattering rain of the monsoon.

Inland, the shock wave reached a mountain ridge that protruded through the glacier. A sheet of superheated water spurted skyward along the Mawson Escarpment, freezing in midair to fall in a delicate frost. The glittering shower fell not upon ice but naked rock, rock that had not felt the breath of air since dinosaurs walked the Earth.

The ice had begun to slide.

A mountain range of ice larger than entire countries shuddered and boomed and broke loose from its attachments. With a long, slow undulation it gained speed, tearing the tops off ridges, scouring the ancestral rock clean, driving its leading edge into the southern ocean, pushing the shattered shelf ice ahead of it.

The sea rose in a towering wall a hundred meters high. Soman clawed to get above it, the entire sea writhing toward him. The mem carried him along the crest of the wave as it drove through the vessels, and where millions of tons of shipping had dotted the ocean, Soman gaped at churning froth. No sign of human life remained. Soman sped along with the wave, feeling the sensation again, like a finger penetrating the back of his neck and wriggling into the brain, and he understood the fluid dynamics of tsunami, lengthening as it reached deeper water, giving up height but retaining its energy, energy stored in speed and mass and wavelength. At nine hundred kilometers per hour, Soman rushed north with the undulation, a wrinkle in the ocean's skin.

India would soon get its water.

He flashed past shipping in the Indian Ocean, vessels experiencing a slight rise as the long, low wave passed, crew looking around as if at some unseen disturbance in the air, then settling back to their tasks with an uneasy shake of the head. The wave reached southwest Australia first, piling against the coastal shallows, rising two hundred feet as friction slowed the leading edge. Soman watched entire towns inundated, then sucked into the sea. The wave traveled unimpeded over the Java trench and lashed high onto Indonesia's unprotected coast before pulling millions into the Indian Ocean to feed the sharks and lesser fishes.

And then the Indian subcontinent loomed before him.

The wave front funneled symmetrically into the Bay of Bengal. Beneath Soman, the mouths of the Ganges rose in fury, roaring a hundred miles inland. In an hour it washed clean the seething masses of Kolkata. Already the Indian plan had reduced the water needs of the population.

The finger pressed deeper into Soman's brain; he shrank away: two hundred ships sunk, a few million people drowned. A small beginning for the disaster.

Slowly, the mem turned Soman back toward Antarctica, and from a great distance he watched a continent in paroxysm. The immense new ice pack in the Southern Ocean had raised sea levels by a few precious millimeters. Tsunami reflections spilled more water upon the Antarctic coast. Shelf ice groaned. Great sheets of glacier broke free and slid into the ocean. Slither, slither in his brain—few major cities of the world lay more than feet above sea level. Venice, Copenhagen, Istanbul, Shanghai, a hundred more inundated. New Orleans abandoned; its pumps too old, too slow. Seawater threatening even Baton Rouge.

Soman's altitude plummeted. The surface of the ocean neared. He flinched; then tried to claw away. The mem plunged him beneath the waves, to a shocking chill that drove the breath from him, to unimaginable pressure. Then all was still. The cold finger made his skull ache. Ice blocking the southern ocean halted crucial currents, created downdrafts of stable high pressure air. The southern Tradewinds slowed to a whisper. The Easterlies that gave rise to the Gulf Stream faltered. The last vestige of the Gulf Stream slowed, then stopped. Europe would experience its coldest winter in fifty thousand years.

Winter it would remain.

The sun crossed the equinox; Earth sped along its orbit. Soman stood in a frozen wheat field in Manitoba, witnessing a spring that brought the first inkling of the true scale of the disaster. The Canadians planted no wheat; their soil never thawed. In the Year of our Lord 2098, spring would never arrive in the Northern hemisphere, where most of the world's food was grown. Africa, taught by decades of marketing to love the taste of bread, depended on the grains of the north. They were the first to starve as nations hoarded their silos.

The mem pumped Soman high above the globe. Great migrations began, dark stains against the frost. Canadians moving south. Ukrainians moving west. Siberians surging into the fragile republics. Anarchy spreading across the world. The finger penetrated hard, insistent, the base of Soman's skull tender, throbbing. As he descended past the glitter of cold sunlight on the Black Sea, he knew something terrible would occur there.

A Russian army moved across Ukraine, trailed by caravans of desperate citizens. The Ukrainians were gone. A rumor of stockpiles in Georgia. The horde surged south. Millions converging into the bottleneck between the Black and Caspian Seas.

The Georgians had enjoyed a good crop. It was eaten in a week.

Armenians and Azerbaijanis fought side by side for the first time in centuries. Their stand lasted four days. Then their staples were consumed.

The Iranians, blessed with the warm waters from the Persian Gulf and the Arabian Sea, warned their desperate northern neighbors to stay home. Baku was burning; pestilence spread through the Caucasus; millions surged south along the Caspian shore. The Persians watched the lands to the north devastated by the human wave as completely as the tsunami had destroyed Calcutta the year before. Soman witnessed the gathering of grave-faced Ayatollahs. As the ache in his skull grew, Soman knew they had taken the decision: the threat could still be contained in the narrow northern corridor.

The first country to cross the line since 1945, Iran in March 2099 detonated six nuclear devices, sealing their northern border. Soman saw the flash and watched his bones glow through melting flesh. He screamed as the nuclear wind vaporized everything around him, melting the sand to glass, hurling him northward like a meteor. History would record that the Iranian decision saved an important remnant of culture for the future world. The Iranians wrote this history.

Descending over Poland, Soman witnessed a second flash—the Germans devastating eastern Poland and Slovakia. The mushroom clouds and their searing updraft hurled him into the stratosphere, where he tasted the poison and knew it would circle the globe for a hundred generations.

The Germans earned only six months; there was no natural bottleneck into the Fatherland. By September, with winter approaching and the bulging European food supply depleted, the Germans joined the rest of northern Europe in its futile trek south, to die against the placid Mediterranean.

Soman swirled in a daze over North America, through radioactive dust and greasy smoke; the ash of the waning industrial age. The lights of Chicago winked out under deepening, silent snow.

Soman heard a sound rising from the world, a wail of a billion voices in agony; it had finally happened, and it was too late.

Forty-three years had passed since *Sorcerer* departed.

And somewhere in the Central America isthmus, a man and his ragtag band moved south through the jungle.

Everything went dark as if a bulb had burnt out. The residue of the mem swirled through Soman like wreckage on the tide, the base of his skull throbbing. Someone shook him—Marya, gesturing urgently. Soman flopped and crawled over the lip. The attendant peeled off the suit. Marya ran to him from the other room, his clothing in her arms. "We must go." In her haste she tripped over the cable and slammed to the floor with a yelp. Soman stooped to help; she shoved the clothes at him. "Hurry!"

Chapter 22

Marya pulled Soman from the building. He stumbled in her grasp, images from the mem flickering.

They emerged into the evening cool. Twilight deepened over Alta; the first stars hung like jewels. Marya was speaking; something about a vehicle. A throng of people blocked their way, their voices joined in ululation, wailing at his presence. At the far side of the crowd stood Kolar beside an olden, gazing at the mountains with the vacant expression of a man who has learned of a death in the family. In the east an unnatural radiance lit the sky, not the warm glow of sunset, but blue-white and stark, betraying an energy source greater than any in Alta.

Soman pointed. "What's that?"

"The Monar have come."

Soman froze. Fast machines that explode, Marya had said yesterday. And The LEV stood in those eastern hills. He plowed through the throng toward the olden.

The crowd pressed close; arms reaching for him, expressions spellbound. The noise swelled, a choir of a hundred moans. The faithful, come to see their Prodigal Child. This was not going to go over big with Mordano. Each person touching Soman fell instantly, giving in to rapture, to be replaced by someone from behind. Then Soman grasped that their collapse was their Maro snuffing out their ecstasy. No euphoria allowed in Alta.

But the blazing eastern sky frightened Soman even more. The entire city in motion, people running, oldens racing, cycles buzzing like hornets, all fleeing the same direction—away from the stark light in the east. And overhead, that quarter moon blazing. He recalled the fuzzy view of Colony One through the telescope, a ship standing at airlock, the surface around littered with wrecks.

They reached the olden. Marya tugged him up the steps. "Come. We take you to a safe place." The motor stirred; Soman tasted ozone as the olden carved a path through the crowd, turning to join the convoy of oldens heading west. Over the din Soman yelled, "No. I have to get to my ship."

"You must hide!" Marya grabbed his shirt and pulled him toward a seat, crouching as if the hiding must start immediately. The olden accelerated; the last of the faithful dropped behind.

Soman pushed free of her and leapt to the front, kicking the door open. "Stop the bus!"

Marya screamed.

"Tell the driver to stop. I'm getting off." The olden ground to a squealing halt. The faithful surged forward. Soman pointed resolutely at Kolar. "Tell Kolar we must drive to the LEV."

Marya shouted to Kolar; Kolar shook his head.

Soman looked around. The mob was only yards away. But there, up the street—he yanked Marya out of the olden and ran, his hand clamped around her wrist, dragging her along, her wail adding to the roar of the mob.

In the east, the sky shone like a false sunrise.

A man sat on a cycle, trying to work his way into the fleeing masses, frozen as he watched Soman and Marya approach, trailed by the mob. Soman pulled the man off the cycle and leaped on, keeping his grip on Marya's wrist. "Get on!" he shouted. He raised his leg, looking for a starter. Nothing. Of course, it's electric. He felt a pad under his right thumb, and pressed it. Nothing. "Marya! Show me!" She struggled to get away. Hooking her waistband, he lifted her onto the narrow seat. The first of the crowd was almost upon them. The owner tapped Soman politely on the arm. Down the street, the olden had started with a whir and now gained speed toward them.

Soman pressed the thumbpad again, this time from the side. The bike jumped ahead. Marya clutched him to keep from catapulting backward. "Hang on!" he yelled, and jammed the thumbpad farther. The cycle sped forward. Soman looked back at the owner's incredulous expression. Poor guy had no concept of theft.

Soman accelerated, heading east. Suddenly the road bent. A building loomed dead ahead. Soman leaned to turn and flailed for handbrakes— but there were no brake handles. "Marya, how does it stop?" Feeling with his foot for a pedal. The building grew large, blotting out the sky.

Her arms locked around his waist, Marya shouted, "Your knee. You...oh, the word—"

The cycle bounced over the curb. Soman leaned into as tight a turn as he dared. Instinctively he gripped the bike with his legs, and miraculously the vehicle screeched to a halt, skidding across the grass and stopping inches from a wall of yellow stone. He shifted Marya back onto the seat.

"The word is squeeze," he said. Clever. Thumb slide to go, knee squeeze to stop. He swung around and drove away, careful with the throttle, resisting the urge for speed. Don't go all the way to Eridani and back, and then die on a motorcycle, like Lawrence of Arabia. Eventually something gets you.

Marya made incoherent sounds, her hold weakening, forcing Soman to reach back to keep her from falling off. The road forked. "Marya, which way." She could only moan, her head lolling. Suddenly Soman recognized the symptoms—overwhelmed by runaway emotion, her Maro was shutting her down, and she tipped off the back of the cycle. Soman squeezed with his knees and grabbed her with one hand. He skidded the cycle to a halt. "Come on, Marya, wake up, Which way?"

"You cannot go there," she said.

"I have to go. You wait here."

"No!"

"I'll be careful."

"I stay with you."

Soman saw determination in her eyes. "Okay then, which way?"

Marya pointed down the right fork. They raced through the outskirts of Alta and entered the undulating country of the ancient spaceport.

At the last rise before the rubble of the landing pad, two large oldens blocked the road. Dozens of beige-clad people huddled behind, shouting and pointing, radios crackling. Two sounds from the landing site filled the night air: a high-pitched whine and a low pounding like heavy surf. And the acrid, unmistakable smell of burning rocket fuel.

Soman tried to maneuver around the oldens, but a man moved in the way, shouting, forcing Soman to turn sharply. The cycle tipped, throwing Soman and Marya to the ground. The man grabbed Soman as he regained his feet. Soman tried to wrest free, shoving with his forearm, clipping the man's jaw with his elbow, his gore rising. "Marya, tell him to let me go."

Marya shouted.

The man scuffled and yelled back.

Soman balled a fist, but lassitude put an end to it; Soman found himself sitting on the gravel, every muscle loosening. The man also faltered, his grip slackening, and he hunched as if Soman had actually punched him. Marya tottered, supporting herself on Soman. All three staggered under the onslaught of their Maro.

Soman fought the Maro's weakness, enough energy only to register that the Altans were incapable of fighting in anger. Perhaps they could wield weapons in a dispassionate way, as Solin had, but they would be no match for an enemy with fury as its ally. Sora had told the truth—these people were incapable of murder. So how would they ever defend themselves—or him.

His energy returning, Soman stood carefully. Beside him the man crouched and watched, but made no new attempt to restrain Soman. "What's going on down there?" Soman asked Marya.

Marya covered her ears against the whine and shouted, "The Monar landed in a vehicle."

It took a moment to sink in. That's the high-pitched noise, an idling turbine. His trained ear detected unevenness in the whine, a periodic clatter. Worn blades. Going to disintegrate if it doesn't get service.

Marya touched his sleeve. "We must hide."

He tried to work his tired brain.

Marya threw her arms around him. "Let them destroy your vehicle. You are home now."

Light glinted off a thousand highlights in her hair. He hugged her fiercely, lifting her clear of the ground, and she gasped as he crushed the air from her lungs. Then he released her before his Maro could paralyze him. He backed away a few stumbling steps, leaving her reaching for support. Then he whirled and yanked the cycle upright, running with it, searching for the button with his finger, slipping in the loose soil beside the roadbed. The man gave chase. Soman felt a hand on his shoulder as he found the accelerator and spun through the dirt around the end of the olden, into the dark.

Marya shouted, but the scream of the turbine erased her words.

The tip of the LEV poked above the hill, silhouetted against eye-searing brightness. He ditched the cycle short of the crest, wanting to get closer without being seen. Running just behind the ridgeline, he tried to remember the terrain. There was an old roadbed that might provide cover. His stomach grumbled and he felt light-headed: no food since breakfast. So much for catching up on sleep tonight. And the worst headache of his life, as if the mem had shoved a piece of pipe up his cranium. He slowed to a jog to save his thin reserves. Not the way to go into battle: a sleepless night, an empty stomach, and an implant that cuts you down the instant you even think about hurting someone.

He reached a vantage point. Illuminating the LEV were the powerful floodlights of a spaceship not two hundred yards away, its heat shield glowing orange. The second sound, the low roar, seemed to come from the LEV, where figures scurried away, thin, frail, dressed in black.

The low-pitched sound stopped. Flames shot from the LEV's nacelle. Soman clambered up the scree and ran for his ship. Someone was starting the engine—they were going to launch. But the ramp hadn't yet been retracted—he raced toward it. As he reached the shadow cast by the LEV in the Monar search beam, a detonation flattened him. The LEV settled, tilting, landing struts bending, screeching like wounded animals. The ship quivered, then teetered toward him, slowly at first, accelerating, metal howling as it fell. Its shadow caught Soman staring up, frozen.

He scrambled to his feet and ran from the rushing shadow, dodging through the ruins of the old spaceport, like running in a dream, legs of glue. Then a thunderous concussion flung him to the ground. The earth behind him convulsed. Soman's world flicked out. Quiet, black. For a few seconds, the peace of oblivion. Then tranquility burst—the world returned with searing pain in his head, grit in his eyeballs, rough concrete against his cheek.

He opened his eyes. Ten yards away lay a wall of bent and jagged metal.

Squinting through the pain, Soman spotted the Monar. One had fallen, two others helped. And in the lead, a solitary figure barely fifty yards from the ramp of their ship. Soman smelled rocket fuel. A dark stain spread beneath the LEV, vapors shuddering upward. Going to be one hell of a fire here when the Monar ship lights its engine.

In an instant he was up and running, making a wide arc around the Monar. The coming minutes would see the only liftoff from Earth in this lifetime. He had to be on it.

Angling toward the Monar, he fixed his sight on the lead man. The Maro fought him; he stumbled. As he fell he lowered a shoulder. With a thud and a grunt, he caught the man square in the back and they sprawled together onto the jagged concrete.

Soman squirmed against slack muscles, clutching his aching skull, sucking air, willing the Maro to give back control before the Monar unholstered their weapons. The man he'd taken down didn't move. Soman crawled to the inert figure, gasping for breath, looking for a gun. Nothing. How do you recognize a gun in the fifty-fourth century.

Muscles strengthening each second, Soman pulled the lifeless man to his feet, surprised by the ease of the lift. A bag of bones. Voices approached. Pinning the man's arms behind him, Soman turned to face the other Monar, the floodlights of their ship directly behind him. The man moaned. The others neared, three herky-jerky figures in black, holding their hands up against the glare of the light. They shouted out, and Soman made out a woman's voice, then a man's.

Something sounded familiar in that voice. It took a moment to sink in—He was sure there were some English words in there. How did they know—

"My world," a woman said. She hunched down, hands on knees, as if burdened by a great weight. Her skin was deeply lined, her figure androgynous. The two men beside her swayed like drunks in the gleam of a police flashlight, one round-faced, the other gaunt with deep-set eyes.

"Drop your weapons!" Soman shouted.

The woman looked at the round-faced man. "Do he spoken English?"

"Now!" Soman shook his hostage for emphasis.

"No weapons," the woman blurted.

"Joni, stoop!" shouted round face.

Soman looked closely, then stared—at the first white people he'd seen on Earth. But look at them, staggering, panting. They're exhausted. No wonder, trying to move around in six times their usual gravity. Their simple black jumpsuits betrayed no bulges, no clips for a gun. The Altans could have taken these guys, Maro or no. Just walk up and push them over. Soman looked back up the hill toward Alta. Smoke still curled lazily from the LEV. "You wrecked my ship!" he screamed.

The eyes of the Monar grew large. They understood him. Their language was English, no doubt; not the halting speech of the Altans but fluid sentences, clearly English though drifted over the centuries.

Joni shouted, "Smit, Smit, er you hart?"

Soman shook the man in his grasp. This must be Smit. He wanted to throw Smit as far as he could, wanted to smash his head against the battered hull of the LEV, douse him with leaking fuel. But at the thought he wobbled, his legs giving way. Easy man. He breathed deeply; the Maro eased its grip, teaching self-control better than any parent.

Stillness hung over the ruins of the spaceport. "I'm going with you," he said, hefting Smit over his shoulder and starting up the hill toward the Monar ship.

They looked at each other. "Did he say…" Joni said.

"Bad idea," round face said as he stumbled after Soman.

Soman took in the silhouette of the Monar ship, hauntingly familiar. He stopped dead. An M620. They hadn't improved the design since *Sorcerer* left, except for that Mark nine slung underneath.

Round face seemed to be the boss, so Soman made him stay below while he and the others entered the elevator. He wanted no funny business in the cabin while they prepared for launch. He called down, "What's your name?"

"Flip." The man crouched, standing clearly painful.

"Flip, you cross me up, I'll cram your skinny ass out the airlock so fast you won't know what happened."

Flip kept his eyes on the hilltop, as if expecting Altan infantry to appear.

The elevator started with a grind and clatter, smelling of lube oil, fuel, and sweat. Soman looked down on the Monar, not one of them taller than five-five.

"Poor Smit." Joni said. Shying away from Soman and avoiding eye contact, she lifted the chin of the inert man and touched his bleeding face, her hands shaking. The lift groaned, then clanged home. Easing Smit into a seat in the cramped cockpit, Soman turned to the other two. "Okay, get this thing ready to launch. Anything out of line, we leave Flip behind." He made an effort to put spine in his voice, but he heard the tremor.

They staggered to the console.

Soman watched them. God, the LEV. Gone. Goddamn. Then he noticed Joni and the man speaking low and fast. "And no tricks—I know how to launch an M620. Done it many times." The two exchanged a look of bewilderment and terror. As Soman listened to them talking through the checklist, he gained a sense of their pronunciation. Then he looked around the dimly-lit space—his stomach turned. A crack in the bulkhead, filled with a yellow material like dried snot. Suit racks empty. Switches on the control console a dozen different shapes; the originals all missing. And it struck him. It wasn't just an old design unchanged through the years—this could be an actual ship left over since time forgotten. A ship Hakim might have flown. Soman leaned against the bulkhead, dizzy with nostalgia, terrified by the risk.

Liftoff drove him deeply into a makeshift seat of cushions—only four seats in an M620. The patched bulkhead rattled as the engine's whine grew to a roar, its turbine clattering. Cloud layers streaked by, flashing orange. What must Marya think, watching this fireball, leaking fuel incinerating the LEV, the Prodigal Child disappearing in a conflagration.

Somewhere a pump rattled. The engine went silent. Soman floated up in the cushion, scrambling for a restraint. Flip swore. Joni leaped for the control panel.

"Gotta reset!" The gaunt man shouted.

"That's what I'm doing, Dave," she screamed back. She jabbed a button with both thumbs and screamed, "Reset!"

No one breathed.

"Come on, reset," she pleaded.

Weightlessness was suddenly terrifying. Free fall short of escape velocity, the ship an artillery shell in parabolic trajectory, Earth's unforgiving crust seconds below. Involuntarily Soman curled into a ball, arms around his head.

A burble from below deck. The engine coughed. The ship shuddered. Then the sweet roar of igniting fuel. Thrust returned, pinning Soman to the cushion.

Flip grinned. "Damn, now I gotta re-calculate the burn." He looked over at Joni. "Hey, remind me to buy a new fuel pump when we get back, will you?" Flip laughed, Joni shivered.

Soman knew from Joni's face that there were no new pumps where they were going.

The ship staggered into orbit. Flip shut the engine down, the nozzle clanking as it cooled. Smit remained unconscious, strapped to his seat, twitching occasionally as if trapped in a bad dream. Flip huddled over calculations, then lit the drive again.

"Wait," Soman said, trying to raise himself from the cushion, thrust sucking him back.

Flip looked over.

Through pain and exhaustion, Soman tried to think. "Where...where are we going?" Wanting options, knowing there were none.

Flip's expression turned incredulous. "Where do you think? Home."

Soman looked out the viewport, listening to the rattling turbine, knowing it would shred the cabin if it flew apart. The ship rolled. Earth slid past, a brilliant starfield taking its place. Home. The moon. But...where was home for Soman. Home was...a place and time that no longer existed, unreachable, unrecoverable. After all the centuries, home was a thousand scattered memories. The expanse of prairie from the cockpit at thirty thousand feet. The house in Waterloo. Parents whose faces would barely come to mind. A screech of tires on cobblestone. The contents of Julian's antique chest. And in a tunnel deep under the ice, waiting in her descroid, someone who would call him Daddy.

Engine shutdown. Soman's limbs began to shake. He hugged himself, trying to stop the tremor, but it shook him as if the engine still thundered. He knew why—eighteen hours since the last meal. "Got a sandwich or something?" he asked, trying to sound casual.

Flip and the crew froze over their checklists.

Maybe there's no such thing as a sandwich anymore. "You know, something to eat. I'm st—." Their expressions stopped him. "Come on, you must have provisions aboard."

"Rations must be approved by the Council," Flip said.

Soman realized that the Monar never looked him in the eye. Even among themselves, they rarely made eye contact; they looked at each others' chests. Soman tried to remember what they reminded him of. Then it came: Jakarta. People crammed together, eye contact a violation of personal space. Until Ley depopulated the place.

Smit moaned. Joni pulled herself along the console rail and dabbed his oozing cheek. Smit turned and flashed Soman a venomous look.

For the first time Soman saw the injury to Smit's face, the left side swelling into an ugly bruise. "I'm really sorry," he said. "I thought you were an armed party. But I…really need something to eat." Hearing desperation in his voice, unable to quell it.

"It has nothing to do with that." Flip scanned his instruments. "I can't issue rations without approval. And I'm not breaking radio silence. That's the rules."

"Radio? What about the quan?"

"Quan?"

"You know…" Soman stopped. If it had to be explained, it was gone into the depths of time. They were back to using radio, tolerating the delay, the interference, the wide angle signal. No wonder no one heard *Sorcerer's* incoming hails. But hunger was insistent. "You…you'd be punished for giving me food?"

No one spoke. They studied the controls. He took in their emaciated bodies. "Are you all starving?"

Flip bristled. "We're fine. You're the one's way overweight." Then he added, "This mission's using a lot of energy. Fuel, food, heat, water, it's all energy. Everyone's on short rations because of you."

"Me? I didn't ask you to destroy my LEV!"

Flip pointed at Soman, making eye contact briefly then watching the floor as he spoke. "How'd you hide the program so long?"

"Huh?"

"That ship didn't spring up overnight. Where do you hide everything?"

"Hiding? I landed three weeks ago."

"Yeah, we spotted that. Pretty dumb, letting it sit there in the open. Engine problem?"

At Soman's empty stare, Flip said, "Come off it, we know you're Ikrit."

"No, my name's Soman."

Exasperated, Flip pulled out a clipboard. "Look, we both know the Altans can't build a ship like that. It'll go better for you if you tell the truth."

A kernel of fear kindled in Soman. *It'll go better for you.* Then he realized what Flip had called him—Ikrit. "Flip, Alta hasn't heard from Ik in years."

Dave and Joni exchanged a glance. For the first time, Flip had nothing to say.

"I'm from *Sorcerer.* Ever hear of—"

The Monar crew froze.

Soman swallowed. They knew.

"Don't give me that bullshit!" Flip shouted. "They've been dead a…" He faltered. "A thousand years."

"Three thousand, most of them," Soman whispered.

Flip's eyes narrowed. "I don't have time for fairy tales." He turned to Dave. "Come on. Gotta transfer that fuel." They disappeared through a hatch.

Soman caught Joni studying him, her head tilted slightly. She looked quickly away, eyebrows knitted in concentration. In the dark Soman nodded off, though he'd knew it might be dangerous to sleep. A sound woke him with a start. The crew were eating, each holding a small block of dark, crumbly material. Floating in front of them were globes of water, which they sucked from a nipple.

Soman's stomach lurched at the sight. His sore tongue stuck to the roof of his mouth. "How about water."

"As soon as you contribute," Flip told him.

Joni looked to Soman, then at her crewmates. She pushed off and glided his way. "Me first. You can go next—whoops—" She plowed into him with a tangle of limbs and hair; he grabbed her in self-defense. "Sorry," she said. She grasped his hand where he'd grabbed her thigh to keep from piling into the bulkhead. "This," she said, removing his hand, "probably violates some regulation. Anyway I don't know you that well yet."

Soman looked into her gaunt face, shocked how easily he'd wrapped a hand around her thigh with room to spare.

Flip guffawed. "Get fucked in space, you join an elite club."

"A club none of *you* will ever join," she shot back.

Everyone's attention on her scrawny ass, she pressed something into Soman's palm.

As she pushed away, he closed his fist over the chunk of green

In the tiny, ammonia-saturated head, Soman made the morsel last, a few flakes the consistency of pressed spinach, like eating air, leaving him feeling hungrier from the tease. He licked the last bits from grimy fingers. When he squeezed out of the urinal, Smit eyed him. Soman almost reached to brush off stray crumbs, stopping just in time.

Soman gave in again to sleep, unable to fight the lethargy of a second day without real food. Joni woke him in the dead of the sleep period to slip him another scrap, the cabin black, stars outside the port like fireworks. He grew weaker as his body digested itself, cell by cell, hallucinating that the ship approached Epsilon Eridani, the star grown huge and red, Ley waiting for him on a planet of volcanoes and smoke.

He woke to Joni shaking him. "Tell us about *Sorcerer*," she said.

Flip made a dismissive noise.

"Let's hear him out. It'll be easy to prove, one way or the other. We look for the ship."

Flip blinked. "We torched the ship."

Joni shook her head. "That's not how it worked. I looked it up. If he's really from *Sorcerer*, that was just his lander. The starship would be in orbit."

Soman dare not move. They hadn't found *Sorcerer*. Not yet.

Joni scanned her crewmates. "If there's an orbiter, we'll know he's not Ikrit."

Soman could understand how one bit of metal would easily go undetected, unless they deliberately trained the instrumentation on its orbital path. But the LEV's re-entry burn must have glowed like a nuke.

Flip turned to Soman with a half smile. "Okay, then tell us where the ship is."

Soman feared to say anything. Prove he'd been telling the truth, but expose the location of *Sorcerer*.

"There's no damn starship," Flip said.

"Flip," Joni said. "If he's Ikrit he wouldn't have come with us. He'd have waited there for someone to get him. And he knew this was an M620."

Flip considered, then looked at Soman. "Give us the orbit, then."

Soman shook his head.

"We'll find it. Just take longer."

Something occurred to Soman. "There was a light flash from Epsilon."

Now Flip looked at Soman steadily.

"You saw it, then?"

"We did," he said.

"Man alive," Joni said. "I told you." Then her face grew grave. "But the Council…this isn't good."

Flip shook his head. "Why did you come?"

"I…I had decided the Altans couldn't help me. Tomorrow I was going to launch and come looking for you."

Flip laughed. "Good thing we showed up. You wouldn't have survived that."

Joni asked, "Why look for us?"

Something told him not to evade. He left out nothing: Anoka, the mission, everything. He closed his eyes, exhausted from the effort, from the unaccustomed act of opening himself. "I was hoping, I mean…you must have a way to get down onto the ice."

Flip snorted. "You're kidding, right?"

Soman shook his head, weakly.

Flip spread his arms and laughed. "Man, you're lookin' at our entire air force here. Land this on the ice, we melt a hole to bedrock and drown."

Soman's gut knotted. How could it be—the Altans seemed to think the Monar were all-powerful, implacable, dangerous. When they had just this one ship, these puny commandos. Somehow the Monar had managed to terrorize the Earth through reputation and an occasional volley of missiles from a far limb of the moon.

All this time, all that risk, the ruination of *Sorcerer's* crew, and there was no one on Earth or moon who could reach Anoka. Soman tore the cushion from its restraints and hurled it across the cabin. He held weakly to the hatch handle, the Maro shutting him down, the Monar staring at him as the room blacked out. When Soman regained a sense of his surroundings, Flip asked, "What was that all about?" Too weak to answer, Soman watched the deck, its metal surface riddled with cracks.

An alarm beeped. Flip swung into his seat. "Okay, people, descent."

Joni heaved the cushion back at Soman and, hands trembling from starvation, he secured himself for landing. The bubble of Colony One grew. A horrible wreckage of ships ringed the dome—hulls split open, huge tortured chunks of ship scattered about. The rail launcher swung into view, curved like a scythe, gleaming. And piled beside it, needle-shaped projectiles stacked row upon row. "Those your missiles?" he asked Flip.

Flip didn't look up from the controls. "Yeah."

"High explosive tip from what the Altans tell me."

Flip turned to Soman, seeming to consider how much to say. Then he grinned. "Speed those things hit, you don't need explosive."

Soman looked again. Sure, those needle points were too thin to house a warhead. Then he noticed the colored pattern, lines of alternating bars that shimmered and changed as the Monar ship descended. Moiré pattern. Multiple layers. "Ablative coating?"

Flip nodded.

Preserve the maximum mass for the impact area. Their ship's a wreck, their people starving, but their weapons are top notch. Nothing had changed in three thousand years.

Within minutes the ship clanged home at the airlock. Flip donned a headset. Soman couldn't catch the words, only the terse tone as Flip bent over the console. Smit leaned close as if making certain Flip told the truth. Sounds outside the hatch. Clanging, tools on bolts.

Soman unstrapped and tried to stand. Despite all the loads he'd ferried to the moon, he'd never gone to the surface. Now he felt 1/6 gravity for the first time. Soman swayed, only the weak gravity allowing him to remain upright.

Flip's conversation ended abruptly. "We'll see," he said to no one in particular.

The hatch opened. A dozen people in black jumpsuits entered. The air wafting in with them carried a foul odor of unwashed bodies, human waste, and rotting soil. Soman's hollow stomach stirred. Monar surrounded him, hands clutching. He stumbled out of the ship and into dark corridors, firmly in their grasp.

Chapter 23

Soman lay in the cell, a basalt cave, small, cold and dark. The floor was too small to stretch out, so he curled into a ball. Cold soaked from the bare rock of the lifeless moon, hurtling a quarter million miles from Earth.

Dim light from a small grate high in the door revealed a pattern on the ceiling. Tool markings in the rock. Soman wondered about the man who'd done the work. Dead long ago, the Universe moving implacably on.

The little black-suited people had driven Soman from the cockpit of the M620, men restraining his arms, their leader clearing the curious from the path, gray gaunt peering faces. As Soman passed, a low murmur rippled through the watching Monar. A tiny round-eyed child peeked from behind a mother's leg. A teenage boy weighing no more than forty pounds snatched at Soman's pants, then ran off.

Their footfalls echoed through dim unlit corridors, traveling by the faint emanations of light from distant chambers, along tunnels of once-rough rock smoothed by centuries of hands rubbing past. The men wore miner's lights but flicked them on only in the darkest of corridors. Passing through airlocks with evidence of many repairs, the men handled the hardware with reverence, opening and closing hatches gently, working mechanisms with a delicate touch.

Soman assumed they were taking him to the Council. Then an abrupt turn, a dead-end, the low cell door already open. It took a moment for the realization to hit. Soman pulled up, dragging his escort to a halt with a sound of feet scrabbling against the unforgiving stone of the floor. "I want to see the Council," he said.

Grunting, the men strained to push the giant into his cell. The leader kicked the back of Soman's knee, and pitched Soman headfirst into the open cell door. The lintel struck him above the eye, drawing blood from an old, old scar.

Pressing his sleeve against the wound to stanch the bleeding, breathing the stink of three days in the same clothes, Soman moaned, imagining that moment when he'd stood between the LEV and the Monar ship. It had seemed the only choice.

The cell spun like a re-entry gone wrong, a swirl of regret. No one would ever know what happened. Soman thought of Selen, unaccounted for. What had she thought in her final instant; where did that thought reside now. And what of Anoka's short lifetime of thoughts, locked now in a frozen residue of nerve, a ghost of electrons.

Soman lost track of time: seconds, minutes, hours indistinguishable. Beneath the surface of the moon, encased in rock, the quiet was complete. Only the squirm and squabble of his body eating itself.

A noise. Soman raised his head. Footsteps approaching, the sound ringing though the silence like an alarm. A voice. Soman stood in a rush, striking his head on the ceiling, fresh pain from the gash above the eye. A man stood facing the door, the man who had marched him to the cell, who had kicked him through the door. Beside him, Flip studied his shoes, his eyes sad.

Flip looked up. "What happened to you?"

Soman touched the wound. "Not the welcome I expected."

The silence drew out. Finally the policeman spoke, maintaining his focus on the dull metal of the door. Reminding Soman of an old calculus professor who had lectured while looking at the floor, erasing with his left hand as fast as he wrote formulae with his right. Not very social here.

"The Council has decided," the man said.

Soman's skin prickled. "Decided? They haven't heard me yet."

The officer closed his mouth, then drew breath to start again.

Soman interrupted. "Flip?"

Flip rubbed the back of his neck.

The officer continued. "You are an enemy of the colony. You may not live here."

"I don't want to live here!"

"You entered the colony without permission."

"I just want to get back to my ship!"

"You constructed a vessel of war."

"I…" wanting to say more, anything to prevent the man from continuing the litany, from reaching the end, from ending any chance for rebuttal. But his voice trailed into incoherency.

"The penalty is death. The Council has decided." The man turned and walked away.

The words circled. Soman fought to stop them from penetrating. The buzz in his head grew. His knees shook. The words speared him clean and cold.

Flip rubbed his toe on the floor.

"You kill people without a hearing?" Soman's voice low and hoarse.

"Everyone's terrified."

"Terrified? Of one person?" Soman's fingers turned white on the ledge below the window.

"They figure you're Ikrit."

"What do you think?"

Silence drew out. Flip looked behind him. "Doesn't matter what I think." He turned back. "One of the leaf vats is fouled, has to be taken down…we're already on short ration because of fuel for the mission. Everyone's edgy."

"Edgy. *There's* a reason to kill someone."

"They almost destroyed us."

"Who?"

"You don't understand, do you?" Flip glanced down the corridor, listening. Everything was quiet. He turned back to Soman. "After The Disaster, the English speakers, you know, what was that country? Big one in North America."

Soman hung onto the bars. The United States beyond memory. He couldn't form the words.

"Anyway, they went south. Tried to move in and run the place. But there was a little backlash from the locals. I guess our ancestors weren't always so kind to their southern neighbors."

Soman held the window ledge to keep from sliding to the floor, picturing how Latin America would have responded to having the upper hand with the gringos after three centuries of exploitation.

"They hunted down anyone with white skin. Anyone speaking English."

No wonder a white guy from space asking for someone who spoke English had been suspect. Why Julian Weaver had passed himself off as mulatto, immortalized in stained glass as a dark-skinned prophet.

"The people with money grabbed whatever ships they could and headed for the only place that wasn't in chaos."

Soman tried to imagine what it must have been like, lifting off through toxic clouds, the world burning, heading for refuge in tunnels beneath the moon's surface.

"Colony Four had all the amenities. That's what saved One—we were the backwater, just mining and rail launchers. The systems at Four couldn't keep up. The new guys were used to unlimited air, lots of water, eating like pigs. They didn't want to cut back.

"There was a crisis at Four. People dying. Next thing you know, all the crawlers are headed for Three. And more ships from Earth. With all the extra people, the engineers at Colony Three figured out they had four days left. People eating their clothes, sleeping in toilets, waiting for a fucking miracle.

"There was a revolt. The Council at Three decided to send all the immigrants back to Earth. But the new guys had brought their guns—" Flip's voice grew venomous— "People dead, holes in the bubble, total fucking mess. And the guys who knew how to keep things running were dead. A compressor gives out and—" Flip made a slashing motion across his throat— "everybody's fightin' for the airlocks, just like at Four. But it was too far to One and Two for the crawlers, so now they're taking ships, leaving people behind to die."

Flip's eyes drifted into the distance, as if he could see the ships rising from the bleak lunar horizon. "That was Sunday morning."

"Well, our ancestors at One were miners and mechanics. They re-jiggered the rail launchers, and when the ships came into sight they warned 'em off, told 'em they'd be shot down if they tried to dock. Most of the ships slipped over to Two. The leaders at Two dithered around 'till it was too late. Big fight over dock C, and poof, the whole thing goes." Flip made an explosion with his hands. "Pieces of the dome scattered ten miles."

When Soman had spotted that blown dome in the telescope, he'd imagined it simply abandoned. War brought to the moon inconceivable.

Flip's chalky face splotched red.

"So first ship even looks like it might come towards One, those rail launchers hummed. Bam, knocked 'em out of the sky." Flip glared ferociously at Soman, his easy-going manner buried beneath this old outrage.

Soman understood. Eventually everyone gets into that spot where there's only one thing to do. Jump, fight, die, give up, whatever. Choose sides. Caught in the trap, you fight. Unless you wear the Maro. Shorter options list then.

A long silence, distant sounds of humanity drifting down the corridor, faint voices, brief laughter, the squall of a baby.

"You tell it like it happened last week," Soman said.

Flip looked up. "Every Sunday night, we hold a service. Starts any time now." He listened. "Well, they pounded the launch sites on Earth pretty good to make sure they couldn't keep coming. And whenever they spotted an airfield or anything that looked like one, they pounded that, too. Pretty much they've stopped trying. Once in a while we have to go down to check a suspect site."

Soman shook his head. "Surely the Earth is no threat anymore."

"Soman, the last barrage from the Ikrit was only forty-three years ago. That missile in '23 caught us by surprise. Near miss, they call it. Wasn't a miss for the people in the collapsed tunnels." Flip looked Soman in the eye. "A hundred thirty three of them. So we pounded them again, so hard we starved for a year. Then nothing for forty-three years, until a ship shows up in Alta. Nothing scares people more than Ik and Alta teaming up."

"No chance of that," Soman said. "The Altans throw up you even mention an airplane."

Soman was now truly afraid. These people, taught to hate from birth, taught to fear. Sunday night services honoring the dead for three thousand years. And still the skirmishing went on. It didn't seem possible.

Then Soman remembered: Protestant still fighting Catholic after how long, hundreds of years, most of them unable to say what the hell they were fighting over. Something about the Trinity. Tamil fighting Indian. Black fighting white. Hate learned as a child, reinforced in word and deed, justified in rituals like Sunday night services for the fallen. He pictured the women on the lawn of the shay, gazing rapturously at him, making the sign of the Hawk. They'd fight too, if the Maro didn't stop them.

He looked down at Flip. "Did you try to find *Sorcerer*?"

Flip shook his head. "Still looking. Our sensors aren't that good. Then again, we could be looking in the wrong orbits."

Soman hesitated only a second. Gave him the coordinates.

"Wish I'd known that before," Flip said, studying the wall of solid rock.

Soman watched him. "You believe me, don't you."

Flip traced a crack in the rock with his finger. "Doesn't matter what I believe."

"Doesn't the Council want to look at it, get the files, see what we found? You started out as our assembly station."

"The way they see it, as long as you're breathing, you're taking away the safety margin for everyone."

Soman's mind ricocheted around, searching for a way out. What could he gnaw off to escape. "Flip, think of all the gear you could use from *Sorcerer*. Two years' rations for twenty-three people."

Flip looked behind him. "Yeah, that'd be a shame."

A shame. The end of everything, summed up. The last Prodigal Child. Ambassador of Epsilon Eridani. Sole survivor of *Sorcerer*. Father of the last remaining child of the second millennium.

"I'm sorry. I really am."

Soman leaned against the bars. "How much time do I have?"

Flip scraped the floor with his foot. "Not much. After the service I guess. You, uh, use a lot of oh-two."

Soman's voice came out dry and rasping. "Flip, please, can you get me more time?"

What would it matter, an extra minute, an hour, a week. What to do with it. What purpose would it serve, that time, any time, a minute or a decade. Still we beg.

Flip moved into the corridor.

"Flip."

Flip stopped, turned.

"Tell me…how… how do they do it?"

Flip flashed a wicked smile. "They cram your ass out the airlock." And he was gone.

Soman hung at the edge of the tiny window, measuring it with his eyes, as if he might crawl out. His legs weakened, forcing him to kneel. Faces spun. Lorca, Rami, Moss. Siba, Ley, Cabot. Marya, Kolar. Horg. Images battered him. Wrecked ships littering the moonscape. Joni sneaking food. The night scene at Maracaibo. He replayed it, trying to make it turn out differently. The airlock. What would it be like. Well, he knew. Third time the charm.

Anoka. No one would ever claim her. She lay waiting without knowing it. How is that different than death. Or from life, for that matter, all the time spent submerged in the tedium of routine, in the striving, events and activities. Once in a while waking to a moment of clarity, pausing to look around, to the joy of it, and the terror. Watching the final moment approach, and what happened to all the rest.

Then he heard it. Barely louder than his pounding heart. He couldn't make out the words, only the sweet, slow harmony of the choir, rising to crescendo. Falling to soft and blended melody. To think these runty, mean, fearful people could make this music, the sweetest he had ever heard. It rose in multiple steps, one part chasing the other, sopranos soaring, until all joined in a wondrous, sacred climax.

Silence. Soman breathed raggedly. Sunday night in Colony One, the culmination of the weekly service, celebrating survival so many centuries ago. And the Council won't listen, fear and hatred learned from parents, and from parents before them, taught and hard-wired. The soft melody of peace too faint to hear without the Maro to still the noise. How would the Maro survive. The Altan's greatest advance made them incapable of defending it. Peace cannot be kept by force, it can only be achieved by understanding. Soman felt its unsolvable riddle. Those who use force never develop the understanding. Those who harbor peace cannot defend themselves. Einstein knew the truth, but he didn't know how to get there. The theoreticians always leave the proof to practical men. Practical men who trample the theory, mindless.

Muscles softening, Soman sank to the floor. What to do with this time. How did Rami spend his last minutes: ensuring the return of *Sorcerer*. Siba cared for Ley. Ley explored the planet, documenting to her last breath. How had they overcome the fear that paralyzes. Soman tried to imagine a noble act in his life, and found none. "God..." he moaned, unsure if he was about to pray. He felt around inside for a soul, any inkling of some part that could survive after vacuum tore open the flesh.

Footsteps. The cell door opened. Soman knelt, swaying. A man faced him. "Walk," he said, and pulled Soman to his feet. Darkness. Stumbling down the corridor. Soman tried to speak; someone quieted him. Feeling the importance of each second, time slipping away. They jumped around, these seconds; he couldn't focus on one long enough to use it, to savor it.

Through a hatch, into a large chamber. People watched from dim corners. A hand clamped over his mouth. He tried to twist free, lost his balance, and fell. Arms pulled. Silky black hair brushed his face. Marya. No, it couldn't be.

Another stumble. Hands pushing.

An airlock. He halted; someone barreled into him. Vision turning black.

Rough hands pushed him into the chamber.

The hatch closed, a crowd of people pressed close. A hiss of air. Soman gulped, unable to breathe, covering his eyes as if to stanch the eruption. The hissing faded to empty silence. A hatch slid open, Soman's stomach rising, body tightening.

The hatch clanged shut behind him.

Terrific noise filled his ears.

Chapter 24

A voice. A touch on the shoulder. Soman opened his eyes. A cabin like the aftermath of a plane crash, cushions and clothing and baggage, a mad detritus risen in weightlessness like ghosts of past missions. The hull crackling. A grimy pressure suit strewn across the control panel, one arm waving slowly, resonating to an unseen air current.

"Swallow." Worry lines crossed Joni's emaciated face. She broke off bits of greenbar and slid them past Soman's lips, lips shrunken and cracked. He swallowed. His stomach made gurgling sounds, like leaking fuel.

Torpor held him in a sluggish fog. Joni pushed in the last bits, a finger lingering on his parched tongue. She produced a water globe, and he sucked from its cool nipple. She worked a damp cloth on crusty seepage gluing his eye shut. He turned his head. Through the port shone stars, and he watched them with his good eye, a billion blazing globes so thick they disguised the dark of space, each burning toward some distant end, nova or collapse.

Nearby, a sound of disturbed sleep drew Soman's attention. Starlight reflected from the hairless skull of a little girl, entwined with a companion. She stirred, yawned, stretched, arching her back, small nipples pushing through her thin shirt, hands tapering to delicate fingers. A hint of roundness from waist to hip, a pubescent mound supporting the nipple; she was older than he'd thought, maybe twelve. Then she turned to face him, and Soman was shocked to see a woman's eyes, a woman's sorrow.

A sound. Flip working the console, panel lights flickering across his face. He tried to smile but managed only a thin grimace.

Soman couldn't make his tongue work, lost in the deep corridors of the Monar.

Flip said, "Hope we can find your ship first try—they didn't allow us any provisions. We're counting on yours."

Soman glanced at Joni. That greenbar.

Flip chuckled. "Our little thief."

"I was afraid you wouldn't last that long," she said.

He tried to push words up his throat. The attempt dislodged a plug of phlegm. A fit of coughing. He croaked, "We're going to the ship?" Unable to believe it could be true.

"That's the plan."

Soman knew what he should do: crawl into a descroid and let this pass over, give the world more time, take a rest from the agony of life in this millennium. The descroid less terrifying now. But wait. Orbiting between the Monar and the Earth. How safe would that be…and, "Why did you…?"

Flip said, "Ben's taking back a load of fuel while the rest of us start pulling out what we can use."

They were going to strip *Sorcerer*. The paw he'd been willing to gnaw away. He tried to sit up, but all four limbs had been secured with straps, tied to cleats beyond reach, pinning him to the cushion. He looked to Flip. "You going to let me loose?"

"When we get there."

Every way he'd turned since returning from Epsilon Eridani, he'd been restrained.

A hatch clanged and someone floated through. Soman tried not to stare at the horribly deformed nose and upper lip, a face sliced, melted, and abandoned.

"That's Ben," Flip said.

In a reedy voice, without resonance, Ben said, "I'll de takin' da shik dack."

Soman marveled that Ben could make himself understood at all, with no soft tissue covering his upper teeth and that tangled mass of cartilage at the center of his face like a collapsed building. "What happened to you?"

"Cance'," Ben said.

"I thought…you have a magshield."

"Fucking Ik missile in '23 took it out, Flip said. "Generator was in the west tunnels—yeah I see you know what happens when you work the moon for long without a magshield."

Soman turned to the bald woman. Even her eyebrows were gone, smooth and shiny ridges above large blue eyes. He'd seen that dry hairless skin before, the deep-set eyes, the flesh stretched tight over angular bones. "Cancer, too?" he asked.

She nodded.

Flip said, "That's Heather. And Michael's back there somewhere, oversleeping as usual."

"You sent sick people?"

"We weren't overwhelmed with volunteers. Joni recruited friends and family." Flip winked. "Wonder what she promised."

Soman looked around at the debris littering the cabin, at the decrepit ship holding back the suck of space. The Monar had so estranged themselves from Earth they had no idea that, two days' travel away, medicine existed to save Heather and Ben. The power of the idea lifted Soman from his torpor. Maybe he could end this. With peace between the Altans and Monar, there could be airplanes in this lifetime. A way to reach Anoka. They'd leave *Sorcerer* alone, let him retreat to the descroid for a few decades while the world progressed.

"Flip, we need to go to the surface first."

Sudden stillness in the cabin. Then Flip said, "We got exactly four days to turn Ben around with the fuel, or they crank up the rail and your orbiter is gone. A detour to the surface isn't in the schedule. "

Soman swallowed, calculating. The risk was huge. "We'll need an extra week. Say two weeks total until Ben gets back."

Soman heard mirthless laughter. A man stretched out on the nav seat. "Take two weeks, you're going down with the orbiter," he said. "Me, I'll be back at One." Soman recognized him from the party of Monar who had hauled him to the cell. Unlike the other Monar, this man had no reluctance to make eye contact, eyes hard and humorless.

"Meet James," Flip said.

Heather's companion pulled himself up behind her, his face puffy from sleep. Wrapping his arms around Heather, he squeezed. She leaned into him and smiled over her shoulder.

Soman's resolve strengthened. "I mean it. We can't dock without a transponder."

The room froze.

"And where we gonna find a transponder?"

"My lander."

Flip deflated. "We blew it up."

"We'll have to go back to the Colony," James said, watching Soman.

Soman tried not to show the chill that ran through him. Hadn't thought of that. Never looking away from James' fixed gaze, Soman said, "You only blew an engine. The transponder's in the bow." They wouldn't know about the leaking fuel, wouldn't have noticed the fire in the chaos of lift-off. "It can take a lot more bashing than you gave it."

Flip shook his head. "They'll kill us."

"They couldn't kill you if they wanted to. You know about the Maro?" Blank looks. How to explain that. Fatigue slowed Soman; the energy from the smuggled greenbar had already drained. Concentrate. Don't hold anything back or James'll have the ship heading back to Colony One. "There's another thing you need to know." He let the silence hang for a few seconds. "They can cure cancer."

Heather stirred, her mouth moving silently. Michael gripped her shoulder.

James said, "You expect us to believe that?"

"It's true. No one dies of cancer in Alta." Hope that's not an overstatement.

"It's a trick," James said.

Soman shook his head. "I'm too tired for tricks."

Joni watched him, her head cocked, just as she had after he'd claimed to have returned with *Sorcerer.*

Flip looked to Heather, then Ben. "What do you think?"

Ben was speechless. Heather said, "I'll go."

"Not so fast," James said. "I never volunteered for a drop to the surface."

"They'll never agree to an extra week anyway," Flip said. "But we need those supplies." He pulled on the headset, then hesitated. "I don't think we should mention the cancer thing. Only the transponder."

James grew angry. "You'd lie?"

Soman found himself agreeing with James. "You have to tell them. There's no way they could say no."

Joni spoke up. "No, I think Flip's right. They'll think it's a trick too. It's just too…you have to know the Council."

Flip squeezed his brow. "I think we'll leave it out for now." And then to James: "We have to go down for the transponder anyway. Let's not complicate it."

Tight-lipped, James looked Soman up and down. "How do we know that's even true?"

Soman looked James in the eye. "It's true." Thankful for such skill at evading, at withholding, at lying, practiced and honed over three millennia.

"I'm not falling for this," James said to Flip.

Flip watched James for a moment. Then he said, "On the orbiter, you're the crew chief. But on this ship, I'm in charge." He reached for the microphone.

Soman listened, eyes closed. Urgent explanations, long silences.

"—didn't know."

"…can't expect…"

"Okay, we know that!"

Flip signed off and there was a whispered conversation around the console.

"…put your life in his hands?"

"We already—"

"Far as we can tell, yes…"

"…telling the truth."

Soman opened an eye. Joni was looking at him. He met her gaze; she lifted an eyebrow.

Then quiet and dark as Soman slipped into unconsciousness.

Radio crackle. Soman opened his eyes, unable to tell how long he'd slept. Flip huddled over the panel, pressing the earpiece to his head, James and Joni listening in the pool of instrument light.

"…half tank if we take an orbit before the burn. That'd be four days with no supplies. Or we could burn right now and bring home a fuel reserve of, uh—" he glanced at a display. "Point two one. Almost empty."

Soman held himself still against an awful feeling. They'd discussed a new option while he slept. He almost blurted that he didn't need the transponder. But what would they do if they knew that was a lie, that he could lie so convincingly. Even if the lie might save two lives. No, three.

Flip peeled off the headset, leaving it hovering in their midst. They all looked drained.

"Well?" James asked.

"They'll let us know."

James raised his voice. "Let us know?"

"They're on the edge of losing the CO_2 ratio. Between the refueling and the extra oh-two for the ship…"

Joni's bony fingers clenched white on the edge of a seatback.

"They need that full tank. And…they have to figure out if there's enough oh-two for us right now."

James inclined his head toward Soman without looking at him. "There's sure not enough for him."

Flip chewed his lip. "Yeah, that's part of it. It would …" he looked at Soman.

A fist gripped Soman's heart. If the ship turns around—his eyes flicked involuntarily to the airlock. They wouldn't wait until the ship docked at One. They'd need every precious gasp of oxygen.

Flip saw where Soman was looking, and hurried on. "They may not be able to handle the six of us right now. Someone's calculating."

Joni held back tears.

Soman watched stars outside the port. Life hung on a calculation of O_2, of CO_2 ratio, a math of air and breath, life or extinction. He imagined the ship returning to One after spitting him out, halfway between the Earth and its estranged moon. The dust of Anoka crumbling bit by bit, her preserved thoughts and memories disintegrating, erasing her soul one atom at a time.

The ship rushed toward Earth, the crew watching the growing planet, ice and clouds so bright it hurt the eyes.

In the cabin only time moved—an hour, then two.

He drifted, semi-conscious. Dreams he couldn't fathom, dark shapes swirling.

A crackle of interference. Joni startled. Flip jumped to the com station, snatched the headset from the air.

James sat up, alert.

Flip listened. "Yes sir," he said.

From the corner of his eye Soman watched Flip remove the headset, the only motion in the ship. "There's not enough oh-two reserve. We get two weeks."

James sagged. Ben shrugged. Michael and Heather held each other.

Flip looked hard at Soman. "But they're loading the launcher."

Soman swallowed hard, imagining those needles lined up on the rail. It would only take one ripping through *Sorcerer* at supersonic speed. He couldn't even think about a brace of needles tearing into Alta. All they'd leave is a smoking crater. Worse than Jakarta.

Joni and Flip exchanged a glance. Soman knew they were imagining a different terror—the prospect of another drop into the merciless gravity of enemy territory. And suddenly doubts surfaced in Soman. He'd promised them it would be safe. But what of Ratoul, of Mordano.

Low Earth orbit. Brilliant white, blue, and green turning ponderously beneath them. Delicate fractal coastlines, the great blurred curve of the horizon unfolding fresh slices of planet each ninety minutes. Soman longed for its rich, thick atmosphere, for gravity, for sunshine, for swirling clouds and flying birds, damp and pungent soil.

Soman's turn at the radio. Five orbits before an answer to his hails. Seven more before Alta Central brought Marya. Her manner was cool. Explanations. Misunderstanding the words. Frustration. Pleading. Finally

Marya withdrew, deferring to Ratoul. Soman and the crew waited. Ten more orbits, fifteen. Another day lost of the two weeks.

A call from the surface. Ratoul and Marya. The Monar crew rigid at the sound of Ratoul's voice, steel and authority. Soman made his pitch, prepared during the hours of waiting. "Marya, tell Ratoul the Monar wanted to kill me, but some friends rescued me and we escaped." He squirmed against the restraints. Another lie. "Tell him we have no food, and we need to land."

The line went silent. When Marya came back, she said. "You may land, but not with Monar."

Soman didn't look around. "Marya, we're all in one ship. They saved me. We're starving. Please." Holding back the most desperate plea: let us land or they'll kill the Prodigal Child. That argument would send the Monar back. Tricky, the balance here.

Silence. They were going to lose the signal in a minute, the ship skimming through space above Alta.

"Tell Ratoul there are no weapons—" Soman turned to Flip and mouthed, 'no weapons?'

Flip glanced to the hold, then made the motion of turning a key. The weapons they'd use to prod one large Earthman out the airlock.

Soman turned back to the radio. "Tell Ratoul I have control of the weapons. Anyway, you don't understand, these people can barely walk in Earth gravity. They can't hurt you. And there are only seven of us." Soman looked at the chronometer. Thirty seconds until they lost the signal.

Marya's voice came up to them, tinny and crackling. "You ask a hard thing."

"Marya. Next orbit we have to land. Bring all the guards you want. And bring doctors and nurses. Please."

His only answer was a hiss of ions as the M620 plunged around the world.

At the edge of the atmosphere, turbulence tossed the craft. Soman fought vertigo, closing his eyes against the glare of the globe and the screaming air, as Flip fought a craft that had no business making another re-entry. Somehow he brought it safely down.

The Monar crew lay crushed in the cabin, barely able to lift their heads against the fearful pull of the planet. Soman opened the lower hatch. A breeze carried the pungent odors from the blackened ruins of the LEV. The bitter scent registered in the deepest folds of his brain, flooding him with melancholy.

Weak from starvation, Soman tottered down the ramp. On the hilltop clustered the largest assembly of oldens he'd ever seen. There must be two hundred men crouching behind vehicles. He held to the rail, willing his legs to keep him upright. Suddenly there was Marya, running from the center of the Altan forces, hair flying. Ratoul led a more decorous delegation in her wake.

Ratoul neared, eyebrow raised. He surveyed the scene like a general searching for the high ground. Soman recognized the word for enemy. Marya explained, "He says you bring our enemy."

Soman shook his head. "No. Trust me. They are just friends who need help."

"He says perhaps you have not chosen your friends wisely."

"He say and now you bring another ship. You place the city of Alta in danger."

Again Soman shook his head. "No, the Monar have agreed not to attack. In a week we'll be gone."

At this Marya looked sharply at Soman, an interruption in the translation that caught Ratoul's attention.

Soman said, "Well, they'll be gone. I mean, we'll make another trip to the ship in orbit..." Damn, this was getting too complicated. And Soman had no idea what the next move should be after the week was up. Claws of strain crept across his chest. He gestured to the ship. "We haven't eaten in days." Just the thought of it forced Soman to falter, dropping to a knee. "Two of them have cancer. I was...I'm hoping you can treat them."

Soman heaved himself back up. In desperation, he scanned the crowd. There, a familiar face. "Alla," he called out, "I have a patient for you."

Marya translated haltingly. Still no one would approach.

Soman limped down the hill and into the ship.

A collective gasp from the Altans as he emerged carrying Heather's skeletal form. He walked to Alla.

Alla backed half a step, looking to Ratoul. Ratoul watched but made no sign.

Soman said, "Her name is Heather."

Marya mouthed the name as if feeling its strange sound on her tongue. A breeze brushed strands of hair across her face. She looked at Heather; their gazes flickered over each other.

"Tell them," Soman said.

Everyone craned to listen. And a strange thing happened: Soman heard Marya's words and understood. The language of the new Earth was seeping in.

Alla spoke the name of their enemy, confused, the feared Monar represented by this invalid.

"Tell Alla that Heather has cancer. On the moon they have no cure. She is dying."

Heather swallowed with great effort, looking at Alla in terror and hope.

One by one the Altans turned to Ratoul.

Soman saw that Ratoul grasped the expectation in all those eyes. Finally he spoke. "We will take these Monar. For now. Then we will see." He crossed his arms and waited.

Soman offered Heather, and Alla took the burden.

Chapter 25

Soman reveled in the sensation of food in the belly, juices gurgling, stomach muscle writhing in pleasure. After two meals and twenty hours on the IV, vital fluids pumping into him, he hobbled into the corridor.

He found Ben first. Ben grimaced through drugged sleep. The doctors told him that Ben needed two months' treatment—the best they could hope in a week was remission. Cancer is not a simple disease. A cure is not a magic wand one waves. Ben must return for the remainder of the treatment. Soman watched Ben flattened to the bed by gravity, surgery, and pharmacology, Couldn't imagine him flying the Monar ship back in five days.

Heather lay in another room, limp under sedation, an arm encased in a machine that shot her with monoclones a thousand times a day. Michael sat vigil, stroking her other arm.

The other Monar finished their first meal on Earth. James, sniffing a slab of meat, looked up with distaste. Joni tasted a fruit, overcome by its sweetness, dripping tears and juice in equal parts. Flip grinned ear to ear as he sipped the first chowder of his lifetime. While they ate, propped in bed like scarecrows, Soman tried to answer their questions about the meal, the plants and animals used, how they grew and what they looked like. He could see them struggling with the concept of food from such a wide variety of sources—in the Colony, variety, such as it was, was manufactured from different algae.

The calories lulled the Monar to sleep, a sleep protected for the first time in their lives from the cosmic storm raging across the solar system, sheltered by a planet's magnetic field. As they slept, a steady stream of doctors drew blood, ran tests, analyzed chemistry, and pumped them full of medicine: hydration and immunization, vitamins, gamma globulins, minerals for depleted bone, hormones to stimulate cellular repair.

Marya peeked in the door. "You will come to the shay now."

Dozens of guards in beige stood at the hospital entrance. More sat in vehicles at the curb. Soman wondered what they'd been trained to do, what their Maro would allow. Perhaps there was a police version of the Maro, tweaked to give advantage in a struggle. The Maro programmed to recognize 'enemy', to allow actions prohibited within society. But where would that end. Within a society, the Maro appeared to work. But between societies, maybe there was no technology yet to replace understanding.

In the distance, lightning flashed, black storm clouds building against the southern mountains. He climbed into the olden, and once at the shay, fatigue claimed him.

Soman woke to unease, to a sense that a sound had stirred him. He glanced at the window. A breeze rippled the curtain, the light outside muted and diffuse, as if clouds surrounded the house. A dream chased him, just out of reach. A voice. A face. A conversation. He looked more closely. There on the sill, a scuff of dirt. His scalp prickled.

It had been no dream. Horg had visited him in the black of night.

He had looked up from the confusion of sleep, Horg touching shoulder, a finger to his lips.

"We watch," Horg whispered. "We thought you left us."

Soman swallowed a thick plug of sleep. "I did."

Horg leaned close. "You will come now? We must go before—" Horg glanced at the door. Dim light shone from the hallway, in the quiet before dawn.

Soman thought about the Monar and their faceless Council. About Ik, destroyed. People ready to fight and die for some belief, some fear, a perceived slight or a petty difference. Soman raised up on an elbow. "Is everyone like you, Horg?"

Horg's brow knotted.

"In your group, out there wherever," Soman waved a sleep-heavy arm toward the window. "Is everyone happy, living secretly in the outback?"

Horg looked blankly back at him.

"Or are there hard people. Angry people."

Horg gulped. "I…we have all people. People with…different skills."

Soman grabbed Horg's shirt with both hands and pulled him close, their noses almost touching, Horg leaning back. "Horg." Soman said, increasing the pressure. "We need the Maro. Without it, we'll keep killing each other."

Horg's eyes grew large.

"I'll come see your gang. But I'll tell them what I just told you. Go find out if they still want me." Soman let go. Horg scuttled back, breathing hard.

"Someone has what seems like a good idea, and before long people are fighting over it. Along the way it stops being just a good idea and starts to become a cause. Then we're all in trouble." Soman pointed at

Horg. "Can't you see where it's going to end up?"

Horg looked down.

"Someday people will die for it." When Horg said nothing, Soman asked, "Are you ready to die over the Maro? Is this what you teach your children?"

For the longest time Horg didn't move. In the distance an owl hooted. The breeze billowed the curtains into the room. Finally Horg stepped to the sill and disappeared.

Soman remembered Horg's expression: despair. He rose from bed, showered off the grime of Earth and moon, and walked down the stairs to face his deadline.

It was already afternoon; he'd slept another twenty hours. Marya brought food, and Soman ate. Eggs and meat, the taste of protein cramping his mouth, so hard did glands pump out saliva. Bread, fruit, coffee. Exquisite. A few curious members of the shay drifted past, peering with astonishment at the mountain of plates and bowls.

Finally sated, he asked Marya to walk with him. He peeked out the door into a thick afternoon fog that rolled in from the harbor, and he breathed a sigh of relief; no worshipers present. They strolled, shivering, tendrils of chill mist creeping into their clothing. The rustle of their feet the only sound in the dead air.

"I met a man last night," Soman said.

"Which man?"

"A stranger. He came to my room."

A tightening in her face. "A stranger?"

"He came from far outside the city. He had no Maro."

Marya gasped. "Why did you not call for help?"

"I was in no danger."

"I am so sorry."

"You decided I didn't need to know."

She dropped her eyes. "The Calayan," she said in a whisper.

"He wants me to visit."

"Of course not!"

"They want me to encourage their people. They see me as a spiritual leader. Their... prodigal son."

Marya turned away. "You make fun of me!"

"No. I see a similarity. He takes his beliefs as seriously as you take yours."

"They have no beliefs," she hissed.

"Of course they have beliefs. They're just different than yours."

Marya's face showed shock. "You will join them?"

"No. Three thousand years, and people are still fighting. I'll die, you'll die, and it will still be the same."

"What did you tell him?"

"I told him everyone needs the Maro."

Marya smiled. "Did he believe you?"

"I think so." Soman looked into the mist. Did he believe it himself.

She bowed her head. "You are wise. Something good will start from it."

Soman shivered in the damp air, recalling Horg's parting expression, shaking off a sense of dread.

At Ben's bedside, Soman watched the monitors, remembering his own recovery in a room like this. The doctors had tapped Ben's bones and seeded his marrow. The seeds multiplied and spread through him, identifying the cancer, perhaps ripping off its telomeres. Ben sank into the hospital bed like a country at war. Pain and gravity bore down on him.

Soman entered Heather's room. Michael stood beside a chair, lifting one skinny arm over his head, then the other, then both, grunting from the effort. Regaining his breath, he lifted a foot from the floor. Then the other foot, straining, jaw locked, neck tense. He collapsed into the chair. "I have to build my strength," he said, breathing hard. "We're staying."

Soman frowned. What would the Council think of that.

"We were married six weeks when Heather got sick. She got a treatment, but it only gained her a few months. We don't know anything compared to these people." A hint of anger in Michael's voice. "We had always talked about exploring one of the other colonies, maybe helping start one up, until she got sick. So when Joni came to us about salvaging your ship, we figured, why not." He squeezed Heather's hand. "But now she has a real chance. She needs her food and medicine. If we leave…well…it seems safer here."

Soman watched Heather sleep. What a stunning woman she'll become. A young wife, the chance for a fresh start in a new place.

Michael resumed his training.

Marya burst into the room, breathless. "They found a man sleeping by the water. A man with no identification and no shay." Her eyes fixed on Soman. "And no Maro."

"Where is he?"

"At the police—"

"The police?"

Marya nodded, catching her breath. "Removing the Maro is a crime." She tugged him out the door. "You must tell us if it is the man."

Ratoul met them at a desk manned by two bored men in beige suits. What must police life be like in a city with the Maro. Complaints about barking dogs. Lost children. Cats in trees. How thoroughly he had stirred everything.

They followed Ratoul to a small room, two men standing outside, one in official beige, one in private clothing. Shoulder clasping. A hurried conversation too fast for Soman to follow. Marya pulled Soman to the door of the room. Soman peered in. There sat Horg, head in his hands. He turned to Marya. "That's him."

Murmurs from the police. Marya began to pull Soman away.

"No. I want to talk to him."

The hallway grew clamorous; Ratoul, the jailers, and Marya all talking at once, Soman grasping only the stray word. Ratoul was pointing vigorously at Marya. Marya in turn had a grip on the man in plain clothes, gesturing with her free hand. But even at the height of argument, Soman noticed the discipline, the edge of civility worn like a comfortable suit of clothes that kept the Maro within the confines of its thin disk. Altans quickly learned to argue without taking it too far. Soman reflected that he'd known many people with such self-discipline; it didn't require a Maro. But the Maro made the skill universal. A stunning evolutionary advance for a race driven for thirty thousand years by the hair-trigger responses of hunter and hunted.

With the Altans preoccupied with their debate, Soman stepped quietly to the door and slipped in beside Horg. "How are you, my man?"

Horg smiled like a puppy dog. But his face quickly fell as the door opened and the clamor burst into the room.

"Quiet!" Soman shouted, rewarded with shocked silence even if they didn't understand the word.

"What happened?" Soman asked Horg. "Did you take back my message?"

Horg looked down. "I could not."

"Why?"

"I failed."

"No, you didn't fail. Just tell them what I said."

Horg shook his head. "They will think…that I…"

"That you agree with me, is that it?"

Horg nodded.

"And they won't want you to tell the others what I said."

Another miserable nod.

"Why not just tell them I'm ready to visit, go back and play it safe."

Horg sighed in resignation and looked at Soman with a hangdog face.

"You can't lie like that, can you?"

Horg shook his head. "They would know."

Soman shook Horg's shoulder. "Horg, you're a good man. I'll help you." Soman glanced over his shoulder to the gang in the doorway. "You're in a bit of trouble here."

Horg nodded.

Soman stood and said to the Altans, "This man is my friend." No one moved. "Marya?"

"Oh yes," she said, and translated. Astonished looks from everyone. An arched stare from Ratoul at this new choice of friends.

"He will receive a new Maro, yes?" All heads nodded. "Good." Soman turned to Horg. "Just now I have to take care of my crew. I'll come back for you."

In the hallway, Marya told him that Horg faced years in prison.

"What good will that do?"

"It is the law."

"Give him his new Maro and let him live in peace."

Marya shook her head as she translated. Then Ratoul and the beige suit harangued Soman together, not waiting for Marya. When Soman got them to stop, Marya explained. "The Maro is so important we must not let this violation be without punishment," she said. "People must know it will be so."

Soman shook his head. "Do you want the Calayan to come back and take the Maro again?"

Marya nodded.

"Then you must have an amnesty."

At Marya's blank look, he said, "You must let the Calayan take a new Maro without punishment so they will want to come back. If they know they face prison, they will never come."

The policemen dismissed this idea with both hands. Ratoul looked at Soman as if *he* were the criminal. "You do not understand," Marya said.

"Your intolerance is no different than the Calayan's!" Soman shouted. And another thought occurred to him. "Who says they all need a Maro anyway?"

Marya, looking horrified, glanced at Ratoul.

"What about people whose chemistry is balanced, who learn civilized behavior in the shay." Finally Soman made sense of his tangled feelings about the Maro. It was an amazing advance, but requiring it of everyone was a mistake, the mistake of most societies who try to force everyone to live their lives in the mainstream, legislating the path instead of the outcome. "You're as bad as they are," he said. "You force the Maro on everyone. Who cares if you have a Maro or not, as long as you behave. No wonder some people want to take it out."

Marya gasped. "They have broken the law."

Ratoul watched the exchange.

Soman said, "Tell them what I said."

"I will not!" And then Marya seemed to remember who Soman was; conflict crossed her face. A Prodigal Child challenging a fundamental precept of Altan society. She spun away, her heels clicking down the corridor.

He gathered equipment from the LEV for transfer to the Monar ship, asking Kolar to ride along so he could practice speaking Altan. The LEV was burnt black on the outside, but its heat shield had protected the cabin. Kolar poked around in the gear, asking about the function of salvaged parts, helping ease the transponder from its enclosure. Soman would use it rather than *Sorcerer's* manual entry hatch, to conceal his lie from the Monar.

Soman's vocabulary grew, and he gained the confidence to ask Kolar, "Are you a member of the Church?"

"At one time I was a member."

"What happened?"

Kolar spoke slowly, separating the phrases, using simple words to help Soman understand. "I did not find what I needed there."

"So now you work in the government."

Kolar shook his head. "I was in the government." He smiled. "I did not find it there either."

"What are you looking for?"

"A man my age," he said, scratching his chin. "And still I do not know." He grinned. "Once I find it, then I tell you."

Soman lugged the transponder to the hatchway. How fortunate, in a way, were the people driven by a purpose. Make babies. Write a book. Explore a new continent, a new world. Add to Mankind's knowledge. Burying themselves in life without pondering its ending, all that rushing about leaving no time to ponder. He looked at Kolar. Calm Kolar who seemed not to be caught up in all the striving, all the deception. Better find what you search for soon, old man.

Marya arrived with a warm meal. Soman and Kolar took a break from struggling with language and fell back on Marya. "He asks what you will do once the Monar ship has returned."

"I suppose it depends on how the Monar react to Ben's return."

Kolar shrugged. "History is not hopeful with the Monar."

Soman's appetite was fading. The Monar, like rotten fruit, ruining a good meal. Suddenly he stopped. "Marya. Can you make an appointment with Ratoul? I have an idea."

"Yes. But please do not talk again about am-ness-tee for the Calayan," she warned as she gathered up the leftovers. Soman looked at the food they were about to discard. Wouldn't that be a novel concept for the Monar: leftovers.

An hour later she returned to fetch Soman for their appointment. Through Alta they traveled once again, ending at a plain stone building of five stories. City Hall, Soman supposed, though it lacked the usual acre of stone steps and the Greek columns. He thought it a mark of good sense. In this new world, people didn't spend their wealth so foolishly.

But inside, Ratoul's office was another story. His enclave oozed the grand style of city politicians. The centerpiece a sumptuous wood desk with a view of the harbor. One corner a library, floor to ceiling shelves, study tables, soft chairs. And real books. How much must they be worth, in a city where no one displayed books. Behind the desk, Ratoul towered over them. Ratoul, master of the language of power. Soman settled back into the soft cushions, and began. "I think we've made a start at improving relations with the Monar."

Ratoul's mouth twisted as Marya translated. His reply was curt. "We do not wish for relations with the Monar."

Then Ratoul asked a question, his eyes boring into Soman.

"He asks if you are their ambassador."

Soman frowned, hope for success fading. "I just find myself in a position to help." Soman glanced between Marya and Ratoul, then leaned forward, struggling out of the cushions. "So I had this idea. We pack the ship with supplies. Food, medicine, whatever. It's a chance to turn an enemy into a friend." It had seemed like a good idea, before sitting in Ratoul's daunting presence.

Ratoul laid his palms on the rich grain of the desk, leaned forward and spoke.

"He says you ask him to feed his enemy so he can attack us again."

"That's just it. I don't think they *will* attack again. It will change everything. We can change everything."

When Ratoul next spoke, Marya remained silent. Ratoul glared at her. They exchanged words. Finally Marya nodded in submission. "I will not tell you what he said. Perhaps you should act angry."

"We're even, then," Soman said, remembering their argument over Horg.

But Ratoul had grown distracted. He studied his hands for a moment, eyes distant. Then he rose abruptly and walked to the window. He stood there for a full minute, looking out.

Soman questioned Marya with his hands. She motioned for him to remain silent.

When Ratoul spoke, Marya sat up in her chair. "He asks what kind of food."

Soman looked from Marya to Ratoul, then leaped into the silence. "Bread. Vegetables. Some of those fruit you gave me."

Ratoul turned from the window and addressed Marya.

She flashed Soman a look of triumph. "Ratoul says he will make the arrangements."

Soman knew he should feel pleased with this success, but somehow Ratoul had stolen the pleasure from it.

Six days left. Supplies began to move to the Monar ship. Soman expected Ratoul to change his mind. Instead Ratoul participated, overseeing workers, selecting foods. Ben's incisions healed; he sat up in bed and ate solid food. Soman marveled at the medical technology that could tear a man apart and piece him together in under a week. The doctors bragged to Soman on their progress, then wagged their fingers; Ben needed more time.

Four hours to launch. Everyone had prepared their personal things, ready for transport to the ship. Final medications, exams by the doctors. Ben, Joni, and James already picked up by an olden, Kolar assisting them. Soman talked with Flip as they waited for their ride to the ship. Just small talk, distracted, knowing Marya would arrive within minutes and they must hold a difficult conversation.

She burst through the door, streaming tears. "It's Horg," she wailed.

"What?"

She collapsed against him. "Horg is dead."

"No." Not dead. Impossible. The Altans must have implanted thousands of Maro—millions. It should be routine.

"Someone…oooohhh."

Soman supported her as her legs faltered.

She managed a breath. "They cut his new Maro from him. Blood was everywhere…" With her wail, Soman felt her horror soak into him.

She clutched him. "They placed his Maro in his mouth and…"

Soman grew dizzy. "Who would do such a thing?" Were the Altans that afraid of the Calayan. Could someone fool the Maro for a few violent seconds.

"A note on his chest. It said, *We will not live with the Maro.*"

Finally Soman understood the look on Horg's face that night. Soman never imagined that Horg needed protection from his own people. But Horg knew the Calayan. *We are independent.* No they weren't. They simply lived under a different dogma—a more dangerous one. When would the Calayan and the Altans learn that true freedom meant having a choice, not imposing your self-righteousness on others. Soman leaned his head against the wall. No time to think. No time to bury Horg. The ship must launch. Now.

Except—Soman took in Marya's haggard face. It was a terrible time to do this, but it couldn't wait. He just couldn't let her… "Marya." He held her shoulders, fragile in his hands. "I think you know this already, what I must tell you."

Her eyes welled with tears.

"I am no Prodigal Child. I am just a man. A man searching for his daughter. I left her in a descroid, up in the north. Vawere was no prophet. He was my friend. I don't know why he did this, what he did."

He glanced back at a movement, Flip emerging from the doorway, herky-jerky, legs bending this way and that as he made his agonizing way toward the olden.

Marya streaming tears.

"I'm just a person struggling to get my daughter back and to…" The rest was just too complicated for right now. Watching her fall apart, he was making a terrible mess of it.

Flip drew near.

"Marya…" His voice almost pleading. She stared through the side of the building as if it wasn't there, as if Soman and Flip were ghosts. Flip shuffled up, and almost stopped. One look at Marya's face and he kept going, forcing his muscles through the thick gravity of Earth.

"Mordano is right," Soman said when Flip had passed. "I have no message from God. I don't want to hurt you, I just—"

Flip hollered from the olden.

Marya walked away.

Soman's hand trailed along her arm. "I..." he stopped. The most ridiculous thing he could add was 'I love you'.

Soman ran to the olden. As it accelerated toward the ruins of the ancient spaceport, Flip said, "Quite a way you have with women."

The rocket thundered; blue sky faded to the dark of space. The nearly full moon loomed from the eastern rim of the world. Soman couldn't take his eyes from it, fear stirring, pushing him back in the seat, drying his mouth. The Monar would cut up *Sorcerer*, disassemble it, strip it clean. In that moment he hated the Monar. He wanted to see the Council hauled to Earth, a Maro implanted in every one of them. And Soman began to understand the mechanics of hate. It starts with fear. Fear to hate; such an easy step. Such a hard habit to break.

Someone had to break the habit, stop the cycle. Soman thought about Ratoul. An unlikely peacemaker. Soman closed his eyes, thinking back to Ratoul's change of heart, from denying their landing to sending a mercy mission. It felt miraculous. But Soman didn't believe in miracles.

Chapter 26

Five forms clustered around the Nav one holo. An image floated among them, the moon of the second planet of Epsilon Eridani.

The old pang stabbed Soman. All those crewmates in their shrouds orbiting, silently, eternally. A sound slipped from him.

Joni touched his cheek. "Ghosts?"

He didn't believe in ghosts.

Flip moved around the holo, studying the image from every angle. "You wonder who built it, and what it's for. Someone needs to go back." He glanced at James. "Nothing against the colony, but what I wouldn't give to see that."

James said, "We have a job to do."

Soman looked around the cabin. *Sorcerer* looked as decrepit as the Monar lander, with good reason—they were the same age. Still, it was all the ship he had, and soon it would be stripped to its bones. Unless Ben's run home started something. To James he said, "Can't we wait a bit before we start dismantling?"

James said, "We've got our orders."

"But we don't know what might happen when Ben gets back. They might want to—"

"They'll eat that food and be ready for more. We'd better have it ready. And we're short crew. Fucking Michael." James climbed out of his seat and hobbled toward the hatch, growling to Soman "And find a way to turn this damn gravity off."

"I don't like it any more than you do," he said to James for the fifth time. "But I was the LEV pilot, not the mechanic. It just comes on when there are people aboard." It does now. Took him three minutes on his imcom to program that, as they waited for the transducer to synch the entry hatch.

James fixed Soman with a hard stare.

What new malfunctions could he stage to keep the crew occupied for a few days. A little more time for the supplies Ben carried to reach the Colony, for news of his surgery to spread.

A frozen bay two airlock slowed them, its random recurring decompression alarm keeping everyone on edge, forcing frantic, breath-eating suit drills, robbing them of sleep and disrupting the schedule moving stores from galley to LEV bay. Despite the fact he'd arranged it, Soman couldn't stop his heart from hammering whenever the alarm went off.

Radio, microwave, ultrasonic channels were all open, set to pick up any signal from the Colony. But from the moon, silence.

A pile of rations accumulated in bay two. Soman tried to persuade James that the most valuable of *Sorcerer's* possessions was its damaged LEV. Repair it and you double the space fleet of the Colony.

James appeared tempted. He studied Soman, the gears turning. Finally he said, "Not yet." James must have figured out that Soman was a greater risk with a working LEV aboard.

Soman woke to pounding on the cabin door, James demanding he come to B deck. And there they were, all the Monar, halfway into an electrical enclosure, sweat dripping, food forgotten. Soman slumped against the bulkhead—they'd discovered the ship's magfield generator. Joni glanced up, wiping sweat from her forehead, leaving a slash of grime across her brow. "This has got to go with the first load," she said. She pointed an ancient vom clip at a tangle of wires terminating at a junction block. "I need help with this disconnect—don't want to fry anything, like me for example."

He knew exactly how to disconnect the generator. But without it, the ship was useless for a voyage beyond the planet's magnetic field, billions of cosmic rays tearing up the DNA. A point of no return for *Sorcerer.* The starship would no longer be a starship, just an expensive, beat-up orbital station. He looked from Joni to James, his mind racing.

James eyed Soman unrelentingly. A long silence. His gaze on Soman intensified. "Go ahead. You're the one doing the disconnect. Anyone fries, might as well be you."

All at once an alarm clanged. James jerked around. "What now?"

Soman flicked in and brought up the alarm panel. There: IR spike detect. "There's been a launch from Colony One." Damn, coming for the first load. He pictured *Sorcerer* stripped empty, a cavernous hull holding nothing but echoes. Then something struck him: when the Monar were done, they wouldn't bring him to the Colony, and they'd never waste fuel dropping him back to Alta. He'd end up circling with *Sorcerer,* derelict two hundred miles above Anoka until friction pulled him and the starship screaming back to Earth.

Flip tried to raise the ship. Silence on all frequencies.

James marched them all back to the magfield generator. By the time it sat in the tube awaiting a full crew to muscle it down to LEV bay, the

Monar were exhausted. While they grabbed a couple hours' sleep, Soman slipped down to Bay Two, locked the hatch against entry, and started work on the damaged LEV, confronting the magnitude of the work to be done; he could never complete the job alone. Then he heaved himself up and went to work.

The next day they received a transmission from Ben. "Docking tomorrow." Nothing more.

Soman hunched over the console in Nav One. He'd formed the outline of a plan. Wait until the crews were all at work tearing apart *Sorcerer*. Turn spingrav up to 1.5 gees to flatten the Monar. Take the M620 to Alta. Surely the Monar won't send a barrage to Alta and risk destroying their only ship. It would be a standoff, unless they had another ship hidden away somewhere.

There were nagging problems though. Overcoming the guards they would certainly leave on the lander, and what weapons they might have. Maybe stage an emergency. Soman stole into the Nav tube, his mind working furiously. Avoiding the Monar, he moved supplies to his cabin. A bit of food, spare clothing. Electronics he might need later. At the last minute he added a pressure suit and helmet. Soman's stomach turned. Hope it doesn't come to that.

Then the Monar ship floated outside LEV bay. Soman told James, "I'll go down and start evacuating the bay, so we can open the outer door."

"Just blow it," James said.

"No!" He would need that air later. Hearing the vehemence in his voice, Soman stopped, fearful that James suspected his plan. "We don't have that much air. It's only fifteen minutes to pump to storage, and we save four thousand cubic meters. Never know when you might need it."

James assented. Soman heaved a deep breath.

The Monar ship nosed its way into the bay like a large dog, gently captured on pinions. Climbing the crane, Soman rapped on the airlock hatch. The mechanism made grinding sounds, and the hatch cracked open. It swiveled with a creak. There floated Ben, gray-faced. Soman's stomach turned at the smell spewing from the hatch. Behind Ben hovered many faces, thin and frightened, more people than the ship should hold. They peered around the edge of the airlock, floating and twirling.

"How many do you have in there?"

"Twenty-one."

"They must have been crushed!"

"No choice."

Soman blanched. Twenty-one more people take apart *Sorcerer*.

Ben said, "Get 'en out of heah."

The newcomers settled into the lounge, wolfing down Soman's millennia-old supplies while staring with trepidation at the huge Earth in the terminal screens.

Ben watched them eat. "When a child is naughty, 'e say he's thinking ackles."

Soman frowned.

"Apples," Joni said. "We know it's sinful, that food. We complain about the crap we eat, but we don't want anything to do with apples."

Ben stared into the distance. "Until 'e held an ackle."

There hadn't been any actual apples in the shipment, but the Monar had forgotten so much that to them, any fruit was an apple. Soman felt a trickle of hope, recalling the Amish from his childhood, swallowed up when they could no longer stop the flight of their children to the society surrounding them. The Monar had maintained their culture with a physical separation the Amish would envy. But maybe a crack had just opened…

Joni offered water to a woman unable to muster the strength to drink by herself.

Ben continued. "Had a wiot outside the ai'lock. Had to get out ext'a gua'ds. Woulda to'n the shick ahart. Council cut the O_2 to slow it down."

Joni brought a damp cloth for the woman and laid it across her forehead.

"And then they hea'd adout my cance'. You 'ight, Sonan. All a sudden, a lot wanted to go to Ea'th. All those kids with leukenia? Sixty 'equests in an hou'."

Joni applied the cloth to the woman's neck, then peered down her blouse and looked up in alarm.

Soman said, "But wait. These are all adults."

Joni moved about the room, pressing a hand to foreheads, her face knitted in worry.

Ben said, "The Oh-two consuntion inc'eased two ke'cent the second day."

"Did you say two percent?" James asked.

Ben nodded.

James whistled. "That would be catastrophic." He looked at Soman. "There's no way to generate that much extra oxygen. No wonder they crammed the ship with so many, and adults use more oh-two."

Ben nodded again. "Then all sent to qua'tes and wations cut."

Soman interrupted. "They punished the colony for using too much air?"

James glared at Soman. "Standard policy to reduce metabolism. Everyone resting in quarters and no digestion going on, you get a tick down in oxygen consumption."

"Oah the 'ood they ate. All those ackles."

Soman nodded. Sure, that rich food, the first square meal of a lifetime. Whose metabolism wouldn't rise.

Laying a hand on a woman's forehead, Joni said, "She's burning up." The woman's head lolled limply, sparse hair matted to her forehead, her eyes red and bloodshot, crying out every time she blinked. "These people are sick. Almost everyone has a fever. No wonder their metabolism went up."

Soman peered around the room at the dazed and listless Monar, and felt a spark of hope. This crew wouldn't be tearing apart *Sorcerer* any time soon. And no one was guarding the Monar ship.

"And look at that rash." She pointed at the woman whose blouse she'd opened. A patch of rosy, spotted skin spread across her throat and down her chest. From the corner of her eye trickled a rivulet of blood.

Soman backed down the tube. He casually adjusted a shoe strap, glanced back. No one following. He began a mental list. Pressure suit. Helmet. Uplink transponder. Airframe design files. What else. Think. Speeding up, he reached the nex. His eye fell on an old streak on the bulkhead. Bloodstain—from his wrench, just after clearing this nex and braining three crewmen. Soman crouched there for a long time. Thinking about Flip and Joni, what they'd done for him back at the Colony. "Goddamn!" he whispered. Then dashed toward Nav One.

The radio operator in Alta center couldn't raise Marya. Soman checked the chronometer. The wee hours. "Keep trying." Then back to the lounge. "Joni, let's move the sick into quarters, keep them away from the rest." Soman placed a hand on his forehead, feeling for any sign of fever.

Joni said, "They're all sick. Everyone off the ship has a fever except Ben. Eighteen have the rash. A dozen have nosebleeds, and I've got two bleeding from the rectum." Lowering her voice, she said, "And come look at this." She led him down the corridor to the clinic, joints jerking and straining, breathing hard. But already she was walking better. Spingrav wouldn't stop the Monar for long. He forced away the mental image of the unguarded ship in Bay one, fueled and ready, stilled the voice that said *run for it.*

A woman lay on a gurney, moaning when Joni turned her head for Soman to see. Her eyes shone solid red. Blood dribbled from both eye sockets. Joni bit her lip. "We have to do something, fast."

Soman's auton came to life. Kolar, clearing his throat of sleep, mumbling asides to someone nearby. Soman strained to hear Kolar above the coughs and moans as Joni and Ben moved everyone toward quarters. "Where's Marya?"

"What do you want?" Kolar asked.

In a rush Soman explained the situation in his rudimentary Altan.

Kolar was silent for a moment Then he said, "I will bring a doctor."

Soman headed back to Nav one, unzipping his flight suit to search for signs of rash.

Finally the radio crackled. Kolar, fully awake, urgency now in his voice. He leveled questions from the doctor, unable to translate but at least simplifying the language: symptoms, timing, details of vomit and blood, fever and pain. Joni appeared, and Soman grabbed her to help with answers. The queries grew more detailed, and Soman sensed that the doctor approached an answer.

"Do you or the Monar who were on Earth have this sickness?" Kolar asked.

"Not yet," Soman told him. He felt his forehead again. It seemed warm.

"The doctor thinks it is the bleeding fever."

"What's that?"

"A virus. A very old one."

"Are we going to get it next?"

Kolar spoke to the doctor in hushed tones.

Soman's balance faltered. They might have brought this disease to the moon—the sin of the conquistadors, delivering plague to a virgin population. Isolated from Earth's germs for thousands of years, the Monar must have no antibodies to the diseases of Earth. Or maybe it came with the supplies. What a brilliant idea—take fresh food. Why didn't someone think of that. Ratoul, who was always so cautious, so calculating. But then Soman stopped. Food didn't carry viral disease, animals did. The worst you could get from food was diarrhea. How the hell...and he remembered Ratoul's refusal, his turnaround.

Kolar spoke. "The doctor says you have been inoculated."

"How long do they have?" he shouted to Kolar.

"Treatment must begin within two days after symptoms appear."

"All right, we're in time. I think the symptoms have just started." Unless a jump in metabolism counts. "Okay, we're bringing them down."

By the next orbit, the ship was ready to drop for re-entry—re-fueled, the worst of the vomit cleaned up. Still, there was a stench in the small cabin that Soman feared could never be removed. He tried, in a rushed five minute session, to teach Flip how to maneuver *Sorcerer* in case of attack. But he doubted Flip had learned enough, his eyes wide at the complexity of the systems.

Just in case James got any ideas, Soman programmed spingrav to ramp up to 85% over the coming day, a slow enough rise it shouldn't be noticed.

Kolar was back on the radio. Ratoul would not approve a landing. Soman must keep them in orbit. The doctor would give instructions for their care.

"But we have no medicine here! You said they need treatment within two days."

Silence at first from Kolar. When he spoke, his voice betrayed strain. "Ratoul says we can not be certain this is the same fever. He fears to bring a new disease among us."

"Fuck Ratoul! We brought it to *them*." Soman looked around, grateful that none of the Monar was in Nav One to hear this. "And what do you think?"

Silence from Kolar.

The nex opened and Joni was there, tears streaming down her face. "Carla just died."

Soman flicked in, took the open channel to his implant. "Kolar," he said, his voice quavering, fighting back fulminating anger, "They are dying. We're landing next orbit. You tell Ratoul there had better be a medical team ready for us."

"They won't help," Joni said, her face more ashen than usual.

"Hell, we're going down anyway." Soman headed for the hatch.

She threw her arms around him. "Thank you."

Soman stood at the top of the ramp, staring in disbelief at the empty hillside. Behind him, agony bled from the open hatch, cries of pain doubled by unforgiving gravity. It had been the worst re-entry of Soman's life, each bump of turbulence smashing someone's bleeding face into the deck, squeezing excrement from bodies in extremity. Stepping over the sprawled and contorted forms to reach the ramp, Soman was certain that several were dead. Still, stiff, cooling.

No oldens, no doctors, nothing stirring all the way to the outskirts of Alta. Surely the Altans wouldn't just leave them here to die.

A noise. With sudden hope Soman ran back to the ramp and squinted at the hilltop. In the distance he thought he detected dust rising up the slope. A vehicle. Soman raced down the ramp, then sprinted past the wrecked hulk of the LEV and up the hill to meet it.

The olden stopped, the smallest olden he'd ever seen. A figure emerged.

"Kolar? Where are the—" Kolar's expression grim.

Kolar took a long look down the hill.

"Fuck," yelled Soman. He returned to the Monar ship, fuming. He prepared the patients for transport, lining up the peaceful dead with the suffering. He climbed the hill a second time. Kolar sat on the fender of the olden while the driver remained in his seat, clutching the steering wheel as if afraid the Monar would pry him from the vehicle and tear him apart.

"Is Ratoul going to let them die?" Soman asked Kolar.

Kolar shrugged.

The struggle to communicate fully frustrated Soman. "Where is Marya," he asked.

"That is too difficult for now."

Soman made another round of the cabin, giving water, stepping around pools of blood and vomit, holding a cloth to his nose against the foul odor.

"I think two more are gone," Ben said, then huddled in a corner.

Soman climbed the hill a third time. Nothing. Then Kolar placed a hand on Soman's shoulder. Soman followed Kolar's pointing finger. Dust in the distance. Three oldens, climbing the rise. They pulled to a stop in a whirl of dust. People alighted, faceless men and women in full masks, air tanks slung over their backs, carrying gear; stretchers and blankets, IV stands and monitors. A medical team swathed in personal protection gear as if the all the plagues of Earth threatened Alta. No wonder it had taken so long.

The medical team trotted to the lander, then emerged carrying the moaning, the unconscious, and the inert, everyone slick with excretions, blood, and sweat.

The olden brought them to the back entrance of a hospital. Nurses in masks and white jumpsuits wheeled patients down a ramp and out of sight. A white-suited man led Soman and Ben into the building, and Soman's ears crackled at a slight pressure change as they opened the inner door. Black seals around the doorframe. Soman recognized the design. Airlock. Negative pressure zone. Biohazard facility.

Kolar turned them over to a large masked woman who whisked them into an examining room, its surfaces smooth and white. Bright lights recessed into the ceiling lit the room with a violet tinge. The woman helped Ben onto the table and steadied him before turning to Soman. From her big-boned shape and the crinkles around her eyes, Soman knew it was Alla. She stabbed their fingers and rushed away with blood, clicking the door closed behind her.

Ben sat on the edge of the table, head down. "They got us now," Ben said. The sterile light turned his gray skin blue. "They knew."

"I can't believe..."

Ben slammed a fist on the table, and the clang resounded in the cubicle. "Think a'out the colony."

The Colony. The Monar ship had carried a work crew that had been well on departure, and now all were stricken. Soman's grasp of statistics forced him to face the reality. A group of twenty was a large enough sample to represent what must be happening within Colony One. Every one of the thousand-odd Monar must be fighting for their lives against the bleeding fever.

Alla burst into the room, the mask hanging around her throat, her face brightened by a broad smile that faltered as she looked from Soman to Ben. She placed her arm around Ben's heaving shoulders, speaking to him encouragingly. Soman strained to catch her words. He heard "blood," "good," a few numbers. Mostly he heard her hopeful tone of voice. "Ben, I think our blood tests are okay." He met Alla's eyes. "Good?" he said.

A blank look.

He tried to make the right sound. "Bwon?"

"Si, bowan!" And she was off in a torrent of explanation.

"Ben, we're going to be okay. Our inoculations protected us."

Ben said nothing.

The door opened and Kolar slipped into the room.

From his expression, Soman said, "Bad?"

"Perhaps only three will survive."

Soman grabbed Kolar. "We have to get help to the Colony."

Chapter 27

Soman ran the pre-launch checklist near exhaustion. Stopping for a moment, his gaze drifted to the satchels lashed in the empty seats. Fucking Ratoul. Gone on a visit to the far reaches of Alta, leaving no instructions. The officials remaining in the city wouldn't consider Soman's pleas for doctors until Ratoul's return. Soman fought back rising anger; if the ethic of Alta wouldn't allow Ratoul to fight Soman, it didn't prevent neglect at a moment when time was of the essence. By now the entire colony must be dying. Soman had rushed to Sora, to Lar, to Alla, pleading. No one would travel to the Monar.

He had only wanted to stop the fighting.

He forced himself back to the checklist. Kolar had at least managed to deliver a few medical supplies. That would have to do.

Ben stared at the controls. Finally he spoke; he had family in the Colony. A brother and twin sisters.

Soman set aside the checklist again. "Parents?"

Ben shook his head, looking in astonishment at the notion that one his age could have living parents. The Monar had lived like that for centuries, blinded by hatred and fear from realizing the life they could have. So stupid. As every conflict must appear from a distance.

Suddenly Flip's voice boomed in Soman's implant. "Launch from One."

This second, unauthorized trip to Earth had finally tipped the Council's hand. "How long do those darts take?"

"Not the rail launcher, it was a rocket launch."

"You have another ship?"

"An old one. I didn't think it could fly."

Soman pushed it all from mind. Focus on launch.

The stop at *Sorcerer* was brief, dropping Soman and picking up Joni. Then the craft slipped back into the void between Earth and moon, carrying a sack of medicine, eight med suits, and the first load of supplies from *Sorcerer*.

James and Flip stayed aboard *Sorcerer* to prepare the next load. The job would continue. The colony would need more supplies. Everyone counted on it.

Soman crawled back through the airlock and manned Nav One,

unable to take his mind off what Kolar had explained about the bleeding fever. One of the ancient hemorrhagic fevers, descendant of hanta and Ebola, it had hidden between outbreaks in animal reservoirs, infecting humans during times of disruption: flood, drought, war. Chaotic migration ahead of spreading ice sheets had jumbled animal populations and their viruses, giving rise to ever more virulent strains. Disease claimed more lives than war and famine during the darkest years. Humans and disease eventually settled into an uneasy equilibrium, the virus living benignly among rodents, unable to mutate and explode, held to the edges of human habitation by vaccination.

Only three of the Monar were still alive from the twenty-one, something in their chemistry able to resist the hook and gouge of the virus.

As they had sped to the lander for launch, Kolar had told Soman, "Ratoul is on the way back to Alta." A pause. "He sends his regrets."

"You tell Ratoul—" Never mind.

They worked shifts in Nav One, keeping an eye on the Colony and tracking the two ships—one outbound, one coasting in, passing each other, mute and dark. Ben maintained radio silence, still following the rules, observing the routines of thirty centuries.

Day two. Soman entered Nav One, where Flip dozed, unable to hold out to the end of his shift. Soman checked the position of the approaching Monar craft. "Whoa! They're almost here."

Flip blinked, now fully awake.

"They should be in decel." Soman scanned the data. "Still holding twelve thousand." He looked around. It took only a moment of thought. He set the Nav calculating its trajectory. Can't wait for it. "James, we're locking down. Suit up." He tossed a suit to Flip, then climbed into his, fumbling to latch it tight. "At that speed, the ship is no different than a missile." Soman jumped into a seat and brought up maneuvering controls. "Flip, See if they'll talk to you."

Flip struggled into the suit, then tried to contact the incoming craft.

No answer.

Soman warmed up the maneuvering nozzles and equalized fuel.

The silent Monar ship bore in, accelerated by Earth's pull. Soman finished figuring the trajectory. The incoming ship would pass hundreds of miles from *Sorcerer's* path. If it was a missile, the aim was really bad. And yet they'd dropped their ordnance on Ik with pinpoint precision.

And then it struck Soman: Earth. Oh no. He pulled up a new grid. Where was it going to hit. What if a ship loaded with fuel crashed into the center of Alta. He ran the calculation as he tried to raise the Alta operator. Knowing there was no time to evacuate. Ratoul was away from the city. And where was Marya....

Beside him, Flip shouted into the transceiver. Not a gasp from the incoming ship.

The blip came straight on, never maneuvering to rendezvous, never slowing, no correction to skim into orbit. The ship streaked by then blasted into the atmosphere, sucked by Earth's gravity to a speed of over fifteen thousand miles an hour, glowing brilliantly for a few seconds, disintegrating to molten bits, falling to the ice of central Asia like molten tears.

Soman trained the scope on the largest of the dark splotches as Sorcerer glided overhead, the viewscreen confronting them with every spacer's nightmare—a swirl of black smoke rising from a dirty hole in the ice, jagged cracks radiating from the impact point like spider legs. He tried to understand. Malfunction, or an unmanned missile that missed its target. Or—Soman's breath caught—a second mercy flight, everyone on the ship succumbing to the bleeding fever along the way.

Flip tried continuously to raise someone from the colony until he grew hoarse. Finally James pulled the mike from his hand.

"Can't just sit around," Soman said. He headed for bay two, James and Flip straggling after him. They began banging on the damaged LEV, removing dented panels, replacing struts, dragging out the gear for pressure testing the cabin. James helped with no quarrel.

And then Ben called in. "On the way," was all he would say, despite a tirade from Flip for more information. Until now, Soman had never seen Flip angry. A few days back it would have been funny.

Two more days. Soman, Flip, and James worked round the clock, unable to sleep, unwilling to stop for more than a few minutes, wanting no idle time. The LEV's new panels took shape.

The proximity alarm clanged. Soman and James met the Monar ship at bay one. Ben pushed by without a word, pale, dazed. Joni cowered in the elevator, gripping James fiercely, burying her face in his shoulder as he moved her toward quarters.

Soman peered into the hatch. Three patients lay in med suits. He entered the cabin. The nearest patient lay open-eyed, as if watching Soman.

Soman gasped. "Smit!"

Both eyes shone red, saturated in blood, dried hard over his eyeballs. Smit didn't blink.

"Smit," Soman murmured. He touched Smit's shoulder. Then backed through the hatch, leaving the three forms floating, as still as deep space.

Chapter 28

Soman shielded his eyes from the sun, watching the LEV fade to a flickering point in the sky, the acrid aftertaste of launch still in the air. He steadied himself against a boulder, uncertain how he had made it through the past two weeks.

He flicked into the auton; its whisper filled his skull. "*Sorcerer*," he said. While he waited, he wound his way through the eroded remains of the launch pad toward the waiting Kolar.

"Here." Joni said, her voice lifeless.

"They just lifted off," Soman said. He squinted up at the last glint from the LEV. "That docking routine running okay?"

"We can handle it."

It would be Ben's first docking with the LEV. Soman regretted that the surviving Monar had to stay on the ship, but they weren't ready for activity on Earth. Even the half gee of spingrav wore them down. Anyway, it was impossible just now to bring them into Alta, after what they'd witnessed. Even contact between the work teams now on the way up worried Soman. Ben burned like a fuse, and James…James was hard to figure. He hadn't spoken more than a dozen words in all the time they'd worked on the LEV.

Soman climbed to the hilltop, where Kolar stood gazing at the place in the sky where the LEV had disappeared; wisps of smoke torn by rising morning thermals.

He followed Kolar to the waiting olden, the crunch of dry soil underfoot.

The olden rumbled into Alta. Today Kolar would help him find fuel. *Sorcerer's* tanks were down to 8%. Only a few LEV trips left.

The word "fuel" didn't translate exactly. Kolar brought him, at the end of an hour drive, to an electrical station on a dune overlooking the Caribbean. Fat, finned spikes of insulators covered the equipment like insect armor. Buzzing cables ran away in all directions. In the control room he met a slow-moving, florid woman. Around them equipment hummed. A taste of ozone sharpened the air. Workers in an adjacent room, all wearing the tan tunic, stopped their work to stare at the visitors.

The woman's fleshy face barely moved as she unleashed a torrent of words. After a full minute of discourse from the woman, Kolar pointed to a diagram above the control panel and said simply, "The fuel comes from the ocean." Reducing everything to a schoolchild's language, accommodating Soman's weak grasp of the language. Marya's disappearance leaving more than one hole.

The massive woman watched Soman, her chair bending and groaning to its task. They called it fuel, but Soman could see it was electricity, generated somehow out in the sea.

Soman studied the schematic of the system. Two massive cables crept along the seafloor to thousands of generating arrays. The units appeared to float thirty feet beneath the surface, anchored to the sea floor beneath. Deep enough to avoid the worst wave action but shallow enough to catch the sunlight filtering through the clear tropical water. Each unit held a large surface area exposed to the sun, like solar panels. But these probably weren't solar panels—they'd have placed standard panels on land, without all the expense of anchoring at sea.

A half hour later, following tortured repetitions, crude sketches, and hand motions, he thought he understood: the panels held colonies of algae engineered to produce not molecules, but electrons. The arrays contained no moving parts, no expensive electronics, just mile after square mile of captive organisms generating the electricity that ran the city.

Worthless for rocket fuel. The LEV needed liquid combustibles. And without it—a half-dozen more launches and that's it. Even with the Mark Nine they'd slung beneath the repaired LEV.

The woman swiveled her chair and waved a hand over the diagram, words tumbling from her once again.

"She talks of the gas," Kolar said.

"Gas?" Soman studied the diagram again. Look at that. A separate grid of blue in the background, converging into two lines that disappeared off the screen.

"Yes, for the boats."

Gas for the boats. He clapped Kolar on the shoulder. "Now you're talking about fuel! What kind of gas?"

Kolar's forehead wrinkled. "The gas from water."

"From water?"

"Yes, some of the electricity makes the water into gas. It is unavoidable. We use it for the boats."

"Damn, oxygen and hydrogen?"

Kolar's expression remained blank.

"I want to visit these boats."

Kolar considered. "Tomorrow."

Along the roadway into the city they encountered a throng of worshipers. Apparently Marya hadn't spread the latest word. Or...maybe she had, and no one wanted to listen. At some point, Mordano will put and end to this.

Soman flicked in. Flip responded. "Any progress with the descroids?" Soman asked.

"They've got most of the controls torn apart, if you call that progress. Also one of the pods. Just now they're all standing around a pile of parts like they're ready to shit. I offered to try putting it all back together, but I don't think they can handle my brilliance yet." And yes, Ben and James were staying away from the work crew assessing the worst of *Sorcerer's* eroded fuselage panels for replacement. Soman had decided to scavenge hull plates from the Monar ship. *Sorcerer's* hull had to be shored up, and the M620 had no business making any more re-entries.

"Found us any fuel?" Flip asked.

"Nothing we can put in a rocket tank."

A pause. Then Flip said, his voice low and serious, "Well, if we run out of fuel at least I won't have to worry about coming down there."

"Let's not start that again." Soman recalled that conversation with Flip in the corner of Nav One just before this re-entry.

"Soman, where will we go if you decide to hibernate?" Flip had asked.

Soman noticed that the other Monar had slipped out.

"You know we can't go down there," Flip said, glancing through the port at a sliver of Earth. "We can't go home. What are we supposed to do?"

Soman scraped his toe on the floor. "Don't worry about it yet. I'm going to see how far we can get building airplanes. I thought I'd give it a year. If we haven't got something in the air by then, we'll all take a few decades in the descroid."

"Orbit isn't the safest place. You get 'em started, someone's going to re-invent the missile. And they just might use you for target practice. So let's take her back to Eridani. You get your time, we get the hell out of here and do something interesting." Flip lowered his voice. "You know if we leave James this close to Earth, someone's going to get killed."

"Flip, I'm not doing that trip again."

Kolar made arrangements to visit the boats in the morning. Then they returned to Kolar's shay, Soman afraid, or ashamed, to face the people of

Marya's shay. He knew only that Marya had left the city and had revoked the duro, which he understood to mean the renunciation of her vow. Where she had fled, Kolar didn't know, or was not allowed to say.

After breakfast, Kolar appeared and told Soman they would meet the olden on a side street to avoid the growing throng. Sneaking a spice roll from the table, Kolar led him out the back door and through the garden.

Once underway, Soman flicked in and raised Flip. It was always good to speak English.

"Hey boss."

"Got those descroids working yet?"

Flip laughed. "Only if these things work with parts strewn across the floor. But I think they had some kind of epiphany last night. All of a sudden they acted like they knew what they're doing. Made a list of all the stuff they need."

"What kind of stuff."

"Parts, chemicals, test equipment. They want to send someone down for it."

"No! Don't send anyone yet. We've got to plan every trip carefully. Have them contact Ratoul to get what they need."

At the harbor, the olden slipped past row after row of magnificent wooden boats, cranes swinging loads on deck amid the tang of salt air and the aroma of moldering seaweed. They met a wiry man with white hair and a weathered face, dressed in a drab hooded windbreaker. Studying the jacket, Soman thought it archaic, but he couldn't place why. During introductions it struck him: oilcloth, a garment out of the…what would that be, before plastics, maybe the 1900's.

The man sprang from pier to boat and moved alongside a tank bolted to the deck, using the word Soman recognized as fuel—peen this and peen that—as he laid his hands on the surface of the cylinder. Soman tried to discern the material used to make the tank. The surface seemed to be coated with an impervious glaze. He struck it with a knuckle, expecting a metallic clang. A dull thud, as if tapping wood. Could it be possible, containing hydrogen in a wooden tank. No way—H_2 molecules were too small; they'd leak through the pores.

They struggled with technical terms, Kolar trying to help but clearly out of his element. Soman examined everything, clambering over the equipment, studying valves and piping. Finally he concluded the fuel tanks held hydride—low pressure hydrogen tied up in weak chemical bonds. A safer way to transport hydrogen than compressing it to liquid form, but useless for the LEV.

He tried to describe liquid hydrogen, cooled to minus…minus what. Don't even know what temperature scale they use. They wrangled over that, voices growing tense. Incomprehension from the boatman over hydrogen colder than ice and pumped like water. In the end, the man shrugged dismissively, then sprang to the pier and began organizing his next load.

Soman trudged away, trying to work out how to get all the work at *Sorcerer* completed with the fuel on hand. Then a notion: maybe the Colony's tank still held enough fuel to be worth a trip. Soman shivered over a return visit, a thousand still and frozen bodies inside. James and Joni had blown the air to prevent decomposition, but still…

A woman met them inside the shay with a whispered message to Kolar. Kolar stepped to the wall communicator, then emerged with a frown. "Ratoul is not happy."

"Ratoul is never happy."

"It is about equipment they request for the repairs."

"Yes, I know. Sora is making progress." And unless they found fuel fast, they'd need those descroids soon.

"Ratoul says this is expensive. Alta cannot pay."

"But I need the repairs." The whole idea was to work on the descroids while trying to build an aircraft industry. Cover both bases, just in case the airplane program hits snags. And there was other urgent work needed to keep *Sorcerer* operating, to ensure the ship could manage low-orbit station-keeping for a few decades, just miles above the upper wisps of atmosphere. Soman had counted on Ratoul's support. Good thing he'd held back giving Ratoul those airframe plans—that meeting was scheduled for tomorrow.

Kolar called Ratoul on Soman's behalf. But the leader of Alta was adamant. Enough money had been spent sending supplies to the Monar. The Altans were not a rich people who could donate their expensive medical equipment for one man's use. The comment about supplies to the Monar ran through Soman like a nasty cough.

Soman could see that the coming months and years would be a constant battle as Ratoul tried to get what he wanted and give back as little as possible. Soman was already tired of it.

He called the ship. According to Flip, Sora and her technicians were loading their personal gear for a return to Earth. "No one's going anywhere yet! Tell them to keep working." Ratoul was stealing Anoka from his grasp.

Soman slammed the door of his room behind him, then kicked a chair against the wall. The Maro drove him to his knees, and he sank gratefully into its numbing aura.

Later, kneeling in front of the window, he watched the deepening blue of twilight, pondering who might support the repairs. Scanning the low buildings around the shay, his eyes lit on the towering church spire.

He washed and descended the stairs. Kolar sat on the porch, contemplating the white-robed crowd on the street. "Kolar," Soman said. "Please call Mordano, and tell him we're on the way."

They entered the chilly nave, lit by clusters of flickering candles.

Kolar settled into a pew at the back of the sanctuary.

Soman looked around. No sign of Mordano, only a scattering of worshipers. One or two looked up as the wind banged the door against its latches. Soman moved up a side aisle. Nearing the transept, he halted, uncertain.

A flicker of movement across the sanctuary in the dim light. A head turned; someone had noticed him. A figure slid from the pew and knelt. A rustle of motion like a wave, all heads turning to Soman, all knees striking the floor.

A touch on his elbow; he flinched. Mordano's features wavered in the candlelight, his glance flickering around the sanctuary.

"Wee gew down." He led Soman from the sanctuary, leaving behind a breathless quiet broken only by the moaning of the wind.

Eyes riveted on the chest behind the altar, Soman stumbled as he started down the stairs.

He nodded when Mordano inquired about coffee. Watched the priest perform his ritual with the beans.

Finally Mordano said, "Eeyew are no come warsh…war sh sh—"

"I attended service last Sabbath among the Monar."

Mordano struggled to swallow.

Soman smiled. Mere mention of the Monar still dried the throats of the Altans. "It seems I create a difficulty for the Church."

Mordano nodded.

"The difficulty grows worse every day."

Again the nod.

"The people have been waiting a long time for their Prodigal Children."

Mordano now wary.

"Perhaps the best solution is for me to depart from Earth."

Mordano's eyebrows rose. But in the next instant his eyes narrowed, as if he sensed this was too easy.

Way too easy. "There is a problem. My ship needs repairs." Soman sipped coffee.

Mordano blinked. "We help now. Sora. Something more?"

Soman shook his head. Sipped again. "So I fear I may be required to remain in Alta for an extended time. In that case, we would need to talk about my role in the Church."

Only the creaking of ancient timbers in the wind.

Soman held out his mug. Mordano moved to the sideboard and refilled.

"First we must decide what to do with the contents of the *fundam*."

A tightening of Mordano's lips. "Certainly not."

"You see, Ratoul will not pay for repairs." From the flash in Mordano's eye, Soman saw that Ratoul's disdain for Mordano was mutual. "And of course I have no funds—" for an instant Soman recalled the bank account that should have awaited him, gone like everything of his age.

Mordano folded his hands carefully, then said, "The coost for theese re-pars?"

Soman fought back the grin that threatened to ruin the grave mood. "Sora knows the details."

Mordano studied him. "Perhaps," he said, "the Church assist. I speak Sora."

Soman rocked his head as if considering. "That might work."

They climbed the stair to the sanctuary. Soman stopped at the *fundam* resting in its niche behind the altar. Julian's old chest, his gift across the centuries. Time capsule for the returning crew. When Julian asked all the crew to provide a few treasured mementos, Soman had given him that old San Jose Twins hat. The photo of Anne, Anoka, and Soman sitting like three cowboys in their boots and hats on a length of split rail fence. And the rock: smooth, fist-size, with a painted grin and two button eyes. On the bottom, in the scrawl of a hand just learning to write: *To my Daddy, LOVE*.

More than anything in this world, Soman wanted to open that chest. And he had just relinquished his claim to it.

Chapter 29

Kolar agreed to carry the message to Ratoul. Less chance for misunderstanding that way. Kolar had carried a few innocuous pages of airframe designs, nothing specific, and Soman's schedule of launches and equipment needed to complete the overhaul of descroids and critical equipment on *Sorcerer*.

Sora had expressed confidence that six or seven descroids could be made to function. She needed parts, and chemicals, and a pembron— some kind of diagnostic simulator used to check Maro. In the meantime, Sora was content to admire the view from orbit and to wander the ship, studying its systems, marveling at the city of metal circling her world.

Soman awaited Kolar's return on his shay's porch. If he strolled down the street, he risked becoming the center of a large crowd. For the moment, the shay was his prison.

"Well?" Soman asked when Kolar slid into a chair beside him.

"He says he cannot take the money of the Church."

"He understands Mordano approves it?"

Kolar nodded. "He knows of your meeting with Mordano."

"But Sora is employed by the institute—why can't she just work at Mordano's direction?"

Kolar shook his head. "The Church makes the research, but the budgets are from the state."

Soman considered. "Kolar, is there a legal basis for not accepting money from the Church?"

Kolar's turn to consider. "Of course he is not allowed to take Church money for the normal budget. For this—" Kolar shrugged. "It is a special case. Let us say that he could make it work either way."

"If he wanted."

Kolar nodded.

"And he knows he will get the aircraft designs."

Kolar grimaced. "He says this was already agreed for the current work."

"Ratoul's decision means I must abandon my ship and remain on the planet. Why does Ratoul want me to stay here?"

Soman missed some of Kolar's reply, so he made him repeat, then explain it a different way. The third time through, Soman got it. So

Ratoul sees a way to unbalance the power between government and Church. The faction clamoring for the Prodigal Child grows each day. If Soman stays, it would tear the Church apart. The government would have to step in. In the chaos, Ratoul could find a way to control the Maro. Who received it, how it was programmed. A power held by no head of state in the history of Alta. Of course Ratoul would explain everything as necessary for the good of the people at a time of danger. That's the way it's done. By the time people realized the real danger, it would be too late.

Unless there was something about Ratoul that bred doubt about his motives, about his fitness to lead according to Altan ideals.

Maybe there was.

Soman hesitated. In orbit, helpless in a descroid, he would survive at Ratoul's pleasure. If he took this step, Ratoul would become his enemy. There would be no safe refuge anywhere near the civilized Earth, anywhere within the reach of the technology that Ratoul could develop in his lifetime. Soman held his head. It would mean giving Flip his dream.

Soman touched Kolar's arm. "Kolar, I will see Ratoul now. Can you meet me outside Lar's office in an hour?"

Kolar nodded, called for an olden. A ball skittered across the lawn, children giving chase. Kolar stepped forward nimbly and intercepted it, flipping it with his toe, then bouncing it between toe and heel, the children screaming for him to kick it back. Watching, Soman smiled. Kolar has many talents. He climbed aboard the olden.

Ratoul shifted his chair, its scrape marring the quiet. He concentrated, entering notes into a pad.

Soman cleared his throat.

Ratoul looked up, a flicker of annoyance crossing his face. He held his stylus poised above the pad as if interrupted from a great matter of state.

"Can anyone else hear us?" Soman asked.

Ratoul's eyes flickered. "So now you speak the language?"

"Can anyone hear? Do you record what we say?" Soman interpreted Ratoul's hesitation as surprise at the question, not failure to understand Soman's pronunciation. Soman leaned forward. "It is for your protection."

Finally the raised eyebrow from Ratoul.

"We walk." Soman said.

Ratoul hesitated, as if wondering whether he would need an umbrella, or a guard.

Soman guided Ratoul by the arm, enough steel in the grip to cause discomfort, not enough to wake the Maro, steering Ratoul away from the building, his head throbbing from the irreversibility of this path.

Ratoul resisted Soman's tug, glancing back.

Soman saw the olden gliding thirty meters behind, no doubt Ratoul's security detail, an anomaly in peaceful Alta. He tugged to force Ratoul faster. Keep him off balance. Taking a deep breath, he said, "How will Alta remember Ratoul." He wasn't sure that was exactly what he said, but looking at Ratoul, he sensed comprehension.

"Two ways," Soman continued. He held up a finger. "One, the man who brought the airplane to Alta." He raised a second finger. "Two, the man who killed a thousand people." Soman wiggled his two fingers and said, "Your choice." He knew he was missing the articles and conjunctions and damaging the tenses. But Ratoul seemed to understand.

Soman paused, his brain working furiously to line up words, one by one. "I give you one chance to be that first man."

Ratoul huffed.

"Only one chance. Do not make a mistake in these minutes." Soman waited. He didn't want Ratoul to miss what came next. "Or I make you the second man."

Ratoul's eyes narrowed.

Soman repeated the sentence. Then he added, "Comprehend?"

"I hear the words."

"If you force me to stay on Earth, Ratoul will be remembered as another Solin."

Ratoul stiffened beyond his customary severity, like a general hearing distant artillery.

Soman knew that with the next words he leaped into the dark. Everything depended on this guess. "I made inquiries. I know your role in the blood fever. If I tell, you will be known as a killer greater than Solin."

Ratoul stumbled. Soman steadied him, knowing the feeling, shock disconnecting the muscles from their source of energy, motion faltering. He recalled his reaction in the Monar cell, unable to stand under a sentence of death. And long ago, the same weakness at the doctor's mention of medulloblastoma.

Ratoul leaned on Soman for an instant, then regained his balance.

He had launched the missile without knowing for certain. Now he knew.

Ratoul's mouth started to work. "I…I tried—".

"No talk!" Soman glanced around to be certain there was no one nearby, that the olden kept its distance. Suddenly he worried how much Ratoul might have modulated the Maro of his bodyguards. The streets were empty except for that trailing olden. Perhaps he should have brought Kolar. This meeting should have been held at the shay, among witnesses. Too late.

Soman shook Ratoul's arm, tightening his grip until Ratoul winced. At that, his Maro awoke, and he felt tendrils spreading through him like a narcotic. He smiled. His Maro relaxed its grip. "Listen carefully. Three people know. I can ensure they all depart with me. Take Mordano's money. Repair my ship. Protect your future." Soman released Ratoul before the Maro slowed his step. "Or we will tell a story that will soon reach the far districts of Alta. Solin and Ratoul will be spoken in the same breath. And you will walk this street a beggar."

Soman saw Ratoul recovering from the shock, regaining his composure, calculating. He stopped, looking into Ratoul's eyes. "And if I tell my Monar this story, you are a dead man. They have no Maro to stop them." An alleyway appeared on the right. Soman slipped into it, losing himself into the center of Alta, leaving Ratoul alone on the street.

Calm fell over Soman. Now there was no choice, no hard decision, no balancing of possibilities. Just stay out of Ratoul's way while Sora finishes her work, then go. Give Earth another two hundred fifty years. Not so long, really, in the scheme of things. With all the information he'd leave with Ratoul, they would certainly be capable of mounting a recovery through the ice.

And perhaps there would be another prize—plenty of time for Lar and his successors to figure out the telomere.

Soman slipped through alleys and back streets, deeper into Alta, watching for familiar landmarks. One more task. There. That building; those poppies. Suddenly aware that these were his last minutes on Earth, Soman stopped. He breathed the flowers' aroma, time slowing. Life had become a series of waking bursts between retreats into the descroid. Not so different really from a normal lifetime—a few moments of real awareness rising now and then from the slumber of daily life. It just stretches out longer this way, living a few months each two and a half centuries, seeing how it all turns out without the daily tedium of all the generations.

The hospital came into view. There sat the olden, Kolar's profile in the window. Soman dashed across the street, stepped through the door, slipped past Lar's office, and padded up the stairs. Brushing past clucking nurses, he stopped in the half-light amid a reek of chemicals and rotting flesh.

By the time Lar had been summoned, the glass bubble lay upturned in a corner, the mass of tubes and wires trailing off the platform like severed tentacles.

Soman sat on the floor, cradling Siba in his lap, tears running down his face. Sunlight streamed from the opened shade. Her chest shuddered once, and her final, faint exhalation brushed his lips. She stilled. When Lar tried to pull him away, Soman held her tightly and watched her eyes fade to nothing. Lar would need to get his samples elsewhere.

Stumbling back down the corridor, Soman stopped dead as a man disappeared into a nearby room. It couldn't be.

Soman crept to the doorway. A bubble occupied the center of the room, identical to the one that had housed Siba until moments before. Ratoul sat beside it, a hand placed on the bubble near the perfectly still hand of the woman inside. A thick tube ran from a respirator to the mask covering her face, the frayed white tape running into the raven hair spilling across the pillow. Her chest rose and fell to the hiss of the machine.

Ratoul turned slowly, and before Soman could move, their eyes met. Then he turned back, leaning his head against the enclosure.

At the waiting olden, Kolar took one look and asked, "You are all right?"

"Ratoul was there, in the hospital."

Kolar looked across at the hospital for a long moment. Yes," he said. "Ratoul is often here. He visits his wife."

"What happened to her?"

Kolar sighed. "It was the day you first landed," he said. "We thought the city was in danger. Ratoul ordered an evacuation. In the confusion, Liriana was struck by an olden."

Soman recalled Ratoul's manner that first day. He had written him off from the start as impatient and unkind. Now he could see Ratoul's mood that day for what it was; anger and grief held back. How he must have hated Soman that morning, and yet he managed it. And Soman had never thought to inquire of Ratoul's family, never considered a pause from the contest of wills. It was always how he could get what he needed from Ratoul. Never imagining Ratoul might need anything from him. Never imagining that the return of *Sorcerer* had stolen something from them both.

Part 3: The Dark Beyond the Stars

Chapter 30

James gripped the silver cylinder in gloved hands, shifting his feet for purchase, arms straining to lift. Open channel rasped with his breath and the whirring of suit motors. Shafts of light from helmet lamps lanced the gloom, glinting off a wall towering above them.

Almost imperceptibly, the foot-long bar rose from its cradle.

Soman peered through the dark at the slowly rising ingot glinting in their beams. Three inches in diameter, the length of a man's boot, and so massive it took all a man's strength to overcome its inertia.

James said, "It must have a mass of a couple thousand pounds."

"And only the size of my dick," Flip said.

When the cylinder rose to shoulder height, James said, "Okay, high enough," and clutched it to stop its ascent. The others scrambled to hold him down, hooking boots under the platform.

James' reaching arms reminded Soman of something, an old sculpture in Alta. Another century gone, whistling past on a fierce wind. Soman weakened at the thought of Marya. Her life lived up, even the babies she'd conceived gone, swept away in the storm of time.

"Hold on!" yelled James.

Soman renewed his grip on the present. Four of them grappled James to help stop the cylinder from carrying him into the blackness of the shaft. Finally they halted the upward motion of the cylinder, and James started it moving to the right, toward the second cradle, identical to the first but empty. The others moved in a cluster around James, offering their bodies as firm points of purchase, shuttling ahead like sweepers guiding the rock.

Soman shivered. What would happen when this shaft of tooled alien metal slid into its receptacle. The instructions were clear, despite the lack of language: move the shiny ingot from the cradle on the left to the one on the right. No mention of what happened then. And so the crew had argued over it, as they had argued every move since arriving at Epsilon Eridani.

Sorcerer had emerged from the empty space between stars, a dust grain floating toward Epsilon Eridani. They collected at Nav deck like survivors of a plane crash, heads throbbing, joints scraping, clotted memories loosening. At least this time the updated map of the solar nebula brought them here on time.

Suddenly they realized Kolar was missing, and they raced to descroid deck. Kolar smiled tiredly from his pod. "I thought everyone had forgotten me. I can't seem to catch my breath."

They lifted Kolar from the pod and floated him to the clinic. Ben studied the diagnostic screen as it scrolled one red-lined item after another. Ever since the reconstruction work on his mouth, Ben had been interested in medicine. He'd made a study of the clinic's gear, but he was finding it difficult to understand the details.

With the help of the auton and searches through the database, Ben and Soman assembled the picture none of them wanted to face. The descroid hadn't been kind to Kolar's old organs. Elevated enzymes indicated damage to the heart muscle. A murmur told of regurgitant flow, a valve not closing. The skewed electrolyte balance was diagnostic of pulmonary congestion and low kidney function. His heart functioned at half efficiency, attempting to compensate by a trip-hammer pulse.

Soman placed a hand over Kolar's. "We think it's a leaky heart valve. Did you have it already?"

Kolar nodded weakly.

"I'd say the descroid cycle damaged it further." He indicated the chest socket connecting Kolar to the system. "It's giving you drugs that should help."

Soman knew it was only a palliative, something called ACE, plus a diuretic and a sedative. How long could his weakened heart keep this up. On Earth a new valve was a routine surgery, but Kolar had left all that behind.

Like Kolar, the ship had needed attention. Soman began the checklist. At least there had been no fire. But the collector had taken fresh damage, and the auton flagged a half-dozen components that required an urgent look-see.

The crew assembled in Nav One to plan the work, sipping water from their globes, sucking to replenish parched joints. "We're going to continue on to the planet," Soman said. "We'll need that much time to make repairs. Then we can slingshot around EE2 for an extra push back toward Earth." *Sorcerer* had completed half its job, and Soman was ready to race for home. Ratoul would be long gone. In the century and a quarter since they'd departed, Earth should have progressed from rudimentary flight to space exploration. Humans had made that leap in fifty years the first time. It should go faster now that humanity knew how it could be done.

At the odd quiet around him, Soman looked up. The Monar had stopped drinking. They stared at him in disbelief. James said, "We're not just turning around?"

Flip said, "If you weren't planning to explore once we got here, why come all this way?"

Soman scowled. "This was the voyage programmed into *Sorcerer,* and we knew the exact shape of the gas clouds from the first trip. Any other destination would have been a crap shoot."

"Okay, but dammit, we're here now." Flip slapped Soman's arm. "It's only your second trip here, and you're bored already?"

Soman looked to the holo, where EE2 had grown enough to show a disc. He had no intention of looking around. Then Flip's words struck home. His second trip. Like Cabot.

Flip shook Soman's shoulder. "Don't worry. None of us are going down into that gravity. We don't much like planets. But Ben and I want to take a run with the LEV out to that moon. Moons interest us."

Soman's head throbbed, recalling suits swinging like dead weight from the rack. "It's too dangerous."

Flip laughed. "We come out here in a ship older than dirt, freeze dried in little toilet stalls rebuilt by people who'd never seen one before. And you think a little side trip to the moon is dangerous?"

Soman looked away. Ley had used almost the identical argument, just before heading to the planet.

James said in derision, "I don't recall it was that safe around Earth."

Joni said, "We can't come all this way and not try to find who built all this."

Kolar coughed. Everyone turned to watch him, his med suit tethered above the couch, cheeks sunken, eyes closed, half in another place. He'd insisted on staying with the crew instead of in isolation at the clinic.

Soman said, "We have to get Kolar back where they can do something for him."

"Soman," Ben whispered. "Do you really think he can survive the descroid again?"

Joni whispered. "Let's ask what Kolar wants."

For a moment Kolar contemplated the disk of EE2 in the nav holo. Soman recognized the signs of Kolar's two brains in quiet conversation.

A gentle nudge as the ship made a course correction. The quiet broken only by the soft hum of ship's systems and the occasional 'pung' of the nav probing the approaching planet.

Kolar turned back to them. "It shouldn't be a matter of what I want. It's about what knowledge we could return. What price we've all paid to get here."

Soman watched them. He'd seen the gleam in their eyes as EE2 grew in size. Their unthinking willingness to risk their lives for this. Why couldn't they see the larger goal, why couldn't they grasp what might await them back on Earth. He pushed off for the nex and left them.

As *Sorcerer* approached EE2, Soman left spingrav off, though atrophy had started. Kolar's struggling heart could use a break, and it would be only a week before slipping back into their pods for the return trip. But by the third day, as EE2 loomed and final course corrections had to be made, he realized the repairs were taking longer than planned. With deep reservations, he slipped *Sorcerer* into orbit, knowing the delay would spur the Monar to renew their insistence for an exploration of the Pearl.

The collector work required a team—really two teams working shifts—but Soman didn't have that luxury. Suiting up wore the Monar down—no way could they stand up to the rigors of work on the hull. Soman had trained the Monar in suit operation and made them practice the sixty second drill until they could latch down in under five minutes. They had practiced attentively, no one mentioning the obvious—they were too slow to survive a real emergency.

So Soman exited the C hold airlock alone, a spare suit positioned just inside in case a rescue was needed.

The collector was more damaged than he had realized, many of the booms torn away. After two hours repositioning the remaining units to cover as much area as possible, Soman knew it was time to head back. He rounded the last arm of the collector and paused, taking in the lustrous copper of the planet, breathing deeply to overcome the vertigo. Holding the superstructure with one glove, he drifted alongside the ship, soaking in the view. The suit beeped—thirty minutes' air remaining. Soman hurried around the curve of the hull toward the airlock. Thirty minutes seemed like a long time, but in the bulky suit, moving with caution, even a small issue could boil away a half hour before you realized it.

He almost re-entered without noticing the tatter of cloth. He was about to activate the lock when it caught his eye. Something clinging to the grate work of the platform beneath the outer hatch. A hole in the grate, he thought at first, or a ding from a micrometeor. Hurrying, imagining the ticking clock, he clipped the safety tether to the lower cleat and reached over.

It came loose when he scraped his glove across the grate, a corner of it clinging, then tearing free. He held it in front of his visor. A piece of red fabric, faded, full of holes—no, those weren't holes. It was lace. The most incongruous object imaginable clinging to the outside of a starship. A woman's undergarment.

Now he spotted a dark spatter on the hull. And he knew in an instant that it was a thin glaze of iron pigment, all the proteins sublimed in the two and a half centuries since someone had been forced through this airlock and snagged their panty on the grating as their face splattered blood on the closing hatch. That's the way it must have been. No one voluntarily exits an airlock wearing underpants as an outer garment.

Soman scrambled into the airlock. Selen's underwear. No wind to tear it loose as *Sorcerer* voyaged to Earth and back. What had Bruni done to her, then ejected her, almost naked. Had he been simply freeing up one more descroid, or covering up a rape. And then Siba had happened by. Soman gasped, realizing how close she'd come to sharing Selen's fate.

The air hissed and the inner airlock hatch opened. Someone in a pressure suit blocked his way, and Soman flailed at it before remembering, when it crumpled, empty, that it was the suit he'd left there. Heart pounding, he headed for Nav One. Sliding through the nex, Soman stopped. The Monar were clustered around the console, and from the strained silence Soman knew he'd interrupted something.

"Look," James said, watching the console. "There's time to explore. We know you don't want to. But we're going."

Joni said, "Please, you've got to understand. We don't have anything to return to. This is our life, right here, right now. We won't hold you up for long."

Soman thought about the ruined Colony One, almost everyone Joni had ever known dead inside the silent dome. He glimpsed how the Monar could be more comfortable at Epsilon Eridani than on humanity's home world.

James turned to face Soman. "Your problem Soman is you're afraid to live your life."

"I just…" Just what. What had he been doing the past three thousand years. Life—what is it. What I did yesterday. What I'll do tomorrow. What about the stuff going on incessantly in my head. The suffering, the planning, the anger, the desire. What's that. Is that life, or just a distraction. Soman shook it off. Right now the problem is he's terrified every time he thinks of leaving the ship in a LEV.

The auton beeped. Soman glanced to the console. The green flicker of a notification. "Hang on. I want to check out something on the surface." He pulled up the visual.

The crew looked over his shoulder. "What are we looking for?" Ben asked.

"Ley's lander." He'd known he had to look. One thing about Ley, you could never say she'd been afraid to live her life.

He checked the view angle. Almost ninety degrees. Right over the spot. "Auton, maximum zoom."

The view blurred then regained focus.

Soman studied the center of the image. A dark stain marred the shininess of the surface, the shape familiar from dozens of busy freighter sites—the smudge of a landing burn. No doubt about it, this was where Ley landed. But the LEV was gone.

Soman sat a long time watching the planet turn, trying to imagine the possibilities. Ley was dead. It had been two hundred fifty years. But something had happened here after her final transmission to Siba. This wasn't just some remote station. Someone, some thing, had taken the LEV. Finally he spoke. "Auton."

"Ready."

"Spingrav on, half G."

Flip protested, "Shit, boss, do we need this?"

"If we're staying long enough to explore your moon, we don't have a choice."

Flip smiled broadly. "Show me how to operate that LEV."

Joni settled into the second Nav seat. "Teach me about these sensors. We'll need to know how to operate everything."

Chapter 31

James gauged the cylinder's position second by second, nudging first one side then the other, aligning it with its new receptacle—two rows of curved pins that would hold it in place between gleaming end plates. Moving frantically as the cylinder approached the cradle, James reached underneath to check its alignment.

"Get your hand out of there!" Joni hissed.

"It's gonna miss."

Joni knocked his hand away. "It'll crush you. Let it miss."

It missed, striking crookedly on the left-side pins. Its mass and momentum would have sliced off James' fingers and blown his suit. The cylinder rebounded imperceptibly. James nudged, and it slid home.

Silence. Everyone held their breath. The weapon loaded, the switch turned, the message sent. No idea what they'd just done. Soman looked up at the wall stretching into the darkness, studded with glistening protrusions like a field of diamonds. Expecting a holo to appear there, or a message. His eyes played tricks. He shook his head. Tiny flashes of light in the peripheral vision. Remembering the blue flash, he covered his visor with his arm and clenched his eyes shut. He sensed a grave mistake.

Soman had chosen a trajectory to the moon that would keep the LEV far from a direct line between EE2's mirrors and the Pearl's laser. Flip had run the controls, grinning at Ben as he fired the main engine for the burn across to Pearl's orbit. Joni worked the sensor seat, testing the nav ping, the laser probe, the holo translator, the electromag scan, anything that still worked on the old craft. They reached the small black moon.

Soman said, "Now we're going to start the traverse we should have made last time."

The LEV gained altitude and began a spiral traverse that would give them full coverage of the surface in eight and a half orbits. It didn't take that long. Within ten minutes the LEV hovered five thousand meters above a series of eleven perfect concentric circles, the smallest solid black. "A bulls-eye," Soman said. His heart rate picked up. If Cabot had just made the traverse.

"What's a bulls-eye?" Flip asked.

"An old Earth thing," Soman said.

Flip said, "I guess we're supposed to land there."

"We're not landing anywhere yet," Soman said.

"Where else you going to land?"

"We're not landing anywhere, period, until we complete the traverse we should have done last time."

James spoke up. "Just don't tell us at the end of the traverse that fuel is too low, or some other thing. You know we're going to land there in the end."

"We'll land if it's safe and it looks like our best option." Soman met James' glare. The others occupied themselves with small tasks. "And if we find the missing LEV, we'll put down there instead."

James said nothing more, and the traverse continued.

Except for the circles, the surface was black and featureless, no shade of topography, no variation in chemical concentration, no flash of reflecting metal. Nothing. Barren as the mirror facets of EE2, except that this surface absorbed all radiation, its blackness drawing attention to the concentric rings, to the landing pad at their center.

Thrusters changed pitch. The LEV stopped. Traverse complete.

"Joni. Give us a close-up of the landing spot, plus a full scan for composition, texture, thickness, elastic modulus—"

"Whoa," she said, turning to her screen. "One thing at a time." Within seconds she lifted her hands from the controls. "Okay, what am I doing wrong? I'm getting nothing."

"Laser mapping," Soman said. "Translate to holo."

The holo built its map in green topography. Soman's throat tightened. It was no landing pad after all, but a second entrance into the Pearl.

"No fucking way," Soman said. Every instinct told him to go back to *Sorcerer*, patch it up, and get home.

James turned. "Knew you'd back out."

"You want to land, I'll land! Right next to the edge. Then be my guest. Climb on down."

Flip studied the holo. "Joni, how big is it?"

"Uh, diameter sixteen hundred meters."

Ben said, "Ten times as big as that tunnel on the other side."

Flip grinned at Soman. "Piece of pie. Isn't that what you say?"

"Cake," Soman growled. "It's cake. And there's no such thing out here."

James said, "No need to argue. You don't want to go, we take you to the big ship and come back."

Soman swallowed. Glancing around the cabin, his eyes stopped on

Kolar. He unstrapped and moved to the edge of Kolar's seat. "Kolar," he said, softly.

Kolar searched Soman's eyes. "If you argue about it much longer, I may not live to see it."

Soman looked over his crew. He knew it was an unreasoning fear, this persistent terror left from his first reconnaissance of the Pearl. His palms grew sweaty, thinking back on it. Then something occurred to him. This habitual fear was no different than the fear the Monar harbored for the Earth. Or the Altans for the Monar. Deal with it.

He swung into the pilot's seat. "Training's over. I'm flying. Strap in." While everyone scrambled to secure positions, Soman wiped his palms on his flight suit. Then he grasped the yoke and started down. No one spoke, the quiet cabin broken only by Kolar's soft wheeze, the tinkle of the positioners. Soman brought them down.

"Ben," Soman said. "See those port covers stowed in those rings. Deploy 'em. In case we get a laser flash."

Ben moved about the cabin, covering the ports.

The entry hole grew slowly. They sank into the black moon.

"Joni, how far down are we?"

"Fifty K."

Soman watched the screen. "About as deep as the laser chamber already." They were halfway to the center.

Joni shouted, "There's the bottom!"

He slowed the descent, then glanced at the holo. Sure enough. Ninety-five k down, the cylinder ended at the exact center of the moon.

The bottom of the shaft was lit with eleven smaller concentric circles, closely spaced, not more than ten meters between them. As they watched, the center black ring brightened to a luminous white. If ever there was a symbol for a landing pad, that was it. This was what the original mission had come searching for. Soman felt equal parts wonder and terror.

The bump, the momentary sensation of weight, then the barest rebound of their bodies against restraints.

The message in the panels was clear: four scenes, clearly showing the ingot lifted from the left side cradle, moved to the right and inserted there. But the part of the scene that stayed with Soman, etched into his brain, was the appendages that held the ingot in the illustration. Not fingers, but long curved claws.

A suit hit Soman in the back.

"Here," Flip said. "This one must be yours. It says fat boy size." Flip turned his own suit back and forth. "Show me which end I crawl into."

Soman glided backward in a slow tumble. Vertigo as the chamber spun. The flashes grew. They *were* inside, a pulsating pattern of brilliant light, so perfectly white Soman thought he had never seen white before. Then it retreated, and within moments it faded, leaving a pointillist image of black spray on the retina, and a trembling of the flesh.

Soman opened his eyes, disoriented, unable at first to move, seeing only the wild sweep of helmet lights shooting into the dark from the jumbled crew. His tumble had carried him to the full reach of his tether, thirty meters above the platform. Clicking the annunciator, he realized there was no chatter on open.

The others realized it at the same time, looking around.

How could that be. The quan needed no signal; it used the quantum structure of the universe. Infinitely more reliable than radio. Nothing interrupted the quan.

Soman pointed toward the LEV, and everyone moved toward it.

The sound of wheezing filled the cabin as they tumbled through the airlock. Kolar was pale, his breathing ragged. "Something woke me," he whispered.

Soman watched the monitor. Heart rate 140. A turn for the worse.

"What was that light?" Kolar asked.

"No idea." Soman moved to the driver's seat. "Let's see what *Sorcerer* picked up." He glanced at the com panel and saw only black. Quan dead. No return signal. No system link. No electromag signature. Soman took the controls. Where was *Sorcerer*.

He lifted off, then fought an urge for speed. Back up through the opening. Easy, man. Globules of sweat swirled in a cloud around his face. Meter by meter the walls slid by. The hole at the end of the shaft grew wider, everyone straining to see some detail in the black viewscreen.

Flip shouted, "The ship!" A portion of hull was visible beyond the hole.

Soman knew it couldn't be *Sorcerer*, left behind in orbit around the planet.

The LEV slipped out of the Pearl. Something floated there all right, so huge it could be a planet, its surface so close the LEV must fall to its gravity, yet it didn't. Soman tried to make sense of the texture of the thing, lines and curves like rivers and ridges. As he tried to puzzle out what he was seeing, Joni said, "They came to us."

Chapter 32

The dot of the LEV hung in a sliver of space between the smooth curve of the Pearl and the fissured surface of the thing.

Then, in an eye-blink, the object before them disappeared, the screen dark as a cave, not a pixel anywhere. Blackness where something had floated a moment ago. He pinged—and got an instant return. It was still there. How could an entire planet go dark.

Soman checked again for *Sorcerer's* signature. Nothing.

"Look," Joni said, pointing. A single light had flickered on, directly in front of the LEV.

In the pool of light around it, Soman could make out details on the surface. Now he saw it wasn't rivers and geology. It was much closer than he'd imagined; with a surface of twisting tubes and girders of massive proportion, ovoid modules with broad fins, the whole assembly resembling a termite nest, chaotic in design, a manufactured object the size of a third class asteroid. Yet the LEV hovered half a kilometer above the surface without falling. Soman sat with his mouth open, uncertain which was more frightening—that they might fall, or that they weren't.

Soman knew there was nowhere to go but forward. He drove the LEV closer, alert for any acceleration that would mean gravity had taken hold, a pull that could crush them. A hundred meters from the light he eased back, stopped by an incongruity: a class G dock. He shook his head in mystification, then closed the last hundred meters. That dock was clearly where they wanted him. As he approached, a sense welled up in him—this is what the original *Sorcerer* mission missed.

A solid thunk as the docks mated.

Scanning instruments, Soman said, "It's breathable. No Nox—hey—" he looked up at the hiss of the airlock. James peered through the widening gap. "Wait," Soman called out. "We should still suit up, you never—" But James had slipped through. Joni glanced back for just an instant, then floated after him, Flip following.

Soman hesitated. Every bit of training told him to suit up. No idea what was the right procedure now, far beyond the realm of humans.

"Come on," Ben said, heading for the lock.

For a few seconds, Soman watched Kolar's restless sleep. Then he slipped out after Ben.

A wash of light from the LEV spilled across a large airlock, the chamber spherical, its bulkheads grey and uniform. No, not completely uniform; on a section of the far wall was a dark rectangle, or maybe a gap in the bulkhead. On the curved wall below the rectangle hung a latticework that ran right up to the darkness. Ben pulled himself up the lattice, using it like a ladder. Within seconds he'd disappeared into the dim reaches beyond the last glimmer of light.

Soman pushed across the dock. Where the ladder ended, Soman reached into the dark, beyond the top of a wall—or the edge of a cliff. He touched a surface. It felt smooth and sticky, and he pulled back with a jerk, straining to see into the darkness. He heard rustling ahead as the others fumbled in the dark.

He reached forward again. Once again his hand clung to the surface. Not sticky, really, but attracted, like a magnet to iron. He reached with both hands, and using the stickiness of the wall, he pulled himself beyond the end of the ladder into the pitch black. Instantly his head felt heavy. The surface started to feel like down. Soman crawled, clinging like a bug, clenching his eyes shut to quell vertigo. Drawing his feet under him, he squatted straight out from the wall like an Escher print. Pressure on the soles of the shoes. Just like gravity. He stood, tentatively, arms out for balance. It *was* gravity. Or something that felt like gravity, without the vibration and rumble of spingrav. Gravity that existed only this side of the ladders.

"Look," someone whispered.

A smooth white sphere hung in the near distance, the size of a cue ball held at arm's length. But as soon as he looked straight at it, it disappeared. He reached out. Nothing. When he looked away, he glimpsed the glowing sphere again, but only in peripheral vision. There and not there.

"Six of them," Joni said from close by.

The glowing spheres provided no illumination; the chamber could be a small room or a cavernous space. He reached into the darkness like a blind man and touched Joni's shoulder. She grasped his arm.

From the left a new circle of light appeared, then grew. Joni's profile became visible in the strengthening glow; her thin nose, the curve of lip, a flicker of highlights in her hair. The circle lengthened to an oval, all of them holding up hands against the sudden brightness. The wash of light revealed the space in which they stood, a circular chamber of a dozen meters diameter. They stood at one edge, near the drop to the airlock. On the opposite wall, the bright oval continued to enlarge.

Soman squinted through the glare. Movement in the oval. A glint and a shadow. Something coming through. A figure. Soman drew an involuntary breath. A woman wearing gold fabric, black hair halfway to her waist, oval face with dark almond eyes. Those eyes—recognition weakened his bowels.

She walked toward him, fabric sliding over supple limbs.

Soman stood frozen to the spot, recognizing every detail, knowing it couldn't be his long-dead Anne walking toward him.

A flurry of motion behind the woman. Long spikes and bulbous shapes. Even in that split second before he recognized the forms, an atavistic fear rose in him. Joni stepped back into a crouch, but Soman was unable to move, frozen in place by the woman, and by the spiders behind her, man-size spiders, crowding through the oval port.

The impossibility of encountering a woman gone over three thousand years shook the will from sinew and muscle; Soman swayed as she closed the last few meters. Behind him, Joni had begun to wail, a low warbling noise of terror.

"Well, Mr. Soman, you finally show up."

That voice. Not Anne's but—

"Watch out!" Flip shouted.

A motion too quick to follow. He watched her fist retract from a spot just beneath his eyes. The mass of her hair swung sideways in reaction to the motion, sweeping like a black cape onto her extended arm. She receded; the room spun, light faded. The sickening flash of concussion. Pain in the center of his face. The floor slamming his tailbone. His head striking with a crack. Dark, quiet, life suspended.

Then the world rushed back at him with a roar of tinnitus like a jet engine. He clawed at the air, his nose streaming thick warm liquid, head throbbing. She stood over him, hands on hips.

"Mr. Soman, I've been waiting a long time for that."

Soman couldn't answer, unable to breathe through his smashed nose, impossible to comprehend the woman standing over him, Anne in every detail, the voice Commander Ley's. Scrambling against the smooth surface, he managed to sit up, gasping through his mouth, blood spattering the floor, plop, plop, plop.

Behind the woman the spiders sidestepped back and forth, claws clacking against the floor. One scuttled forward, its short front limbs tipped with a circle of fine talons—the claws from the pictograph inside Pearl. Someone tugged at Soman's arm, but he was unable to get up, unable to move, unable to think. He detected an odor unlike anything he'd experienced on Earth or the ships of men, and a sensation of bone-chilling cold.

"Get away!" someone hollered, and with a glance Soman saw James yanking Joni back. Ben slumped on all fours, a splatter of vomit beneath him.

A shadow fell across Soman. The spider loomed, smooth globular head, four compound eyes on stalks swiveling and dipping. Soman's stomach clenched reflexively. He sat helplessly beneath the creature, head bowed, the buzz of overload filling his skull.

Joni's scream rose in pitch as the spider reached out two sets of pincers.

One chela held a clear globe. The other appendage dabbed Soman's blood where it congealed on the floor.

"It's eating the blood," Joni said with disgust.

The woman laughed. "Just taking samples."

The spider somehow coaxed the darkening fluid through the wall of the globe. Clutching the full vessel in a claw, it sidestepped across the floor and through the portal, the others following.

The woman tossed her hair back and looked Soman in the eye. "First Officer Ley, assuming command of *Sorcerer*," she said.

Soman blinked. Anne. Ley. It couldn't be. They were both dead.

James sidled cautiously to the edge of the portal and peer around the edge where the spider carrying the blood had disappeared.

Ben wiped his mouth on his sleeve.

"But this," the woman continued, running her hands lightly down Anne's torso, smoothing the fabric over taut curvature, "is something else, isn't it. After a lifetime in that old clunk of mine, not quite a man, not quite a woman, I decided to try a new look. I chose something you would appreciate."

Soman's mind whirled. In his confusion he thought to tell her *Sorcerer* was gone. Then it occurred to him: she must have the ship. "How—" He tried to stand. Sucking breath, he aspirated blood and hunched in a fit of coughing.

"Mr. Soman, of course we knew of your late wife. I had seen this image from the Chicago Trib site." She pointed to her temple. "It was up here, we only had to tease it out. There are only so many neurons to hide in." She speared him with a broad smile, though her eyes never flickered. Anne's face, but not her smile. A smile more scary than anything in Ley's old arsenal. "Now I'm interested in the rest of the story. The secrets you never told."

Soman spit blood. He couldn't accept it, and yet it was Ley's voice. "But how…we thought…Siba said…"

"That I was dead?"

"How can you be…"

Ley's eyes faded to the distance. When she spoke, her voice was dead, smooth and level. "I *was* dead. The air ran out. And then there was water…" She stared beyond the light of the empty portal.

Soman searched her face, taking in the familiar, intimate shape of that body. As long as she didn't speak, Soman could persuade himself that his wife stood before him, and all the years of longing burst through, though he knew he couldn't let them, that he'd never get them under control.

Ley's presence returned. "I was shouting," she said. "But the shouting wasn't sound, it was transmissions and data streams and…things I couldn't understand. I was transferred to a machine, then fluxed here. It was like going into a descroid and waking in a new body. And the body is the web. They installed me into one of them." She gestured toward the spiders withdrawing through the portal. "But I couldn't greet you in one of *those*."

Soman strained to breathe; not from pain, but from a realization rising in him.

"Yes, Mr. Soman. You took my life and the Vradra gave me forever."

Wobbling on his feet, Soman glimpsed the long glide to eternity. Of all people, Ley had found it. Ley who had played her life like a two-minute drill. Relief flooded through him; Ley hadn't died. Ley was… "You've been living here for two hundred fifty years," he said.

"I don't think of it like that," Ley said. "Time is…different here."

Goddamn, that meant Siba hadn't needed to…

"Had the courage to tell them what happened, Mr. Soman?" She was scanning Ben up and down.

It knotted Soman's stomach to see Anne's eyes looking at Ben that way.

"He told us," Joni said, as she examined the spot on the floor from which the spider had removed every evidence of Soman's blood, leaving not even a stain.

"Everything, Mr. Soman?"

Soman nodded. Blood ran down his throat, gagging him; a fresh spatter blew out his nose.

From the open portal where the Vradra had disappeared, James called over. "Where did they go?"

"To the lab," Ley answered. "It's not every day we encounter new samples.”

Flip moved to the other side of the portal. “Are they dangerous?” he asked.

Joni made a derisive noise. Throwing a distasteful look at Ley she said, “I’d say *she’s* the dangerous one.”

Ley dismissed Joni with a glance, then asked Soman, “And where is our Siba?”

Soman looked down, unable to speak. Images of Siba spun. Siba making that last log entry, old and feeble. Siba in the life support bubble. Siba striding through the nexport behind Ley, mysterious, young, irresistible. Siba exhaling her last breath as he held her. He couldn’t stop the sobs that burst from him.

“Don’t you tell me—” Ley straightened, spine erect, shoulders back. Ley’s stiff gesture, not a hint of the lissome grace that Anne wore like a slinky dress. Her eyes smoldered, and it seemed she coiled to take a step toward him. “Then who is it you left back in the LEV?”

“Kolar,” he said. Then the realization came to him is a flash. He looked up at Ley. “Kolar. He’s dying. Can you…”

Her dead smile flickered as if a thought amused her. “Of course we can. I want to see the LEV anyway.” Moving toward the ladders, she knelt, leaned into the weightless zone and pulled herself over the edge.

Soman and Ben exchanged a glance. “Can we trust her?” Ben asked.

“Trust her?” Joni mocked.

“I deserved what she did,” Soman said, cradling his dripping nose in his hand. “And we can’t do anything for Kolar.” But what a risk. They knew nothing about this place, and Ley was the last person he’d trust. But they couldn’t just wait for Kolar to die…“If they can do this…” he murmured. A technology beyond anything imaginable. And if the machine wears out, move to a new one. But it was all so fast. God, Kolar.

James shrugged. “He’s your Altan.” He stepped cautiously through the portal and peered after the withdrawing Vradra.

Ben glanced toward the ladders. “I don’t like leaving her alone with the LEV.” He moved after Ley.

Soman followed. By the time he reached the top of the ladders, Ben had descended. Soman stared at the precipice. He went to his knees at the edge, gripping the ladder to keep his hands from shaking. Then plunged over the edge.

Ley had stopped just inside the hatch, hanging there in the zero G of the LEV. “A cockpit like this was my whole life,” she said, stroking the edge of the lock. “Life was so hard, and I never realized it. You just kept going. You knew it could end any time, but you avoided thinking about it." She pushed off and drifted through the cockpit, touching the console. "We avoided thinking about a lot of things. It's amazing how humans lie to themselves, Mr. Soman."

Soman slid past Ley to Kolar. His vital signs had sagged. Heart rate 135, blood pressure dropping. He pushed Kolar's hair out of his eyes, then watched Ley as she fingered the suits floating at the ready. Finally he leaned close and said, "Kolar." Kolar hadn't the strength to turn his head, but his eyes swiveled. He listened as Soman spoke to him, his eyes riveted as he grasped what was offered. Soman saw, in Kolar's expression, dread over the failure of his mortal body in this distant outpost and astonishment over the unexpected opportunity that had been laid before him.

Ben asked Ley, "Are you running the place then?"

Ley grasped the arm of a suit, running her hand along the fabric. "Oh no. Mostly I've shut down to wait out the years until someone made it back out here. I knew more humans would eventually come. Never imagined it would be you. What a treat."

"Who's in charge, then?"

"No one's in charge." She shoved the suit back into its place. "When individuals don't have to compete to stay alive, you no longer need leaders. Just imagine—there's no reason for competition. We tap the limitless dark energy; we have access to all the resources we could ever need. We aren't worried every hour about starving, or having our mates stolen." She looked over at Soman. "Or dying."

Soman waited. Then Kolar met Soman's eyes, and gave a barely perceptible nod.

Soman looked up. "He agrees to the procedure."

Ben's face twisted in anguish. "Soman, I don't know."

"Dammit neither do I! You have a better idea? Look at this display."

Kolar's eyes closed, as if he couldn't bear the debate.

"Shouldn't we find out more about this?" He turned to Ley.

Ley glanced at the med-suit display, then said, "It seems to me he doesn't have much choice." Her focus faded into the distance again, her eyes glazed over.

Ben said, "How does it work?"

But Ley stood immobile and mute.

Soman watched the deteriorating display for a few seconds, then touched Ley's arm. "I think we need to hurry."

Ben gripped Kolar's arm. "Kolar," he said, urgently.

Kolar's eyes re-opened.

"Are you sure you want to do this?"

Again the slight movement of Kolar's head. Up, down.

Ley's presence returned. Her mouth turned up into a smile, but the rest of her face moved not a millimeter. A twitch more than a smile, like a horse's tail flicking flies. "The Vradra are preparing."

"How long?" Soman asked.

"A few minutes," Ley said.

"You can do this so fast?" A thought turned his stomach. "You're putting him in a spider."

Ley chuckled. "No, no. It's not exactly the way I had it planned, but it will be amusing."

Soman tried not to imagine Ley's idea of amusing. With his hand resting on Kolar's head, he felt the heat emanating from him, his life force leaking away.

"And then we'll prepare for you," Ley said, as if reading his thoughts.

At his expression, she said, "You don't want to keep trusting to this flesh and blood, do you? It's highly unreliable." Her gaze lit on Ben's rebuilt face. "I can see you know all about that." stroking his jaw, she rotated his head, studying the work, running a finger along the smooth line. "This is all new, isn't it?"

Her caress of Ben made Soman squirm.

Running her fingers lightly over Ben's new lips, she said, "There's something about real skin that gets my juices going, after all the years. Figuratively speaking, of course. I don't think I have the actual juices now, though we could work on that."

Ben pulled away from her touch.

Soman experienced a momentary shift, as if looking down on his body from a great height. A moment of panic struck him at the thought of leaving this body behind. "How long…to be ready again." Suddenly Soman wanted more time. This was moving too fast. Kolar didn't have a choice, but…this step was starting to feel awfully close to death.

She turned, an eyebrow lifted. "You are most eager, Mr. Soman. As I expected. Siba told me about your obsession."

Of course she had. For a moment the throbbing in his face overcame him. He touched his bloody nose. It had swollen enormously. He could feel the bits of bone embedded deep in his face. It was going to need attention, soon.

Ben glanced back toward the ladders. "Where are the others?"

Soman turned. No one had followed them back to the LEV.

"I suppose they went off exploring the station," Ley said.

"Exploring?" Soman asked. He remembered James standing at the portal, more interested in the Vradra than in Kolar.

"You said station?" Ben asked.

Soman pictured the bulk of it looming above the Pearl. "It's so huge we thought it might be a planet, except—" he peered at her. "How did you get it here so fast?"

Ley cackled. "Get it here?"

"We were only inside for a couple hours."

"Mr. Soman. All that descroid travel has damaged your brain." She laughed. "We may not be able to recover enough from these neurons to help you."

He stilled as she patted his cheek, Anne's hand, Ley's rough touch.

"You don't think you're still there, do you?" she asked.

His mouth hung open as her laugh filled the LEV. Where could they have gone, in almost no time at all. If they weren't at Epsilon Eridani…his skin tingled at the recollection of those lights behind their eyes, the sensations. He pictured *Sorcerer*, derelict, sole satellite now of EE2. Systems still humming, air circulating, coffee cooling in its cups. Its human occupants transported mysteriously, like stories of the Rapture. Never to be manned again, until future voyagers from Earth discover the artifact and wonder.

The med suit beeped. Kolar shuddered.

Soman's attention flew back to the display. "His heart's gone unstable. One eighty, then thirty." He looked at Ley. "Is it ready?"

Ley dismissed Kolar with a wave of her hand. "Don't worry. We have time to do the transfer. Come on, I'll show you where we are." She pushed off toward the hatch.

Kolar's face had turned grey.

"We have to take care of Kolar first," Soman said.

"Mr. Soman, I believe you're afflicted with compassion in your old age."

A clatter behind them. Soman spun to see a spider entering the hatch, the Vradra with all those limbs better suited to weightless maneuvering than humans.

Soman and Ben shrank against the bulkhead as the thing squeezed past. It pulled itself to Kolar with three grabs, legs windmilling, pulling behind it a board with cords trailing from the sides. It fastened the straps to hold Kolar down. Ben slid into position at one end and grabbed the handles. "We're going with him," he said. "Come on, Soman. Take the other end."

After a moment's hesitation, the spider slipped back through the open airlock, smooth and quiet, an elbow brushing Soman on its way past. Soman barely flinched. The obvious sentience of the Vradra quickly overcame his ancient revulsion for their body form.

He and Ben scrambled to their feet at the top of the ladders. The litter carrying Kolar was immune to whatever force held the rest of them to the station floor, floating easily at carrying height.

"Flip?" Soman called out. It was dark once again, the bright portal gone. The six spheres hung there, devilish, seeming to exist when you weren't looking at them, but disappearing at a direct look. Some kind of odd spider art. Maybe suited to those compound eyes.

A portal opened in front of Ley revealing a long tube, its bright walls illuminated. No sign of the rest of the crew. Ley disappeared into the tube and Soman followed, guiding the litter. He hurried to catch up, Kolar's head bobbing limply. "So where are we?" Soman asked.

"You can't figure it out? Mr. Soman, you're the navigator."

He said nothing. Fucking Ley.

"Back there in the observatory," Ley said, "What did you see between the spheres?"

"Observatory? I thought it was a gallery, or..."

Ley laughed. "It's the window to where we are." She gave him a moment to think. "What did you see?"

Soman tried to remember. So compelling were the spheres, nothing else had registered. "I don't know. I didn't notice anything."

"Nothing. Very observant. Total black around the spheres. What does that tell you?"

Soman tried to think. No stars. "We're inside a planetoid."

Ley laughed. "Did you ping anything when you left the moon?"

"Uh, just the station."

"Correct. We're not inside anything. We're outside of everything." She chuckled and said, "A planetoid," derisively. Then she stepped through the portal that marked the end of the tunnel.

Soman followed, then stopped short. He'd stepped into a vast, round chamber—a perfect hemisphere. In the center, glistening, floated a thick metal ring on edge, a meter in diameter. Around it scuttled a crowd of Vradra. Beside the ring, a block rose like a rectangular crystal that could have grown from the floor itself. A human figure lay upright, suspended on the face of the block, naked, white on black. Soman could almost imagine a web of spider silk stretching outward, the dangling figure at its center ready to be sucked dry.

Ben cried, "It's you!"

Soman walked to the figure. Its eyes sagged open, though Soman saw no spark in their blue depth. A good match for his height and build, the effect suggesting Soman, but the details imperfect—art, not photography. His skin crawled with the realization that Ley had been prepared to transfer him to this body. She'd been waiting for him.

Ley slipped a hand around Soman's waist, the softness of Anne's breast against his arm. Longing weakened his knees.

"Not bad, is it?" Ley said. "Of course the network can tease every detail from a memory."

Soman studied the man formed from Ley's memory. The jaw more pronounced, the eyes set deeper, the overall effect more pugnacious than Soman. Memory; what you see, what you want to see, what you wish, all tangled up. And easily tricked. "Why would you do this for me?" Soman asked.

"You don't want to?"

Soman studied the equipment. A slab of black and a plain ring. No controls, no moving parts. No sound but the click of claws on the floor. "How does it work?"

"How can the Vradra explain a million years of principles we can't comprehend?"

A commotion drew Soman's attention. Spiders had positioned Kolar's litter so his head hovered at the center of the ring. Ben walked to the edge of the litter and took Kolar's hand. Then he looked up at Ley. "I don't..." he said. But Ley's pupils had dilated, her eyes vacant, leaving only her shell.

Soman stood before what was to be the new Kolar. Touching an arm, he pinched a bit of skin. Thicker, more resilient than human skin. What did it look like inside. Did it possess the same organs, the same metabolism, or was it a new biology entirely. Or a machine. Its huge pupils disconcerting.

It was about to get confusing, with two of him. Though they wouldn't look exactly alike. Kolar-Soman was missing the scar above the eye, and the hard disk in the belly. And his nose wasn't broken. It dawned on Soman that he could choose any form, any body, any look. No, Anoka needed to see her father. Maybe the Soman of seven years ago, the way he'd looked as Anoka had faded under the narcotic. Younger, without the timeworn look. Soman shook his head to think of all the time that had passed since he'd left Anoka in her pod. Seven years to him. Thirty-three centuries on the calendar.

As Soman stared into the being's eyes, they blinked. The pupils shrank.

Soman teetered backward, away from the thing. The eyes followed him. Soman's own eyes, watching him. A thump. A foot shook; a heel tap tapped against the wall.

"Ben!" Soman shouted, glancing over. Kolar's hand was clamped around Ben's wrist.

A new sound from Kolar-Soman, pinned there like a rare insect. "Omm," it said, lips round, throat quivering. "Omm." Then the lips formed a new shape, a new sound. "Ay." The lips moved silently for a moment. Then it said, "Om. Ay. Sin." Again. And again. The sound changed each time it repeated, more continuous each time. The new Kolar was speaking. "Amazing," it said.

"Ben!"

Ben looked up, anguish on his face. Kolar lay limp and slack. A spider pulled the litter away, and a fresh portal appeared ahead of it.

Ben followed. "Where is he going?"

"Kolar is there now," Ley said, indicating the form hanging from the wall.

"But..." The spider moved Kolar through the portal and it snapped closed behind them.

Ley called to Ben, "The transfer is complete. Come and greet Kolar."

Thumps and murmurings from the figure pinned to the block.

"Where are they taking him?" Ben asked. He stared at the wall where the portal had vanished.

"The Vradra must have their samples," she said. "This is, after all, a research station."

"But..." Ben stopped. Spiders clustered around the new Kolar, easing him to the floor, stretching his new limbs. Ben scanned the chamber, his eyes lighting on the portal in the far wall where they had entered. "I think I'm going to puke," he said.

Ley said, "You look like you need a stiff drink."

Ben stumbled toward the portal.

Kolar sat on the floor, turning his head experimentally, flexing his arms.

Soman hesitated, wanting to see every instant of Kolar's resurrection. What the hell had gotten into Ben! "How long until he's functioning?" he asked Ley.

"A few minutes," she said. "Then, Mr. Soman, I have to prepare for you." Hands on hips, she said, "Though how we'll tell you apart, I don't know. I suppose he'll be the nice one."

Chapter 33

Soman went looking for Ben, found him the LEV, in furious motion. Soman looked back through the hatch. Kolar was back there, coming to life. Snatched from death. An actual way to save a person, instead of what doctors did. They might call it saving a life, but they only staved off the inevitable.

Ben shouted over to Soman, "Come on, man. Get it together."

Soman looked around, alarmed by Ben's vehemence. He worked the control panel like a test pilot in a tailspin.

"What are we doing?" Soman asked.

Ben concentrated on the display. "Powering up the nav." Ben scanned the com screen, glanced to the hatch, then swung around to face Soman. "We have to find the others and get out."

"Get out?"

"Yeah, get out. Before they kill us too."

"Ben they didn't kill him. They saved him. Didn't you hear him tell us 'amazing'? It's Kolar, starting over..."

"They killed him," Ben said. He gripped the console as if he would rip it from its moorings. "I watched him die."

"But...he's in that new body."

"I don't know who that was on the wall, but Kolar looked at me one last time and died. *After* that thing on the wall woke."

Soman stared at Ben. "But..."

"We've got to find our crew."

"But we can..."

"Don't be foolish! Why do you trust her? You've noticed she doesn't like you much."

"I...we saw Kolar take over—"

"It's not Kolar."

"He spoke to me. He *was* Kolar."

"It will talk like Kolar, it will act like Kolar, but it won't be Kolar. Kolar is gone." Ben gripped Soman harder. "Don't fool yourself, man." He released Soman and pushed off. "We've got to find the others." When Soman didn't follow, Ben stopped, halfway to the hatch. "If you do this, we'll be left with a machine looking like Soman that thinks it's you. And you'll be...samples."

"It would be me. I'd have all my memories, everything that makes me—me." With a body like that, a person would be assured of all the time in the Universe. All the worlds to be visited. All the future to be witnessed. The inventions. The unimaginable, the distant future. No more gut-wrench at remembering, before shoving it away in panic, that some day the Universe will flow onward without you. Then for some reason he thought of Lar and his office stacked high with samples.

"Just because someone steals your memories doesn't mean they become you. Your soul is more than a collection of memories."

"I don't believe in a soul."

"Then what are they going to transfer that will make that machine you?" He punched the hatch open panel. The servos wound up.

Soman watched the hatch re-open. Possibly, for this transfer to work, there had to be a soul. But…Soman hesitated. Perhaps belief in immortality is no different than belief in the soul, a vain hope, a long habit hard to break. Then these are truly the only moments allowed a human.

Ben disappeared up the ladders. Soman fled the emptiness of the LEV, and followed.

Standing before a section of wall, Ben said, "Isn't this where the portal was, the one James was looking through?"

The surface was smooth, seamless, and inscrutable. Around them hung the ghostly spheres. Soman was certain he could see them, until he looked. Then he couldn't be sure. Like souls.

They retreated to the LEV, closing the hatch behind them with a whir and thump. Soman touched the back of a seat. Four empty seats. He watched the suits hanging in the rack still as stone.

"Soman," Ben whispered, his voice urgent.

Soman followed Ben's gaze.

A man hovered outside the port, peering in. A large man with a broad chest. "Kolar?" Soman asked.

"Fuck," Ben said.

A whine and a crackle. Both men jumped as motors activated and the hatch cracked open. Kolar slid through, naked and smiling.

Ben turned whiter than Monar pale. "How did you get in?"

Kolar seemed to ponder for a moment, studying the hatch. "The Vradra have a web here. Equipment is easy. I saw the switch in my mind. Just a pulse at the right place and it opened."

It was Kolar's easygoing manner, but Kolar with an advanced degree in the workings of things.

"You speak English," Soman said.

Kolar pushed off and floated toward the suit locker. "Yes, I spoke to you before, don't you remember?"

Of course. He had said 'amazing'. "How?"

Searching through the locker behind the pressure suits, Kolar said, "I suppose now I need the fat boy size." He withdrew a silver flight suit and slipped it on. "All the knowledge of the station is available to me. Though it's hard to navigate through it. Bewildering, really. Most of it I can't fathom. Language, though, seems more or less automatic." He looked at the controls. "On the journey here, I could not comprehend how these worked. Now I see ways to improve them."

Ben punched a button and the hatch wheezed shut. "Why did you come here?"

"The spiders aren't very good company. Neither is the woman. And it was all too much to take in. The web is confusing." Kolar glanced around the interior of the LEV like a tourist. "I wanted to see this place with new eyes." He touched his eyelids. "Literally new eyes." Then he chuckled. Unlike Ley's ominous laugh, Kolar's came with bushy angled eyebrows that gave him a quizzical look.

"Why do you look like me but sound like Kolar?" Soman asked.

"I choose my own voice. Of course I remember the sound." Then his voice changed. "Why would I want to sound like you?"

Soman's skin crawled, hearing his voice imitated perfectly. As if a twin had moved into his flat, answering his phone, using his kitchen, sleeping with his woman.

"Can you tell us apart?" Soman asked Ben.

"His nose isn't broken." Ben said, up against the bulkhead, keeping his distance. Then he said, "I know you're not Kolar."

"Jesus, Ben, anyone can see it's Kolar—I mean, he looks like me, but obviously he's Kolar."

"No, it's a good question," Kolar said. He tugged an earlobe absently, the way Kolar always had. "I ask myself the same question. My brains have much to discuss. But now it is many brains."

Soman said to Ben, "See, only Kolar would say that." It *was* Kolar. Calm, gentle, never prodded to anger. Asking instead of telling.

Kolar looked at Soman. "You are planning to do this?"

"Of course."

Kolar studied the two men. "You have argued over it. Do not be hasty. It is hard to be certain if there are two Kolars or one."

Soman's mouth opened.

"It may be a risk for a man in his prime years. Maybe you awake in an immortal body. If this is one." Kolar raised his arms and considered. "Nothing I have learned yet proves this to be so. But maybe it is no more than donating your experience and your knowledge as you would donate a kidney. For me it is miraculous. But for the man who was once Kolar…I cannot be sure."

"We have to find the others," Ben said.

Soman frowned. There must be a way to distinguish the real Kolar from a copy. Some characteristic that makes him genuinely Kolar, not simply a machine with his routines. That would mean our friends, our lovers, our families could be mimicked by imposters employing a collection of cues. He looked into Kolar's eyes—this being has all Kolar's complexities, and even *he* isn't sure.

"Your arguments are as perfect as Kolar could make them, to convince me you are not Kolar."

"No, I would not try to convince you. I only say I am not sure."

"But—"

Ben pressed Soman. "You can't still want to do this."

Soman faltered. "I…"

Ben said, "Take us to see Kolar. The old Kolar."

Kolar's eyes took on the far-away look they had seen earlier in Ley. He stayed away a long time. When he returned, he said, "I am sorry. I have not learned to navigate well." Once more he faded. Finally he shook his head. "The old Kolar is gone. He is now with the…the chosen."

"The chosen?" Ben asked.

"Kolar nodded with a faraway look. "It is what Vradra means. Chosen." He stared off for a few more seconds. "Certain individuals are chosen for this service, to come here for the transfer, to become…what would we call them…" His eyebrows lifted slightly. "Scientists, I suppose."

"You mean all these Vradra have been transferred?"

Kolar nodded.

"None of these is a…an original?" Ben asked.

For a quiet moment, Kolar fingered the fabric of the seat where he'd lain for days on the edge of death. "No. The chosen travel here to become part of the station."

Ben grabbed Kolar. "Where's the rest of our crew?"

Kolar blinked, and once again his attention faded, disappearing to the inhuman reaches of the station, leaving an empty husk resembling the corpse of Soman, vacant as when it hung from the wall amid clattering

Vradra.

Soman tried to rein in a growing disquiet.

Then Kolar was back, his expression perplexed. "Some factual matters exist on the surface, easy to find. But the workings of the station…it's…" He glanced to the hatch. "Let's try…" he slid out of the LEV. Soman and Ben followed.

"You said scientists," Ben said to Kolar as they approached the ladders. "What are they doing here?"

They started up the ladders. "The station's purpose is research," Kolar said. "Those spheres you can't quite see." He paused. "The Vradra are searching for…I can't tell what."

"What are they?" Soman asked.

"They're…" Kolar cocked his head. "Universes."

"You mean galaxies." Soman said. Kolar was having trouble understanding, raised in Alta without the knowledge of space to comprehend. They reached the chamber, and once again Soman tried to catch a direct glimpse of the things.

"Oh, no. In fact one of these is our universe."

Soman stared. "You can't get outside the Universe," he whispered. But what had Ley said—*We're not inside anything, we're outside everything.*

Kolar shrugged. "Those aren't photons you're detecting. A gravity wave up the flux ripples the edge of your retina. It's an artifact of the flux line, not light from the Universe."

The quan hadn't worked. *Sorcerer* was gone. There were no stars. They were beyond the farthest shore, beyond the most distant shore imaginable. Beyond any recognizable thing.

And soon, beyond death.

A sense of wonder filled Soman. Ley had said the Vradra knew how to control dark energy. That would certainly change the needs of sentient beings—no cruel work of daily living, no more consuming their planet. Devoted to exploration. Not the exploration humans do, stealing resources here and there for brief forays into new territory, scrabbling for yet more resources, ruining whatever they find in its exploitation. This was true exploration, an entire civilization dedicated to research.

Kolar said, "When beings arrive from the beacons, they—we add their knowledge. But I am unable to see the goal of it all. "

Soman looked at Ben. When beings arrive…

"Our friends," Ben said. He shook Kolar. "Can you find them?"

Kolar looked to the wall. A fresh portal grew. Soman jumped through. They stood in a room amid black cylinders like oil drums, spaced several meters apart. Soman ran a hand across one. "Why did you bring us here?" he asked Kolar.

"It seemed this room was connected to them somehow," Kolar said, frowning.

Soman looked back at the still-open portal. "Is this the way they came when they followed the spiders?" he asked.

Kolar shook his head. "It doesn't work that way. There is only one portal. It opens where I wish, where I direct it. Except I am uncertain…"

Ben pulled him back through the portal. "Come on, try again." The portal closed and Kolar once again faded into concentration.

The portal opened again. This time it led them into a long tunnel, like the one that had taken them to the chamber with the ring. Ben began to run.

"How did we get here from the moon," Soman asked Kolar as they jogged to keep up.

"That flux," Kolar said. "The Vradra discovered it, hmm, longer ago than humans have lived, it appears."

"I meant, how does it work, traveling so far in a few moments."

Kolar slowed, while Ben sprinted ahead. "I see information, but there's no translation, I have to…there is a network of these flux lines. The Vradra use them for travel within the galaxy, then between galaxies, and now to this point of…what would it be," he slowed again. "Symmetry. We're at a point of symmetry"

EE2. The beacon. Just enough to tantalize, to ensure that any race with technology and curiosity would make the voyage, then move the ingot from A to B.

Ahead, Ben peered through a new portal. Soman heard the clacking as he drew near, and then the room came into view. Dozens of Vradra lined up on pedestals, their legs dangling, free to grasp and manipulate. Machinery suspended from the ceiling. Fitted around the compound eyes of Vradra on their pedestals were instruments of glass and delicate metal parts. A spider eased itself onto a seat.

"Were they here?" Ben asked.

"I am not sure," Kolar said. "But I see where the woman is. Do you want to go there?"

"No!" Ben said.

Soman became aware that Kolar was staring at something. A spider just settling to its pedestal held something, and they all watched as it turned the object over with two front claws, then held it up to an instrument. A tool of some sort peeled back the chalky white surface layer, like skinning an orange. The shape, familiar somehow, but incongruous.

Then the Vradra turned the item of its study around, and Soman's breath stopped. He looked at Kolar. Kolar stared, eyes blank.

"Ben, it's Kolar's foot," Soman whispered.

"No it isn't!" Ben hissed, "Kolar was a black man."

Soman's gaze flicked back to the thing held delicately in the Vradra's claws. Now it peeled skin from the other side. Somehow the blood had been removed, because there was no tint of pink to the flesh. Soman watched the toes as the Vradra inserted the foot into the jaws of some test equipment. A foot. A human foot. Its skin white, not black. Already, with Kolar inhabiting the white body of Soman, he'd begun thinking of Kolar as a white man. But this was not Kolar's foot.

Soman and Ben fell as they retreated into the tunnel, and then they were running, Kolar stumbling behind them. Kolar struggled to keep up, whether from unfamiliarity with this new flesh or from something he saw in the depths of the web.

They fell through the portal, and it snapped closed behind them.

"Where are they?" Ben hollered, shaking Kolar roughly. Kolar stood like a statue, face drawn, eyes lifeless, gone again. Then his gaze returned, and he stumbled sideways as if the ship had suddenly moved. Gravel ground in his throat, as he moaned.

A new portal opened.

Chapter 34

Oppressive warmth wafted from the portal. Even through his crushed nose Soman choked on the stench—rancid sweat, fecal matter, sulfur. And a sound that singed the skin, a scream of agony and despair. The sound froze him, made it impossible to look up from the floor, the brain struggling to make sense of the scene from shadows. An elliptical shape. A tatter of black fabric; not an article of clothing, but enough of clothing's shape to suggest something once worn. A rectangle. Soman knew that above it hovered a gurney like the one that had carried Kolar to his death—or to his new life. Or both.

He forced his eyes to rise from this geometry.

A ring cast the elliptical shadow, identical to the ring that had encircled Kolar's head, a ring now pushed to the side. The sound of wailing palpated the air of the room; at first Soman didn't connect it to the woman writhing on the hovering litter, not a shred of black jumpsuit remaining to cover her agony. Something marred the symmetry of her body, something important, something so incongruous that Soman could not at first understand because it was more than an arm missing, it was all the attachments of the arm, the shoulder, the collarbone, an entire corner of her torso missing, the skin sewn neatly up; not sewn but melted together, the seam running so deep into her chest that a flap of extra skin dangled and her distended breast occupied a spot below her neck like a lost continent drifted halfway around its world in tectonic nightmare. No structure of bone remaining, the left side of her chest a sack holding a frantically beating heart and a throbbing lung whose purpose was to fill the room with its desperate wail.

A phrase assaulted Soman: The spiders must have their samples.

Ben stumbled to Joni, adding his incoherent cry to hers. At his touch, her eyes opened in a chaos of motion. More shrieks, more screams, which Soman couldn't hear, wouldn't hear, didn't hear, because of the roaring in his ears and the premonition that his guts would throw themselves through his mouth.

Cradling Joni's head, Ben turned to take in the rest of the room.

Soman could not fight the urge to follow Ben's gaze to James, on a second litter, his face a mask of calm, eyes focused a million miles beyond the ceiling, unbothered by the commotion. Soman took comfort in James' peaceful countenance, and he lingered on that placid face, even as he sagged to his knees. James had been the longest of the Monar, almost six feet long in space, six feet tall on the Earth, except Soman would never see James standing on Earth. How unexpected that the torso and head of a full-grown man was only three feet long.

Soman's glance searched under the suspended litter as if he might find James' legs there. Legs and hips, because the spiders had sampled everything of bone below James' ribs, then melted the bag of his abdomen around a stub of spine, the final vertebra protruding where genitalia should have hung, stretched like a golf club wrapped too small.

Joni's wails subsided as Ben held her, until there was only the wheezing sound of breath.

Soman closed his eyes. Eventually something gets us. Never know when someone might blow your air or leave you stranded. Or take a few samples to better understand the meaning of the Universe. Siba and Rami and Hakim and now Joni and James and…Flip. Yes, in a minute. Soman attempted to think only of Heather and…he couldn't remember the boy's name. Thought they were so ignorant, settling for the short human lifetime. Now Soman hoped they enjoyed sunset after sunrise, week after day, decade after year. That Marya found a new shay and grew fat little babies and died peacefully. All those lives finished. He hoped they'd been well-lived.

And Flip. What did you do during your century in space. Well first I donated my memories to the big research project beyond the Universe. The one that's been searching for the meaning of everything for the past million years or so. Then I donated, let's see, all the muscles of my face, one by one, down to the bone, and my nose, both eyes, an ear, and yes I guess I donated my tongue too. Hope the Vradra learn enough from this that Soman's new face will work better than the piece of crap Commander Ley got, well it looks great, that's for sure, but it's damn scary when she tries to smile.

Kolar stood with his head bowed. Soman tried to discern his thoughts—then a chill ran through him. Maybe Kolar was receiving instructions. Maybe, maybe, maybe…always something new to puzzle, mysteries multiplying with each bit of knowledge gained, even when standing beyond the border of an infinite Universe, vast information within reach, the most massive compilation of knowledge ever.

"Kolar," Soman said.

Kolar looked up, slowly, as if his head weighed more than he could manage.

"Are they any closer?"

Kolar stared with dull eyes.

"What have they learned? Have they figured out anything more important than how to get energy from empty space, or how to load us up in a machine?" Looking down at Flip, he could see tiny marks on the bone where the last muscle attachments had been scraped neatly away. The expressions Flip had been so skillful at creating with that thin layer of protein and lipid.

"Are they learning anything except more technology?"

Kolar shook his head.

"Are they done here?"

Again Kolar shook his head.

For the first time, Soman saw three spiders standing near the portal, bodies swelling rhythmically, compound eyes pivoting like moviemakers documenting the scene. Urgency cut through Soman's paralysis. He almost touched Flip's bare skull, then hesitated, his hand inches away. "Is there anything left here to save?"

Kolar shook his head one last time, but Soman couldn't tell if it meant 'no' or 'I don't know'. Just a research station. Gathering knowledge. And there huddled Ben with a trembling woman finally quiet, agony brought to comfort by some magic conjured out of touch and murmur more breathtaking than the flux line back into her universe.

Expecting a flood of Vradra to clatter through the portal, Soman grabbed Flip's gurney. "Hurry!" he shouted.

What must Flip perceive of the world. Crippled sounds. The touch of the gurney, Soman's hand steadying him. Pain perhaps, though he expressed no agony. With no soft parts above the neck, he would never again express agony; the bare skeleton expressed it, nothing else needed. If there was mercy beyond the Universe, the spark called Flip was gone, the connection between his cells disrupted, synapses broken, his beating heart simply an autonomic reaction. Still, it seemed important to save whatever remained.

"Don't stop," he yelled, forced to wait at the top of the ladders while Ben adjusted his grip on Joni. Soman glanced back. Kolar had closed the portal, but another might open any instant. While Kolar and Ben moved their charges down the ladders, Soman considered Flip, searching again for any clue that someone occupied the brain behind that shredded face. No sign of sentience. Maybe he was gone; maybe his soul, whatever made him Flip, *had* been transported. Maybe it was just a bit of human foolishness, this attachment to leftover tissue and bone. For a moment hope flickered in Soman. Maybe the three were already gone to…to where, to bodies somewhere—Soman froze. To those three spider bodies, watching as shipmates carried away their human remains, while they learned to use their new hosts like newborn colts testing spindly limbs. What must they have thought as they watched their former selves sliced and sampled, as they'd listened to that scream.

Soman squeezed Flip's hand. "Hang on, buddy." With that bit of human foolishness he dove into the darkness.

The LEV door closed behind Soman with a thunk. Ben attended to Joni, touching her face, probing her perfectly sealed wounds, finding something to cover her nakedness. Joni's eyes had begun to lose their look of animal terror, sliding into dull shock.

Soman's mind raced. Power up. Back to the Pearl. Reverse the cylinder. Flee back along the flux. He secured Flip's gurney to the suit rack. How would they ever care for these fragments. No time to figure. Just get them to *Sorcerer*.

"Kolar," he called out.

Kolar looked up from lashing James onto a seat. He had pulled James half into a flight suit. The empty pant legs floated crazily in the air currents.

"God, tie those down, will you please?" An edge of hysteria in Ben's voice.

At a sudden thought, Soman asked, "Kolar, How long can you last away from the station?"

"I do not know. I think much longer than you."

Soman stared. This version of Kolar, looking like Anoka's father, would live longer than…just maybe…in a hot instant, desire for this swept through Soman. Instead of swinging into the pilot's seat, he hesitated, one part of his mind urging speed, another part caught by the lure—

Kolar grabbed Soman's arm.

A face approached the port. The breath went out of Soman. He'd forgotten about Ley.

<h1 style="text-align:center">Chapter 35</h1>

The hatch opened with a clang. Soman faced Ley. Or, was it Ley. Was it Kolar; was the station a posting of borrowed souls, or stolen. Or no souls at all. Stardust, Siba had said. We are stardust.

Ben looked up, an arm splayed across Joni's chest as if he could protect her.

Ley, floating just outside the hatch, flashed her wicked smile. "Mr. Soman. We're ready to do your transfer." At his expression she said, "What? If it's good enough for me, it's good enough for you."

The suits undulated gently in the rustle of air from the hatch opening, and the LEV's station keeping monitor beeped softly, every ten seconds.

"You won't have another chance. You want to gamble on Earth?"

Soman tried to weigh the gamble, but the brain seized up at the enormity.

Beep.

Ley's smile broadened, a grin of delicious proportion. "Here's the deal. You and Kolar go. Leave the others here. There's nothing left to them anyway."

He glanced at the three Monar. What was really left inside these husks. James, no spark behind the vacant stare. Flip, lolling from side to side like an asylum inmate, a reflex like a smashed snake writhing on the road. Joni, catatonic.

Ben's eyes bore into Soman.

Soman froze. Ben. What about Ben.

Flip's head rolled back and forth, disturbing the stillness of the cabin. Then it slowed, and stopped.

Beep.

Flip's hands rose, haltingly, tapping along the gurney, inching up his torso, finally reaching the surface of raw skull bone, his movements intentional, searching. His fingers quivered; a guttural sound broke from him.

He'd thought Flip was transferred to one of the spiders. Then…who is this, moving Flip's hands.

He looked to Kolar. What would he…but Kolar floated motionless, eyes far back in his head. His body began to tilt ever so slightly from inattention to its position in space.

Beep.

"Kolar."

"I have Kolar occupied just now," Ley said. She grinned. "Go back to Earth. For two and a half centuries I've wondered what a man would pay for immortality." She gestured to the Monar, where Flip's hands trembled across the bone. "Leave them with the Vradra." She nodded at Ben. "And if you're lucky, you'll have eternity to think about it." She stroked the surface of the LEV. "I think I'll come along, see how things turn out."

Beep.

Earth, the blue-white globe turning beneath an orbiting vessel, the green of endless forest, the random meandering of rivers, the geometry of grain fields, the glint of sun on the curve of vast oceans. And perhaps Anoka waiting, ready to resume her life. He had to believe in that.

He had to take Ley's offer. For Anoka.

Beep.

Soman couldn't breathe. His mind raced, flailing. Ben's eyes on him. Three unknowns but only two equations, a math not even Rami could solve.

Then Kolar was back, steadying himself against the console, his hard gaze on Ley. And Soman knew that, while Kolar's presence had returned, this was Soman's own knot to untie.

A warble rose in his ears, the sound from the Monar cell, of death drawing near, the closing down of choices. And now death was not just a word, not a literary allusion, not a poet's lofty ideal, but imminence, finality. A shard of memory transported him back, Soman in his pressure suit, grasping the bloody wrench, crewmen sprawled on the deck, his rational mind shut away somewhere. His reason, his humanity, suspended by fear. In fear we give up the chance to find a better way. So we fight, we go to war, people die. But just maybe…there's a third path.

Another echo of Siba: …*inside we know. This knowledge makes our choices worth something.* Soman felt an opening inside, a release of barriers, as if circulation had been restored to regions of his mind long unused.

Beep.

But…Anoka. In a rush of blood Soman solved it. Of course. If you can't find a third equation, eliminate one of the unknowns. He gazed through the open hatch, his head pounding, recoiling from the perfect logic of it. *Anoka would never know the difference.*

In that moment Soman seemed to hang in space, far above the LEV, watching. Heard himself shout, "Ben! Get them back!" Observed himself punch the hatch close button, then squeeze through the narrowing gap just ahead of Kolar. It slammed closed. "No!" Kolar yelled.

Then Soman re-entered his body, facing Ley. "Take my crew home," he told Ley, as she opened her arms and gathered him in. His heart constricted, Anne's face so close, her breath carrying not a woman's deepest juices, but dust and ozone and chemistry unfathomable.

"Mr. Soman! My, my." A moment of uncertainty. She gazed through the port at the furious commotion inside the LEV.

Then, with an easy shrug, she shook it off.

A meter away, Kolar and Ben pounded on the hatch button and the viewport. The faint noise of their shouting carried through. Then Kolar stepped back from the port and his eyes focused on the hatch mechanism. The hatch remained closed.

Ley winked at Kolar though the port. With a satisfied chuckle she led Soman away and up the ladders. The racket from the LEV rose. Then it receded as Soman and Ley reached the chamber with the six glowing universes. They crossed to the portal opening before them. Soman tried to organize a plan, while he mustered hope for a soul, just in case.

The portal led once again to the cavernous room. Soman stumbled across the floor in Ley's grasp, a quickening buzz in his ears, the buzz of the LEV spinning toward the inner crust of the Pearl.

A halo of light circled a waiting ring, and a block with its new body. Spiders scuttled around the equipment, dozens of them, a hundred of them, clattering rhythmically. Eyes on stalks twirled and waved. Mouth parts glinted. Soman studied them, trying to discern through some gesture, some intention, some glint of eye, the spark of souls inside.

His words to Siba floated up: *If you're wrong it's too late.*

The human form stuck to the surface of the block matched Soman in every detail, not an imperfect copy from Ley's memory—the face chiseled asymmetrically, the old scar above one eye, worry lines across the forehead. Its unclothed flesh hung flaccid, stomach concave, eyes closed, mouth agape. Tabula rasa, soon etched. How did it hang there. He reached out. The block attracted his hand—local gravity along the wall. A place where gravity could come at you from any direction, 'up' and 'down' flickering on and off in a heartbeat. All the unknowable in the Universe crowded in on Soman, his chest pulling as if against three atmospheres' pressure.

"What will it be like in that…body?" he asked.

Ley considered. "Do you ever try to imagine eternity?"

Soman found no energy to speak, halted by the dizzy

incomprehensibility of time.

"Of course you try," she said. "We all did. And you can't do it. You can't make the leap from the finite to the infinite." She touched the double's cheek. "Once you know you're never going to die, your mind expands to consider eternity." She ran a finger down its breastbone, the skin dimpling beneath her touch. "But…" her voice faltered for an instant before continuing. "It's just as terrifying to realize you could be part of eternity as to know you won't."

"Will it be me in there?"

"Mr. Soman. You always get tangled in the minutiae."

Soman's chest ached with longing. Just maybe…

Ley tugged him to the machine. She laid him on the hovering platform beside the ring. His senses heightened, he noticed the pellucid light of the chamber; the inhuman aroma of the Vradra moving around the equipment; Ley's hands upon him, pressing him down. He concentrated on a last thought: we must be on that LEV when it departs. For Anoka.

The ring slid into view above him, a subsonic vibration resonated through his skull. Soman raced through the memories of two voyages, images burning across his brain like an old-time projector.

Then a rushing river flowed through him, a wild cataract flushing his innermost parts. His body shook. The power built, overwhelming sensation; the rush grew beyond imagining, and he surrendered to it.

The rising flood broke. He sensed it coagulating, like the energy of the big bang condensing into matter. The coagulum became entities moving through him, shadowy quanta hopping from level to level, freeing the essence of him from its convoluted framework. Uncountable bits rose, torn away into the dark, the loosened particles plunging him into nostalgia. A patter of rain. The call of a loon. Mother offering a cookie. His mind expanded in their wake, reaching for the end of the Universe and beyond, stretching for infinity, nearing the barrier uncrossable by mortals. Sensation grew sluggish as if nearing the speed of light, growing infinitely heavy, time slowing, slowing, grinding to a halt.

Then bits of coagulum skipped and arranged themselves, burrowing to their rightful places. There was again a singularity, an identity, a self separate from the nothingness. Time sputtered into motion.

Voices from the void. Patterns of light and dark. The light disappeared, sprang back. Disappeared again. Something he had done. He did it again. Colors assaulted him, as if color had materialized a moment ago. Again he blinked. Shapes. A person. More rearrangement of the fragments. The angles confused. He recalled the position of the new body against its gravity wall. Suddenly Soman wondered which gravity gripped him—that fact all-important. He tried to make sense of the room, of the shadows, the milling spiders.

Anne leaned close, peering, speaking. The timbre of her voice brought a stab of recollection, then disappointment. Ley, not Anne. But there was an odd thing. Something about her face—it glistened in a new way. Wet streaks marred her smooth complexion. Then she walked away.

In the distance stood the block. Not the blank place he expected, but a man. A sensation of out of body experience filled Soman. The man blinked; his eyes rotated in a moment of disorientation. Soman watched the familiar face, and he registered its unbroken nose. The man's eyes, lighting on Soman, struggling to focus. Confusion. Then a flash of understanding. And Soman knew it had searched Soman's memories, recognized Soman's damaged face, and made the calculation: he had crossed over. Soman's mind tried to resume the race outward to infinity, reaching to complete the journey, straining to cross that gap of a few feet to the man on the wall. He stopped short in hard realization.

Regret detonated in Soman like a grenade. Now he knew, had always known; consciousness was an emergent property of neuron and bone, of synapse and fleeting chemical. Delicate and ephemeral, collapsing when the brief storm passes, like a fading rainbow. It shook Soman by the throat.

The creature on the block gazed one last time at Soman with eyes grown deep and aware, a haunting look as one road split in two. With a heave it flopped from the block. Soman tried to say go, go, but nothing would come out. Crawling, scrabbling with new limbs, it followed Ley with frantic flailing motions to the far end of the chamber. It was slow; it fell behind. Ley disappeared through the portal.

The Vradra clattered around Soman. He fought off the torpor. Go, go. He tried to stand, but muscles wouldn't work. He tried to speak. No words would form. He fixed his gaze on the nearest compound eyes. He reached out, grasped a limb. The eyes swiveled down.

The man from the wall had not yet reached the portal when the opening began to close, the circle of light it cast on the floor of the chamber shrinking each second. With a lunge it managed to reach the portal. A windmilling of arms and a final spasmodic thrust of legs, and it fell through the portal as it closed.

Soman's platform began to move. He gripped the Vradra, held its gaze. Something flickered in there. How to...such a chasm. This would take time. Time he didn't have. He knew Ley would be firing up the LEV any minute. Come on; he couldn't speak, couldn't move from the bed. They passed through a portal. Finally he lifted his tongue, gained control of his lips. Never releasing his gaze into the Vradra's eyes, he spoke. "I…am…Soman."

Around him the Vradra clattered. Their eyes flitted across his features. He fell back, weak with surrender. This was taking too long. It could take days, or years. The project of a lifetime.

Chapter 36

Joni sits before the viewscreen, her empty sleeve wrapped into a turban, her solitary hand resting on James's chest. James gazes beyond the shimmer of the blue-green aurora outside *Sorcerer* with eyes unmoved by the planet filling the screen. The night side of the world sparkles with the glow of cities. Spingrav groans at ¾ g, all the strength left in it. The ship whirs, circulating air heavy with the stink of old wounds.

A keyboard clatters. Flip raps away, a sound like all the exposed bones of his face rattling.

Ley growls, "Mister, you keep up that racket, I'm not letting them give you a new tongue." It is a matter of faith that, two hundred fifty years beyond the Maro, miracles await.

Ben scans Flip's typing, his eyes reflecting the marching line of letters on the screen. He shakes his head and slides Flip's hands one key to the left. "Try it now."

Flip's face cannot show if he feels frustration. He bends to the task. A mistake of half an inch in the placement of fingers makes all the difference. Half an inch or the distance to Epsilon Eridani.

Wheezing its age, the nex rattles.

The form of Soman stops just inside Nav One, hesitating, feet rooted to the deck. It happens every time he approaches Nav deck—mortality haunts the place. He peers into the dim cabin, points of light on instrument panels clustering like cities in the night. An orange indicator on the panel flashes on and off. He watches it, avoiding Ley's gaze.

Flip stops. Freed of their task, his hands rise to his face. Ben seizes Flip's fingers to keep them from probing every detail yet again. He reads Flip's message and says, "Yes. The colonies are back on the moon. Six of them now." Flip's jaw trembles and sounds emerge, primitive vocalizations testing the limits of the mouth to form speech without its soft parts.

Involuntarily, Soman's tongue probes teeth, a tongue taken for granted, used for a lifetime without thought, like a friend or a shipmate. Those colonies won't be home, Flip. They won't be Monar. Strangers from a new age now dwell in the deep tunnels of the moon. They will have dark skin; they will not speak English. Soman forms a mental image of Alta, of Marya and Kolar—the old Kolar—of a shay on a quiet street.

Forget it. All human, all mortal, all gone. A glow from behind the Earth promises the line of dawn soon, but for now the cold beyond the hull penetrates. A vision comes over him, of blowing snow and vast open prairies.

Joni calls softly. "Come in." Sometimes she must prod. He steps in.

The nex crackles again. Another form resembling Soman enters. Kolar. They call him Kolar anyway. He acts like Kolar; he uses Kolar's memories. Impossible to stop the mind from following old habits, from responding to familiar things in the usual way, even knowing that Kolar is dead and dismembered, sampled and left behind—it's too much information. Easier to keep it simple. Call it Kolar. Call it Soman.

Kolar says, "The LEV is ready."

"We won't need it."

"Why?"

Soman nods toward the flashing orange alarm. "Vessel on the way." He punches a button. The orange light stops flashing. "Flip, tell the system to track and zoom." Cabot used to brag: control systems so advanced even a blind man could fly the ship. Even blind and mute, even a crew with parts scattered beyond the Universe.

Flip types. An image flickers among them, fuzzy but clearly a vessel, with engine pods and a bulbous bow, cockpit low in the front, a design different from anything Soman has ever seen. Ben draws an audible breath. "How have they made so much progress?"

"Two hundred fifty years is a long time," Soman says. In the two and a half centuries before *Sorcerer's* first departure, the world went from sailing ships and barber-surgeons to starships and the descroid. But Soman understands Ben's astonishment: Ben lived at the close of three thousand years of decline. Progress among the Monar meant living to see tomorrow, thwarting the next raid. Progress that finally stumbled. Eventually something gets you.

But now Soman sees the great curve of the future spreading forward in millennia, in epochs, in the swirl of colliding galaxies. He allows his awareness to enlarge, swelling to the limits of human comprehension, breaking past that ancient barrier, sweeping beyond the momentary confusion to ponder the glow of the infinite. A hundred twenty five years spent dormant in a corner of the starship was nothing, a century nap, while the humans aboard risked the descroid to stem their swift decline.

A world glitters before them. A fierce glow surrounds the Lago de Maracaibo. Satellites race in tight circles. Orbital platforms hang above the last wisps of atmosphere. Dark holes bored through the ice, a world recovering its past. A world of progress beyond imagining. The one they counted on the first time, Soman and Anoka. The wait is over.

He smiles inwardly, at peace in the one certainty: the new Soman, even if it carries no spark of human soul, will follow an unshakable obsession: recover Anoka. Soman knew it would be so. The way to save crew and daughter both, the equation solvable only with one unknown eliminated, the mystery faced, finally, in the dark beyond the stars.

Anoka will never know the difference. At least not until she grows old while he does not. She will face the moment of realization that he is immortal while she is flesh, that he is not fully her father but an echo of him. He must watch her grow old and die—unless Lar's descendants have mastered the telomere. More than anything now in this second return, he wants immortality for the daughter of Soman.

His eyes glaze, and he goes to that place, far away and nowhere at all, an infinity of interconnection, of crosstalk, of pure knowledge, a whizzing of alien transmission like missiles through the ether, the Vradra web. He has detected something important in the synthesis of knowledge, tendrils leading to elusive patterns, the trail tantalizing. Somewhere in the labyrinth, there is something important, for him, about him. But with the return voyage spent in dormancy, he has had little practice navigating the vast web across the flux line arcing to infinity. It must be what an infant experiences, trying to make sense of a city street from a speeding levitron. Now, he senses a presence in the web, moving just beyond reach. And a second one. Dragging back to the physical, he finds Ley in the cabin gloom. She wears her sly smile; he knows it was her sentience.

Kolar says, "Leave it alone. He will find it with time."

Ley casts a derisive look. "You would withhold the truth?"

"It is not necessary to speak all truths."

Soman looks from Ley to Kolar. What truth. Kolar's expression unnerves him.

"Was it you lost your tongue, Mr. Soman?"

Soman finds he is holding his breath, and he wonders if he must breathe in this life. Maybe breathing is simply a habit that won't die even in this new body, built into this construct to give the appearance of humanity.

"I knew from the start you were keeping a secret," she says. "With your memories joining ours, finally I have it. A daughter left behind. Damn you."

Soman presses his temples. "Get out of my head!" he howls at Ley.

Ley laughs. "Mr. Soman, you're losing your grip. I'm not in your head. I'm right here with Kolar." She laughs long and hard.

Kolar watches Ley with silent disdain.

Soman feels anger flash white-hot at Ley, but he is quick, cutting it off before—and then he realizes he has no Maro, all that left behind. And yet he mastered his anger without it, its teaching finally complete, like a vaccination that finally took. And when everyone can be inoculated, the germ of violence eliminated, no one will need the Maro.

Images stumble past. Anoka on a fence rail, Anoka making snow angels, Anoka smiling, holding down the beret while the wind blows her into the sky, wisp by wisp. Anoka and Soman kneeling, heads bowed before a granite slab poking through snow. Anoka amid pure white sheets, gripping his hand, smiling, trusting. "See you Daddy," as her eyes close that final time.

The approaching ship looms now, and Soman can see figures on the bridge, peering at the scarred starship.

Ley leans toward Soman. "Do you think Julian made that trek just to deliver a few trinkets for the returning crew? What do you think he was doing for that year? Hanging out on a mountain top, waiting for God to speak through his auton?"

Soman stares at her. He doesn't want to know.

"Mr. Soman, with Kolar's knowledge of the Church, and your memories of Julian, the facts strongly suggest that Julian spent the year retrieving his goddaughter's descroid before snow buried the world, then establishing it as the foundation of a church. That word 'fundam' is more than a metaphor; it has a literal meaning—the physical base that supports the building. The writings of the Church are full of references to what the Prodigal Children will discover in the foundation of the Church, and that the contents of the fundam will guide them to it. Somewhere deep in the bowels of the cathedral you will discover an ancient descroid, preserved for as long as it might take for your return."

"God," Soman says. Twice he stood before Julian's treasure chest, touching the enclosure, Anoka deep beneath his feet, the key to finding her inches away among the artifacts of another time and place, the possessions of a vanished crew. Anoka awaited the return of the Prodigal Children along with all the faithful. Soman slumps into a seat. It is too much; there seems to be a real heart breaking in his chest. He could have enjoyed a lifetime with Anoka. Instead he relinquished the gift to Mordano, his fear of death driving him as far from his daughter as a man could flee.

Ley says, "It's sad, really. Soman passed up living his life."

Soman watches the planet. When did Soman forget there was a life to be lived, days to be filled, meaning to be crafted from each moment. And he knows the answer, because Soman passed along every urge and memory, all his knowledge and foolishness. It happened in the hour after committing Anoka to the vault, Soman's life suspended as surely as the descroid interrupted hers.

He gazes at the dark mass of the nighttime Earth. Soon a sliver of dawn will boil the rim of the globe. No more regrets. No more vain hopes; not another moment wasted. Soman passed along an obligation before departing to wherever generations without counting disappear. Now there's an appointment to keep, a life to live.